Marry Me... Again!

There are *some* men you never forget!

They're handsome and sexy.
They're demanding—unreasonable.
You know the type....

But while they may be hard to live *with*,
they're *impossible* to live without.

So when a man like that says

Marry Me... Again!

there's only one answer.
Yes!

Relive the romance...

Three complete novels by your favorite authors!

About the Authors

Rebecca Winters—Award-winning author of over a dozen books. Rebecca's deeply emotional stories have gained her fans worldwide. She is a graduate of the University of Utah, and has also studied at schools in Switzerland and France, including the Sorbonne. A teacher and a mother of four, Rebecca makes her home in Salt Lake City, Utah.

Jasmine Cresswell—This multitalented, award-winning author of well over forty contemporary and historical romances, Regencies, mysteries and mainstream novels has an international background. Born in Wales and educated in England, Jasmine met her husband while working at the British Embassy in Rio de Janeiro. Her latest book, *Desires & Deceptions,* will be published in the spring by Mira Books.

Suzanne Simms—Bestselling author of almost thirty contemporary and historical novels, Suzanne also contributed to *Dangerous Men and Adventurous Women,* a collection of essays by romance writers, edited by Jayne Ann Krentz. Suzanne currently lives with her husband, her son and her cat, Merlin, in Fort Wayne, Indiana.

Marry Me... Again!

REBECCA WINTERS
JASMINE CRESSWELL
SUZANNE SIMMS

Harlequin Books

TORONTO • NEW YORK • LONDON
AMSTERDAM • PARIS • SYDNEY • HAMBURG
STOCKHOLM • ATHENS • TOKYO • MILAN
MADRID • WARSAW • BUDAPEST • AUCKLAND

HARLEQUIN BOOKS

by Request—Marry Me... Again!

ISBN 0-373-20105-2

This edition published by arrangement with Harlequin Enterprises B. V.

Printed in U.S.A.

CONTENTS

She's never stopped loving her ex-husband.
And now, after three long years,
she's determined to fight fire with fire
and win him back!

FULLY INVOLVED

Rebecca Winters

CHAPTER ONE

"CAPTAIN SIMPSON? Regina Lindsay reporting for duty." She checked her gold watch nervously and noted with satisfaction that there were still two minutes to go until the new shift took over. After all her planning, she couldn't afford to make any mistakes now.

The smell of frying bacon from the interior of the station reached her nostrils, making her feel slightly nauseated. She hadn't slept well, anticipating this moment, and couldn't eat breakfast. Her emotions were tying her in knots.

The darkly attractive man seated at the desk put down the copy of *Fire Command* he'd been reading and lifted his head. He was wearing his luxuriant black hair shorter than she remembered. In his days as a newspaper foreign correspondent, he rarely found the time to get it cut. She'd always liked his hair longer because it had a tendency to curl, reminding her of a gypsy's.

Slowly his gray eyes took in the regulation black pants and gray shirt she wore, then shot her a cold, dispassionate glance. Not by a twitch of the tiny scar at the corner of his mouth did he let her know that her presence affected him.

"Gina. I'm not even going to try to guess why you've shown up here—let alone outfitted like that. I'm on duty for the next twenty-four hours. If this has something to do with alimony payments, call your attorney. He's still in the phone book. Presuming you plan to be in town that long."

He reached for his magazine again, but she noted with satisfaction that his gaze fell on the hurry-ups propped next to her shoes, and his dark brows furrowed in displeasure. She had his attention at last! The standard-issue black boots, pants, helmet and yellow coat stood ready beside her. As if in slow motion his stormy eyes played over her face and figure once more, fastening on her slender waist where she'd attached her walkie-talkie.

At this point he rose to his full six feet two inches, looking leaner and fitter than she'd ever seen him. In full dress uniform he was heartbreakingly handsome. "If this is some kind of joke, I'm not amused."

She cleared her throat. "You asked for a replacement while Whittaker is on a leave of absence. I'm swinging in from Engine House Number 3. Call Captain Carrera if you want."

He scowled. "Captain Carrera is a pushover for a pretty face. What's going on, Gina?" he asked in a wintry tone. "Where did you get that turnout gear?"

"In San Francisco, when I graduated and started to work." She pulled her badge out of her shirt pocket and put it on top of the magazine. He stared at the official insignia of the Salt Lake City Fire Department as if he'd never seen it before. His hand closed over the badge.

"Your approach is very novel, Gina, but enough's enough. I'm warning you—"

"Hey, Grady! I'm in!" One of the fire fighters poked his head inside the door, took one look at Gina and grinned. "Oops! Sorry, Captain. Just wanted you to know I'm here." Gina couldn't look at Grady as the fire fighter walked through the engine house calling, "Eighty-six! Eighty-six!" It was the code that meant a woman was on the premises. Everyone would be on his best behavior.

"Captain?" A man who seemed close to fifty knocked on the door and then came in without asking. "I'm going to fuel the truck unless you have other work assigned for me right now."

"Go ahead," Grady muttered.

"Ma'am." The older fire fighter nodded politely to Gina before leaving them alone once more. Following his exit four other men came into Grady's office on the pretext of checking in, but Gina was well aware of the real reason, and she had an idea that Grady was, too. Her gilt-blond hair drew attention wherever she went. In an effort to minimize her attractiveness, she wore it in a ponytail while on duty, but she had no way of hiding her unusual violet eyes with their dark lashes. As Grady had once told her, no other woman he'd ever met possessed her unique coloring—then he'd whispered that she was some kind of miracle as he pulled her into his arms. But she knew those memories had no place here today.

"All right, now that you've gained the attention of the entire department," he said, pointedly eyeing the last man out of the door before flicking her a hostile glance, "I'm afraid you'll have to leave."

Gina stood her ground but Grady would never know what it cost her to remain upright when her legs felt like buckling. "You requested a replacement because you're a person short. I'm the one who's been sent."

His eyes narrowed to silvery slits. "If you're a fire fighter, I'm Mary Poppins!"

Warmth suffused her cheeks. "Call headquarters. They'll verify my status as a paramedic, as well."

"I don't have time to listen to this," he bit out. "Goodbye, Gina. Whatever it is you want can be accomplished through the mail. I believe I've made myself clear. The door is be—"

"Ladder 1 respond to concession fire in Liberty Park area." The dispatcher's voice over the gong accomplished what nothing else could have. A fire fighter's sole function was to respond to the alarm once it sounded. Grady left her standing there as if she didn't exist and ran to the truck. Already she could hear the revving of the engine and shouts from the men. And she could feel the familiar surge of adrenaline that fills every fire fighter's veins once a call comes. It was as natural as breathing for her to want to respond, but she'd been assigned to engine 1. So therefore she had no choice but to go inside and settle in until the gong sounded for their rescue unit.

The truck left the station, its siren wailing, within twenty seconds of the time the alarm had come in. Anything under a minute was good, Gina mused, feeling inordinately proud of the work Grady did. So many times in their short-lived marriage, he'd tried to explain this pride and sense of exhilaration to her, but she hadn't understood. In all honesty, she hadn't wanted to. Out of fear that he might get killed, she'd accused him of trying to be a macho man who got his kicks from playing with fire.

How wrong she'd been. How little she'd understood what motivated him. Not until she'd been through the rigorous training herself had she begun to comprehend his love of fire fighting. It gave him a natural high that not even his work as a correspondent, covering explosive situations in the Middle East and Central America, had offered. That high was contagious and had finally infected her. But how to make *him* see that?

She reached down for her turnout gear, aware that seeing Grady for the first time since the divorce had shaken her badly. She'd rehearsed the moment a thousand times in her mind, imagining—fearing—it would go exactly as it did. But his indifference to her physical presence managed to twist the knife a little deeper, dissolving her hopes that somewhere inside him he still cared.

If he'd been told ahead of time that she worked for the fire department and was being sent to his station, he'd have been on the phone to the battalion chief to protest. She wouldn't have been able to get near him. This way, she had the slight advantage of cornering him in his own territory. She knew enough about her ex-husband to realize he detested making his private business public. He wouldn't be able to get rid of her in front of the others without creating an embarrassing scene.

So when he came back and found her in residence, he'd have to live with the fact until they could be completely alone. A shiver crept along her spine at the thought of that confrontation, but too much was at stake for her to back down now.

As a friend had once innocently said when Gina admitted she was still in love with Grady, "Then stop moaning about it. Go after him! Fight fire with fire!" Gina had done exactly that. And she'd come face-to-face with a man whose eyes were as dead to her as the ashes of last winter's grate fire.

Someone's tuneless whistle broke in on her thoughts. One of the men she'd seen a few minutes ago came into the office on a lope, but he stopped short when he noticed her gear. His light blue eyes smiled. "Hi. I'm Lieutenant Corby. You must be Ron Whittaker's replacement."

"That's right. I'm Gina Lindsay." She shook his outstretched hand with difficulty because of the helmet and boots she carried, and they both laughed. The sandy-haired man didn't seem to take himself too seriously. Gina liked that.

"Since the captain's not here, I'll show you around. For a minute there, we all thought you were his latest conquest." Relieving her of the boots, he grinned in a mischievous manner that exuded confidence.

Gina fought to keep the smile pasted on her face. "The captain has a reputation, does he?" she asked as she followed him into the large room behind the office that served as a living room cum lounge.

"Only after hours. He's a stickler for the rules. Fortunately for me, I'm not. You married?"

"You're straightforward, I'll grant you that, Lieutenant, so I'll return the favor. I'm not married but I made an ironclad rule when I became a fire fighter—no mingling with the crew except on a professional basis." In fact, she hadn't accepted a date since her return to Salt Lake and generally preferred the company of Susan Orr, a fire fighter from engine 5.

"Not ever?" His mock expression of pain made her laugh again, and this in turn brought two other men out of the kitchen, carrying mugs of coffee.

"Howard? Ed? Meet Gina. She's the swing-in for Whittaker."

The men said hello and eyed her speculatively, but not with the same glimmer of male admiration they'd displayed earlier when they thought she was a visitor. She'd come to expect this reaction from her male co-workers. Only in recent years had women intruded on their all-male fraternity.

Gina tried hard to blend into the background and not call attention to herself. Most of the fire fighters she knew were becoming accustomed to females in the department, but a few still had trouble accepting women in the traditionally male role. She could understand their feelings. She was a woman, and that made a difference in their eyes. It always would. The only thing to do was try to get along, and for the most part Gina had succeeded. But it took time to ease in and become a part of the family.

"You can bunk in that bed next to the wall," the lieutenant continued, setting her boots down beside it. He gave her a quick tour of the kitchen, bathroom and dorm. "We've all eaten breakfast, but there's plenty left if you're hungry."

"Thanks. I might take you up on that after I settle in."

"Grab it while you can. We get busy around here. Working under the captain, you'll learn stuff that wasn't in the textbooks. Here. Let me put your coat and helmet out by the truck, and call me Bob when the captain's not around. Okay?"

"Okay." Once again, she relinquished her things to him without the argument that she could do it herself. Some men couldn't break the habit of treating her like a woman instead of simply a co-worker. She didn't mind at all.

Once alone, she surveyed her kingdom. Eight beds and eight individual lockers took up most of the dorm's space. She straightened her hurry-ups and threw her small overnight bag on the bed, pulling out a pair of coveralls before she went into the bathroom to dress. She expected to be uncomfortably warm; the weatherman predicted ninety-eight degrees by midafternoon, a typical July day. However, she liked the dry heat of Utah after the dampness of the Coast.

Gina forced herself to eat a light breakfast, but any second she expected to hear the truck returning to the station and the sound of Grady's deep voice issuing orders. She decided to do without coffee because she didn't need a stimulant. The dispatcher's voice coming periodically over the radio kept her adrenaline flowing at a fairly steady pace. That, combined with the fact that she'd be working with Grady, had her heart pumping overtime as it was.

"We're going to play tennis before it gets too hot," Bob called out from the next room. "You ready?"

"I'll be right there." She finished putting her dishes in the cupboard and ran out of the kitchen. Howard and Ed were already on board the engine. Bob held the door open for her, but to her dismay she could hear the ladder truck already entering the bay.

"Ms Lindsay. If I could have a word with you," Grady ordered as he jumped off the rig that had backed into the station. He tossed his helmet on the peg and walked over to her, his eyes a smoldering black. He was her superior, so Gina had no choice but to obey. She removed her booted foot from the step.

"Next time," Bob promised. The other men waved and the engine roared off.

Gina followed Grady to his office with trepidation, while the other men headed for the kitchen. She sensed Grady had now had time for the shock to wear off. Inside the office, he turned around and leaned against the door, arms folded. His silence, ominous and unforgiving, made her feel uneasy, and she sought refuge in one of the chairs facing his desk.

"I hoped you'd be gone when we came back, but I suppose it was too much to ask for. You've got exactly one minute to tell me what this is all about." She heard the underlying threat in his tone.

"I'm not the person you should be asking since I have no validity in your eyes," she answered calmly. "Call anybody at number 3. I've been working there for two months, and before that, in Carmel and San Francisco. Yesterday Captain Carrera told me my orders were to report here this morning."

A nasty smile pulled at the corner of his mouth. "Are you honestly trying to tell me that the woman I divorced because of irreconcilable differences to do with my job—among other things—is now a fully certified fire fighter?"

"Yes." Her chin lifted a fraction.

"Forgive me, but my imagination simply won't stretch that far."

Gina got to her feet, needing to choose her words carefully. "Grady, I don't blame you for being incredulous, but a lot has happened in the past three years."

A dark brow quirked disdainfully. "You're asking too much if you expect me to believe you've become an entirely different person in that period of time. The word *fire* used to scare the life out of you."

"That's true," she said forcefully, "until I sought professional help."

"That's an interesting revelation, considering the fact that you point-blank refused to get help all the time we were married." The cords stood out in his bronzed neck. "I begged you to talk to someone. I'd have done anything if I thought it would do any good, but you weren't interested."

"You're wrong, Grady. I was too *frightened*." She wiped her moist palms against her hips in an unconscious gesture of frustration and uncertainty. "Don't you see? If I couldn't be helped, then it would have been worse than ever! I was afraid of the answer."

His mouth thinned to a white line. "But *after* our divorce you suddenly found the courage. That pretty well says it all, doesn't it, Gina?"

"Engine 1 respond to medical assist at 1495 Washington Boulevard."

Grady unexpectedly reached out and grasped her wrist. "Let's find out what kind of fire fighter you've become...with paramedic training to boot! And when we get back you can further enlighten me as to why you've returned to the scene of the crime. I'm not through with you, Gina. Not by a long shot!"

He perforce had to let go of her arm as they entered the lounge. "Winn? You'll ride engine for now. I'm going on this assist." He rapped out the order as they hurried to the ladder truck. Gina could still feel the imprint of Grady's hand on her wrist by the time they arrived at their destination on the west side of town.

Grady rarely lost control in any situation, and the ferocity of his grip told her she'd hit a nerve, one that ran deep.

Rico drove the truck. Next to him sat Frank, then Gina. Grady got in last and shut the door. She was almost sick with excitement at being this close to him after all these years. His body remained rigid. No one in the department would ever have guessed how intimate she and their revered captain had once been. He showed no feelings for her now except a residue of bitterness that her presence had suddenly evoked.

Still, she was where she'd wanted desperately to be. There'd been times during the past few years when she wondered if she'd ever realize her dream of being with Grady again.

As they pulled up to a white frame bungalow Grady made the assignments. "Gina will be patient man, Rico, you stay with the rig. Frank, you and I will supply backup. Let's go."

Gina followed Grady off the truck and strode quickly to the front porch, where a middle-aged woman stood waiting just inside the screen door. She held up her left hand, and Gina could see that her ring finger was swollen twice its size, constricted by her wedding rings.

"Thank heavens you came," she blurted out, white with pain. "I didn't know what to do. Once in a while I break out in hives, but this sneaked up on me. I can't get my rings off and I'm afraid I'll lose my finger."

"We're here in plenty of time to prevent that from happening," Gina assured her. "Let's go into the kitchen. The table is a perfect place for you to lie down while we get those rings off. I'll just grab a pillow off your couch, and Frank will go out to the truck to get the cutter. What's your name?" As Gina conversed with the woman, Grady stood a few feet away scrutinizing her every move.

"Mary Fernandez." The woman sighed as she climbed up on the table with Gina's help and lay flat on her back.

"Well, Mary Fernandez," Gina said, smiling, "we'll have you comfortable within a half hour. What have you taken for the pain?"

"Aspirin."

"Good. That will help."

"Is it bad?" the woman asked anxiously.

"Swelling often seems worse than it really is. What I don't like to do is cut into your rings. They're beautiful."

"I think so," Mary said. "My husband's away on business. He won't believe this."

"Well, now you'll have something exciting to tell him," Gina soothed, taking the cutter from Frank. "It will hurt for a while because I have to get the underside of the saw around the band. I'm going to cut through in three places. If you want to scream, I won't mind."

"I had five children and never screamed." She chuckled, but Gina could see the way the woman was biting her lip.

As incident commander, Grady had to write a report, and he made notes, asking a few questions while Gina continued to saw carefully through the gold bands. Twenty minutes later, the swollen red finger was free of the constriction.

"Ah..." The woman moaned her relief, and her eyes filled with tears. "You're an angel from heaven and you look like one, too. Thank you."

"You're welcome." Gina assisted the woman to her feet and handed her the pieces of her wedding bands. "These can be made to look like new again."

The older woman smiled. "It doesn't matter. My finger's more important."

"Indeed it is. Do you know what causes your hives?"

"No, but I'm going to call a doctor and find out so nothing like this ever happens again."

"Well, you take care of yourself, Mary. Call us again if you're ever in trouble."

"I will," she murmured, walking them to the door. "What's your name? I want to write a letter to the department to let them know how grateful I am for what you did."

"Just call us station 1. Goodbye, Mary." Gina shook hands with the woman before going outside to the truck. By now a medium-sized crowd had gathered around. This time, Gina was last to climb onto the rig.

"How many times have you done that maneuver?" Frank wanted to know as they drove into the mainstream of traffic.

"That was my first."

"You could have fooled me. You have a real nice way about you, Gina. Welcome aboard."

"Thanks. Actually, the woman was wonderful. That had to hurt!"

"Rico, pull over at the next supermarket. We'll grab a bite of lunch." Grady's suggestion effectively changed the topic of conversation.

"Will do, Captain. Who wants to go in on barbecued spareribs?"

"I do." Gina and Frank both spoke at the same time. Under normal circumstances, Gina had a healthy appetite but was fortunate to have a metabolism that kept her nicely rounded figure on the slender side. When she worked a particularly busy and demanding shift, she ate what the men did. Fire fighting devoured calories.

"How about you, Captain?" Rico inquired.

"I don't know. I'll wait till I get in there."

Rico parked in an alley and they all went inside the store. They'd just made their purchases when another call came through on their walkie-talkies. By the time they reached the scene of a car that was on fire, it had burned itself out. Grady made a preliminary report, and then they headed back to the station, eating their food on the way.

Since the bathroom wasn't in use when they returned, Gina slipped inside to wash up, thinking she'd relax on her bunk for a while and read the latest issue of *Firework*. But when she walked into the dorm, her cot wasn't there. Puzzled, she went over to the locker, but all her belongings had disappeared.

"I took the liberty of moving your bed and gear to my office, in case you were wondering."

Gina whirled around. "Why would you do that?"

"Because there's no way you're sleeping with seven men," Grady said in an authoritative voice that brooked no argument. They were still alone in the dorm.

"I've never asked for special privileges and I don't intend to start now. It's bad for morale, and I don't want to be singled out."

"In this station, you do it my way, Gina."

"At number 3 the four of us slept in the same room."

His gray eyes glittered dangerously. "Perhaps now that you've left, they'll be able to get some sleep."

"There are five women in the department and—"

"Half of my crew is married." His face wore a shuttered expression. "I won't allow you to create any undue stress among the wives by sleeping in the same room with their husbands."

"Do you think I'd intentionally try to cause trouble?" Her chest heaved with indignation.

"It follows you, Gina."

"When we were married I don't recall making a fuss because you slept in the same room with female fire fighters."

His mouth twisted in a mockery of a smile. "You have a short memory. When we were married, there were no women in the department. It made life a whole lot easier."

His tone made her wonder if he was one of those men who didn't approve of female fire fighters on principle, but this was not the time to get into that particular discussion. "The crew will know something's wrong."

He paused on his way out the door. "Don't lose any sleep over it. By your next shift, you'll be back at engine 3," he stated with familiar arrogance.

"You can't do that, Grady!" she retorted without thinking. She'd only been on duty seven hours and already he wanted her as far away from him as possible.

"Can't I!" He fixed her with a glacial stare. "Just watch me!"

"I didn't mean it that way." She took a deep breath. "I understand Whittaker will be out several more weeks."

"How typical of you, Gina. Now you're certified, you think you're the only paramedic in the department."

She bit her lip in an effort not to rise to the bait. "I don't want to be switched back before the allotted time because it won't look good on my record," she lied. Under no circumstances could she tell Grady the real reason.

"Don't worry." He grimaced and looked at his watch. "Seventeen more hours—after that you're home free. Captain Carrera will understand when I tell him I've found someone else with more years in the department to fill in."

"So you won't give me a chance!" She fought to keep her voice steady.

A nerve twitched alongside his strong jaw. "I'm giving you the same chance you gave *us*, Gina. And now you have approximately five minutes before you're to report to the lounge. We're going to discuss a variety of prefire plans, and we'd all be fascinated by a contribution from you."

Her delicate brows furrowed. "What do you mean?"

"You trained in San Francisco. Maybe there's something you can teach us," he muttered sarcastically.

"Grady..." Her eyes pleaded for a little understanding.

"Captain Simpson to you, *Ms Lindsay*." He passed a couple of the men on his way out of the dorm. Gina could hear their voices pitched low, then suddenly something Grady said made them burst out laughing. It shouldn't have hurt, but it did....

CHAPTER TWO

WITH ONLY A FEW MINUTES to go until the next shift reported for duty, Gina got up and dressed, made her bed and slipped out the front door of the station carrying her turnout gear.

She hurried to the private parking lot out back and put her things in the Honda, not wanting to be cornered by Grady. Her first twenty-four hours at station 1 had been enlightening. Fortunately, both the engine and the ladder were kept busy throughout the night, preventing Grady from catching her alone. From time to time, she'd sensed his gaze on her, eyes narrowed in anger, but she didn't acknowledge him unless directly addressed.

A car passed her in the driveway as she pulled out into the street. She expelled a sigh, relieved that she'd managed to escape him, but she knew it was only a temporary respite. Still, she couldn't face him right now. Too many emotions and memories were tearing her apart. She needed a little distance to regain her perspective before he forced a confrontation—and knowing Grady, there would be one. . . .

Traffic was fairly heavy with people anxious to get to work. While she waited through the third red light at the same intersection, she happened to glance in the rearview mirror. The black Audi several cars behind her wasn't familiar, but she recognized the man at the wheel.

Her heart did a funny kick. Was it coincidence or was Grady following her?

Three quarters of the way home to her apartment on the East bench, he still pursued her. Evidently he wanted to get their talk out of the way as soon as possible. A thrill of fear darted through her. His anger had been growing since she reported for duty the morning before. Right now she imagined that one wrong word from her might rip away that civilized veneer to reveal the bitter, uncompromising man who'd divorced her.

When she drove into the carport of the duplex she rented, Grady was out of his car and opening her door before she could pull the key from the ignition. "You still drive too fast, Gina."

"Apparently not fast enough," she muttered, sliding out of the driver's seat.

"Something told me I wouldn't find you at home if I came by later." He accompanied her to the front door and stood there, patiently waiting for her to unlock it. She was dismayed to find that her hand trembled. This was *Grady* about to enter her house. She'd imagined it so many times—but not when they'd both just come off duty, dead tired and still wearing their uniforms. Now was not the time for the kind of talk Grady had in mind.

"Come in." She finally found her voice, wondering too late what he would think about her gallery of photographs, covering two entire walls. Many of the pictures were of him, some taken on their honeymoon in Egypt, others in Carmel during a visit to her parents. But he walked into her small living room without looking around him, his attention focused solely on her. He gave nothing away. His study of her face was almost clinical.

Unable to help herself, Gina stared at him. The first thing she noticed was that he needed a shave. His beard was as black as his curly hair. It gave him a slightly dissipated air that added to his masculine appeal. Without her intending them to, her eyes roamed over the familiar lines and angles of his features and settled on his mouth, a mouth that could curve with a sensuality so beguiling she'd forget everything else.

Three years hadn't changed him, not really. It was more in the way he responded to the people around him that be betrayed a new hardness and cynicism. But maybe it was just with her that he exhibited this dark side. She wondered if the laughing, loving Grady she adored had gone for good—and worse, if she'd been the person to rob him of that joie de vivre.

The tempestuous battles leading up to their divorce had killed all the love he'd felt for her. In three years he hadn't once tried to contact her by phone or letter. Like flash fire, their love had burned hot, out of control, sweeping them along in a euphoric blaze. Then suddenly it blew itself out, and she wakened to a nightmare.

"Would you like something to eat or drink?"

"Gina—" he bit out, quickly losing patience with her as he lodged against the arm of the couch. She sat down on the matching sofa across from him. His eyes were a startling gray, impaling her like lasers. "What's going on? What are you doing back in Salt Lake? I'd like an honest answer."

Gina settled back against the cushions and crossed her legs, trying to assume a nonchalance she didn't feel. He wanted honesty but she didn't dare give him that. Not once in twenty-four hours had he shown the least sign that he still had any feelings for her.

All this time she'd held the hope that seeing her again would trigger some kind of positive reaction, however small, however ambivalent.

"I used to live here, Grady."

"More to the point, you died here," he came back in a harsh tone of voice. "The person you were, the marriage we had . . . all dead."

She swallowed hard. "It felt that way at the time—until I sought counseling and started examining the reasons for my so-called phobia."

"Which were?"

"We married without really knowing anything about each other. There I was, teaching English in Beirut, then suddenly I met you and within six weeks we were husband and wife. Our married life in the Middle East was like one long, extended honeymoon with no home base and—"

"And dangerous," he inserted icily. "Certainly as life-threatening as any work I do now, but I don't recall your giving it a thought. If I remember correctly, you were more than eager to be my bride."

Gina averted her eyes. "Grady—" her voice trembled "—you told me that the newspaper you worked for had offered you an editor's job and that you intended to take it so we could start a family. I thought that was why we made our home in Salt Lake. You told me you craved a little domesticity. But after sitting at that desk for a few weeks, you dropped a bomb on me. Without discussing any of it, you resigned and told me you were going to go back to your old job of fire fighting." She got to her feet and began pacing. "I didn't even know you'd been a fire fighter. I thought you'd always been a newspaperman."

"I believe we covered this ground three years ago, Gina."

"And I'm trying to explain to you that I was too young and immature at the time to understand your needs. You were right when you accused me of being spoiled, incapable of giving support or comfort to my husband. It wasn't just my fears of your job. I've never told you this before but I was jealous of your friendship with the crew. I felt like you loved the fire fighters more than you loved me."

Something flickered in the recesses of his eyes, but he let her go on talking. For the first time she felt that maybe he was listening.

"Don't you see? I wanted to fulfill you in every way, but when you started fire fighting again, I thought you must have fallen out of love with me, that I no longer brought you the kind of happiness you needed. As a result, I felt totally inadequate. The psychologist explained that I used the fear of fire to mask my *real* fear of losing you. Perhaps that doesn't make sense to you, but it opened my eyes."

"Go on."

She took a deep breath. "Further along in therapy, I was challenged to explore my fear of fire. The psychologist suggested I observe a fire fighter training session. You see, long after we divorced I was plagued by nightmares, all having to do with fire."

He rubbed the back of his bronzed neck as she spoke. The fact that he didn't interrupt told her he was absorbed in what she had to say.

"Well, I went to a few training sessions and watched and learned. Incredibly, my nightmares went away and I actually found myself wanting to be a participant. The psychologist was right after all. I didn't have a fear of fire. Eventually, one of the trainers suggested I take the examination to see if I could qualify for the school. This didn't happen overnight, of course, but in time I took it and passed, and went on from there."

Grady stared at her for timeless minutes without saying anything. She couldn't imagine what he was thinking.

"Do you remember telling me what it was like to fight and the indescribable feeling you got from helping people?" Her violet eyes beseeched his understanding. "I couldn't relate to that at all. It just made me feel more isolated from you than ever, but—"

"But another miracle occurred and now you understand me completely," he mocked.

"Not completely," she answered, struggling to keep her voice calm, "but I can honestly say I share your love of fire fighting."

His face closed up. "So why didn't you stay in California?"

If only she dared tell Grady what was in her heart, but the very remoteness of his expression prevented her from blurting out her love for him. "I—I suppose deep down I wanted to show you that I had overcome my fear. I knew you'd never believe me unless you actually saw me on the job."

"You're right about that," he said thickly.

"Grady," she began, her voice almost a whisper, "I discovered something else in my counseling sessions. You and I parted with a great deal of bitterness, for which I take most of the blame." She watched his dark brows draw together. "I hoped that if I came back to Salt Lake we could meet as friends and bury past hurts."

He got to his feet, holding himself rigid. "That's asking the impossible, Gina."

She bit her lip and nodded. "Then I'll just have to accept that. I realize our marriage failed mostly because of me. I had this idea that if you heard me say it, it might help to heal some of the wounds. Despite everything, I've always wanted your happiness. And I've always hoped you didn't blame yourself for problems that weren't your fault. You're a fire fighter's fire fighter. I was a naive little fool to expect you to quit and find something safe and sane to do for the rest of your life. Perhaps a part of me wants your forgiveness."

His eyes were shuttered. "Forgiveness doesn't come into it, Gina. I was insensitive to your fears and needs, too." She had the impression he was about to say something else and then changed his mind. "I'm glad you got the counseling you needed, but I'm sorry you made the move to Salt Lake to prove something that wasn't necessary. I followed you here because I was afraid you'd come to Utah with the mistaken notion that we could pick up where we left off three years ago."

She felt like dying. "No. We're both different people now. Firehouse gossip says you have interests elsewhere."

Grady's intent gaze swept over her. "You've grown up, Gina, and it's all to the good. But it doesn't change the way I feel about your working at station 1."

She thrust out her chin. "I figured that was why you followed me home. Well, where do I report for duty tomorrow, or should I call headquarters?"

He didn't say anything for a minute. In the past she'd fought him on everything. Right now he was probably in shock that she was being so amenable. "There will be talk if I switch you to another station before Whittaker comes back, particularly as there were no complaints about your performance. Far be it from me to give you a black mark on your record after one shift because of personal considerations. You can stay on, Gina, until Whittaker reports back, which should be two weeks at the most. But in the meantime, I suggest you bid another couple of stations if you intend to live in Salt Lake."

Two weeks at the most to accomplish the impossible! "I'll take your advice. Thank you, Grady," she whispered, suppressing her joy that he hadn't seen fit to send her out of his domain just yet.

For some reason, Grady didn't seem to like this new side of her, or at least, he didn't seem to know how to respond to her levelheaded behavior. "When you report in the morning, you'll be treated exactly like everyone else."

"Of course."

"Stay away from Frank. He already thinks he's in love with you. He's got a sweet wife at home."

She blinked. "Anything else?"

"Corby's been telling everybody that you don't date fire fighters, but he's going to be the first one to make you break your rule. Don't do it, Gina. It can ruin lives."

They stared at each other across the expanse. "I never have and I never will. Is that good enough for you?"

"You're the one I'm worried about. To be a professional means never to mix business with pleasure. To be a woman in this profession makes it that much more difficult."

Gina smiled. "Do I take it you don't approve of female fire fighters?"

He started walking toward the front door. "Did I say that?" he shot back.

"I'm not sure. I don't remember you expressing your opinion one way or the other when we were married."

"The issue never came up." He gave her an enigmatic look.

"Now that it has, would you tell me your honest feelings?" She'd heard every opinion under the sun, but Grady's was the only one that mattered to her.

He appeared to consider her question for a minute. "If a woman can do her job well, it makes no difference to me."

"But—" Gina added, sensing a certain hesitancy on his part.

He rubbed the back of his neck thoughtfully. "But I still prefer to retain the image of a woman as I see her. Soft, curvaceous, warm, sweet-smelling . . .

"I'm afraid a woman in turnout gear with a mask and Nomex hood loses something in the translation. Particularly when her ears are singed, her knees burned beyond recognition and her face blackened with third-degree burns that never heal properly."

Gina was inordinately pleased with his answer. She cocked her head to the side. "It's a cosmetic thing with you, then."

"I suppose. However, you proved today that you could do the job. So admirably, in fact, that both crews want to hear more from you the next time we discuss prefire procedures. Your comment about always wearing your mask to the scene of a car fire made an impact. In the crew's words, you're all right. High praise indeed after only one shift. Does that answer your question?" He sounded bored with the whole discussion.

"Yes, but I have one more. Have you told anyone—does anyone know about—"

"About us?" he interjected sternly. "No, Gina, and I see no reason for it to ever become public knowledge."

She lowered her eyes. "No. Of course not." Her bottom lip quivered and she bit it. "What shall I call you at the station? Captain or Grady? The men call you both, depending on circumstances."

He reached for the front doorknob. "Do whatever moves you, Gina."

She drew closer, smiling inside. She wondered what he'd do if she ever called him "darling" or "sweetheart," the way she used to. Neither of them would be able to live it down in front of the crew, but right now she was tempted. "Well, I'll see you in the morning."

Grady's pewter eyes played over her features once more before he nodded. Then he was out the door.

She started to shut it but left it open a crack so she could watch him as he strode quickly toward his car and drove away. She hungered for the sight of him and wondered how she would make it through the next twenty hours until she could be with him again.

He'd never know how close she'd come to walking over and putting her arms around him. No matter what their problems, they'd never had trouble communicating physically. As soon as they were within touching distance, the cares of the world would vanish. Grady was a passionate lover, always tender and seemingly insatiable. She'd never been intimate with a man until Grady came into her life. After three years, she still couldn't imagine being with anyone else. He'd ruined her for other men; if it was too late for her and Grady now, she had the strong conviction she'd remain single for the rest of her life.

Tears spilled down her cheeks. She missed him terribly. He was the most wonderful thing ever to come into her life, but she'd been too insecure to handle the fact that he lived another life apart from her—a dangerous one.

That was why, at thirty-three, he had an enviable collection of medals for heroism, according to Captain Carrera, and a reputation throughout the city that few men could equal.

Only the most aggressive fire fighters would bid for the kind of action he and others like him faced every time they reported for duty. That reality had paralyzed Gina with fear throughout their marriage. Now she quietly preened at all the praise heaped on her ex-husband.

If she didn't have to keep her former relationship with Grady a secret, she could entertain the guys with several hair-raising accounts of his daring in Beirut and Nicaragua during his war correspondent days. They'd never hear about it otherwise, because Grady was so modest—always had been. He couldn't see that what he did was in any way out of the ordinary.

To Gina, her husband had been bigger than life. But she'd loved Grady with a possessive love and lost him. If he'd only give them another chance, she longed to show him how different their marriage could be. There had to be a way to reach him, and she'd find it no matter how long that took!

Naturally Grady would have been with other women since their divorce, but so far no other woman had captivated him to the point that he'd proposed marriage. As far as Gina was concerned, her ex-husband was fair game and she would break any rule to win him back. With luck, Whittaker wouldn't return as quickly as Grady envisioned, giving her more time to rekindle his interest. Then maybe he'd learn to like the woman she'd become—enough to want to see her off duty.

Happier than she'd been in three years, Gina cleaned her apartment from top to bottom, showered, then took a long nap. Later in the day she went to dinner and a movie with her friend, Sue.

They'd met when a fellow fire fighter was injured and taken to the burn unit at University Hospital. During their all-night vigil they hit it off famously. When they had free days at the same time, they often watched videos and ordered pizza. Susan was down on policemen at the moment, having dated one who turned out to be married.

She and Susan had quite a lot in common, personally and professionally, and it amazed Gina now to think that during the months she lived in Salt Lake with Grady, she'd never once gone down to the station house or met any of his crew. She hadn't made any new friends, particularly avoiding people connected with Grady's line of work. Her life had been far too insular, always waiting for Grady to come home. She hadn't wanted anyone else if she couldn't have him. He must have felt so trapped, she mused sadly.

When Gina reported for work the next morning, she could hardly contain her excitement, because she and Grady would be spending the next twenty-four hours under the same roof. Her eyes searched for him hungrily as she let herself in the front door of the station, dressed in coveralls. He and the others had already started their routine jobs of checking out the apparatus. Everything had to work, from the siren to the lights. All the breathing equipment had to be in perfect condition.

"Good morning," she called out. The men turned in her direction to greet her. She was conscious of their staring, but it was Grady's gray eyes she sought. To make sure he never forgot that she was a warm, sweet-smelling, curvaceous woman, she'd left her hair long and brushed it until it gleamed a silvery gold. Behind her ears she'd applied a new, expensive perfume Grady wouldn't recognize, but she wore little makeup except lipstick. She returned everyone's smiles, noting that Grady was the only one who merely glanced at her and nodded while he continued to inspect the pump gauges.

"What's my assignment for this morning, Captain?"

"You can start with the windows in the station."

"All right." She headed for the kitchen to fill a pan with hot water and vinegar. No fire fighter loved doing the station's housekeeping duties, but washing windows was definitely the most abhorrent and demeaning assignment of all. Bathrooms rated higher.

Gina settled down to her task with a vengeance. Grady knew exactly what he was doing—and he wasn't playing fair. He said he'd treat her like the others, but that obviously wasn't the case. There were enough windows in the place to keep her busy and isolated all day, which was exactly his intention. He purposely didn't assign any of the men to help with the job because he didn't want her fraternizing with one individual. She knew Grady was determined to keep her as far away from him as possible, without letting the crew suspect his intentions. And his word was law.

When the gong sounded for engine 1 to respond to a medical assist because of a family fight, Gina had to leave her window washing unfinished and hurry out to the truck. Grady had warned them that the Fourth of July holiday would bring a lot of calls. Unfortunately Grady rode ladder, which meant she'd see him only in passing. But even in that assumption she was wrong. After they'd assisted at the stabbing, their engine went immediately to a vacant lot where some children had started a fire while trying to light their "snakes."

The few times the engine returned to the station, the ladder truck was out. By eight that evening, the engine had responded to over twenty calls. Gina grabbed a bite to eat and quickly put the window-washing equipment away before another call came through. She'd have to finish the job on her next shift.

Around eleven, they were called to a house fire on the lower avenues. Grady's ladder was already in position when they pulled up to the scene. Gina gathered from Bob's conversation with the batallion chief over the walkie-talkie that the roof had caught fire from an illegal bottle rocket.

The sounds of fireworks and cherry bombs, the popping of firecrackers and the shrill whistling of noisemakers filled the hot night air. Everyone in Salt Lake seemed to be outside, which made driving to the scene much more difficult and gave Howard nightmares that he might run over someone's child suddenly darting into the street.

Smoke was pouring out the upstairs window and attic area of the huge old house. The enormous pine trees surrounding it could easily catch fire, something they all feared. Grady was up on the roof with the chain saw to ventilate. She could see his tall body silhouetted against the orange-red glow of the flames. The fire was becoming fully involved, which meant that every part of the structure was burning. Grady and his backup man would have to relinquish their position soon.

Gina was nozzle-handler and Ed, leadoff man. She entered the house with the empty hose; it was easier to manipulate without any water in it. She dashed up the old staircase to the second floor, then sent Ed back to tell the pump man to turn on the water. Another engine had been called to assist, and several hoses were going at once. It didn't take long to contain the fire.

Outside, while they were putting the hoses away a little while later, Gina glanced at the ladder truck but couldn't see Grady. She excused herself for a minute and hurried over to Frank. "Where's the captain?"

His perpetual grin was missing. "They hauled him to Holy Cross Hospital."

It felt as though a giant hand had squeezed her insides. "What happened?"

"I don't know. I was at the other end of the roof when it collapsed."

That was all Gina needed to hear. *Dear God,* she murmured to herself as she hurried back to the engine. "Howard, the captain's been injured."

"Yeah, I heard," he said when they'd all climbed inside. "We'll go by the hospital on the way back to the station and check up on him." No one spoke as they drove away from the scene. The bond between fire fighters was as strong as any blood ties could ever be, and she knew how the crew members felt about Grady.

All Gina could think about was that at least he hadn't been trapped inside the attic or wasn't still missing. Grady had often reminded them that no two fires were alike. The element of surprise lurking at every crisis made their work challenging and often dangerous. Gina tried to mask her feelings and let the others lead as they entered the emergency room.

To her surprise and everlasting gratitude, Grady was sitting on the end of the hospital bed being treated for smoke inhalation. As far as she could see nothing else was wrong.

The sight of four grubby, foul-smelling fire fighters drew everyone's attention, including Grady's. "Get out of here, you guys." He sounded strong and completely like himself. Gina sent up a silent prayer.

"We're going." Bob grinned and punched him in the shoulder. One way or another, all the men managed to give a physical manifestation of their affection and relief by a nudge or some other gesture. Gina kept her distance.

"I'll ride ladder if you'll finish washing my windows when we get back to the station." She spoke boldly with a smile that lit up her violet eyes. "I'd rather be treated for what you've got than these dishpan hands."

The guys hooted and hollered with laughter. Grady's steady gaze met hers. "No thanks. I'm on to a good thing and I know it. Those windows haven't been that squeaky clean since the place was built." A half smile lifted the corner of his mouth and her heart turned over. It was the first genuine, spontaneous smile he'd given her. If only he knew how she'd been waiting for that much of a response. Even if it had taken this crisis to make him forget for a little while the enmity between them, she was thankful. "I'll see you guys later," he muttered.

"Your captain won't be coming to work for at least forty-eight hours," the attending physician broke in. "It's home and total bed rest." Grady grimaced as the oxygen mask was put over his face again, but Gina rejoiced that the doctor had taken charge.

The ride to the station was entirely different from the earlier journey to the hospital. The men jabbered back and forth, releasing the nervous tension that had gripped them when they thought something might be seriously wrong with Grady. Gina felt positively euphoric and suggested they drop by the Pagoda for Chinese takeout—an idea applauded by everyone.

The station house was quiet after their last run. The men took their turns in the shower and when they'd finished, Gina took hers. Her thoughts ran constantly to Grady. He'd need some nursing when he got back to his condo. Was there a woman in his life, someone close enough to be there when he really needed help?

That question went around in her head all night. The hours dragged on endlessly. Except for one interruption—a call to put out a brush fire in the foothills—she should have had a good sleep by the time the shift ended at eight o'clock. Nothing could have been further from the truth. And judging from the looks on the faces of the crew, they, too, were concerned about Grady. When a couple of them said they were going to run by the captain's place before going home, she volunteered to go with them, adding that she knew a wonderful hot toddy recipe that soothed sore throats. They grinned at the idea of sampling her brew themselves, and as it turned out, all eight of them decided to visit their revered captain en masse. Gina could have hugged them. This way, she could see for herself that Grady was being looked after, and he couldn't possibly object to her presence—at least, not outwardly.

CHAPTER THREE

GRADY STILL LIVED in the condo Gina had shared with him during their brief marriage. Situated on a steep hill on the avenues high above Lindsay Gardens, its four floors of wood and glass looked out over the Salt Lake Valley in every direction. The stupendous view still had the power to take Gina's breath instantly, reviving a host of memories too painful to examine.

Winn did the phoning to gain them access, and one by one they filed up two flights of the spiral staircases to the third level, which Grady used as a living room cum lounge. Everything looked so exactly the same, Gina could scarcely believe it was three years since she'd stepped into this room with its café au lait and dark chocolate-brown accents. The fabulous Armenian rug they'd picked up on their travels still graced the parquet floor.

Standing in the corridor, she could see Grady lying on the brown leather couch in his familiar striped robe—one she'd worn as often as he after a passion-filled night of lovemaking. From this vantage point she couldn't tell his condition, but at least he was talking to the men. Needing to help, she went into the kitchen to make the drink of hot tea with touches of sugar, lemon and rum. She'd stopped at a store for the ingredients on the way, but had to rely on Grady's stock of spirits for the rum. Fortunately he had a quarter of a bottle on the shelf. She used it liberally then put it back, hoping no one would walk in on her in the process. The crew would become suspicious, to say the least, if they saw their newest rookie making herself at home in a strange kitchen, acting as if she belonged there.

She rummaged in the cupboard for a large mug. It didn't surprise her that the kitchen was immaculate. Grady had always kept a cleaner house than most women, with everything neatly in its place. She found a blue mug and poured the steaming liquid into it before hurrying upstairs, passing some of the crew on the way.

"I made enough for all of you," she called over her shoulder and walked toward Grady, now sitting up, propped against the cushions. The pupils of his eyes dilated in surprise at her approach. Apparently he hadn't known she'd come in with the others. She handed him the mug, taking care not to brush his fingers. "Try this, Captain. It's a proved remedy for what ails you."

He stared at her over the rim of the mug before taking a sip. "On whose authority?" At this point some of the others came up from the kitchen with drinks in their hands, ready to propose a toast to the captain's health.

"Mine. A couple of us were treated for smoke inhalation a few months ago. My buddy made this for me, and it really helped."

"It's not half-bad." Frank gave his seal of approval. The others took tentative tastes and echoed his opinion, then began drinking enthusiastically. Gina wondered if she was the only one who noticed the stillness that came over Grady after her explanation. He lifted the mug to his lips, but his unsmiling eyes didn't leave her face, almost as if the unexpected news had suddenly made him realize the dangers she'd been exposing herself to all this time. Was it her imagination, or did she detect a brief flash of anxiety in those gray eyes?

"You're not having any?" he asked after draining his mug. Everyone else was laughing and joking around, seemingly unaware of the tension between them.

Her mouth curved upward. "This stuff is potent. I have to be able to drive home."

"That's no problem. I'll see you get home safely," Bob piped up, bringing a roar of laughter from the crew.

"Don't you believe it," Howard whispered in her ear conspiratorially.

"Come on, guys," Bob bellowed. "Give me a break, will ya?"

Grady's mouth was pinched to a pencil-thin line, and Gina couldn't tell if it was the conversation or discomfort caused by his condition that produced the reaction. Either way, Gina didn't want their visit to add to his stress, and she began gathering mugs, including Grady's, to take back to the kitchen.

"Want some help?" Bob asked to the accompaniment of more laughter. He didn't know when to quit, she thought in annoyance.

She shook her head. "Don't you think one set of dishpan hands is enough, Lieutenant? You wouldn't want to ruin that macho image at this stage, would you?" This provoked more laughter, allowing her to escape Grady's unswerving stare and Bob's sudden frown.

She cleaned up the kitchen after preparing Grady a breakfast of eggs and toast. When Ed made an appearance with his mug she asked him to take Grady the plate of food. "Make sure he eats it, Ed. I've got to get going."

"Sure," he said, obviously surprised that she was leaving. But he didn't say anything else as she hurried from the kitchen and down the stairs to the front door.

A wall of heat enveloped her the moment she left Grady's air-conditioned condo to walk to her car. Salt Lake was experiencing an intense heat wave with no signs of letting up. Swimming in the pool at Susan's apartment building seemed an appealing prospect as Gina got into her car and drove home. This was her long weekend off, and already she could tell that she'd better fill it with activities or she'd go crazy thinking about Grady all alone in the condo. Or worse, with one of his girlfriends dropping by to keep him company. The pictures that filled her mind made her forget what she was doing, and it took a siren directly behind her to bring her back to awareness.

She glanced in her rearview mirror to see a police car signaling her to pull over. With a groan, she moved to the side of the boulevard above the cemetery and waited. A female officer approached the car and greeted Gina with a wry smile. Then the officer issued her a speeding ticket, her first since returning to Salt Lake. When she was free to go, she headed for Susan's apartment. They could both complain about the police—anything to take her mind off Grady.

As it turned out, Gina didn't get back to her own apartment until late that night, when she fell into a deep sleep almost before her head touched the pillow. She slept around the clock and awakened late in the morning to the sound of her mother's voice. The answering machine was still on. A twinge of guilt soon had Gina dialing her mother's number in Carmel. She hadn't written or phoned in more than three weeks, and she knew her mother worried.

They had a fairly long chat but by tacit agreement didn't discuss Grady. Her mother didn't approve of Gina's plan to insinuate herself into his life again. She'd argued from the beginning that Grady had married her under false pretenses, and as far as she was concerned, their marriage had been doomed at the outset because he hadn't revealed his love for fire fighting to Gina. Gina's father kept quiet on the subject, but she knew his opinion was the same as her mother's. They both hated her work.

The conversation ended after they made tentative plans for Gina to fly to California for the Labor Day weekend—one of the few holidays she didn't have to work.

Before she took a shower, Gina played back the tape to see if she had any other messages. It annoyed her to hear Bob Corby's voice asking her to go out with him. He'd left his home number so she could call him back with her answer.

She felt the best thing to do was ignore the message, and the next time he approached her in person, reiterate her rules. In time, he had to get the point! She'd told Grady she didn't date the men she worked with, and she meant it. What Grady didn't know was that no man she'd ever met measured up to *him*—so there was no temptation, not even with the undeniably attractive Lieutenant Corby.

It took all Gina's self control not to call Grady or go by the condo to see if he was all right. When her next shift began, she arrived fifteen minutes early, only to discover that Grady wouldn't be in for a while. He had to be seen by a doctor before he could report for duty. Her spirits plummeted as she began housekeeping duties along with the others. She purposely avoided Bob, who followed her with his eyes. He was fast becoming a nuisance, but it wasn't until the gong sounded that she realized how angry he felt with her for not returning his call or even acknowledging it.

"Frank?" he shot out, issuing orders as the second in command. "Ms Lindsay will replace you on ladder this run."

Gina didn't know who was more surprised, she or Frank. The poor man looked as if Bob had just slapped him in the face. Clearly he wasn't happy about the sudden switch of assignment, but Gina understood. Bob had decided to set her up for failure. His ego couldn't stand being dented.

Handling ladders was difficult work, even for someone of Frank's brawn. Bob wanted her to look inadequate, unequal to the job.

Rico drove them out of the truck bay to the downtown area. It was noon, the worst possible time of day, with the heavy traffic impeding their progress. Bob got on his walkie-talkie with the battalion chief. They were discussing methods to proceed when Gina spotted smoke pouring out of a fourth-story window of the Duncan office building.

Engine 2 was first in, but the alarm had sounded for more help. This was it for Gina. If she made a mistake at the fire ground now, the other men would know it and possibly suffer as a result. She'd never be assigned to Ladder Number 1 again, and Grady would make sure she was relocated to the station that made the lowest number of runs. News of her failure would spread throughout the department. And this was exactly what Bob wanted to happen.

"Gina, you'll work with Winn, Rico with me. Let's go!"

Whether he'd set her up or not, right then Gina had a fire to fight. For the time being she forgot their personal battle and ran to the back of the truck. "I'll get the poles," she called out to Winn, who nodded and started pulling the ladder off the truck.

The trick with this kind of ladder was to attach the poles to the ladder on the ground and through leverage, hoist the ladder against the building. More than one person was needed to accomplish the maneuver. Gina had done it in training more times than she wanted to think about, but she'd hardly ever had to put it into practice during a real call.

Out of the corner of her eye she saw another ladder pull up to the fire ground. Already a couple of men from the engine truck had gone into the building with the hoses.

"Ready?" Winn shouted. Gina gave the sign and together they placed the ladder in an alley that gave access to the building and set it against the wall. Next she worked the rope that raised the extension so they could reach the fourth floor. She couldn't believe it but they managed the whole procedure without problems. Winn flashed her a quick smile that showed his relief. Normally it would have been Frank helping with the equipment, and she knew Winn had been holding his breath.

Gina grabbed her pack, then put the mask over her face before starting up the ladder. Her job was to hunt for any unconscious or injured people trapped in the building. She had no idea how involved the fire had become, but smoke continued to pour out of the fourth-floor windows and the atmosphere grew darker the higher she climbed.

Her turnout gear felt like a lead weight as she approached the top of the ladder to climb in one of the window frames, the glass blown out by the fire. She could only hope most of the people had left their offices to go to lunch before the outbreak.

The number 2 ladder truck working farther down the alley was having a tough time opening up the side of the building to ventilate. The smoke was really heavy now. Gina's intuition told her the hoses had probably extinguished most of the fire and what she was seeing was a lot of smoke from burned electrical insulation.

Finally she reached the window and wriggled in on her stomach. She started crawling around, going into one room and then another. It seemed like an eternity that she and Winn, who wasn't far behind, had been going around in circles. Except for the shout of a fire fighter and the sound of the hoses, she thought everyone else must have cleared the building. It was then she heard a low moan. The adrenaline surged through her.

Gina veered left and her gloved hand suddenly felt a body huddled up against the remains of a file cabinet. With the smoke as thick as mud Gina had no way of knowing it it was a woman or a man. But the body was definitely too heavy to lift.

Squatting, she grabbed the body under the arms and began to drag it, convinced the person was taller than her own five foot six.

The ventilation must have started working, because the smoke was now being drawn away from her. Gina inched along in the opposite direction, pulling the deadweight slowly down a watery, debris-filled corridor. She'd performed this maneuver hundreds of times in practice drills, but this was only her third live rescue. The instructors had told the class that there was no way to simulate the real thing, because practice drills didn't drain you emotionally and psychologically in quite the same way. They knew what they were talking about.

She encountered a nozzle-handler when she rounded a corner leading to a stairwell. Somewhere along the way she and Winn had become separated, so she was thankful when the man signaled to someone farther down the stairs on the hose to come and assist. The smoke had cleared sufficiently for her to see that she'd been dragging a man almost as big as Frank and completely unconscious. She and the other fire fighter managed to get the man down three flights of stairs and outside to the street.

Gina immediately pulled off her mask and put it on him. She flipped it on bypass to give the man air. He eventually started to come to as an ambulance crew took over and carted him away to a hospital. Clutching the mask she made her way back to the truck looking for Winn, but Rico said he hadn't come out yet.

With a sick feeling in the pit of her stomach, Gina hurried into the building again and raced up the stairs as fast as her turnout boots would allow. Dodging hoses, she replaced her mask and hurried along the floating wreckage, calling out for Winn. They worked on the buddy system. She wouldn't leave the building until she found him!

Panicking because she didn't get a response when she shouted, Gina moved quickly to the area where she'd entered through the window. A dozen different things could have gone wrong, and Winn could be anywhere, hurt or unconscious. She turned one corner on a run and careered into another fire fighter, the collision almost knocking the wind out of her. Her mask fell off. "Winn?" she cried out as the man holding her steady whisked off his own mask. "Grady!"

There was an indescribable look on his blackened face. She must have imagined he said, "Thank God," in a reverent whisper, because in the next instant he was giving her an order. "Go out to the truck, Gina."

"But I have to find Winn!"

"He's out on the ladder lifting someone to the ground right now. Do as I say!"

"But—"

"Don't argue with me," he thundered. "You've caused enough trouble already. Winn said you were up that ladder before he could stop you. You little fool. It wasn't intended that you enter the building on this run."

"But Lieutenant Corby—"

He muttered an epithet beneath his breath, and his hands tightened on her arms before releasing them. "I'll deal with Corby later," he said in a fierce voice, as he handed Gina her mask.

She sucked in her breath. "Yes, sir, Captain, sir!" Anyone overhearing them would automatically assume she was being chastised on the spot by her superior. With cheeks blazing red beneath the grime and soot, she left Grady to his job of filling in the incident report and went back downstairs. She scanned the fire ground for Lieutenant Corby and saw him standing by engine 1. Apparently Grady was now in command of ladder 1. Joining the others in the process of cleaning up, she walked over to help Winn, who was bringing down the extension. A man with a video camera sporting the Channel 8 logo intercepted her.

"I'd like to interview you for a minute, if I could?"

"Ask him." Gina nodded toward Winn. "He lifted a victim from the fourth floor down a fifty-five-foot extension ladder without being able to see an inch in front of him."

The cameraman scratched his head. "But somebody said a wo—"

"You'll have to clear the area." Grady's voice broke in. "My crew has a lot of cleanup work to do. You could get hurt."

Gina looked at Grady standing there in full turnout gear with his hands on his hips and couldn't imagine anyone defying him. To her relief, he seemed fully recovered and ready for action. The cameraman backed off and went elsewhere for a story while Gina helped Winn with the ladder.

The crew worked in silence. Back at the station when everyone relaxed, the men loved to chat, but on the job, Gina noticed that most of them didn't talk. They simply went about their work in a methodical, orderly manner, unlike a lot of women she'd met, who needed to dissect and discuss every step of the way. Gina enjoyed the difference.

She avoided looking at Grady, and grew more uneasy after they all climbed into the truck and headed back to the station. She purposely scooted in next to Rico and practised her high school Spanish with him in an effort to expend some of her excess energy. Rico had an entertaining personality and kept things light. That prevented her from thinking about the inevitable moment when Grady would tell her she'd been assigned somewhere else for her next shift. She could feel the vibrations coming from him even though Winn sat between them.

Much to her relief, another call sent them out to contain a fire near the airport. It was after ten at night before both the engine and the ladder finally pulled into the station. Everyone was ravenous and stormed the kitchen.

Gina decided this was the best time to take her shower. Her real motive was to stay out of Grady's way. So far her plan to go nice and easy had backfired. She hadn't counted on the torrent of emotions his nearness evoked, and it appeared that her entry into his world had upset him so much he couldn't wait to be rid of her.

Turning off the taps, Gina reached for a towel and stepped from the shower just as the bathroom door opened.

"Grady!" she cried out in shock, hurriedly wrapping the towel around her body. But she hadn't been quick enough to escape the intimate appraisal of his eyes. "I—I thought the door was locked. I *know* I locked it!"

His gaze traveled once more over her silvery-gold hair still wet from a shampoo and came to rest on the little pulse that pounded mercilessly in the scented hollow of her throat. He closed the door, sealing them off from the others.

"How many times has this happened before?" His eyes were mere slits but she saw a telltale flush on his cheeks.

"This is the first. I swear it," she replied. He didn't say anything, though he made no move to leave. "I thought I'd shower while everyone ate. I always pick a time when I think it's safe, but for some reason, the lock didn't engage. I don't know why." Her voice trailed off because she had the impression he wasn't listening.

"This could cost you your badge."

"It was an accident, Grady." Her skin flamed with the heat of embarrassment and anger.

"If I didn't know we'd had trouble with this lock before, I'd think you were being deliberately provocative."

Her jaw clenched. "You know me better than that!"

"I thought I did," he ground out, sounding breathless. "If any other man had walked in here tonight and had seen what I saw—" He broke off. Gina looked away.

"While you're at station 1, you'll refrain from showering or bathing on the premises, and that's an order."

She hitched the towel a little higher and glanced over at him. "I know what you must think but—"

"You haven't the slightest idea," he fired back. Gina's violet eyes played over his face. It had an unnatural pallor and his eyelids drooped. He shouldn't have come back to work this soon. He hadn't fully recovered from his earlier ordeal, she realized now. Compassion for the man she loved made her want to hold out her arms and enfold him. Instead, she averted her eyes.

"If you'll excuse me, I'll get dressed and go to bed," she muttered.

"Before I go I want your promise about not showering."

"You have it." She swallowed hard. "Grady? You don't look well," she said impulsively. "Why didn't you stay home for a few more days?"

He drew in his breath and reached for the doorknob. "It's a good thing I didn't, wouldn't you say? Corby's panting for an opportunity just like this."

"You've made your point, Grady."

"I haven't even started," he growled and left the bathroom. She heard the lock click as he closed the door behind him.

For a moment, the bathroom seemed to tilt and Gina gripped the edge of the sink with both hands. She didn't blame Grady. The coincidence of his walking in just then, of the lock slipping at that very moment, was almost too improbable to believe.

She bit her lip in an effort to stem the tears. Of all the stupid things to have happened, this was the worst. Grady was an extremely private person. This kind of situation could only offend him—the last thing she wanted to do.

The gong sounded for engine 1 and she threw on her clothes, only to be waylaid by Grady as she opened the door. Apparently he wasn't taking any chances on that lock. "Frank's filling in on this assist," he said coldly. "I want you to go to bed, and I suggest you go there now!"

It was on the tip of her tongue to take issue with his orders, but the angry look in his eye made her reconsider. Without a word, she walked through the station to his dimly lit office and lay down on the bunk, her heart pounding hard. As soon as the engine had left the bay, Grady appeared in the room. He shut the door, and for what seemed like an eternity he stood there, not saying anything.

She couldn't stand the silence any longer. "Am I being punished—sent to my room?"

"Gang fights are no place for a woman, and I wouldn't care if you held ten black belts in karate. One jab of a stiletto in a vulnerable spot could mean a permanent disability."

Gina sat up, tucking her legs beneath her. "You told me at my apartment that you were going to treat me exactly like the others."

"I intended to until you broke all the rules."

She tossed her head. "The Grady I used to know knew how to forgive—particularly an unavoidable accident."

Even in the half-light, she could feel the menace in his expression. "Apparently the job has brought out a dark side in both of us."

"That's not true, Grady." Her voice trembled. "I'm sorry for what happened earlier. Can't we let it go at that?"

"Once again, you're asking the impossible, Gina."

"Oh, for heaven's sake, Grady. We used to be married. It isn't as if you haven't seen me in the shower before. Naturally I'm thankful it was you who happened to walk in on me. If it had been anyone else, I would have died of embarrassment."

She heard a noise come out of him that sounded like ripping silk. "I thought you did a fairly convincing imitation of embarrassment when I walked in. As many times as you've blushed in my arms, I've never seen you look quite that . . . disturbed before."

Gina sank back on the mattress and turned her head away from him. "I don't want to think about it anymore."

"So help me, I don't want to think about it, either," he whispered. Abruptly he paced several steps and when he spoke again, his voice was brisk. "You'll ride ladder the rest of the shift."

"Yes, sir."

"Gina?"

"What else have I done wrong?" she asked, sighing wearily.

"Confine your hair to a ponytail while you're on duty. Don't flaunt your beauty in front of the men. Corby lost it this morning when you arrived for work. He's angry because you rebuffed him in front of everyone at the condo. That's why he assigned you to ladder."

"I know." She heaved another sigh. "He phoned me at the apartment, but I didn't return his call and I guess that added fuel to the fire."

"To your credit, the crew is recommending you for a medal for that rescue today, which will only make Corby more determined to get even with you. Be careful, Gina."

"What more can I do? I've told him point-blank I don't date fire fighters."

"Just being who you are is problem enough," he murmured enigmatically. "Stay out of his way until Whittaker gets back."

She raised herself up on one elbow. "You're making me out to be some kind of femme fatale." She laughed nervously.

"Come off it, Gina. You've always been a knockout, and you know it. If anything, the turnout gear emphasizes your femininity. There's nothing you can do about the way nature made you, but for the good of the station, try not to draw undue attention to yourself."

"Maybe I should get my hair cut."

"Unfortunately that wouldn't change a thing."

The fact that he still found her attractive should have thrilled her, but his voice sounded ragged and she couldn't stop worrying about his physical condition. "You're tired, Grady. Why not lie down and rest?"

"Is that an invitation, Gina?" he mocked in that hateful manner.

"Would you like it to be?" she taunted, after a long silence.

He swore softly, then wheeled from the room. His abrupt departure pleased her. The idea that Grady wasn't as much in control as he'd led her to believe brought a satisfied smile to her lips. There'd been no need for him to follow her back to his office. He'd instigated this last conversation as if he hadn't been able to help himself.

She turned onto her stomach and hugged the pillow. It was the first sign that maybe, just maybe, she was getting under his skin. In fact, she'd begun to think that lasting this long at station 1 was a miracle in itself.

CHAPTER FOUR

TENNIS AND SWIMMING were Gina's favorite ways of keeping in shape, but some of those activities had to be curtailed during the next week to make time for singing rehearsals. She would be taking part in the entertainment at the annual Fire Fighters' Ball.

Nancy Byington, a fire fighter from station 5, had been made cochair of the ball, and she was out to revolutionize what had always been an event sponsored by the men and their wives. Nancy's reputation as a pioneer in forging the way for more female fire fighters preceded her. When Gina received a call from Nancy asking for help, she was delighted to oblige, particularly as the ball was being held at the soon-to-close Hotel Olympus.

Besides being in charge of the intermission activities, Nancy planned to emcee the dance and to force people to mingle and get to know one another. Her plan to remove a few barriers was met with enthusiasm by other veterans in the department. Preball publicity infiltrated all the stations, urging everyone to attend, with or without a partner. This was one event in which all personnel were expected to participate.

The foyer of the famous old hotel had been transformed into a palace garden. Three-tiered topiary trees strung with thousands of tiny white lights, interspersed with baskets of roses and petunias, created a magical mood, enhanced by the magnificent crystal chandelier shimmering above the marble dance floor below. Nancy jokingly told Gina and the others taking part in the entertainment that they wanted to bring down the house, but "please *not* the chandelier."

On one side of the raised platform where the intermission activities would be performed were the buffet tables. Enough room had been left on the other side to accommodate the orchestra. The tables bordering the dance floor had been reserved for VIPs within the various departments, as well as visiting dignitaries in state and local government.

As the time approached for intermission, Gina looked down from her vantage point on the mezzanine floor. The group was highly animated, encouraged, no doubt, by Nancy's guidance. So far, they'd done a conga line, a Virginia reel, break dancing for the more daring, a waltz for all people more than fifty and a fox-trot for everyone between forty and fifty. The list of innovative ways to get everyone involved went on and on. And all the while, Gina's eyes had been searching for Grady. So far she hadn't seen him. Maybe he'd decided not to come, and stayed on at the station with the skeleton crew.

"Can't you find him?" Susan asked in a low voice. She was the only person in the department who knew about Grady.

"Not yet."

"Will I do?"

Gina turned around and began to laugh, and the sound caught the attention of the other two female fire fighters. The four of them were dressed like male fire fighters, in turnout coats and pants several sizes too large to accommodate their evening gowns. In gloves, air masks and helmets pulled down to disguise their hair, no one would know they were women. They stood tall in their huge boots, since they were wearing high heels. So far, no one had any idea who they were.

With a great deal of difficulty, they moved down the staircase and walked out onto the platform when Nancy gave the signal. A ripple of laughter started among the audience and began to build as they approached the microphone. Gina could hear several boisterous asides telling them to go back to the station.

Her heart started to run away with her as she quickly scanned the audience now seated at tables to watch the floor show. Several hundred salaried fire fighters and volunteers, with their partners, were assembled, wearing tuxedos and evening gowns. It was when she looked beneath the overhang where she'd been standing before the show that she saw Grady with a good-looking brunette sparkling up at him. As Grady was one of the VIPs, he sat at a table near the buffet and dance floor, so close she could detect his slightly bored smile. He looked devastatingly handsome, but not nearly as animated as his date. A duty affair like this was not his favorite activity, and she had an idea he'd only come for appearance's sake. How Gina longed to wipe that world-weary expression from his face. Frank sat at Grady's table with a petite redhead. A few tables away she saw Howard and Ed with their wives. No matter how hard Nancy tried to force people to mix, the men tended to stick together.

"Since you guys gate-crashed this party, you're going to have to sing for your supper," Nancy began her introduction as the lights dimmed and the spotlight came on to blind the performers. "What do you say, audience?"

A huge cheer went up from the crowd.

"All right, Firebrands. Take it away!"

Someone behind the scenes started the tape recorder and the women lipsynched and mimed their way through

"Smoke Gets in Your Eyes," "Ring of Fire" and "Heat Wave."

The choice of songs was a huge success. When the singers finished, the men in the audience got to their feet and clapped for three minutes. A fire fighter planted in the crowd shouted, "We want to hear what they really sound like!" This brought on a chorus of shouts and joking.

"So you want the real thing, do you?" Nancy's voice rang out.

"Yes!" the audience responded.

"All right. But remember! You asked for it!" When Nancy turned to the women, it was their cue to disrobe. Synchronizing their actions, they removed their helmets, masks and gloves, undid their turnout coats and pants, kicked off their boots and wriggled out of everything to step forward dressed in crimson chiffon, calf-length evening gowns. "The Firebrands," Nancy said, motioning them closer to the microphone.

The clapping and whistling started. The men were on their feet once more. No one had guessed who'd been hidden beneath the turnout gear. The quick-change-artist routine was an unqualified success, and it took time for everyone to quiet down.

"I'm going to ask each of the women to step forward as I say her name and identify her station," Nancy continued. "Believe it or not, these ladies are some of the intrepid fire fighters protecting our city. Station 7's representative is Karen Slogowski, station 5's is Susan Orr, station 4, Mavis Carr and, last but not least, from our famous station 1, representing Grady's bunch—Gina Lindsay."

Pandemonium broke out with more cheering and clapping. Finally it subsided as the group began singing to a recorded background music tape of the Beach Boys' hit, "Kokomo." Gina's voice supplied first alto, and for a bunch of amateurs, she felt they performed rather well. The song was a favorite and the long applause at the end of the number reflected the crowd's approval.

"All right, folks. You've heard from the Firebrands. Now we're going to have them bring back the dancing by starting out with Ladies' Choice. Now, confidentially," Nancy told the audience, "our performers haven't rehearsed this part of the program. In fact, they have no idea what's going to happen next."

A hush fell over Gina and the others. Susan's eyebrows quirked while Gina held her breath, wondering what Nancy was about to pull. She wasn't the emcee for nothing!

"You know," Nancy continued, "these ladies take a lot of orders from their superiors day in and day out. I think it would be kind of nice to turn the tables for a change. Where are the captains of these personifications of courage and pulchritude? Come on—stand up! That's an order! Let's have the lights on."

While pandemonium reigned once more, Gina felt faint and flashed a distress signal at Susan, who winked conspiratorially. Gina suspected Susan was behind this, but could do absolutely nothing about it as the glittering chandelier illuminated the room.

"Ladies, go find your captains and let the dancing begin! And all you wives and sweethearts out there, once these four have taken a twirl around the dance floor, it's your turn to pick a new partner and *mingle*!" When Nancy finished her spiel, Sue whispered to Gina that this was her chance.

Flushed with a feverish excitement, Gina made her way slowly across the gleaming marble floor toward Grady.

On the periphery, she could see the other women approaching their captains, who stood up amid continued cheering and joking, awaiting their fate. The orchestra had started to play a bossa nova number that lighted a fire in her blood. What was meant to be simply good fun had turned into something else, at least for Gina. The realization that within seconds she'd be in Grady's strong arms caused a tremor to rock her body.

Grady's eyes ignited to a quicksilver color as she drew closer. His unsmiling gaze roamed over her face and hair, then fell lower to the curves swathed in crimson chiffon, and lower still to her jeweled high-heeled sandals sparkling like the diamond earrings she wore—the ones he'd given her for a wedding present.

She'd brushed her hair till it gleamed white-gold and curved under her chin from a center part. She wore a peach lip gloss and a touch of lavender eye shadow that matched the deeper violet irises. Not even on her wedding night had she wanted to look as beautiful for Grady as she did now. Her cheeks needed no blusher. Hectic color made her skin hot, and she had difficulty breathing as she finally stopped in front of him.

Other people were at the table, but it seemed to her that a nimbus surrounded Grady, blotting out everyone else. He stood tall and straight, like a prince—magnificent in black with a pearly-gray cummerbund, which matched his crystalline eyes. His indecently long black lashes gave them their particular incandescent quality. For a brief moment his expression sent out a message of sensual awareness that Gina felt to the depths of her being.

"Captain Simpson? May I have this dance?"

His half smile was a slash of white in his bronzed face. "What would you do if I said no?" he asked, his voice mocking, and her heart began to knock in her breast.

Nervously, she moistened her glistening lips. "Then I guess I'd have to ask your second in command."

She'd said it teasingly, but a dull flush suddenly tinged his cheeks as he gathered her in his arms and swung her out onto the dance floor.

During their marriage, their bodies had been so perfectly attuned, that even now Gina's hand slid automatically toward his neck. Then, when she remembered where they were, she quickly moved it to his broad shoulder, in a clumsy, betraying motion. His chest heaved as if he, too, had momentarily gone back in time. In Cairo they'd danced the nights away during their brief honeymoon. Right now, it seemed the most natural thing in the world for Gina to melt against him and make a kind of slow-motion love to him as they danced.... But of course they couldn't do that in sight of hundreds of people—including his date for the evening.

As if by tacit agreement, Grady circled her around the floor at a discreet distance, while other couples started to join in. Gina happened to be wearing Grady's favorite French perfume, and that, combined with the male tang of his body and the hint of musk he wore, intoxicated her. Her eyes were level with his chin where she saw a little telltale nerve throbbing madly near the tiny scar at the corner of his mouth. Whatever his feelings were for her at this point, her nearness disturbed him. She'd been married to him too long not to know the signs. This response of his was something to cherish.

"It's sinful how beautiful you are," he grated, and her eyes flashed upward, in confusion—and hope. For an unguarded moment his eyes blazed with the old hunger that made her knees go weak.

"I could tell you the same thing," she whispered in a husky voice, not realizing she was caressing the palm of his hand with her thumb until she heard his quick intake of breath and felt the pressure of his hand forcing her to stop the teasing motion. "I'm sorry."

He didn't pretend to misunderstand her. "It comes as naturally to you as breathing, doesn't it, Gina?"

The censure in his tone caused her to stiffen and she almost missed her step. "What do you mean?"

"You're a born temptress. The first time I saw you, you flashed those incredible violet eyes at me and I fell a thousand feet without knowing what in the hell had hit me."

She swallowed hard. "I—I felt the same way. You were bigger than life."

"For a little while, we tasted paradise," he murmured with a tinge of sadness in his deep voice, "but apparently it wasn't meant to be a steady diet." He cocked his dark head to the side. "Is that what your floor show was all about? A trip down memory lane?" His smile was more cynical than anything else and didn't reach his eyes. "If so, you succeeded admirably."

His words made her spirits plummet sharply. He might have been in love with her once, but no longer. Searing pain almost immobilized her as she understood what he was telling her—it was too late....

"This whole thing may have looked contrived, but Nancy spoke the truth. Dancing with our captains was her idea. She's determined to promote better relations between the men and the women. She had no way of knowing how...abhorrent it would be to you."

There was a long pause, then, "Never abhorrent, Gina. You're the stuff men's dreams are made of, didn't you know?"

But not your dreams, she agonized inwardly. "I think we've danced long enough to satisfy protocol. Your date will be waiting."

Grady stopped dancing even though the orchestra still played. A strange tension emanated from him. "Where's your date? I'll deliver you back to him."

Ever the gentleman . . . but his offer had the effect of plunging a dagger in her heart. She would have loved to produce such a person for him, but she'd come alone and would go home alone. She found she couldn't lie to him. "Those of us performing didn't have dates. We need to be on hand to clean up after everything's over. Have a nice evening, Captain Simpson," she whispered, unable to look up at him. If she hadn't known better, she would have thought he let go of her arms reluctantly as she slipped away and moved across the crowded floor toward the buffet. At the moment she desperately needed a cold glass of punch.

Once again Nancy's voice sounded through the mike, announcing that the next dance was for people without partners. Gina grimaced at the irony and swallowed the rest of her punch.

"Do I dare ask for a dance?" The familiar voice came from directly behind her.

"Lieutenant Corby," Gina finally acknowledged him, surprising an unexpected look of contrition shining out of his light blue eyes.

"I did a dumb thing the other day, assigning you to ladder, and I'd like to apologize."

Gina folded her arms. "I'm certified to ride ladder, Bob. No apologies are necessary."

"I know." He nodded, and there was a moment's uncharacteristic hesitation. "It's my reasons for doing it that I'd like to explain."

Gina took a deep breath. "Did the captain ask you to?"

He looked affronted. "We exchanged a few words, but this apology is my own idea." Something in his tone forced Gina to believe him. "I don't usually have trouble getting a woman to go out with me." He scratched his ear. "I know that sounds conceited, but it's true."

"I can believe it," she interjected good-naturedly.

He stared at her for a moment. "It ticked me off that I couldn't get to first base with you. In fact, I'm still having a hard time seeing you as one of the crew."

"You and all the others." She smiled.

He shook his head. "No. . . some of the guys are further along than I am. I guess I just don't want to fight fires with a woman. There are a lot of other things I'd rather do with her." He grinned.

"I admire your honesty. I suppose if a man started coming to my all-female sewing club, I'd feel uncomfortable about it myself."

His brows quirked. "That's not the best analogy I've ever heard."

Gina laughed. "I know, but I can't think of a better one. Women fire fighters are unprecedented—"

"Particularly ones who look like you," he broke in. "I thought Captain Simpson was immune, judging by the way he's treated you at the station, but after tonight, I can see he's as vulnerable as the rest of us."

"He was ordered to dance with me," she retorted to cover the sudden fluttering of her pulse.

His lips twitched. "Would it take an order to get you out on that dance floor now? I purposely didn't bring a date because I hoped you'd take pity on me." His hands lifted in a gesture of comical despair. "I promise this won't obligate you to anything else."

"Sure, why not?" she answered and allowed him to guide her onto the floor.

"Do you samba?" The orchestra was doing a whole series of Latin dance numbers. Gina nodded. "All right, then."

Bob Corby turned out to be an accomplished dancer, challenging Gina's ability to keep up with him. The first dance was over so soon that he begged for another. Soon Gina forgot to count. She hadn't had this good a time in ages. She'd have the rest of the night—the rest of her life—to torture herself with thoughts of Grady and all she'd lost.

She purposely kept her attention on Bob so she wouldn't be tempted to stare at Grady. But when he suddenly gripped Bob's shoulder during their last dance, Gina was forced to meet gray eyes as dark as storm clouds. Why he should look that angry she had no idea. Dancing with Bob didn't constitute high treason, nor did it mean she'd accept a date with him. She'd already made that promise to Grady, so she couldn't understand what kind of feelings could produce such hostile emotion.

"Captain?" Bob turned to him with the same happy smile he'd been wearing as they danced. "Are you trying to cut in on me?" Gina could hear the crackle of the walkie-talkie.

Something flickered in the recesses of Grady's eyes. "We're all needed back at the station. A tire warehouse was set on fire by arsonists. They're calling for additional units. Did you both bring cars?" They nodded.

Even as he spoke, she could see various crews walking away from the tables. It was amazing the ball had gone as long as it had without interruption.

"Gina?" He used her first name, which was a shock. "You'll ride back to the station with me. Someone can help you collect your car later." Gina felt too surprised to respond.

"I'll meet you there, Captain." Bob was all business now and took off at a run.

Gina wondered what had happened to Grady's date, but experienced a sudden, unholy surge of joy that he wouldn't be spending the rest of the night in the other woman's arms. She wouldn't allow herself to dwell on the pictures that immediately filled her mind.

Gina ran to keep up with Grady as they took a side exit and raced down two levels to the underground car park where he'd left the Audi. He helped her in before coming around to the driver's side and starting the engine. With the economy of movement she'd always admired, he backed out and they were off to the station, less than a mile away.

"In case you're wondering why I insisted you come with me, I thought this might be my only opportunity to talk to you privately before we go off duty."

"If this is about Lieutenant Corby, I've already told you I don't date fire fighters."

"I believe you, Gina, but I want to give you a warning. Corby's been bragging to the guys that he's going to have you in bed by the time Whittaker returns to duty."

She rubbed her forehead, where she could feel the beginnings of a headache. "Well, he can brag all he wants. His boast is meaningless," she said disgustedly.

Grady's hands tightened on the steering wheel, his knuckles turning white. "You and I may know it's pure fantasy, but the crew is another matter altogether, and your dancing with him all night adds credence. Once a rumor starts, it can fly out of control and no amount of truth can set it right."

"Are you telling me you're worried about my reputation?" she asked in amazement.

"I'm worried about problems with my crew, Gina. When a crack forms in the foundation, the whole place can come crashing down if you're not careful. We were all getting along fine—"

"Until I came to replace Whittaker." She finished the words for him. "It's no longer a mystery why you wanted this little tête-à-tête. Is this your polite way of getting me to bow out gracefully? Am I supposed to do the noble thing?"

Grady literally stood on his brakes as the car pulled into the parking area behind the station. He jerked his head around and glared at her. "Do you know a better way? Corby has seven years' seniority over you."

"And would bring a nasty lawsuit against you if you had him switched to another station for no good reason," she shot back bitterly. "But of course no one would expect me to bring a suit against him for sexual harassment, because women don't belong in the department to start with." Her eyes flashed purple in the dim interior. "Nancy's right. This department still lives in the dark ages!" On that note she got out of the car and slammed the door before she could hear Grady's response.

"Gina?" he called after her, slamming his own door. He ran to catch up with her. "I'm not through with you." He reached out and grabbed her arm, closing his hand over soft, warm flesh.

She whirled around, causing the chiffon to swing lovingly around her long, shapely legs. "Is that an order, Captain?" The blood was pounding in her temples, and her diamond earrings glittered with every heartbeat.

Grady's face had lost some of its color, and his mouth thinned into an uncompromising line of aggression. But before he could say anything else, they both heard the sound of the back door opening. Grady let go of her arm as if her skin had scalded him. "It's the captain!" one of the crew shouted. "Let's get ready to roll."

Gina wasted no time hurrying inside and changing into her coveralls and boots.

"You forgot something," Bob muttered as they all dived for their turnout coats on the hooks in the bay.

"What?" she asked almost impatiently, growing more and more resentful of Bob for being the cause of the latest confrontation between her and Grady.

"These." His fingers reached into the silken strands of her hair and removed the earrings. "They look real enough that I'd hate to see you lose them." The brazen gesture suggested an intimacy they didn't share. To her consternation, Grady had witnessed the byplay. There was a murderous gleam in his eyes that reminded her of their conversation in the car. His furious glance reiterated his earlier accusation—that her mere presence created a problem. And worse—it brought to mind the night Grady had given her those earrings. Now was not the time to recall those hours of ecstasy....

Gina took her earrings from Bob without saying anything and put them in one of her pockets. Earlier in the evening she'd been prepared to forget any friction and make a friend of him, but no longer. Unfortunately, he was her superior on the engine, which meant spending the rest of the shift in his company.

Other units were already battling the blaze when Gina's engine pulled up to the fire ground. Bob ordered Gina to lead in with the hose and start spraying the exterior of the warehouse to reduce the temperatures for the men on ladders. Ed worked with her, anticipating her movements as they carried the unwieldy hose across the crowded pavement surrounding the building.

Black smoke billowed from the roof, filling the air with hot fumes that burned her lungs. The place was a roaring inferno, singeing her brows and lashes as she trained the powerful spray on the wall of flame threatening the man above her on the ladder. At times she could scarcely see a foot in front of her.

When she heard a shout coming from somewhere overhead, she lifted her face instinctively. And that was the moment something glanced off her helmet, knocking her into oblivion.

"SHE'S COMING AROUND. Other than a gigantic headache, I think she's going to be okay."

Gina was cognizant of several things at once. Cool fresh air was being forced into her starving lungs and she could hear voices around her, one of them Grady's.

She pushed the mask away from her face and opened her eyes to discover she was inside an ambulance. She immediately focused on Grady's blackened face, but what impressed her most was the look of pain in his eyes.

"Don't move, Gina. Just lie still and take it easy."

She couldn't understand why he was there. "What happened? I heard a noise and suddenly everything went black."

He closed his eyes tightly for a minute, apparently held in the grip of some intense emotion. "A man from ladder 3 was overcome and his hose slipped," Grady started to explain. "His backup man braced to keep the hose from snaking, but you were standing in its path." His voice shook. "We can thank God it was only the hose and not the nozzle that sent you flying."

She sighed. A full hose running under pressure could break bones, or worse. "Sorry to leave you a man short, Captain." She gave Grady a wan smile.

"Gina..." he whispered in an agonized voice. She'd never heard Grady sound like that before and warmth surged through her heart, quickening her entire body. She no longer felt any pain. Somewhere deep inside him he still had feelings. Feelings for her. The knowledge caused her eyes to fill with tears. She blinked them away.

"You shouldn't be here, Captain. I'm fine. How's the other guy?"

His eyes played over her features for a long moment before he spoke, as if he were having trouble getting his emotions under control. His vulnerability was a revelation to Gina. Did he have any idea how hard he was squeezing her hand?

"I don't know," he finally answered in a thick voice. "We'll find out when we get to Emergency."

"I heard the attendant tell you I was going to be okay."

"You are." His relief was undisguised. "But I want an X ray to find out if you've suffered a concussion."

Gina moved her head tentatively. It was sore at the crown. "I don't feel sick to my stomach. I think that's a pretty good indication it's not serious. Are my pupils still dilated?"

An epithet escaped his taut lips. "You know too much for your own good."

Her smile was impish. "Does that annoy you?"

Her question seemed to catch him off guard. "Do you want the truth?"

"Nothing but."

"I prefer to think of you the way you were a few hours ago, but I'll confess that you're a good fire fighter, with more courage than I've seen in a number of men."

"That's high praise indeed coming from the illustrious Captain Grady."

With that remark his expression sobered. "Whatever the prognosis once we get to the hospital, you're exempted from duty for a while."

Her eyes searched his for reasons. "Why?"

"To give you a chance to fully recover—and to cool an explosive situation with Corby."

Gina ran a shaky hand through her hair. Grady still held on to the other, and it seemed completely natural. "What he did back at the station was inexcusable."

He sucked in his breath. "In all fairness to him, what he did he couldn't help. You're pretty well irresistible to the male of the species, Gina."

"Loyal to your male crew to the bitter end, aren't you, Grady."

"Realistic," he retorted solemnly. "All eyes were on you at the hotel. They couldn't help but be anywhere else. Men are the weaker sex, didn't you know that? Your smile can twist a man into knots and have him begging for more. Corby's no different from any other man in that regard."

"And he's the best fire fighter in the city next to you."

His dark brows furrowed. "He's *one* of the best."

But if it were a choice between her and Lieutenant Corby, Gina knew in her heart which one of them Grady would choose. There was no contest. Suddenly all the fight seemed to go out of her.

"Gina?" He sounded alarmed when he heard the small moan that escaped her lips. "Are you feeling ill?"

"I think I'm tired." Which was the truth, but more than that, she knew she'd lost the battle and the war. Grady couldn't have spelled it out any more plainly, and their conversation had the effect of numbing her.

"I shouldn't have allowed you to talk so long," he muttered.

"I'm glad you did. It's put everything into perspective." Her eyelids fluttered closed but not before she glimpsed the puzzled frown on his face, the uncertainty. It was a rare sight and one that would haunt her over the next few days.

CHAPTER FIVE

THE X RAY REVEALED a minor concussion, and Gina was ordered to bed for a few days. Sue and Nancy both came by the apartment several times to visit and help out. The guys at the station sent Gina a get-well card. All the signatures were there, including Grady's.

Bob called, leaving a message on the answering machine. He didn't press for a date. All he wanted was to wish her well; he also confessed that everyone missed her around station 1.

On her fourth day, she felt pretty much back to normal, except for an occasional headache. Anxious to be back on the job, she called the station and asked for Grady. If he didn't want her returning to his station, then she needed his permission to call headquarters and get reassigned. Someone she didn't know answered and said Captain Grady was off duty on his long weekend. Frustrated, Gina phoned Grady's condo. She didn't have to look up his number; he'd kept their old one. To her chagrin, he didn't answer and hadn't switched on his answering machine—if he even owned an answering machine. She didn't know.

At loose ends, she wandered out to the small patio off her dining room and lay down on the lounger to sunbathe. The heat was too intense to stay out for long, but it felt good.

She drank lemonade and listened to the radio. Reading still bothered her, but the doctor said that was a common side effect and would clear up in another day or two.

With one side of her body tinged a faint pink, she decided to turn over on her stomach and start tanning the backs of her legs. She closed her eyes, resting her head on her folded arms. She'd been lying in that position for only a few minutes when she felt a shadow fall over her. It was such a surprise, she jerked around and almost fell off the lounger. "Grady!"

"I'm sorry if I frightened you. I rang the front doorbell but I guess you didn't hear it."

She tugged the straps of her faded black one-piece bathing suit a little higher in a self-conscious gesture and switched off the radio. He stood there with his hands on his hips, legs slightly apart. No one looked better in a T-shirt and shorts than Grady. She swallowed hard and scrambled to her feet. "I—I'm glad you dropped by. I've been trying to reach you. Why don't we go inside? It's too hot out here."

Aware of his eyes on her, she almost ran into her bedroom for a toweling robe. Anything to cover herself. She ran a brush through her hair, willing her heart to stop pounding so hard. When she returned to the front room she found him planted in front of her photographs. Many were of him, in various situations; others showed the two of them together. If he found it odd that she still held on to them, he didn't say anything and she didn't explain.

He cast her a level glance over his shoulder. The mocking smile that tugged the corners of his mouth made her feel a need to hide behind her robe.

"Would you like some lemonade?" she asked hastily.

"Only if you don't go to a lot of trouble."

"It's already made."

He drew one bronzed hand through his dark hair. "You look too good for someone recovering from a concussion."

"I feel good. I still have a headache but it's slowly letting up." She hurried into the kitchen and poured them each a glass of lemonade. When she turned around, he was blocking the doorway, and his tall, lean frame seemed to dwarf her compact, tidy kitchen. There was something different about Grady—an intangible quality that stole the ground out from under her. All his pent-up anger seemed to be missing.

"I received the card. Tell everyone thank-you." She handed him a glass, which he took and immediately drained then held out for a refill. The action reminded her so much of the old days she broke into a full-bodied smile, which miraculously he reciprocated.

"The card was Frank's contribution. I think he's gone into mourning that you're not around."

"He's not the only one." She poured the last drop of lemonade from the pitcher into Grady's glass and handed it back. "I'm not used to this much inactivity and I'm going a little stir-crazy."

His devastating smile faded to be replaced by a more serious expression. "That's what I came over to talk to you about—and, of course, to see if you were feeling better."

She tucked a loose strand of hair behind her ear with unconscious allure. "As you can see, I'm fine and eager to get back to work."

He stared hard at her as he finished his second drink. "How would you like to take a drive up into the mountains for the rest of the day? It'll give you a break from this enforced idleness. And we'll have a chance to discuss your future with the department."

His last statement sounded ominous, but the joy she experienced at his invitation superseded all other thoughts. She had to fight to control her reactions. She hadn't seen Grady this mellow since long before the divorce and didn't want to do anything to disturb this momentary truce. "I—I'd love to get out of this heat. Do you mind if I take a quick shower first?"

For the merest fraction of a second, their eyes met in shared remembrance of the countless times he'd joined her there as a prelude to something else equally consuming and intimate. When she realized where her thoughts had wandered, she looked away. Grady shifted his weight as if he, too, had to make a determined effort to keep those memories in the past.

"Take all the time you need. I'll wait for you in the car."

She nodded. "I'll hurry."

Less than ten minutes later, she joined Grady. She'd dressed carefully, choosing white linen shorts and a lavender-blue crocheted top that fit at the waist and had puffed sleeves. A white silk scarf kept the hair out of her eyes as the Audi's open sunroof let in an exhilarating breeze.

Gina had little inclination to talk and apparently Grady felt the same way. When they entered Parley's Canyon for the steep climb to the summit, she was flooded by a bittersweet sense of déjà vu. They'd traveled this section of highway so many times in the past, on their way to picnics in the mountains. The tantalizing scent of his musk after-shave blended with the refreshing aroma of pine, and it took her back to those exquisite early days when they could hardly bear to be apart, even for an hour or two.

"I don't know about you but I'm hungry," he said as he took the turnoff for Midway, their favorite spot.

"So am I. Are you in the mood for hamburgers or pizza?"

"Actually, I had a picnic in mind. It's packed in the trunk."

Gina's eyes widened in amazement. "I haven't been on a picnic s—in a long time," she amended, struggling to keep her composure. Like a revelation, it came to her that he'd planned this outing. She couldn't help but wonder where he was taking them and could hardly breathe from excitement.

The back side of Timpanogos Mountain with its snow-crested peaks dominated the Swiss-like countryside. Gina felt a piercingly sweet ache of such longing, she was afraid to look at Grady. This was one time she couldn't disguise her emotions.

He was strangely silent as he drove through the tiny hamlet of Midway, past the post office. When he suddenly turned the corner and stopped in front of her favorite red-and-white gingerbread house—a type of architecture for which Midway was famous—she didn't understand. The little house with its pointed roof and lacy white scrollwork peered out from four giant blue spruce trees, like some enchanted cottage in the Black Forest. The lawn was a velvety spring green, and the white fence looked freshly painted.

Gina turned to Grady. "Are we going to have our picnic *here*?" she asked incredulously.

His smile was mysterious. "Every time we went past this house, you told me you wanted to have a picnic under those trees. Today I'm granting you your wish."

Her cry of joy could not be restrained. "Did you arrange this with the owners?"

"I did," he affirmed, as he levered himself out of the car. Gina jumped from her side and gazed all around at the magnificent view of the mountains surrounding them. She thought she might die of happiness to have Grady all to herself in this paradise. Her ecstatic glance darted to him.

"Let me help." She reached in the trunk for the blanket while he lifted out the basket of food, then she followed him through the little gate to a nest of spruce needles beneath the largest tree. Gina spread out the blanket and they sat down, reveling in the cool shade.

"Are the people away? How did you manage it?" She threw him one question after another as he began to fill her plate with chicken and potato salad. She, in turn, opened a bottle of sparkling white wine he'd provided and poured it into paper cups, sneaking a taste.

Grady sat cross-legged, munching on a drumstick. "I own it, Gina," he said matter-of-factly. Her motions abrupt, she put down the wine bottle, her violet eyes searching his for what seemed a timeless moment. "About six months after our divorce became final, my realtor called me and told me it had finally come on the market. I told him to start the paperwork immediately."

Tears came to her eyes unbidden. This little house had been their dream—their fantasy. To think that all this time, he'd been the owner, had taken care of it, lived in it, *without her*.

The wine no longer tasted sweet.

Grady blinked when he saw that she wasn't eating. He wiped the edge of his mouth with a napkin. "What's wrong, Gina? Are you feeling ill?"

"No." She shook her head and looked down. "I'm just surprised the people would sell it. You'd think a family would want to keep it for generations to come."

"The man who owned it died without leaving any heirs."

"You must have been thrilled," she said, studying her nails.

Grady looked pensive. "It's just a house, Gina. A place I come to relax and write—when I can find the time."

She hugged her arms to her chest. "The place looks immaculate."

"I have a caretaker who does odd jobs and house-sits when I'm not here. So far, the arrangement has worked out well."

As far as Gina could tell, Grady's bachelor life-style suited him perfectly. He had no need for permanent entanglements, no romantic notions to complicate his well-ordered existence. Had he brought her up here to demonstrate just how smoothly he'd made the transition from bondage to freedom? She hadn't suspected he had a deliberately cruel side.

"Would you like to come inside and have a look around? I bought it furnished because I haven't had the time to take on a redecorating project."

"Of course I'd like to see it." She rose to her feet and accompanied Grady up the walk to the front porch with its old-fashioned swing. The interior of the house had the makings of a turn-of-the-century museum, from a grandfather clock to a cane-backed rocking chair by the hearth. With a few improvements, it could be a veritable showplace.

Grady had turned the parlor into a den. While he sorted through a pile of manuscripts, Gina went upstairs to survey the two quaint bedrooms. Each window had a view of the mountains. The house was as adorable inside as it was out. And Grady owned it!

Gina felt as if someone had played a cruel trick on her. She'd been allowed a glimpse of paradise before it was gone from sight forever. "Does the reality live up to the fantasy?" Gina hadn't heard him come up the stairs and frantically brushed away the tears with the back of her hand.

"I think you already know the answer to that question." Her voice shook. "Can I ask you one?"

"Fire away."

"Why did you bring me here?"

She could feel the warmth of his body and knew he couldn't be standing more than a few inches away.

"I wanted to talk to you in a favorable ambience—away from everyone else—where we could communicate for once, instead of hurling abuse at each other."

She bowed her head, acknowledging his reasons. For so long their marriage had been little more than a battleground. She had to reach far back to remember times like this. "You didn't need to go to such elaborate lengths to soften me, Grady. I know I'm a complication you can't wait to be rid of." She took a deep breath. "I called you this morning to tell you I'm willing to take the next available posting, if that's what you want. It's not necessary for me to be at station 1. Whether you believe me or not, I find no joy in coming between you and your men. Grady's bunch is legendary, you know."

She expected anything but the dark silence that followed her statement.

"I told you in the ambulance that you do good work, Gina," he finally said. "Another station will be lucky to get you, and I mean that sincerely. I'll make it clear on the transfer that the reason for the change is due to Whittaker's return. He'll be back a week from Monday. Your time at the station has only been cut by four days as it is. We can get by with three men on the engine crew for that short a time."

She rubbed her arms as if she were cold. "Then I'll call headquarters in the morning."

"I understand station 6 needs a paramedic. It's a quieter station, not so many runs. You'd be happy there."

Heat filled her cheeks as she whirled around. "I prefer heavier action, Grady. The more runs, the better."

He frowned, the lines marring his handsome face. "The risk of danger takes a quantum leap in a station like number 1. You're still recovering from a concussion. You'd be a fool to go back for more of the same," he said, his voice strained now as the tension began to build.

Her jaw stiffened. "I remember telling you the same thing when we were married."

He gave a short, angry laugh. "I'm a man, Gina. Don't try making comparisons."

"So we're back to that again. For your information, *I* was out there doing my job when a *man* lost his hose and I got the brunt of it."

"Do you think I'll ever forget that?" He suddenly grasped her upper arms in firm hands and shook her. "The sight of your beautiful body knocked ten feet through the air before crashing against solid concrete? Or the blood in your hair when only an hour before it shimmered like gossamer? How about those stunning eyes closed to me, possibly forever? How about your luscious mouth blistered beyond recognition by heat so intense, a dozen men went to Emergency suffering exhaustion?" His chest heaved. "Do you honestly believe I'll be able to put that picture out of my mind?"

"Grady—" Her voice came out on a gasp. She placed her palms against the warmth of his chest, too shocked by his emotional outpouring to think coherently. His heart galloped beneath her hand.

"Touch me," he begged, covering her hands with his own to slide them around his neck. "Kiss me, Gina. I've needed to feel you like this for too long," he confessed, his voice ragged, breathless. Gina couldn't believe any of this was happening and lifted tremulous eyes to her ex-husband. The eyes staring back were hot coals of desire, blazing for her. "If anything, I want you more now than when we were married."

His dark head lowered, blotting out what little light there was in the bedroom. With a low moan, Gina surrendered her mouth to his, giving herself up wholly to the one man she loved—loved beyond comprehension. The hunger for him grew, even as it was being appeased. She felt that her bloodstream was full of shooting stars as he deepened their kiss, literally swallowing her alive. She had no idea how long they tried to devour each other.

Grady couldn't seem to get enough of her. His magic hands slid into her silky hair, cupping her head to give him easier access to her eyes and mouth.

Her lips chased after his, allowing him no respite as they both clung, delirious with wanting. Like water bursting over a dam, they were caught in a force beyond their control.

"I've dreamed of this so many times," she whispered feverishly, pressing hot kisses against his neck, drowning in the feel and scent of him.

He crushed her voluptuous warmth against him. "I never believed the reality could surpass the dreaming. I'm not going to lie to you, Gina. I want you. So much, it's agony."

"I know. I feel the pain clear to the palms of my hands. I've been in this condition longer than you can imagine."

He groaned at her admission and picked her up in his arms. "Can't you see you were made to be loved? Your skin and hair, everything about you was created to entice me! I can't function any longer without lying in your arms again. Only you can put out the fire that's burning within me, Gina. Help me," he cried out.

His voice shook with raw need. Gina was no more immune to his pleadings than she was to his caresses. How many nights for years had her body been racked with a longing that only his loving could assuage? She wrapped her arms tightly around his neck as he carried her the short distance to the bed, burying her face in his black hair, glorying in the right to be loving him like this again.

"Promise me you'll always stay this way, Gina. I couldn't bear to think of you maimed or disfigured for no good reason. You're so beautiful it hurts," he whispered against her mouth as he placed her gently on the bed and moved to join her. "I'll fix it with Captain Blaylock at station 6. It'll minimize the dangers tremendously. I couldn't do my job the way I'm supposed to if I constantly thought I had to worry about you."

A gentle finger traced the fine-boned oval of her face before his lips followed the same path. "This exquisite face, this body, was meant for *me*." On that note he covered her mouth with smothering force to begin his lovemaking in earnest.

At first Gina was too entrapped by her own needs to think coherently. It might have been an hour instead of three years since they'd last made love; it was as if they'd never been apart. But slowly the realization dawned that they were no longer married and that Grady was assuming she'd abide by his conditions. She needed clarification on one crucial issue before Grady became her whole world once again.

She caught his face in her hands, but when she saw the degree of entrancement that held him, she almost couldn't ask the question.

"What?" he murmured, reading her expression with uncanny perception, kissing her bottom lip with a tenderness that was almost her undoing.

She swallowed hard. "Let's agree to worry about each other on the job. But you weren't really serious about what station I should bid or your ability to perform your own job, were you?"

Instantly a stillness settled over Grady. She watched the glaze of desire diminish until it was no longer there. Suddenly he looked older again, harder. A shudder racked her body, because she'd been the one to extinguish the light.

"I'm deadly serious, Gina," he finally answered, but she knew that already. Slowly he removed her hands from his face and slid off the bed, rubbing the back of his neck in a distracted manner that revealed his turmoil.

She got to her knees. "We're not married anymore, Grady. I have to live the life I've made for myself. Isn't that what you told me when I tried to dictate yours?"

His face was ashen. "So now the shoe's on the other foot," he said in a haunted whisper.

"No. That isn't the way it has to be," she cried out in despair. "Haven't we learned anything from past mistakes? I found out how wrong it was to try to make you into something you're not. We fought day and night because of it. Now I'm begging for your understanding. Why is this so different?"

Grady's intelligent face was a study in pain. "It just is."

"So now I'm going to have to bear the burden of guilt because the work I do affects *your* performance?" Her tightly controlled voice cracked before she could finish the sentence.

"Your coming back to Salt Lake has knocked my world sideways, Gina!"

She buried her face in her hands, wondering how to reach him. "In other words I should have stayed in California."

"It was a hell I could have endured," he muttered bleakly. He moved over to the window to stare out at the mountains. "Now it wouldn't matter where you went. You'd be in the thick of the action. Your chances of ending up a casualty are only outnumbered by the chances of ending up a quadriplegic. Or enduring a series of skin grafts and marrow transplants—for starters."

In a daze, Gina slithered off the bed. "We could both be killed in a car accident on the way home today. I learned in therapy that this kind of thinking is a useless expenditure of energy."

"If you're hinting that I need to visit a shrink, then you're way off base."

His words affected her like a slap in the face. "I wouldn't presume to make a suggestion like that. Only a wife has that prerogative."

He spun around. "Meaning that since I'm no longer your husband, I have no right to demand anything of you!" he lashed out. "You're right, Gina. We're both free to pursue our lives and our careers without interference from the other. As long as you're not at my station and you're out of my sight, you're at liberty to skydive if you want to."

"As it happens, I don't." She tried to inject a note of levity into the conversation. "Look, Grady. You said you brought me here hoping the atmosphere was conducive to some real communication. Isn't it possible for us to coexist in the same city without turning everything into a shouting match? We're bound to run into each other occasionally. I don't want to cower every time I see you coming." Her hands lifted in a pleading gesture. "On the strength of the love we once had for each other, can't we pretend to be civil and rational about this?"

His hands tightened into fists and the blood drained from his face. "You just don't understand, do you, Gina? And there's no way I can explain. I wish—"

Gina's head lifted, as she waited for him to finish. When he turned away from her without saying anything, she spoke for him. "I used to say that word like a litany when you went back to fighting fires. In my heart, I'd repeat over and over—I wish we lived somewhere else... I wish we'd never come home from the Middle East... I wish I could send you off to fight fires every day with a kiss and a sack lunch...I wish I had your baby..."

Her last statement hovered in the air like a live wire, sending out sparks. A flash of pain came and went in his gray eyes so fast, Gina wasn't sure she'd seen it.

"We can thank providence that's one mistake we didn't make," he said in thick tones.

Gina couldn't take any more and hurried out of the room and down the narrow staircase. They'd trespassed on quicksand at the mention of a baby. She fought the tears but it was a losing battle. To fill this adorable cottage with Grady's children had been her greatest secret longing. She closed her eyes in pain. So many dreams gone.

Cleaning up the remains of their picnic gave her something to do. Grady came down the front porch steps as she folded the blanket. His face was devoid of animation. She couldn't remember who had said that nothing was deader than a marriage that had ended, but the thought sprang to Gina's mind as she gazed at her ex-husband's face. Every time she thought she was making a little progress with Grady, the gulf seemed to widen even more. Yet, ironically, they were more physically compatible than ever. But physical desire alone couldn't compensate for everything else that was wrong. It might bring gratification for periods of time, but in the long run, giving in to their longings would only destroy them both. And Gina knew that any kind of relationship with Grady other than marriage would never satisfy her.

Grady put the picnic things in the trunk while she climbed into the passenger seat. "As long as we've come this far, I'd like to drive past Bridal Veil Falls on our way home," he said equably once he was in front of the steering wheel. "Any objections, or are you in a hurry to get back?" He spoke as calmly and matter-of-factly as if the scene in the upstairs bedroom had never taken place.

She took her cue from him. "I'd like that. My air conditioner at the apartment isn't working that well. I don't want to go back until absolutely necessary."

Grady nodded and started the engine. "Here." He handed her the scarf that she'd somehow lost on the bed and forgotten about. She thanked him and put it on, along with a pair of sunglasses, hoping to detach herself. But nothing could erase the sexual tension radiating between them. A fire had been started in the bedroom and only one fire fighter could put it out, she thought with a glimmer of ironic amusement. Then she sighed. It had been bad enough to work beside him day after day, but since he'd touched her, since she'd experienced the ecstasy of being in his arms again, this was agony in a new dimension.

Beneath his cool, implacable exterior, she wondered if he was suffering one tenth of her frustrations. Worse, she feared that he might slake his longings with that brunette he'd brought to the ball. Gina couldn't stand the thought of someone else being the recipient of his lovemaking. Not now...

She rested her head on the back of the seat and closed her eyes. It took every bit of self-control she possessed not to slide over and wrap her arms around his shoulders. She needed his kiss so badly....

He turned on the radio and fiddled with the tuner until he located a station playing soft rock. She found it merely distracting until the Beach Boys started to sing "Kokomo." Grady flipped to another station before she could ask him, and that one motion betrayed that his nerves were as taut as hers after all.

When they arrived at the turnoff for Provo Canyon and the falls, he suddenly turned left toward Salt Lake. She started to say something, but he silenced her. "I've changed my mind. Is that okay with you?" he practically growled at her. Even if it hadn't been okay, she wouldn't have dared argue with him in this mood. The atmosphere was explosive.

They arrived at her apartment an hour later. She got out of his car the minute he pulled to a stop in the driveway. She couldn't tolerate being in his company another minute.

To her amazement he got out of the car and followed her to the door. "I might as well take a look at your air-conditioning unit before I go."

"Th-That's all right, Grady. I've told my landlord about it. He'll be over in the morning to fix it."

He stroked his chin where the beginnings of a beard had started to show. "So...I'll leave it to you then to call headquarters and start bidding another station."

She nodded. "Thank you for the picnic. It was delicious."

He scowled. "It was a disaster and we both know it. No more games, Gina."

Her chin lifted. "I was thanking you for the food and the beautiful drive." Her voice quivered slightly.

In a totally unexpected move, he pulled off her sunglasses and stared at her face for a long moment. She didn't understand and her expression must have reflected it. "I'm taking one last, hard look at you, Gina. It's possible that the next time we happen to see each other, your face and body might be changed beyond all recognition."

He thrust the sunglasses into her hand and strode off toward the car. She could still hear the screech of tires a block away as she entered the apartment and collapsed on the couch, her body shaken by deep, racking sobs. The tears weren't just for what they'd lost. She also wept for Grady, because he'd just discovered what it was like to be afraid for someone else. It was the most isolated, lonely, horrifying feeling in the world.

CHAPTER SIX

SUSAN REACHED across the table and stabbed the rest of Gina's burrito with her fork. "May I?" she asked after the fact, swallowing the last of their Mexican-food lunch.

"Be my guest." Gina chuckled and finished off her Coke. Normally she had a healthy appetite, but since her trip to Midway with Grady she'd been too upset to eat much of anything.

"I take it you're not thrilled about being assigned to station 6," Susan said gently. "I'm sorry things are so bad between you and Grady. But maybe it's better not to be around him all the time under the circumstances."

"At first I thought so, too. But it's been almost three weeks since I last saw him. We haven't even bumped into each other at a fire. I spend the majority of my time going on building inspections. Nothing ever goes on at number 6. Would you believe I'm actually hooked on *Days of Our Lives*?"

Susan burst into good-natured laughter, which was so contagious Gina finally joined in. "What other stations did you bid?"

"Two and three."

"There'll be an opening at one of them pretty soon," she offered supportively. "If you don't mind my changing the subject, let's talk about our trip to Las Vegas. I told Nancy you and I would be rooming together. She and Karen want to be together, which leaves Mavis as the odd woman out."

"She can room with us. We'll request a triple. I like Mavis. She's a born comedian."

"So do I. Then it's settled." Susan smoothed her brown bangs away from her eyes. "I can hardly wait for the weekend. I've got fifty dollars' worth of nickels to play on the slot machines."

Chuckling, Gina shook her head. "You fool! Don't you know it's all rigged?"

"I don't care. A slot machine is kind of like a mountain. You climb it because it's there."

Gina grinned. "You're right. Just make sure you stick to nickels. Frankly, I think Las Vegas is the last place they should hold the union convention. We're all underpaid as it is."

"Too true." Sue cocked her pert head to the side. "Don't you like Las Vegas?"

"I think it's awful. In fact, I avoid it whenever possible."

"But Grady might be there. . . ."

Gina averted her eyes. "If he does show up, he'll stay away from me. You don't know Grady when he digs in his heels."

Susan was silent a moment, her expression pensive. "For what it's worth, hang in there, Gina. I watched the two of you dancing at the ball." Her warm brown eyes softened. "If a man ever looked at me like that I think I'd die. He may try to act indifferent, but believe me, he was giving off the vibes."

"The situation has deteriorated since the dance," she murmured. "If you don't mind, I'd rather not talk about him." She cleared her throat. "What's happened with Ron?"

"I have no idea. Since I found out he has a wife, I've bowed out of the picture. He keeps leaving messages and I keep not returning them," she said in a bleak tone of voice. She eyed Gina soulfully. "We're a real pair, you know that?"

A sigh escaped Gina's lips. "Why don't we go play some tennis and burn these calories off?"

"Good idea. Let's go."

The heat was too intense for them to play more than one game, so they opted to swim and succeeded in wearing themselves out to the point that Gina fell asleep as soon as her head touched the pillow later that night.

She had only one more shift to go before the trip. Mavis called her at the station and offered to drive everyone to Nevada in her van. Her husband and children would have to get along with the Volkswagen for two days. The arrangement suited Gina just fine. She was sick of her own company. With Mavis entertaining them along the way, the time would pass quickly. For at least the weekend, Gina resolved to ward off all thoughts of Grady.

Fire fighters from around the country poured in to the hotels within walking distance of the convention center. The union planned to deal with issues ranging from employee benefits to the latest safety features in turnout gear. This year a session had been added to address the challenges facing female fire fighters.

Since there were too many workshops for one person to attend, Nancy divided up their group so the entire convention was covered and asked them to take notes. They could exchange information afterward. However, all of them planned to attend the women's session.

Gina enjoyed that session the most. It gave her an opportunity to meet women from every part of the country. The one point that emerged loud and clear was that it would take another generation before women were accepted as an integral part of the system. The guest speaker—a feisty Puerto Rican from the Bronx—brought the house down with her closing remark. "The old guard will have to die off first," she said, "but we'll handle it in the meantime. Right?"

The crowd went crazy, but Gina noticed that a few of the men in attendance were clearly not pleased. The very issue the women had been discussing was brought home a dozen times throughout the day. Loud comments and snickers, rude asides, came from corners of the room at every session Gina attended. Only a small number of men were responsible, but they managed to cast a pall over the activities.

After being propositioned for the third time just walking from one session to the next, Gina had had it and decided to go up to the room to wait for the others.

A couple of men were loitering by the elevator. They threw her furtive glances, then smiled. Angry at this point, Gina needed a release for the adrenaline flowing through her system and dashed up the stairs to the tenth floor.

"Is it my imagination, or are we getting unduly harassed out there?" she burst out the minute she entered their suite.

"I figured something like this might happen," Mavis said. "In fact, my captain warned me about it."

Sue didn't look too happy, either. "Nancy just phoned and said the same thing was happening to her and Karen. It's a put-up job. She thinks we ought to just stay in our rooms for the rest of the night and have dinner delivered."

"I agree," Gina said, nodding. "There's no way I'm willing to face that again."

They heard a knock on the door, and Sue, who was closest, answered it. Gina recognized the man as one of the two down by the elevators. "Is this where the party is?" he asked in a distinctly Southern drawl.

"Not unless you're into karate!" Mavis yelled out as Sue slammed the door in his face.

"I'm calling security," Gina announced, but before she could pick up the receiver, the phone rang. Her eyes darted to Sue. "What do you think?"

Mavis made a face. "It could be my husband."

"I hope it is," Gina said angrily. "Ask him to report the problem."

Mavis nodded and gingerly picked up the receiver. She put the phone to her ear, then held it out in front of her for anyone who cared to listen before putting it back on the hook. "Well, ladies. Shades of the Salem witch hunt."

"It's disgusting," Gina muttered. She tried to call the front desk but the line was busy. After five minutes of unsuccessfully trying to reach someone, her anger started to turn into resignation. She looked at the others and saw the same expression on their faces.

"I'd like to leave Las Vegas. The sooner the better," Sue stated unequivocally. Gina tried the phone again, even as Sue spoke. It was still busy.

There was another knock at the door. By tacit agreement no one moved. Gina kept phoning. The knock grew more persistent. "Gina? Are you in there?" a male voice demanded anxiously.

Gina's eyes locked with Sue's as the receiver slipped out of her hand. "Grady." Her heart in her throat, she flew across the room and opened the door. By the greatest strength of will she kept herself from leaping into his arms.

His penetrating gaze swept over her in one all-encompassing motion. "Are you all right? The trouble-makers have been rounded up and dealt with. I tried to get through to your room but the line was busy."

Gina swallowed hard. "I was trying to phone security."

If he noted her pallor, he didn't say anything.

"It's good to see you, Captain Simpson," Mavis greeted him with a broad smile. Sue's eyes communicated a private signal to Gina before she joined Mavis in saying hello to Grady. Her glance clearly said "I told you so."

Grady was at his most charming, dressed informally in a cream sport shirt and dark gray pants. "Ladies, I'm afraid that sort of element will always be present at a function like this. Don't let it put you off. The night's still young." His dazzling smile took Gina's breath.

"Good," Sue piped up. "I'm ready to go hit the slot machines. Come on, Mavis. You can help me lose all my gambling money."

"I'm real good at doing that. Show me the way." They were out of the room so fast Gina didn't have a chance to say anything. She couldn't. After three weeks' separation, it was heaven just to look at Grady.

A slow heat invaded her body as his eyes took in the raw silk dress she wore, its color the exact shade of her violet eyes. "Did anyone approach you, Gina?"

"Yes," she answered in a breathy voice.

His eyes narrowed perceptibly. "Could you identify him?"

"You mean all three?"

She heard him say something unintelligible under his breath. "The hotel security officers are holding them downstairs. If you're able to make a positive identification, you can lay formal charges against them."

She rubbed her temples. "Much as I hate the whole idea, I'll do it. No women in any line of work should have to put up with that."

"I agree. Word will spread and—let's hope—prevent this from happening again next year. A couple of other women are also willing to cooperate. Would you like me to go down with you?"

"Please." Her eyes implored him.

"Then why don't we get it over with right now?"

Gina nodded gratefully and went downstairs with Grady. The whole process took only a couple of minutes. There was strength in numbers, and the other women showed no hesitation in picking out the men responsible for casting a blight on the conference. One positive outcome of the incident manifested itself in the tremendous sense of bonding Gina felt with the other women, and men, determined to stamp out this kind of behavior.

"Do you have plans for the evening?" He'd accompanied her to the door of her suite. She almost fainted at the question. The last time they were together he'd walked away from her in anger.

"No. You know how I feel about Las Vegas. I'd rather go back to Salt Lake tonight. The only reason I came was because Nancy said it would be a good experience and she's been at this a lot longer than I have."

His dark brows quirked. "And was it a good experience, apart from the obvious?"

She gave him a full, unguarded smile. "Yes. It did my heart good to see so many female fire fighters all assembled. The speaker in our section said there are more than forty women assigned in New York City alone. That's impressive, and it makes me more certain than ever that there's room for everyone if we're given half a chance."

His lips quirked. "That was quite a speech. You almost convince me."

She inhaled a deep breath. "To quote you, I'd be a liar if I said anything else. I used to love teaching school, but nothing compares with that moment when the gong sounds and the adrenaline spurts through your veins. You don't know what you're going to find till you get there, but you know somebody needs help. Instead of standing idly by listening to the sirens go down the street, you're able to respond. Qualified to respond. No wonder you quit your job at the newspaper."

They looked into each other's eyes for a long, silent moment. She couldn't read his enigmatic expression. But it was his next statement that really shook her. "I have to get back to Salt Lake tonight. You're welcome to ride with me. I'm leaving now."

She couldn't believe he'd made such an offer, not when every time they were together ended in pain and bitterness. She knew what she *should* do, but where Grady was concerned, she was willing to undergo anything to be with him. Even if they fought every step of the way. Grady left a void in her life nothing or no one could fill.

"Just give me long enough to gather my things and write a note to the girls."

He nodded his head, though his solemn expression made her wonder if he regretted the offer already. "I'll go down for the car and meet you in the breezeway."

She put a hand on his arm. "Thank you, Grady, and I don't just mean for the lift home."

A distinct frown marred his handsome features. "I guess it would do no good at this stage to point out to you that a female fire fighter faces drawbacks a man never encounters."

"You mean you've never been propositioned?" she asked with a sparkle in her eyes, trying to keep the conversation light. Already he'd introduced a sensitive subject, and he seemed determined to press on it, like repeatedly probing a sore tooth with your tongue.

A smile broke out, dazzling her with its brilliance. "Touché," he murmured mysteriously, removing her hand.

Her eyes narrowed. "I seem to remember a certain black-eyed belly dancer in Istanbul lying in wait for you on several occasions."

"Were you jealous?" he quipped playfully.

"I hated her."

Grady burst out laughing, the deep, rich kind of laughter that took her back to those heavenly days when they'd first fallen in love. "Believe me, sweetheart, she hated you much more."

The endearment was a slip of the tongue but it had the power to rob her of breath. And it caused Grady to revert to his inscrutable self. "I'll meet you downstairs in ten minutes."

Her hands literally shook as she hurriedly packed and dashed off a note to Sue and Mavis. She left a twenty-dollar bill on top of the note to pay her share of the gas. With a large family, she knew Mavis didn't have extra money to squander. Although she couldn't hope to fool Sue, she indicated in the note that the incident had upset her and Captain Simpson was willing to drive her home because he had to leave early for business reasons, anyway.

Grady stood by the Audi and put her things in the trunk before helping her into the car. "We'll grab a hamburger on the way out of town."

Suddenly a hamburger sounded divine. If they took the time to go to dinner at a restaurant, they wouldn't get served for an hour. And she couldn't wait to get away from people.

The stark beauty of the desert held Gina entranced for a long time. They rode in companionable silence until they reached St. George, where Grady filled the tank with gas.

Traces of fatigue fanned out from his eyes. Gina handed him a Coke and bought one for herself while he paid the attendant. "Would you trust me to drive your car for a while? You look like you could use a nap."

After a moment of uncharacteristic hesitation, he finally shook his head. "We usually end up with a speeding ticket when you drive. I'm not in the mood to be pulled over tonight."

Gina had the grace to blush, and Grady, ever alert, noticed.

"How many tickets have you had since you came to Utah? The truth now."

"Only one." The day she'd gone to see him...

He finished off his Coke and threw the can in the wastebasket. "That's one too many."

On that succinct note they got back into the car and drove on. Ironically, it was Gina who fell asleep en route and awoke a while later to discover that Grady had pulled off the freeway onto a side road at the exit leading to her apartment building.

"What's the matter?" she whispered, still disoriented from sleep. She raised her head from the window, rubbing her stiff neck. "Is something wrong with the car?"

"No."

That one word delivered in a still-familiar husky timbre set her pulses racing and she woke up fully. "Are you too tired to drive any farther?" she asked in a quiet voice, unconsciously running her palm up and down her silk-clad thigh.

"No."

A strange tension filled the car and she was acutely aware of his whipcord-lean body inches from her own. The ache that never truly left her throbbed to life, and she didn't know where to look or what to say.

"I want to make love to you tonight, Gina."

A moan escaped her throat. "Here?" She almost choked getting the question out. Was she dreaming?

"If this weren't such a public place, I'd say yes. I brought you back to Salt Lake tonight for that very reason. I want to take you home with me. If your answer is no, then I'll drive you to your apartment."

She couldn't believe any of it. "Grady—" She turned her head to stare at him. "I—I don't understand."

He was half lounging against the door, with one hand resting on the steering wheel. It was dark inside the car and she could scarcely make out his features. "What could you possibly not understand?" he asked wryly. "It's a simple yes or no."

Her mouth had gone so dry she couldn't swallow. "Nothing's simple where our relationship is concerned."

"We don't have a relationship."

Her cheeks burned crimson. "Then there's a name for what you're asking," she whispered.

He stifled an epithet and sat up. "I asked you for an answer, not a cross-examination."

She folded her arms across her stomach. "The answer is no."

He started the engine immediately. "That's all I need to hear." He drove back onto the freeway, and within a minute they were pulling up the driveway of her building.

"Grady—" her voice shook with emotion "—I don't know you like this."

He left the motor running and stared straight ahead. "Surely you don't put me in the same category with the other men in your life?"

It was on the tip of her tongue to tell him there were no other men in her life, but she didn't want to give him that satisfaction. The fact that he expected her to sleep with him—because *he* suddenly wanted to—hurt her deeply. Maybe she'd have flung herself at him if he'd asked her that question in the beginning, but by now too much had happened and she wanted more than a night of passion with him. She wanted all his nights for the rest of their lives. "If you mean that having been married to me once gives you special privileges, then you're mistaken. If we were dating again, it might be different, but we're not. As you said, we haven't got a relationship."

She heard the mocking tone of his laughter. "So if I were to begin courting you again, you just might condescend to offer me the pleasure of your delectable body?"

"If you started dating me again, I'd know why. The answer would still be no."

"Can you actually conceive of my ever asking you for a date? Because if you can, your imagination is more creative than mine."

She grasped the door handle. "You offered me a ride home from Las Vegas, for which I'm thankful. Let's leave it at that. What you want can be had anytime, anywhere, with anyone."

She got out of the car, slammed the door and walked around to the trunk, then realized it needed a key to open. Grady suddenly appeared. The moonlight revealed that the sarcastic smile was gone from his face, replaced by an expressionless mask. He handed her the bag and shut the trunk.

"Just so we understand each other, Gina. Tonight I wanted that total communion of body and soul we always managed to achieve in bed together, despite our problems. I thought you wanted it, too. Forgive me if it sounded like I was insulting you. I'll never ask you again."

Quickly Gina turned her head away. If he'd said *that* to her in *those* words, she couldn't possibly have refused him. Just when she thought she understood him, he changed everything around, making her feel the guilty party. It should have thrilled her that Grady could admit he still craved the intense, passionate bond they'd shared. But that wasn't enough. They probably wouldn't be able to stop at one night. In the end she'd be his mistress. From wife to mistress. It defied logic!

"It isn't possible to achieve a total communion when so much else is wrong, Grady. We found that out while we were married. You're choosing to ignore that part."

His gaze slanted toward her in the remote manner she'd grown to fear during their marriage. "You've changed, Gina. I've been looking for some vestige of the woman I married, but she's not there."

Gina blinked. "You divorced that woman, Grady."

His deep sigh seemed to reverberate beneath her heated skin. "A paradox within a paradox," he muttered cryptically, then reached into his trouser pocket. "I had rather elaborate plans for returning these to you tonight, but under the circumstances I'll just give them back now."

Gina couldn't imagine what he was talking about until he took her hand and dropped her diamond earrings into the palm. The moonlight turned them into a thousand little prisms. The significance of what he said hit her so hard she stood there like a statue. Grady had wanted to recreate their wedding night. Had he been planning this since her accident, the night of the ball?

"Did you even know they were missing?" he asked in a dull voice.

She put them carefully in her purse. "I assumed they were still in my turnout coat."

His smile was one of self-mockery. "A fitting place for them."

She couldn't let Grady think she was that callous. "I decided my turnout coat was the best hiding place for something so valuable. For your information, I bought a new turnout coat to wear at station 6. My old one is hanging in my bedroom closet. I had no idea you'd removed the earrings at the hospital, and since I've had no occasion to wear them, I had no reason to be—" She stopped and took a deep breath. "Why am I bothering to explain? You think the worst, no matter what I say or do."

"Am I that bad, Gina?" The teasing gruffness of his tone startled her, but it also told her Grady was satisfied with her explanation. Those earrings were sacred to her—and perhaps to him.

"You're much worse, actually. I have trouble understanding how you inspire such fierce loyalty among your crew."

He rubbed his lower lip with the pad of his thumb. "Then you should be grateful to have Captain Blaylock giving you orders."

"What orders? Rescuing kittens from trees, or dispensing plastic leaf-bags?"

His smile was complacent. "Look on the bright side. You've still got all your body parts in all the right places."

Gina ran a nervous hand through her hair. "If I don't get transferred soon, I'll be going someplace else to look for work."

"Where?" He fired the question abruptly.

"I'm going to California for the Labor Day weekend. If there's an opening at my old station in San Francisco, I'll take it."

There was a slight pause. "What's the attraction, apart from the fact that your parents live there?"

"I've always loved to swim, as you know. My station covered the harbor, boat fires, oil rigs, that sort of thing. I got into quite a bit of underwater rescue work, which beats watching soap operas in the afternoon."

He drew himself up, and she could see his muscles tauten. "What's this about, Gina? A little moral blackmail so I'll find a place for you at station 1?"

"I thought you were beyond blackmail of any kind, Grady. This may come as a surprise, but working at station 1 is not my aim in life. I'm planning for my future and I've been checking out all the possibilities here and in Northern California. Since none of the busy stations have openings here, and since it doesn't look like there'll be any in the near or distant future—for political reasons or otherwise—I don't have any choice but to go back."

She expected Grady to hurl some retort, but he remained unexpectedly silent.

"To be honest, it's not as hard to make it as a female fire fighter in California," she went on. "There are more of us down there and we're more accepted. I'm afraid Salt Lake is man's last bastion. You're in your element, Grady Simpson."

"You've changed almost beyond recognition, Gina."

"Then I have you to thank. To think if I hadn't met you, I'd probably be—"

"Dead! Blown up by a terrorist bomb. The American school where you taught has been a target many times in the past few years. The fact that you didn't leave Beirut when the government was urging all Americans to go should have warned me that you have an unhealthy sense of adventure."

Gina was incredulous. "Do you mean to tell me that all the time I was worried about you getting killed behind enemy lines, you were worried about *me*?"

"I felt that anxiety in the pit of my stomach from the moment we met." His voice rang with the truth.

"I can't believe it. You never said anything. I never knew."

"I never intended you to know. A man doesn't like to admit that kind of fear, not even to himself. All I knew was that I wanted you for my wife and dreamed about you becoming the mother of my children. I couldn't get you out of the Middle East fast enough."

She drew closer. "If you hadn't met me, would you still be over there?"

"In all probability, I'd still be a war correspondent somewhere on the globe."

Gina was aghast. "Did you love it so much?"

"I only loved one thing more," he whispered.

"Grady." She shook her head in a daze. "Why didn't you tell me any of this? When you found out you couldn't tolerate that desk job, why didn't you say something? I'd have gone anywhere with you."

He absently rubbed the back of his neck. "I wanted us to have roots, Gina. A real home, not some hotel room for two weeks at a time with five minutes' notice to evacuate. Fire fighting gave me the adventure I craved, and a home base as well. The best part was that I had my wife to come home to after a twenty-four shift. She smelled like flowers, was beautiful beyond description and held me in her arms at night. I knew that when I was away from her, she wouldn't be kidnapped or blown up or shot." Or knocked unconscious by a runaway fire hose...

Gina sagged against the fender of the car, unable to take it all in. He'd given up so much for her, only to be alone now. "Grady—after our divorce, why didn't you go back to the newspaper?"

"That only appealed while I was a headstrong bachelor without responsibilities. When you work in a war zone, you live on the edge. For me, that time has passed, Gina. Now you couldn't lure me away from the department. When I came back to Salt Lake, I came home, literally."

There was too much to absorb. Gina needed some time to herself to sort everything through. Grady had just revealed a side of himself she hadn't known about. He was more vulnerable than she'd ever imagined. His fears were as real as hers had been. Their lives were like a jigsaw puzzle with a piece askew. And every time you tried to fit it back in place, another piece was moved out of position until you couldn't remember how to put it all back together again. "I wish you'd told me all this three years ago."

His mouth thinned. "All the talk in the world wouldn't have affected the outcome." The air hung heavy with his parting comment, made all the more devastating because it was the truth. "See you around, Gina."

She let herself in the front door, then fell limp against it. *See you around, Gina.* To hear that from him after all they'd shared and lived through. It wasn't fair. She should never have come back to Salt Lake. Doing that had only plunged them deeper into pain. It was best for her to go back to California. Right now she couldn't relate to the Gina who'd reported to Captain Simpson one beautiful summer morning full of bright hope and expectations. . . .

CHAPTER SEVEN

"Ms Lindsay. The phone's for you."

"Thanks, Captain." Gina took the receiver from Captain Blaylock, a man the same age as her father with the same loving disposition and warm, caring spirit. "This is Gina Lindsay."

"Gina—thank heaven I reached you before you went off duty. Remember Jay, that fire fighter from engine 7 I met in Las Vegas? He took me to breakfast?"

"Remember?" Gina said, laughing, "he's all you've talked about for the past two weeks!"

"Well," Sue drawled, "he finally swung a shift that gave him today off. He wants to spend the whole day with me. And if everything goes the way I hope it does, we'll end up at my place for dinner."

"That's wonderful." Gina was really thrilled for her.

"And he has a friend. Another fire fighter you once swung shift with, Stephen Panos. Remember him?"

"Yes. He could pass for a younger Omar Sharif."

"You noticed!"

"I noticed. He's nice."

"Well, he noticed you, but he's never been able to work up the courage to ask you out, because your blasted rules precede you."

"You know why I've had to stick to them, Sue. I haven't wanted to give Grady a reason not to trust me."

"Look, I don't mean to sound cruel, but does it really matter any more what he thinks? You haven't seen or heard from him since he drove you home from Las Vegas. You admitted to me that it's really, truly over this time. So break your rules and come out with us today. Please. How long has it been since you went out on a real date, Gina?"

"A date?" she repeated.

The captain smiled, forcing Gina to turn her back on him. She sighed. "A long time, since before I came back to Salt Lake."

"*That* long?" Susan gasped. "You're way past due, my friend. We're going to play a little tennis, swim, get acquainted. That's all. What do you say?"

"Well..."

"Do it," the captain barked without lifting his head from his stack of paperwork. "That's an order."

Gina laughed. "Sue? Did you hear? Captain Blaylock just ordered me to go with you. How about that?"

"Tell him he'll receive a medal for cooperation in the line of duty. Gina—do you mean it? You'll come?"

She took a deep breath. "Why not? I probably won't be working in Salt Lake much longer anyway."

The captain's head came up. "What's that?" He frowned. She really had his attention now and could have kicked herself for what she'd said.

"Nothing, Captain."

"I didn't like the sound of that. You and I need to have a talk before you go on vacation."

"Gina, the guys will be by for me in a few minutes, then we'll come for you. You can leave your car there, can't you?" Sue's voice dragged Gina back to their conversation.

"Sure. That's fine. But remember that I've been on duty twenty-four hours. And I look it."

"That's the beauty of keeping it in the family. We all look awful. Who cares? They appreciate us on the inside."

Gina started to chuckle. "Wouldn't it be nice if that were true?"

"It's going to make Stephen's day, Gina. You might even enjoy yourself. Thanks for being a good friend. See you in a little while." Gina mumbled her goodbyes and hung up the phone with trepidation.

The captain looked at her for a full minute, waiting for an explanation. "It's obvious you're not happy here, so we need to discuss the problem," he finally said. "Go have fun today, but remember that you and I will have a talk." He sounded just like her father and was every bit as kind. Best of all, the captain was one man who didn't have a problem with female fire fighters. What a difference that feeling of acceptance made. "Thanks, Captain. I promise we will."

In the bathroom she changed into Jamaica shorts and a T-shirt. With a little effort, she soon felt halfway presentable. It seemed so strange to be getting ready for a date. She wondered if she'd ever overcome the pangs of guilt, the sense of being disloyal to Grady by going out with another man.

The new shift arrived as Gina was walking out the door to put her things in the car and lock up. They exchanged greetings and kidded around until Sue arrived in Jay's car. Stephen got out of the back and ambled slowly toward Gina.

"What do you know," he said, giving her a wide smile. "Everyone said it couldn't be done, but here you are in the flesh, Ms Lindsay. Unless Sue's putting me on, she says you're willing to spend an entire day with me. Is that true?"

Gina always thought of Stephen as the strong, silent type, but he had absolutely no trouble communicating and was even more attractive than she remembered. "Only if it's what you want, Mr. Panos."

He eyed her appreciatively. "I've been wanting a date with you since your first day on the rig. I'm not even going to ask why the fates have suddenly decided to deliver you into my hands."

"We can thank Sue, I believe." She smiled back.

"Oh, I do." He nodded his head slowly. "I don't know about you, but I have the feeling this could be the start of a memorable relationship. Shall we go?"

In some ways Stephen reminded her a little of Bob Corby. He was confident and at ease with women but didn't have Bob's arrogance. Gina liked that about Stephen and realized that if she weren't so deeply in love with Grady, Stephen could be a man she'd be interested in.

Sue introduced Jay to Gina, and plans were made to go to breakfast. Over waffles and sausage they mapped out their day, which they filled to the brim with tennis, swimming, videos and some napping in between activities—inevitable, since they'd all been up for twenty-four hours before that.

It was almost ten o'clock by the time they called an end to their relaxing, fun-filled day. Stephen borrowed Jay's car long enough to drive Gina back to the station for her own car. He seemed reluctant to let her go.

"I'm off duty the day after tomorrow. Will you spend it with me? My folks have a cabin on Bear Lake. We could water-ski."

Gina rubbed her eyes with the palms of her hands. "If I weren't going out of town, I'd love to."

"Where are you going? For how long?"

"I'm going to spend Labor Day with my folks in Carmel, then go on to San Francisco. I'll be gone about a week."

"A week, huh?" He frowned. "I guess I can last that long. Barely," he amended.

"You're very nice, Stephen. I've enjoyed this day a lot. I'll call you when I get back. All right?" She couldn't believe she was saying that to him. Maybe she was just using him because she was in so much pain over Grady. If that was true, then it wouldn't be fair to Stephen, but she wasn't in a position to have a perspective on her emotions right now. Stephen had been divorced for five years, and unlike her, didn't seem to have any obsessions about the past. At least, not outwardly.

"I wish this weren't our first date, Gina. I'd like to kiss you good-night." Stephen was always direct. In that respect, at least, he reminded her of Grady.

She flashed him a smile. "Didn't someone once say that getting there was half the fun?"

He had an attractive chuckle. "Whoever said it was right, but I can assure you I'm going to get there, Ms Lindsay."

"Is that a warning?"

"It's a promise." His black eyes sparkled.

He started to get out of the car but she put a detaining hand on his arm. "Don't bother. My car's right next to us. Good night."

"Good night," he said reluctantly, gently squeezing her arm. She got out of the car and shut the door, then threw him a cheerful wave. He tooted the horn a couple of times and drove away while she started to unlock her car.

"I thought he'd never leave," someone muttered behind her. Gina whirled around in stunned surprise.

"Grady?" she cried out as her heart began to thud unmercifully. "How long have you been standing there?"

In the moonlight, his eyes glittered silver. "Long enough to feel sorry for the poor devil. He could hardly keep his hands off you."

"It's not nice to spy on people." She said the first thing that came into her mind, too disturbed to think coherently.

"Your protracted good-night was done in plain view of anyone who happened to be in the parking lot. The fact that I've spent two hours here waiting for you has nothing to do with it."

"Two hours? What could be that important? I'm tired, Grady, and it's been a long day."

"I'll just bet it has," he bit out fiercely.

She opened her car door. "Why don't you say what's on your mind so I can go home?" All day she'd actually managed to subdue the inevitable thoughts of Grady and she'd had a pleasant time for once. Now, within seconds, he'd reduced her to a trembling mass of nerves and desires. "I'll follow you. What I've got to say is going to take awhile."

"No, Grady." She swung around, the light catching the purple sparks in her eyes. "We've said it all. Over and over again. I can't take it anymore."

"And you think I can?" he lashed out, sounding breathless. "You've got your choice. We can talk here where someone from the station is sure to see us, or we leave and go someplace private. Preferably the condo. It's a lot closer than your apartment."

In truth, the condo *was* closer. And she had her car; she could leave whenever she wanted. She couldn't imagine what he wanted to talk to her about, but judging by his anger, it wouldn't be pleasant. "I'll follow you," she agreed at last.

He couldn't be jealous of her date with Stephen. That would imply that he still cared for her, which he didn't. Maybe he intended to upbraid her for breaking her promise not to get involved with a fire fighter. The questions plagued her until she wanted to scream. But what terrified her most of all was this tremendous power Grady had over her. All he had to do was beckon and she came running. He was her obsession and the longer she allowed the situation to continue, the less chance she'd have of ever carving out a little happiness for herself. Her plan to win him back had blown up in her face, just as her mother had predicted.

In a few minutes she'd parked her car and was following him up the stairs as he took them two at a time to the living room of the condo. She unwillingly admired the fit of his Levi's. He had a magnificent body and he moved with fluid grace. Every motion, even the way he ate his food, intrigued her.

"Can I offer you a drink? Some wine?" Suddenly he'd turned into the urbane host and it confused her.

"No, thank you," she murmured, sitting down on the small love seat opposite the leather couch. "Please say what you have to say, Grady. I'm exhausted."

His eyes played over her suntanned face as he stood in front of her with his hands on his hips. "I can tell. Under the circumstances it might be better if we made you more comfortable." Lightning fast, he swooped down and picked her up in his arms. Her cry of surprise was smothered by the mouth that closed over hers, demanding a response. He carried her to the couch and sat down with Gina still in his arms, lying across his lap.

He hadn't given her time to think. She only knew that this was Grady holding her, kissing her as if he were trying to summon the very breath from her body. The terrible thing was that Gina gave him what he wanted, because it was what she wanted, too.

"Grady—love me. Please love me," she begged, burying her face in his black curls, curving her body against him. His strong legs wrapped around hers and ignited something deep inside that made her body go molten.

His hands entwined in the silk of her hair and he held her fast. That incredible translucence was there in his eyes. "I want to do much more than that, Gina," he said thickly. "I want to marry you."

Silence fell over the room, and the only sound Gina could hear was the pounding of her heart.

She traced the outline of his sensuous mouth with her finger, as if bewitched. Her eyes were twin fires of purple gazing up at him. "Do you have any idea how long I've been waiting to hear you say that? Grady—" She grasped his face between her hands and searched hungrily for his mouth, giving him her answer.

Suddenly Grady crushed her to him and buried his face in her neck, holding her so tight there was no space between them. "Sweetheart," he whispered with the old tenderness and the trace of tears in his voice. Gina was already in tears and they fell between her dark lashes, wetting them both.

"If I die tonight, it will be from too much happiness," she confessed.

"Don't die on me now." His body shuddered as his mouth found hers and feasted on it till Gina felt drugged with desire. "I have plans for us," he whispered at last, brushing his lips against her eyes and nose.

"So do I."

He caught her hand to his mouth and kissed the palm before putting it against his heart. "Can you feel that?" His mouth curved in that half smile that always sent her into shock with its male beauty. She nodded in a daze. "It beats for *you*, Gina."

A new radiance illuminated her face. "I came back here—to Salt Lake—for you, Grady. You're the most precious thing in my life."

"Thank God you did." His eyes blazed with a silver fire. "I was a fool to ever let you go." His voice shook with urgency and with a self-recrimination that wounded her.

Gina's eyes searched his. "We had a lot to work out, Grady. But we've found each other again. Our marriage will be much stronger than it was before."

His face sobered. "I came to California so many times you never knew about. I even watched you riding horseback along the beach one day, but I could never bring myself to let you know I was there."

"What?" Gina's heart leaped in her breast. "I thought you'd forgotten all about me. Never a phone call or a letter. I've never known such pain."

"Gina..." He buried his face in the silken profusion of her hair. "What have we done to each other? These past three years have been an eternity. I've been surviving, but you wouldn't call it living. I don't think I could describe how it felt to see you standing there at the desk. You were the most beautiful sight I ever saw in my life."

"Then you're the greatest actor alive, my love." His head lifted at that. "I was literally sick to my stomach, I was so frightened by what you'd say or do." Her eyes glistened. "I couldn't bear to think it was really over between us. I had to find out."

"I told you once how courageous you are. I'm in awe of it, Gina," he confessed, his voice softened by an unfamiliar humbleness. "I don't deserve a second chance, but because of you I've got it and I'm not going to do anything that will ever hurt you again. At least, not knowingly."

Gina stared long and hard at him. "I love you, Grady."

He swallowed visibly. "I love you. Will you accept the house in Midway as a belated wedding present? I bought it hoping that one day, by some miracle, you'd live in it with me. I never gave up on us, Gina. I just didn't know how to reach out to you. Every way I turned there was a stumbling block."

"Grady..." She played with the black tendrils curling over his bronzed forehead. "Let's not dwell on the past anymore. The time's too short. Can we have a baby right away? It's all I can think about since we drove to Midway."

"Why do you think I drove you there, if not to torture you with the idea? If you couldn't be the mother of my children, then I didn't want anyone else. But first—" he tousled her hair with his hand and kissed her mouth firmly "—I'm planning to fly down to California with you. I want to formally ask for your hand in marriage. I couldn't do that the first time around since we were out of the country."

She grasped one of his hands between hers. "Mother told me I was crazy to try and win you back. She couldn't see that going to Salt Lake would accomplish anything but more pain. It's going to be a shock for Mom and Dad when you come home with me."

"A good one, I hope."

"They love you, Grady. They'll be ecstatic. It's the fire fighting they hate."

"Somebody has to do it."

"I know." She laughed playfully. "But they're more resigned to the idea than they used to be."

"Would you like to be married in California?"

"No, my home is here with you," she said firmly. "I'd like to be married in a church, with all our friends from the various stations joining us."

Grady groaned. "I'm not sure any of my crew will be speaking to me when they find out you were really my ex-wife. I even have it in my heart to feel sorry for Corby—despite the fact that I could have strangled him with my bare hands the night of the ball. He can thank providence you stuck to your rules."

Gina looked sheepish. "Except for Stephen Panos."

His eyes glittered possessively. "How many times have you been out with him, Gina?"

"Today was the first."

His chest heaved as he played with a strand of her hair. "I figured as much. Otherwise he wouldn't have let you go so easily."

Stephen was going to be shocked when he heard the news. She'd given him no clue that anyone else was in the picture. "I'll have to tell him soon." She slanted a provocative glance at him. "What about that brunette? From what I saw, you're going to have a slightly harder time of it."

"Don't worry about that," he murmured against her mouth.

"It's worse than I thought," she shot back.

"I love it when you act jealous. But I'll tell you a secret. Among my many sins throughout our marriage, infidelity was never one."

Gina's heart raced. "And after the divorce?"

Grady tousled her silken hair. "After a time I dated my fair share of women, but compared to you, Gina, there's simply no contest." His eyes narrowed and he caught her face between his hands. "Has there been a man in your life?"

She gazed at him tenderly. "Yes. There was one."

He blinked and she saw a brief flash of pain in his eyes. "You don't have to tell me. I don't think I want to know."

"Darling." She lowered her mouth to his. "It was you. Some women can only love one man. It's the way I'm made."

Grady let out a long, sustained breath and the beautiful smile that broke out on his face made him look ten years younger. "Gina—" He began to shake his head, and suddenly she was crushed in his arms once more. "You've made me the happiest man alive." Gina clung to him for fear he was an illusion and might disappear at any moment. "Let's get married over the holiday. As soon as possible."

She nodded, rubbing her cheek lovingly against the slight rasp of his. "We can get our blood tests in the morning."

"Do you want to live here at the condo, or shall we find a place closer to Midway, so we can get there sooner on our days off?"

"We'll never find a better view of the valley than the one we have right here. Let's stay here for the time being. Maybe when our third baby is on the way we can look for a bigger place."

"It looks like I'm going to have to keep you busy in that bed if we're going to produce all those children," he whispered against her ear, biting the lobe gently.

"That's the part I'm looking forward to." Her voice was suddenly choked with tears. "I've missed you so terribly, Grady."

"I can't even talk about it," he admitted. "Let's go upstairs. I'll show you what it's been like for me."

Gina's answer was to nestle closer as he picked her up in his arms and started for the spiral staircase leading to the master bedroom. He paused on the way up to drink deeply from her mouth.

"Grady," she whispered, raising passion-glazed eyes to him. "Do you think you could throw some weight around at headquarters so that our schedules are the same? We're going to need all those days off together if we're going to have that big family."

His smile was mysterious. "Sweetheart, you don't need to keep up the pretense any longer. Tomorrow you'll hand in your resignation. You're going to be my wife again. That's all that's important." He continued on up the stairs and strode into the bedroom, carrying her over to the window so they could look at the view together.

"What pretense are you talking about?" She kissed the side of his neck. "What resignation?"

Grady gently lowered her until her feet touched the floor. He pressed her against him and put his hands on her shoulders. "Gina, you've proved to me that you've overcome your fears. You're the most amazing woman I've ever known. But there's only going to be one fire fighter in this family. I want you home, safe and sound, loving me and our children. I don't know another woman who would have gone to the lengths you did to fight for her marriage, but the fight is over, sweetheart. You've won. Thank God nothing serious ever happened to you before we found our way back to each other. Now, no more talk. I'm going to love you all night long. I need to love you." His voice shook with naked emotion.

The blood drained from Gina's face and she felt lightheaded. When he started to draw her toward the bed she resisted. She felt as if a steel vise trapped her, constricting her breath. The plunge from heaven to hell was swift.

Grady's brow furrowed in concern and genuine surprise. "What is it? Your skin's gone so pale."

"Hold me, Grady," she cried out. "Hold me and listen."

He clutched her to him and for a few seconds, she rested in the strength of his arms. "What's wrong, Gina? Are you ill?" He sounded anxious.

"Yes. I'm ill." She tried to swallow. She didn't know how to say what needed to be said. "How do I tell you this without the pain starting all over again?"

He didn't have to say a word, but she felt some intangible energy leave his body. He didn't stop holding her, but the oneness had stopped flowing between them, leaving her bereft once more.

"I don't want to resign, Grady. I love my work. I—I thought you understood. I thought you'd come to terms with it. And all this time you thought it was a pretense." He started to pull away from her, but she held on to him fiercely and wouldn't let him go. "Listen. Please."

"No!" he cried out, shaking his head. Now his skin looked like parchment. "Don't tell me this now. I can't take it." She'd only seen tears in his eyes on one other occasion—the day he'd told her he couldn't go on, that he was divorcing her. With almost superhuman strength he broke free of her arms and took a step backward, as if he were dazed. "I *refuse* to believe you love the job enough to let it come between us, Gina. You *couldn't* love it. It's the most dangerous job in the world! It's dirty and hard and exhausting and often terrifying. It's no place for my wife!'' His face had a pinched look.

''Why isn't it?'' Gina's chest heaved. ''Am I exempt from the more unpleasant aspects of life?''

''Come off it, Gina. *The more unpleasant aspects of life,*'' he yelled. ''Have you ever seen the charred remains of a buddy when you couldn't get to him in time? *Have you?*'' The tension that gripped him made the cords stand out in his neck. ''Well, I *have!*'' he answered without waiting for a response. ''I've seen five men vaporize in a fireball and I couldn't do a damn thing about it. I'm still haunted by those memories. It could happen to you, any time, any day of the week.''

''Of course there are risks, Grady. *You* take them every time you go on duty. But think of the good we do, the service. There's no other feeling like it. I hoped we could always be together, work together. I thought you'd changed and wanted that, too.''

''Then you were wrong.''

She closed her eyes in pain. ''I love you, Grady. I'll always love you, but I guess this really is goodbye.''

''Don't ever come near me again.'' Eyes of flint pierced through her as he delivered his ultimatum.

That moment would stand out in Gina's mind and heart as the blackest of her life. She never remembered her flight from the bedroom or her drive back to the apartment.

CHAPTER EIGHT

"CAPTAIN BLAYLOCK?" Gina poked her head into one of the offices at headquarters, gratified to find the captain alone. Sunglasses hid her puffy eyes.

"Good. You're here. Come on in, Gina. I know you're getting ready to go on vacation, but I thought we'd better have things out before you go away." Gina nodded and entered the room, finding a seat opposite the desk. She felt like death and hadn't slept all night. Like a person in shock, she'd sat on the couch staring into the darkness. Captain Blaylock's phone call was the only thing to rouse her from a near-catatonic state.

He sat back in the swivel chair and touched the tips of his fingers together, eyeing her curiously. "I raised five daughters," he started off without preamble, "which qualifies me to read between the lines. You're a fine fire fighter and getting better all the time. But you have a big problem in your personal life." Gina averted her head, not so much surprised by his frank speaking as by his astute observation. "Nothing you tell me will ever go beyond this room, but I want to know what's going on. In time, this problem will start to affect your job and then we're all in trouble. I heard you mention Grady Simpson's name on the phone. Let's start with him."

Gina tried to find words but nothing would come out, and to her humiliation, giant tears rolled down her cheeks. She took off the glasses to brush them away. The captain sat forward.

"I've known Grady a long time and they don't come any better, but if I don't miss my guess, something's going on between the two of you."

The captain saw too much, Gina mused brokenheartedly, but she still couldn't talk as she attempted to stifle the sobs.

"I checked with Captain Carrera this morning and he had no complaints about your work, professionally or otherwise, which leads me to believe the trouble started when you went to station 1. Are you in love with Simpson?"

Gina's gasp resounded in the room and the captain nodded. "I thought as much after watching the two of you at the Fire Fighters' Ball. My wife made the comment that she'd never seen two people who looked so much in love and I agreed with her." He paused. "Have you quarreled? Is that what this is all about? Because if it is, you need to straighten things out for both your sakes and the good of the department. Gina? You're a lot like my daughter Kathy. You're proud and you try to stay cool, but inside you're mush." Gina's strangled laugh broke the tension. "Forget I'm your superior and just talk to me as a friend."

"You should have been a psychiatrist." She sniffed hard. "In order for you to understand, I'll have to tell everything and I'd hate to keep you that long when it's your day off."

"Why do you think I'm here?" He chuckled. "I'll be retiring in October and to be honest, I'm dreading it. I've been at this job forty-five years. It's all I know. There's nothing else I'd rather do than try to be of help."

Gina could tell he meant it. "You're one in a million, Captain."

He smiled kindly. "Well, if that's true then you know you have nothing to fear from me."

"I know," she said, nodding. "Well...it all started in Beirut," she began, as if that explained everything.

His eyes crinkled. "As in Lebanon?"

"Yes," she replied, running an unsteady hand through her hair. "That's where Grady and I first met and fell in love." Having said that, Gina felt as if the barriers had come down, and she bared her soul. Except for the intimate details of their life, the captain knew everything by the time she was through speaking. She'd even told him about her plan to look for work in California.

He stared at her for a long time, just as her father always did when he was mulling over an important decision. "What was it John Paul Jones said when all looked hopeless? *'I have not yet begun to fight!'*" Gina blinked in absolute amazement. "Where's your courage, my girl? Are you going to run away when the going gets rough? Where's the fighter who crawled around in all that smoke to rescue a two-hundred-pound man without batting an eye?"

Gina clasped her hands together. "You don't know Grady. His fears are much worse now than mine were in the beginning."

His brows lifted. "And then again, maybe they also hide something else. Have you thought of that?"

Their eyes met. "Like what, Captain?"

He shook his head. "I don't know. But maybe you ought to think about that while you're visiting your folks. Then come home and show what you're made of. No one knows what the future holds, Gina, but if you don't come back, you'll never find out."

The captain had given her a lot to think about. "I appreciate your advice. Your daughters are lucky. I wish all the men in the department were like you. You're not threatened by women."

His bark of laughter resounded in the room. "You didn't know me in the days Nancy Byington came to the department. I was her first captain out of school and we lasted exactly one shift together."

"What?" Gina cried out incredulously.

"That's right. I didn't believe in women doing men's work. We'd never had a female on the force before. I thought it was a big joke. But that was before my Betsy went into engineering and Kathy into medicine. They managed to turn their old dad's thinking around in a big hurry. Give Grady some time. You're young, both of you. Anything can happen. But if it doesn't—" he lifted a finger "—you'll have the satisfaction of knowing that you gave it all you had. That way, you can go on."

Unable to stay seated any longer, Gina covered the distance in half a dozen quick steps to give him a hug. "You're wonderful, Captain."

"That's what I like to hear." He laughed jovially, patting her hands. "Now go on down to Carmel and have a good time."

"I will." She squeezed his shoulder in gratitude, then started for the door, feeling strangely at peace. She wouldn't have thought it possible when he summoned her that morning.

"And Gina?"

"Yes?" She whirled around in the open doorway.

"We may not see as much action at number 6 as you did at station 1, but in order to be the best fire fighter there is, you need to experience it all. You'll learn things with us that you need to know, things you won't learn anywhere else."

How did he get so wise? "I already have, sir. I don't know how you've put up with me. I'll see you next Tuesday morning."

A broad smile broke out on his face. "I knew you were a fighter!"

The idea that Grady's fear masked something else stayed in Gina's mind constantly all the time she was in California. The reunion with her parents shed no new light, even after a lot of discussion, but she returned to Salt Lake after four days of pampering, determined to stick things out for the time being, to see where it all led. Captain Blaylock was right about one thing. If she didn't give Grady more time, she would always have a question, and it could mar any future happiness, period! Grady expected her to remain in California. She wondered what his reaction would be when he found out she'd decided to return to station 6. He'd told her never to come near him again, but if they both happened to be fighting the same fire, he'd be forced to acknowledge her presence, if only to himself. Right now, this was her only hope of reaching Grady, and she clutched at it like a drowning man gasping for air. It could be one hour or six weeks before an alarm went off that brought the two of them together, but she was beginning to learn the value of patience—thanks to Captain Blaylock.

Station 6 was located in a residential area on the northwest side of Salt Lake. Most of the runs involved heart attack victims or incinerator fires, accidents that happened in and around the home. Gina ignored the dispatcher's voice when the first alarm went out signaling a fire in City Creek Canyon, about three miles away.

But strong winds hitting the valley were hampering rescue efforts and more units were called out.

"Let's go," the captain shouted, and Gina jumped into her boots and turnout gear before boarding the rig with Ted and Marty. Captain Blaylock called the battalion chief for more instructions as they crested Capitol Hill, where they could see flames licking up the steep gully. A string of expensive condominiums on top were threatened, and a call had gone out to drop chemicals from the air.

Gina's gaze took in the engines and ladder trucks already assembled, knowing that Grady might be among them, and her heart started to knock in her breast. It was three weeks since her return from Carmel, and she ached for the sight of him.

"Ted? You heard the chief. Drive down to Second Avenue and we'll swing up A Street. Gina, you and Marty go in with the hose and keep that garage watered down till more units arrive."

"Right, Captain," Gina murmured along with the others. When they arrived on the scene moments later, the end condominium was in the greatest danger of going up in flames. Other units were attacking the fire in the gully below.

The captain pulled the plug—attached the hose to the hydrant—with the efficiency of long experience as Gina glanced around and caught sight of a boy of eleven or twelve, standing next to his parents and sobbing his heart out. At least she assumed they were his parents, judging by the way they all held on to each other.

"We'll try to save your place," Gina shouted, reaching for the hose. "Is your car in there?" she asked the father.

"Yes." His voice shook with emotion.

"Any gas cans?"

"One. But there's also my son's new puppy—he crawled under the car and won't come out."

Gina could remember her first puppy and she darted compassionate eyes at the boy. "What's his name?"

"Chester," he said on a half sob. "He's howling in there."

"We'll try to get him out. Ready, Marty?" she called over her shoulder. Marty gave the thumbs-up signal, and they began to pour water on the garage.

"Captain?" Gina asked as he approached to survey the situation. "We've got an animal in there, sir. I'd like permission to go in and get him. I can slide under the car more easily than anyone."

Captain Blaylock nodded his head. "I'll give you two minutes. That's it. If you haven't found the animal in that time, get out of there."

He took over her position on hose. Gina ran to the truck and put on her air mask, then hurried toward the garage.

Flames were licking around it and on the roof, but all Gina could see was the boy's heartbroken expression. She lifted the electric door manually. As soon as she did, she could hear the puppy's hysterical yelping and feel the intense buildup of heat. Gina groaned to herself when she considered inching her way under the gleaming red Porsche 911. Why didn't they own a Wagoneer instead?

She crouched on the cement and started calling to Chester. The puppy yelped a little harder when it heard her voice. "Come here, boy. Come on." She lay flat on her back and wriggled partially underneath the car. Her mask prevented her from going any farther, and she needed another couple of inches to grab the dog. Taking a deep breath, she removed her mask and glove and felt all around. Gratified when the dog's warm tongue started to lick at her fingers, she urged him on. "Come on. That's it," she crooned to him, and finally caught hold of an ear. He had to be a basset hound. She could hear the captain shouting to her.

"I don't like this any better than you do," she muttered, pulling the puppy out by the ear. He howled his head off, but she finally managed to get her arm around his wriggling body. He began to lick her face as she grabbed her mask and glove and dashed out of the garage, needing air before her lungs burst.

By now three hoses were trained on the garage and condo, containing the blaze. Gina's eyes searched out the boy, and she walked over to him, passing a group of other fire fighters.

"Chester!" The boy screamed with joy and hugged the puppy to him. His eyes were like stars as they looked up at Gina. "Thanks." That was all he said, but it was enough.

"You don't know how much this means...." The mother started to cry, leaning against her husband, who was talking to the captain.

"I think I do." Gina smiled as she watched the boy kissing his dog, murmuring baby talk to it.

"Our family dog died last month and we didn't think Max would ever get over it, but Jerry brought this puppy home the other night and it was love at first sight. If anything had happened to this one, I just don't know." She shook her head. "You've saved our house, too, and the car. We'll never be able to thank you enough. It's a good thing you're a woman," she added. "My husband was going to try and get down under the car, but he's too big and bulky."

"Did you hear that, Captain?" Gina winked, observing the cleanup operation out of the corner of her eye. But whatever the captain said in response faded away as her gaze connected with Grady's. He was standing patiently next to the boy, Max, listening to him and petting the puppy. *Where had he come from?*

"She's the one!" The boy pointed to Gina. "My dad couldn't get under the car, but *she* did." He ran over to her. "Do you want to hold Chester. He wants to thank you."

"I'd love to." Gina took the wriggling puppy in her arms, and he immediately proceeded to wet the front of her turnout coat. Gina started to laugh and couldn't stop.

Grady moved closer, his lips twitching. "It looks like you'll have to get your old turnout coat out of mothballs."

"Will you come to my school?" Max asked excitedly, unaware of any undercurrents. Gina tried hard to concentrate on the boy, which was almost impossible with Grady standing only a foot away. She couldn't have described the expression on his face, but he didn't resemble that other man who'd told her to leave and never come near him again. Her heart gave a kick. At least in front of his crew and the public, he'd decided to be civil to her and she could be thankful for that much positive reaction.

"You didn't answer his question," Grady prodded.

"Oh!" She looked away and tried to gather her wits. "You want me to come and give a talk?" She handed the dog back to him.

"Some of the kids get their parents to come if they have neat jobs. My mom works in a dumb office. I wish she rode a fire engine like you. Will you come?"

"Sure. Call station 6 and I'll see what can be arranged. I can do it on my day off."

"Cool!" A big grin spread on his face. "Hey, Mom! Dad!" He ran off to tell them, leaving Gina alone with Grady for a moment. There was activity all around them, but for some reason, Grady didn't seem to be in any hurry to get back to his crew. She should have been helping Marty with the hoses but she couldn't move. Again that tension streamed between the two of them, holding her fast.

"What are you doing back in Salt Lake, Gina? Wasn't there an opening in California?" Now that no one was around, the polite veneer had disappeared.

She tipped back her helmet so she could look at him squarely. "Captain Blaylock pointed out to me that I could learn a lot from working at station 6, so I didn't go to San Francisco. I'm going to stay in Salt Lake."

He cursed beneath his breath, but for one brief moment a haunted look lurked in his eyes before he recovered from the shock. "I hope you don't mean permanently."

"As permanent as one can be about anything, barring unforeseen circumstances." She stood her ground.

"I thought station 6 was too tame for you." He sounded angry.

"I was wrong."

His face darkened and his voice was dangerously quiet now. "What are you playing at, Gina?"

"Rescuing puppies from burning garages."

Another epithet escaped. "And underneath a car with a full tank of gas just ready to explode!"

"You know that's not true, Grady. That tank wasn't close to igniting. The—"

He cut her off rudely. "You know where you should be, don't you? You should be that woman standing there with a son of your own, dammit!"

She started to shake. "It would help if there were a *man* standing next to me, first!"

"I don't believe what I'm hearing." His hands tightened into fists.

"Believe it."

"We're ready to roll," Marty called to her.

"Tell him to go to blazes," Grady muttered. "I'm not through talking to you."

"I shouldn't have to remind you of all people that I'm still on duty, Captain." She'd never seen him lose control in front of anyone before, and the fact that he had was exhilarating to Gina.

"I'm warning you, Gina. Just stay out of my way."

Her chin lifted. "I'm trying to, but you won't let me, Captain, sir."

His eyes had gone black with anger. "So help me, Gina—"

She didn't stay to hear the rest. Everyone was on the rig waiting. Captain Blaylock eyed her flushed cheeks with interest as she climbed on board, and he gave her his secret smile. Nothing escaped the captain's notice. But if he thought Gina had some progress to report about her situation with Grady, he was mistaken. Grady was furious about her decision to stay in Salt Lake. Beyond that, she couldn't read his mind or his heart.

There was a message from Stephen Panos on her answering machine when she got home the next morning. She'd been putting him off since she came back from vacation. Although she liked him, she knew she could never feel more than that, and she had no desire to hurt him. Yet if she continued to put him off, she could easily end up living her life alone, something her parents harped on over and over again.

She finally called him back around three and he asked her to double with Sue and Jay for the fire fighters' annual Lagoon celebration. Besides the Lagoon Amusement Park attractions, there were going to be games and competitions among the crews, with a big barbecue in the evening and a dance to follow. She decided to accept the invitation. It wasn't an intimate dinner, after all. If she could keep things friendly and light, Stephen wouldn't be able to read any more into the relationship than was there. And if her real underlying motive for going with Stephen was to make Grady jealous, then she wasn't admitting to it.

Gina loved Indian summer in Salt Lake; September was her favorite month of the year. The days were hot and the nights cool. She dressed in a navy-and-white sailor top and white shorts for the outing and caught her hair into two ponytails. Stephen said teasingly that she looked sixteen, but the male appreciation in his eyes told her he wasn't complaining.

Sue and Jay had already fallen in love and seemed oblivious to most of what went on around them. Gina watched them with envy. Their relationship appeared uncomplicated and secure. Jay had no hang-ups about Sue's work. Again Gina was reminded of Captain Blaylock's statement that something else could be behind Grady's fears, but her frustration grew because she had no contact with him. She'd seen him twice since the episode with the puppy—once at headquarters when they passed each other in the hallway, and then at the downtown mall while she was doing some shopping. He walked by her both times without acknowledging her presence. That had never happened before, not even when they were both at their angriest during the divorce.

As each day drew to a close, Gina felt less and less confident that there could ever be a future with Grady. Maybe she was a fool to keep on hoping and longing for a sign, she thought. Then, at Lagoon, she saw him feeding cotton candy to the same brunette he'd taken to the dance, and she felt another bit of hope die out. Gina and Stephen had strolled along the path toward the picnic area where the competitions were being held, when she spotted Grady's curly black head among the crowd. In white aviator pants and shirt, contrasting with his bronzed skin, he made every other man around him pale into insignificance.

This time Gina paused to satisfy her curiosity about the woman who held his attention. She was Grady's age, sophisticated and attractive in a dark, almost Spanish way. Gina felt something snap inside her as the woman stood on tiptoe and kissed Grady's mouth after giving him back some cotton candy. In excruciating pain, Gina looked away but not quickly enough. Grady's startling gray eyes penetrated hers for an instant, their look triumphant.

Embarrassed to have been caught staring so openly, Gina turned to Stephen and suggested they sign up for the three-legged race. Jealousy tore at her insides; Grady knew how to get to her. The outing had lost its appeal and Gina wanted to go home. But because she couldn't, she assumed an artificial gaiety, trying desperately to put Grady out of her mind for the rest of the afternoon and evening. She encouraged Stephen to enter all the events with her. Two hours later, they were exhausted.

"How about a swim before the barbecue?" Stephen suggested. "Let's just lie back in the cool water and relax. How does that sound?"

"Heavenly."

"Good. I'm a little tired of crowds and I'd like to get you all to myself, even if it means underwater."

Gina chuckled nervously, recognizing certain signs. Apparently Grady had no difficulty enjoying a physical relationship with a woman even if his heart wasn't involved, but Gina couldn't give physical affection without love.

Under her clothes she wore a one-piece white bathing suit, so it took only seconds to remove her shorts and top and dive into the deep end of the Olympic-size pool. Stephen wasn't far behind. There weren't very many people in the water at this hour. Most of the guests had started eating over at the picnic tables.

They swam for a while, then Stephen grabbed hold of Gina's ankles and forced her to tread water. "I've got a terrific idea. Why don't I go get us a couple of plates of food and bring them back here? We can dance by the side of the pool and avoid the crush."

Gina had second thoughts but didn't express them. She took advantage of the time he was gone to get dressed in her top and shorts. Stephen looked slightly surprised when he returned with the food, but Gina barely registered his reaction because Grady was directly behind him, with the dark-haired woman clutching his arm. Apparently Grady had also decided to escape the crowds—at least that was what she thought at first, until he found a poolside table close enough to her and Stephen to be able to hear them talking. Gina suspected that Grady had intentionally set out to ruin her evening. He didn't want Gina, but he didn't want her paying attention to anyone else, either. Still, the niggling thought that maybe he was worried about her interest in Stephen gave her a whole new set of possibilities to consider.

He'd told her to stay away from him, yet he seemed to go to great lengths to make his presence known whenever they were in the same place together. Was he trying to force her out of his life by flaunting the other woman? Grady knew how deeply Gina loved him, and his amorous attentions to his date seemed calculated to make Gina miserable.

After a few minutes of trying to ignore Grady, Gina couldn't take any more and suggested to Stephen that they head back to Salt Lake. He readily agreed, probably because he hadn't managed to spend any time alone with her, after all.

"Stephen," she began as he pulled into her driveway, "I haven't been the greatest company in the world today. I could make up a million reasons, but the truth is, I'm still in love with someone else and until I can do something about it one way or the other, it isn't fair to go on seeing you. You're too nice, and I like you too much."

Stephen tapped the steering wheel with the heel of one hand. "I figured as much. Who's the lucky man?"

"It doesn't really matter, does it?"

"It might. Don't be angry if I wormed something out of Sue, Gina. She told me you'd once been married. If you're still in mourning, I'll wait until that period has passed. There's a difference between being in love and grieving, you know. I can speak with some authority on the subject."

"I know, Sue told me," Gina answered gently. "I'll be honest with you. I've never stopped loving my husband and I'm hoping that one day we'll get back together. It may not be possible, but I refuse to give up."

Stephen fastened his dark eyes on her. "Have you let him know you want him back? Does he realize you haven't given up?"

His questions surprised her. "We still have something to resolve. It may be insurmountable."

Stephen nodded and then got out of the car, coming around to her side to accompany her to the apartment. "You know where to find me if you ever decide things won't work out with him. I'm not going anywhere." He kissed her forehead and walked away.

Why couldn't she fall in love with someone as nice and uncomplicated as Stephen? Gina asked herself. Someone mellow and steady. Maybe she was crazy to go on loving Grady when nothing could come of it.

Her nerves were wearing thin, yet she had no one to blame but herself. Grady would marry her in an instant if she'd give up fire fighting, but what would she do with those empty hours while he was out on the job? Teaching school could never hold her now. If they had a baby, naturally she'd stay home with the child as long as possible and then resume part-time work with the department, but what if they didn't have a baby right away? During their five months of marriage she hadn't become pregnant. She and Grady would be right back where they started, but this time he'd be leaving her at home to go and do the work they both loved.

Gina knew herself too well. The boredom and the sense of loss would cause a fissure that would grow into another break, perhaps more devastating the second time around. To remarry only to separate again—she couldn't tolerate that. If she could just make Grady understand.

As she started getting ready for bed, an idea came to her. It was the only potential solution she could think of, thanks to what Stephen had said in passing about letting Grady know she wanted a reconciliation.

After a long debate with herself, Gina summoned the courage to phone Grady. Maybe he wasn't home, or maybe his girlfriend was there with him. Gina didn't know, but she had to talk to him while she still felt brave enough. He'd warned her to stay away, but a phone call maintained a distance between them. He could hang up on her, but something stronger than fear of rejection compelled her to try to reach him.

He answered on the fifth ring and sounded as if she'd wakened him from sleep. "Grady?"

The silence lasted so long, she thought he'd simply put the receiver on the side table and left it there so he could go back to sleep without fear of being disturbed by her again.

"What is it, Gina?" he finally asked in a flat voice.

"A—are you alone?"

He cursed violently and she quailed at his anger. "That's none of your business."

Her hand gripped the cord tightly. "I only meant that I wanted to talk to you for a little while, and if this is a bad time, I'll try to call you later."

"I'm on duty in six hours. Since no time is a good time for whatever it is you want, say what you have to say and get it over with!"

"I shouldn't have called. You're obviously not in any frame of mind to listen."

"Don't you dare hang up now!" he warned. "Let's get this over with once and for all. You have my undivided attention. What is it?"

She gulped, wondering where she'd found the temerity to approach him in the first place. "Grady—I've been thinking about us since the other night."

"There is no 'us,' Gina," he said on such a bitter note she could have wept.

"Maybe there could be if you'd just listen for a minute."

A small silence ensued. "When you hand in your resignation to the fire department, then we'll talk. Not before."

"What if I make a permanent home at station 6? What if I don't bid any other stations or do any swing shifts to busier stations? Could you live with that?" she asked with her heart in her throat. It was a compromise, but one that would allow her to do the work she loved and live with the man she loved.

"No, Gina. So don't ask."

His flat-out refusal to consider any options made her indignant. "But why? I thought it was the amount of action and the danger you objected to. If I'm willing to work at the quietest station in the city, why can't you accept that?"

"Because I want you home. Period."

Gina frowned. There was a world of emotion in his voice. She felt she was getting closer to the real problem. Her intuition told her something wasn't right here. On a sudden burst of inspiration, she asked, "Grady...does this have something to do with the fact that your mother wasn't home for you as a child?"

"Don't start psychoanalyzing me. Goodbye, Gina." With a simple click of the phone, their conversation was terminated. Gina sat on the bed in a daze. Her thoughts were flying.

Grady's parents had worked at the Salt Lake *Tribune* when he was a boy. But later on there had been a divorce, and his mother had gone to live on the East Coast, where she remarried. She still lived there, and as far as Gina knew, Grady had little to do with her. As for Grady's father, he'd remained with the newspaper until he died of a heart attack. Gina had never met either one of them.

Though Grady had told her everything about his life as a war correspondent, he'd been reticent about telling her the details of his family life. She knew it caused him pain, so she never pried.

Haunted by the little bit she knew, Gina tried to imagine what it would be like to have both parents working all the time, at emotionally draining, all-consuming jobs. Then, during the sensitive adolescent years, to have to deal with a divorce... Apparently he'd chosen to stay with his father when his mother left.

Was Grady afraid their children would suffer if Gina was a working mother?

Captain Blaylock suggested there might be something behind Grady's irrational fear of Gina's getting injured. She was beginning to think he was right. Grady didn't care that she'd been willing to compromise and stay on at station 6. To quote Grady, *he wanted her home. Period.*

Another thought occurred to her as she recalled how jealous and excluded she had felt when Grady spent so much time with the fire fighters. In those early days, she'd hated that other family. Was it possible that Grady felt excluded now that Gina had another life at the station?

She tried to think back to when they first got married. Had resigning from the school where she'd been teaching been her own idea or Grady's? Their whirlwind courtship had blotted out all other considerations, but she was quite sure Grady had asked her to quit so she would be free to travel with him. It made sense at the time; otherwise they couldn't have been together every possible minute. Besides, Grady had admitted his fear of her being injured if she stayed in Beirut.

Her mind spinning with unanswered questions, Gina flopped on her stomach and stared into the darkness.

Somehow, some way, she had to force Grady to open up. Only he held the key to the riddle. Until she got to the bottom of this, there would never be a future with Grady. Never.

CHAPTER NINE

A WEEK WENT BY but Gina didn't see or hear from Grady. She was almost out of her mind with pain and made up projects to do at the station when they weren't out on calls. On one of her days off she made an appearance at the grade school attended by Max, the boy who owned the puppy Gina had rescued. Usually, she enjoyed visits with schoolchildren; they forced her to put aside her anxieties for a while. But watching these lively, carefree boys and girls only seemed to deepen her longing for a child of her own, and she returned to the apartment even more depressed than she'd been before. The phone was ringing as she walked through the front door, and she could hear Captain Blaylock's voice on the machine, asking her to call station 6 as soon as possible.

This was their day off, so she knew it had to be important for him to be at work. She dialed his number immediately. He didn't waste time talking but simply asked if she was free to help with an emergency. She rejoiced at the opportunity—anything to keep busy so she wouldn't think about Grady.

"Captain?" Gina entered the station in her coveralls and hurried right into his office. He was conferring with the captain of the other shift. They both looked up when she walked in.

"Sit down, Gina. Captain Michaels and I called you because we need your expertise. There's been a bad accident involving a truck and car—they've both gone into the Jordan River. We don't know any details but people are trapped underwater. A call has gone out requesting scuba divers."

"I'm on my way, Captain."

"Good. I'm coming with you." They all boarded the engine and headed west toward the river. "A rescue unit with special scuba gear is headed for the scene of the accident right now," Captain Blaylock explained.

It was a fairly warm September afternoon. At least, the weather was cooperating, Gina thought. Rescues at night required lighting and everything became even more complicated and difficult.

The crew listened to the battalion chief's directives as they roared down the driveway. Police had already cordoned off the accident site. Approaching the area where the vehicles had gone over the edge into the water, they could see the truck's skid marks. A little farther on, Gina saw the big semi lying in the river, three-fourths of it submerged on the driver's side. The other car was about ten yards downstream and totally submerged. The river wasn't swift, but if the people had been knocked unconscious at impact, the danger of drowning was just as great.

She saw a ladder truck farther down the road and knew it was Grady's. Station 1 would have been the first to respond. Heart pounding, Gina jumped down from the rig and ran the hundred yards to the rescue unit, where she would change into a wet suit and tanks. Gina had learned to scuba dive when she was a girl in California. It was second nature to her, and never had she been more thankful for those hours of training than now, when so many lives were at stake.

The battalion chief was waiting for her as she approached the jump-off point. "There were no witnesses when the accident happened so we don't know how many people are down there. Captain Simpson's already in the water with one of his crew, but they need help."

Gina nodded and did a somersault over the edge, carrying an extra set of tanks. Once she had her bearings, she gave a kick and headed for the truck, swimming around to the front where she could see Bob Corby extricating the driver without any problem. He was already giving the man air from his tank and motioned for her to go help Grady farther downstream. She nodded and shoved off once more, employing her strongest kick to cover the distance as quickly as possible.

The car was jammed against some boulders. It was a white Buick four-door, and as far as she could tell, the windows were closed. If the driver had been running the air-conditioning, there could still be enough air inside the car to keep the person—or persons—alive.

As she rounded the side she saw Grady using an underwater torch to get the door open. In the driver's seat was a young man and strapped next to him in a car seat, a baby. They appeared to be dead, but Gina knew you couldn't be sure until you took vital signs.

Grady was too intent on his work to realize who she was. When he could see that help had arrived, he pointed to the door and she immediately rested her tanks on a boulder and started to pull on the handle, lodging her right foot against the body for leverage.

At first the door wouldn't budge, but after a few more pulls it gave way. Grady went in first and unfastened the young man's seat belt while Gina grabbed the extra tank. She put the mouthpiece into the man's mouth as Grady pulled him out. As soon as the opening was clear, Gina dived into the car and put her mouthpiece into the baby's mouth while she unstrapped the car seat.

Then, tucking the baby under her left arm, she carefully backed out the same way she'd come in and started swimming toward the surface with her precious bundle. It had taken longer than she'd expected to go through the maneuver. Her lungs were screaming for air by the time she surfaced.

An ambulance attendant stood ready to take the baby from her, and Captain Blaylock put out his hands for her to grasp as she climbed up the riverbank and collapsed on the dirt for a minute, drinking in fresh air. When she felt recovered, she put on the mask and mouthpiece and dived once more to recover the torch equipment and check for more victims. There could have been another child or even an adult on the floor of the back seat. The impact of a car accident could sometimes cause amazing situations.

Gina entered the interior of the car, but to her relief there were no more bodies or any sign of a pet. As she backed out, she felt a hand on her thigh. Grady had come back, presumably to get the equipment he'd brought down with him.

As she maneuvered her way around, their eyes met. He motioned at the dashboard of the car and pointed to the keys. Since they were nearest her, she pulled them out of the ignition. Grady took them from her and swam to the rear of the car. Gina followed and helped him to raise the lid once he'd inserted the key in the lock. All they found were a couple of suitcases and a camera, to her relief.

Grady pulled everything out of the trunk while Gina reached for the torch equipment, and then together they kicked toward the surface. Gina felt a rapport so strong and binding with Grady that she didn't want to leave the water. This was the first time they'd actually worked side by side as a team. It was an exhilarating experience, something she'd been waiting for since she began her training.

"Nice work," the battalion commander saluted as Gina was helped from the water, Grady not far behind.

"Did anyone survive?" Gina asked as she whipped off her mask and removed her scuba gear.

"All three are breathing on their own, Ms Lindsay. I understand you were called in for this rescue on your day off. I'm recommending you for a medal. Your second with the Salt Lake Fire Department. We're happy to have you with us."

"Thank you," Gina beamed, shaking his hand.

"Grady..." he extended his hand "...you and Bob Corby did excellent work, too. Congratulations. The three of you did the cleanest, fastest work I've ever seen in a situation like this. I'm recommending medals for you."

Gina looked over her shoulder to see Grady's reaction. To her shock, he only nodded at the battalion chief and spared her a brief, impersonal glance before walking away toward the truck.

The blood drained from her face at his abrupt departure. Here she'd been feeling this incredible harmony and oneness with him, had hardly been able to restrain herself from throwing her arms around him and shouting for joy because they'd saved lives together. And all Grady felt like doing was walking away.

A pain too deep for tears weighed her down as she walked over to the rescue unit and changed back into her coveralls. Cleanup procedures were starting, and a tow truck had arrived by the time the engine pulled away from the scene and headed back to the station.

"That was beautiful, Gina," Captain Blaylock said, patting her hand. The others joined in with complimentary remarks. "I'm proud of you. That young father and his baby were on their way home from the airport for a reunion with his wife. Now it can be a happy one. This is what it's all about, eh, Gina?"

She couldn't speak, so she patted his arm instead. Right now she was fighting tears for herself, for Grady, for the plunge from happiness to despair. If Grady couldn't respond after a moment like this, she felt as if she'd come to the end of a very long journey.

It was dusk before Gina left station 6, but instead of going home, she turned toward the mountains. She needed to get away and really think. This was her long weekend off and it didn't matter how long she was gone or if she even told anybody where she went.

When she reached Heber City, she pulled into the Wagon Wheel Café for dinner. No one served better veal cutlets than the Wagon Wheel. The rescue had depleted her energies, and she ate everything she was served, including a piece of homemade rhubarb pie.

Full at last, Gina checked in at her favorite motel down the street, then took a walk through the center of town, savoring the crisp mountain air.

She'd come to a crossroads in her life. She could not go on working in Salt Lake. This had been Grady's territory first. She was the intruder, and Grady couldn't have made it more apparent. Even if he cared, which she seriously doubted now, he was deeply disturbed by something that he couldn't share with her, couldn't talk about. That left Gina no choice but to walk out of his life for good.

At a little past ten Gina went back to the motel to go to bed. Only a few miles away sat the little gingerbread house. For all she knew, Grady was there now. All she had to do was get into her car and drive there to find out. But it would profit her nothing and might result in an even more devastating conflict.

She tossed and turned most of the night, then sat at the table of her room and wrote out her resignation on the motel stationery. She had an obligation to give the department two weeks' notice. At nine, she left for Salt Lake.

After going to headquarters to leave her resignation for Captain Blaylock, she stopped by Sue's place but her friend wasn't home. Despondent, Gina went back to her apartment and put in a call to the movers to make arrangements for her return to California in two weeks. She requested some boxes, which were dropped off the next day so she could begin the arduous task of packing. Sue called her that night and they went out to dinner. Gina's friend was disappointed when she heard the news, but thought it the wisest course of action. At least that way, Gina could get on with her life. Gina promised to come back at Thanksgiving for Sue and Jay's wedding.

"I received your resignation, Gina," the captain said as soon as Gina reported for duty on the following Tuesday. "I'm sorry things didn't work out for you and Grady."

"Me, too." She heaved a sigh. "But he refuses to talk about what's really wrong. I've tried everything."

"Not everything, Gina. You could do what he wants and quit fire fighting if he means that much to you."

"I know. But without knowing *why* he wants me to quit working altogether, I'm as much in the dark as ever. Captain, you're right about Grady. There's more bothering him than just my job. I think it has to do with family problems, something that happened in his past, but he's never been able to open up to me about it. Without total honesty, we can't have a future together."

"You're right. So it appears I'm going to lose one of the best fire fighters I've ever had at station 6. But until that time comes, there's work to be done. Because it's such nice weather this morning, several of the stations have decided to go do practice drills out by the airport. Let's check out the rig and go on over."

Practice drills were killers, especially when you were wearing full turnout gear. Gina immediately spotted Mavis plugging a hydrant.

"Let's show these guys how it's done," Mavis whispered as Gina unrolled hose alongside her.

"Why not?" Gina chuckled. Mavis was like a breath of fresh air right now. A little friendly competition with the men would help keep her mind off Grady. But in that regard she was mistaken. The next time she looked up, there was Grady talking to some of the drill instructors. Apparently his crew had decided to join in.

"Hey, Gina!" The guys from station 1 all waved and shouted to her. She watched them take their place in the lines and had to admit Grady's bunch was an impressive group. She waved back and kept on working with Mavis. A little later the drill instructor announced that everyone would have to climb a ladder to the third-story window of the vacant building and bring down a live victim in a fireman's lift. *"A live victim?"* Gina muttered to Mavis in shock.

Mavis had the light of battle in her hazel eyes. "I guess they're trying to show us up, Gina girl. They'll be sorry!"

These were timed drills and every move and procedure was noted and marked. Mavis winked at Gina and off they went. Gina positioned her hands and feet as she'd learned in countless practice sessions, then started up the ladder. On the other drills, she'd beaten almost everyone's time; she wanted to come out first in this one, too. Maybe it was because Grady was here that she felt this sudden excess energy. Whatever the reason, she scurried up the steps as if her feet had wings. Her victim would be lying on the floor inside the window and she'd have to hoist him over her shoulder and then bring him down the ladder.

In a real fire, Gina would have to determine the weight of the victim before deciding which approach to take, but in practice drills, a dummy was usually provided. Evidently not this time!

She spotted her victim lying facedown on the floor as she swung her leg inside the building. First she had to take off his turnout coat and heavy boots to lighten the load.

"Grady!" she cried out in shock as she turned him over. "What's going on?"

"I'm supposed to be unconscious," he replied in a no-nonsense voice. But his eyes were smiling, something she hadn't seen for so long she almost forgot what she was doing. "You're losing precious seconds. Undress me," he whispered in a voice she hadn't heard since that night at the condo. With shaking hands she knelt down and began to unfasten his turnout coat.

"This isn't fair, Grady. I was supposed to be provided with a victim I could manage," she said quietly, easing his arm out of one sleeve with difficulty because she was getting no cooperation from Grady.

"Don't tell me that now, Gina. A fire fighter needs to have confidence that his buddy can get him out of trouble in any situation."

"If this were a real fire, I'd try to get you out even if I died in the process, but a practice drill is something else again."

His eyes narrowed provocatively. "Everyone's going to be watching you, Gina. If you can't bring me down now, I think you can imagine what the guys are going to say."

Her face went beet red. "If I crumple from the weight, we'll both end up in the hospital."

His sudden smile mocked her. "I thought you were the woman willing to take any risks. If I'm game, what's the problem?"

"There's no problem," she whispered, but inside her anxiety had reached its peak. "You'll have to cooperate, Grady, or else this will be terribly dangerous."

"Of course. What do you want me to do?" He appeared to be enjoying himself as she pulled off the other sleeve and turned toward his feet to undo the boots. "I'd like those to stay on, if you don't mind." He moved his feet away.

"But they weigh too much. Besides, you're supposed to be unconscious—so you can't talk back."

"You'll have to do it my way, Gina, or we won't do it at all," he said in a tone that brooked no argument.

She bowed her head as a shudder racked her body. "I'm afraid you'll get hurt, Grady."

"Is that all that's holding you back? Come on, Gina. Where's your sense of adventure?"

His goading drove her to action and she rolled him on his side. Next, she crouched in front of him and placed his arms over her left shoulder, then raised herself on to her left knee with her right foot flat on the floor. She counted to three and started to stand up, clutching him around the thighs, but suddenly she was pushed to the floor, flat on her back. Grady's body covered hers from head to foot. Even through the thick padding of her turnout coat, she could feel the pounding of their hearts.

"You did that on purpose," she cried out, furious with him and far too aware of their closeness.

"That's right." She felt his warm breath against her mouth and she forgot where they were or what they were supposed to be doing. "Never underestimate your victim. He might become uncontrollable, like this." In a lightning move, Grady's mouth descended on hers, and she almost lost consciousness under its driving force. He didn't allow her a breath. He pinned her hands to the floor on either side of her head, and she twisted and turned to elude him.

"Someone will see us!" she cried frantically.

His low chuckle sent chills through her quivering body. "No, they won't. I arranged it so you'd be last up the ladder." Again, his lips covered hers with smothering force and he slowly and expertly began drawing a response from her.

Gina couldn't believe this was happening, that Grady was actually making love to her on the floor of an abandoned building at the fire department's practice site. "Grady," she begged when he gave her a moment's respite, "why are you doing this now?"

His answer was to kiss her again, over and over till she wasn't aware of her surroundings.

"You know what, Gina? You ask too many questions, but this is one I'll answer." He finally lifted his head and stared down at her intently. "I'm going away on a leave of absence, and I'm not at all certain that I'm coming back to Utah. I wanted to see you before I left and this seemed as good a time as any."

"What?" she raised her head from the floor, but he held her down with the pressure of his hands on her shoulders. "Grady—where are you going? Why?" Her eyes searched his for answers but they remained a blank gray.

"You're a fine fire fighter, Gina. After our dive in the river the other day, I realized just how fine. You'll go a long way in the department, because you've made a reputation for yourself already. You can have a secure future here." His hand caressed her chin. "I'm proud of you, Gina, and I happen to know that if I'd cooperated, you would have lifted me down that ladder today. I have no doubts."

Gina's body was racked with fresh pain. "There's no need for you to leave, Grady. I handed in my resignation the other day. I'm moving back to California on the tenth. I should never have come here in the first place. It's disrupted your whole life." Hot tears trickled out of the corners of her eyes. "Please don't go away on my account."

"I'm not," he murmured, sounding very faraway. "I'm going for me. Whether you stay here or move to California is immaterial at this point."

She sensed the finality of his words, and there was nothing more to say. Gina got to her feet and reached for her helmet while Grady shrugged into his turnout coat. He faced her with a look of incredible tenderness shining out of his eyes.' "For old times' sake, I'm going to carry you over the threshold. It won't be exactly the same as in Beirut, but if we don't get back down that ladder, someone's going to come looking for us."

He gave her an almost wistful smile, then softly kissed her lips before hoisting her over his shoulder like so much fluff. With his usual economy of movement, he stepped over the ledge to the cheers of everyone below. His arms held her securely around the thighs and her head bobbed as he descended the ladder. He wasn't even out of breath when they reached the ground.

Gina had to put on the performance of her life, smiling as everyone started in with the comments and the ribbing about who was rescuing whom. Grady still held her in his arms.

"I'm afraid I played a little joke on Ms Lindsay," he explained to anyone listening, "but she took it like a man." The guys laughed and joked with Grady, who stood grinning among his crew.

As he lowered her to the ground their eyes met for a brief moment. His said goodbye. She turned away abruptly, needing to escape before she fell apart.

"Gina? Wait up," Mavis called out. "What happened up there?" She hurried to catch up with Gina, who was walking quickly toward the engine.

"I'll call you later and tell you all about it," Gina shouted over her shoulder. Mavis didn't pursue the issue. She eyed Gina thoughtfully for a moment before walking over to her engine.

"Can we go back to the station, Captain?" Gina asked quietly.

Blaylock gave her a shrewd look and nodded. "Sure. We're just waiting for Marty. Are you okay, Gina?"

She couldn't answer him.

CHAPTER TEN

UNBEKNOWNST TO GINA, Captain Blaylock had planned a surprise dinner in honor of her last night with the station. Someone had gone out to Bountiful to bring her favorite Chinese food from the Mandarin, while the others had decorated the lounge with crepe paper streamers. A huge chocolate cake with chocolate frosting stood in the center of the table. An enormous package was propped on the floor.

Captain Carrera and some of the crew from station 3, as well as Frank and Bob from 1, joined in the festivities. Gina could hardly believe her eyes when she returned from a run to find everyone assembled and all the goodies waiting on the table.

It was growing dark outside by the time they'd eaten. Gina finally unwrapped her gift, anxious to see what on earth was inside something so huge. A beautiful black-and-white stuffed Dalmatian dog appeared as she pulled the paper away. The fireman's mascot. And that wasn't all. An exquisite gold locket hung around its neck on a gold chain. Engraved on the back were the words *You're the best. Stations 1, 3 and 6.*

Gina promptly made a fool of herself and wept, but her tears turned to laughter as those present "roasted" her, leaving out nothing embarrassing, including Grady's lift down the ladder.

At the mention of Grady, she sobered. Neither Bob nor Frank had any idea where their captain had gone. They didn't seem the least bit happy about it. Bob was acting captain in Grady's place. Now that Whittaker was back, he'd taken over engine, and they'd swung in a new guy to cover ladder while Grady was gone.

Grady had told them the same thing he'd told Gina—that he didn't know if he was coming back.

Everyone in the group speculated on the reasons for Grady's sudden departure. Everyone except Captain Blaylock and Gina. She couldn't help but wonder if he'd gone overseas to see about working as a foreign correspondent again. It was the only thing that made sense. Captain Blaylock kept his ideas to himself, but he gazed at her with compassion several times throughout the dinner.

The gong sounded, effectively ending the festivities. "Ladder 1, respond to assist at fire in progress at Hotel Olympus."

"Hotel Olympus!" everyone muttered at once. There'd been talk of reprisals since the building was closed down permanently, shortly after the fire fighters' ball. Some of them had jokingly commented that they wouldn't be surprised if an arsonist set it ablaze to get even. Many businesses in downtown Salt Lake were worried that the closure of the hotel would adversely affect their incomes. Maybe the joking wasn't so far-fetched after all.

Frank and Bob got up from the table and each gave Gina a hug, telling her she'd better come back to Salt Lake to visit soon. Then they hurried out of the station.

In another few seconds the gong sounded again. More stations were called in to assist, including engine 6.

"That's us. Let's go." Leaving everything exactly as it was, Gina hurried out to the bay with the others, jumped into her boots and put on her turnout coat and helmet.

Gina found it incredible that the hotel was billowing black smoke as they pulled up to the fire ground a few minutes later. Every available unit in the city and county had been called in. Not long ago, she'd danced in Grady's arms in this exquisite foyer. Now everything—not just her dreams—was going up in smoke.

"We've got a fire that's fully involved," she heard the battalion chief saying to the captain over the walkie-talkie. The place swarmed with fire fighters.

The captain began giving orders. "Marty, you're nozzle-handler and Gina is leadoff man."

They jumped down from the rig and started pulling the hose forward through the main entrance to the hotel. From what Gina could gather over the radio, an arsonist had started the fire on the mezzanine floor, where the most beautiful and famous rooms of the hotel were located. If it had been on the upper floors the fire wouldn't have been so devastating.

She felt thankful there were no people in the hotel, but it was a showplace and one of the main tourist attractions of the city. There wasn't another hotel like it west of the Mississippi. Gina could have wept to see the intricate cornices and moldings melting in the blaze.

More than a dozen hoses were going at once. When Marty was in place, Gina ran back outside to tell Joe to start the pump.

It was when she reentered the building and started across the marble floor toward Marty that she heard a bloodcurdling scream. *"Gina! Run for cover! Run, Gina!"*

It was Grady! She was so stunned to hear his voice above the chaos of sirens and hoses, she thought she must be dreaming. But some instinct propelled her to obey his anguished cry. She began to run back toward the entrance when she heard the tremendous crash behind her. Instantly waves of shattered crystal sprayed out in all directions. The air was filled with shards of the once magnificent chandelier.

Gina lost her footing and was swept forward through the entry as if she were riding the surf. Without her mask and gloves, she'd have been cut to pieces.

A couple of ambulance crews ran past her to search for victims beneath the twisted, glittering wreckage. "Marty!" she screamed, picking herself up, intent on going in to find him. Captain Blaylock held her fast.

"Easy, Gina. Come on out to the rig. We'll know in a minute how he is."

"Grady's here," she said, sobbing, "and he shouted to me."

"I know." The captain nodded, ushering Gina onto the engine. "He's up on the mezzanine with the ladder. He must have seen the chandelier going."

"H-he saved my life."

"That he did. Now you sit here, Gina, and that's an order. I'm going inside for a minute."

"I'm coming with you. I've got to know about Marty."

She didn't have long to wait. Just as the captain reluctantly agreed to let Gina go in with him, Marty was carted out on a stretcher.

Gina ran over to him and cried even more when Marty gave her a weak smile. "I'm all right, Gina. Just some glass in my leg. Whoever called out to you saved my life, too. I just started running like hell."

"Thank God!" She bent over and kissed his forehead before the ambulance crew took over. As they carried him out to the ambulance, Marty held out a gloved hand.

"Will you call Carol? Let her down easy," Marty pleaded with Gina. "She's terrified something bad will happen to me. You know how to talk to her."

"I'll call her right now." She turned to the driver. "What hospital are you taking him to?"

"L.D.S."

"Captain Blaylock? Could you ask for a police officer to take me back to the station so I can call Marty's wife?"

"That won't be necessary." Gina heard a familiar male voice directly behind her. "I'll drive you."

Gina spun around and stared up at Grady. His blackened face was the most beautiful sight she'd ever seen. "Captain Simpson? Whether I have your permission or not, I'm going to kiss you for saving both of our lives." Gina flung her arms around his neck and pressed her mouth to his, standing on tiptoe to do it.

Miraculously Grady's arms came around her and he lifted her off the ground.

So many emotions were bursting inside Gina, she didn't stop to think who might be watching. This was Grady, warm and vital and alive in her arms, kissing her back, tasting of smoke and soot. Tasting divine...

"You came back!" she murmured against his mouth.

"That's right," he whispered. "I flew in from the East Coast a few hours ago. I came to look for you. When I heard about the fire, I drove on over here, knowing I'd find you."

Her body shook with delayed reaction. "If you hadn't come—"

"Don't think about it." He crushed her in his arms, kissing the very life out of her.

Captain Blaylock began clearing his throat. "I think maybe you two better carry on some place else, or you'll find yourselves on the front page of the morning newspaper."

Slowly Grady broke their kiss and let her down gently. "Come on, Gina. Let's get out of here. We need to call Carol and then I want to talk to you."

"Do I have your permiss—"

"You have it," Captain Blaylock broke in with a huge smile.

Grady held Gina's elbow as he ushered her through the maze of hoses and equipment to his car, which was parked next to the ladder. He opened the trunk. "Let's get rid of these." He took off his turnout coat while she took off hers, and they tossed them inside. He helped her into the car, then went around to the driver's side.

Instead of going west, Grady turned north to Second Avenue. "This isn't the way to the station," she said, puzzled.

"I'm taking you home, Gina."

She watched him, studying his unique profile, the way he handled the car as they drove through the avenues to the condo. Her heart was hammering so loudly she was positive he could hear every beat.

By tacit agreement they went upstairs to the lounge and immediately phoned Marty's wife. Grady was all charm and diplomacy on the phone, before he passed it to Gina. Then it was her turn to reassure Carol, who broke down sobbing and said she'd leave for the hospital immediately. Gina told her that she and Grady would come by later.

"Next order of business," Grady stated as Gina replaced the receiver. "Come with me." He took her hand and led her up the stairs to the master bath. "I'm going to take a bath downstairs while you shower up here. Don't be too long."

His manner was mysterious but Gina didn't mind. She didn't want to say or do anything to alter Grady's mood. Maybe this time they could really talk.

"I'll hurry. I promise."

He seemed reluctant to leave her, but finally strode out of the bathroom.

Taking a deep breath, Gina undressed and got into the shower, reveling in the hot water. She washed her hair with Grady's shampoo, loving the smell because it reminded her of him. When she stepped out of the stall a few minutes later, she reached for his striped, toweling robe that hung on the hook behind the door. A sense of déjà vu assailed her.

She wrapped her hair in a towel and left the bathroom. Grady stood in the living room in a clean pair of shorts and T-shirt pouring them each a drink.

"Have a little wine," he suggested, passing her a glass. With only one lamp on, his handsome face was shadowed, yet she caught the slightest tinge of a flush on his cheeks. If she hadn't known better, she'd have said he was nervous, and never in their entire married life had she seen him nervous.

His black curls were still damp from the shower and fell in tendrils over his forehead and around his neck. To Gina, he was the most beautiful man she'd ever known, and never more so than right now, with his gray eyes playing over her face as if he couldn't get enough of her. He tugged on the towel to bring her white-gold hair cascading to her shoulders. Putting down his wineglass, he took the towel in his hands and began drying the strands as if he'd been given a precious task.

Gina felt his touch and it sent shivers of ecstasy through her body. "Grady—" She spoke before it became impossible to do so. "I have a thousand questions to ask, but before I do, I have something to tell you." His hands stopped caressing her hair, but he didn't remove them.

"Until tonight, I felt that if you couldn't tell me the real reason why you didn't want me to work—whether at fire fighting or anything else—then I couldn't accept that and couldn't imagine our marriage succeeding. But now—" her voice broke "—I don't care anymore. If you want me to stay home and wait for you every day, hold you in my arms every night, smell like flowers for you—if that will make you happy, then that's what I want, too. I love you, Grady. Let me be your wife again, and I promise I'll make you the happiest man alive. But please give me another chance to be the kind of mate I should have been in the first place. You're all that's important to me."

His hands slid around her from behind and he kissed the tender nape of her neck. "Gina..." The emotion in that one word caused her to tremble. "I don't deserve you or the sacrifices you've made for me. Come here, sweetheart."

He drew her to the couch, then gently urged her to sit. He remained standing. "I want to tell you everything. It's something I should have done before we were married, but even I didn't know how deeply I'd been affected until it was too late for us." His voice sounded haunted.

"My mother and father were both news reporters working for the same paper. You know that. But what you don't know is that my mother got involved with another reporter on the staff and they had an affair." Gina held herself rigid as the revelations unfolded. "I was caught between my parents. Apparently it was an ugly and bitter divorce. Mother went back East with the man and married him. My father retained custody of me and raised me. I was nine when she left. It was an impressionable, sensitive age, and all I heard from the time she left was that you couldn't trust a woman, let alone a working woman, especially a career woman."

"Until the day my father died, he warned me to find myself a docile little woman, a homebody, and settle down. Let her know who's boss, he told me. Keep her home, keep her pregnant." Grady sighed. "I know it must all sound outrageous to you, but that was the kind of man my father was. He thought my mother would quit her job on the paper when they got married. He was making plenty of money and couldn't understand why she felt the need to work. They argued incessantly.

"After the divorce, my mother came to Salt Lake quite often to visit me, but as I got older, I felt estranged from her and I'm afraid I viewed her through my father's eyes. I'm the reason we stopped having any communication."

Gina felt sick. She'd had no idea.

"Then I met you," he said thickly. "You were the embodiment of all that is sweet and gentle and beautiful. I wanted to be your hero. I wanted to be the kind of husband that my father had envisioned."

"Oh, Grady—" Gina hid her face in her hands.

There was a long pause.

"Gina . . . I didn't know how much of my father's bias had rubbed off on me until you insisted on staying on with the department. But it was more than the fear of you getting hurt. I've realized that somewhere deep in my psyche I was afraid you'd fall in love with one of the guys and run off and leave me. That I'd turn out like my father, bitter and alone."

Gina couldn't stand any more. She jumped up from the couch and threw her arms around him. "Are you still afraid, Grady?" she whispered against his cheek.

"Maybe. That's why I went to see my mother."

Gina closed her eyes tightly. So that was where he'd gone.

"She painted a rather different picture from the one my father had drawn, but what came out of her talk was that my father was too authoritarian for her to live with any longer. She felt caught in a trap. They had no happiness, Gina. That's why she left, and her feelings of guilt over the adultery were so terrible, she didn't fight my father for custody."

Gina drew him closer. "So you found out she really did love you very much."

"Yes." He nodded into her neck. "I'm afraid my father did a lot of damage to her, as well as to me. Now I can see reasons for the way things happened in our lives. That's why I came back."

He lifted his head and grasped Gina by the shoulders. "I know there are no guarantees in this life, but I want you for my wife, Gina. Not the way my father envisioned. I want you to be happy, too. You need your freedom. Talking to Mother made me realize that. You can't put your wife in a box the way my father wanted. It doesn't work like that—but what did he know? It wasn't all his fault. He was raised by Victorian standards and didn't have a clue about a woman's needs. Gina—I'm trying to understand—"

"Are you asking me to marry you, Grady Simpson?" Her violet eyes shimmered as they gazed up at him.

"You know I am, Regina Lindsay. But only on conditions we can both accept. Fair enough?"

"Grady..." she whispered achingly, loving him too much.

"I happen to know Captain Blaylock is retiring in a few weeks. Could you live with me being captain of station 6 and you as one of the crew?"

"Grady!" she shrieked with joy.

"I've done nothing but think for the past week. Barring unforeseen dangers, we should be able to live a long, healthy life at 6. And when the children come, you can decide the number of hours you want. Do you think you could be happy?"

The earnestness of his pleading was Gina's undoing. "I've already told you that just being your wife is all that matters."

He shook his head. "No—that isn't all that matters. I adore you for being willing to sacrifice, but I don't want our life to be like that. I want us to both be fulfilled. If I move to 6, I'll have more time to write free-lance. I still have that urge in my blood."

She gave him her most beguiling smile. "Who knows? Maybe you'll write a bestselling novel about a married couple's life with the fire department. We can retire in luxury."

His smile faded to be replaced by a look of such tenderness, it almost overwhelmed her. "Gina...my mother wants to meet you."

"I want to meet her. I'm thrilled with the idea that you have family. I wanted to get to know her ages ago, but you never offered and I hated to pry."

"Gina, I swear. No more secrets. From here on, we talk over everything, no matter how painful. Agreed?"

"Agreed, my darling." She nestled against him.

His hands played with her hair. "Do you have any idea how utterly desirable you are, standing there in my robe with your hair smelling like sunshine?"

She cocked her head to the side and ran her hands over his broad chest. "I think I'd have a better idea if you showed me."

The devastating smile that always took her breath flashed for her now. "Oh, I'm going to show you all right, but we're not married yet."

"Well, you're the captain." She kissed the end of his nose and moved out of his arms. "Whatever you say goes." She started to laugh at the horrified expression on his face and ran for the stairs.

"You'll pay for that, my lovely," he warned, chasing her up the steps, but he was too late. She'd shut the door and locked it.

"Gina?" He pounded on the door. "Let me in."

"No. I always obey my captain's orders."

"I'm not your captain, I'm your husband," he shouted.

"Not yet, you aren't. Right now you're my fiancé."

"Gina—"

"I want a *white* wedding."

"Don't do this to me," he begged in a hoarse voice.

"And I want you in full dress uniform."

"We'll talk about it when you open the door."

"Absolutely no one looks better than you do in uniform, Grady."

"Well, I'm happy you feel that way, sweetheart. Now open the door."

"What will you do if I open it?"

"That, my love, is for me to know and you to find out."

"I'm frightened, Grady."

There was silence. "Of what? Me?"

"I haven't been married for a long time. What if I'm a big disappointment to you?"

"In what way?"

"What if you decide you like that brunette better than you like me?"

"I thought you'd overcome your jealous tendencies?"

"Well, I haven't."

"What if I told you I've been faithful to you since our divorce?"

The lock clicked and the door opened a crack. Grady helped a little with the palm of his hand. Gina's gaze locked with his. "Is that the truth?"

"Do you even have to ask, Gina? My fate was sealed the first moment I saw you. Come to me, sweetheart. We have so much to make up for."

Gina ran into his arms and gloried in her right to be there. "Someone once told me that if I wanted you back, I'd have to fight fire with fire."

Grady's eyes smoldered. "I'd like to meet that someone and say thank-you, because from now on we're going to be fully involved. Some fires are like that, sweetheart. They're meant to burn forever."

There's only one man she can turn to for help.
A man who *may* be a murderer.
Her ex-husband.

FREE FALL

Jasmine Cresswell

Chapter One

Liz saw the crowd outside her apartment building as soon as she turned the corner from the bus stop. Her mouth went dry and her stomach lurched in horrified recognition. Her hands cradled her waist.

"Oh no! Please, no!"

She wasn't sure if she spoke aloud. Blood drummed in her ears, cutting off sound. Inside her silent world, the lights of the squad cars flashed with hypnotic brilliance, glazing the falling snow with orange glitter. One, two, three. Three whirling lights. Three blue-and-white Denver police cars.

Last time, in Seattle, they'd only sent two.

Liz read the neat copperplate inscription on the door of the car nearest her: To Serve and Protect. A great motto, much favored by police departments. It looked so much better than To Harass and Intimidate.

Her gaze raced feverishly over the neon-lit scene. Two dozen spectators, three squad cars, a half-dozen cops—but no ambulance.

No ambulance, and no paramedics. Hope flared briefly. Maybe this time there never had been an ambulance. Maybe the police were here to investigate a burglary. Liz started running.

She saw the chalk outline on the pavement as soon as she'd elbowed her way through the crowd. The spring snow wasn't settling, and the chalk shone white and clean in the evening darkness, a wet gingerbread figure sketched on asphalt. A child's drawing, except for the blood.

Fear clawed at her throat. Liz swayed, grasping the police barricade for support. Dear God, it had happened again.

"You sure missed a horrible sight," commented the woman next to her. "They only moved the body ten minutes ago. The side of her face was smashed right in from where she fell. Terrible tragedy." The conventional words of grief didn't succeed in masking the relish in the woman's voice.

Liz fought to control the sickness welling up inside her. "Was it a young wo—? Do they know who it was?"

"A girl from one of the apartments. Look, you can see the open window up there on the top floor. That's where she fell from. Or jumped."

Liz didn't look up; she didn't need to. Her stomach gave another warning heave, and she pushed through the barricade, barely making it to the corner of her apartment building before she vomited.

When she finally stopped retching, she straightened to discover herself surrounded by three uniformed police officers. One of them—a sergeant—held out a wad of tissues. She wiped her mouth. The policemen watched, their eyes hard.

"The victim a friend of yours, Miss?" The inquiry was polite but cold.

"Maybe.... I think so.... I don't know.... I live here."

"Terrible for you to come home to all this." The sergeant's voice had warmed, now that he knew she wasn't just an overcurious bystander with a weak stomach. "Which apartment is yours? I'll see that the officer guarding the entrance lets you in."

She glanced up, finally allowing herself to look at the open window, a big bay in the center of the sixth floor. It was hers, of course. Hers and Karen Zeit's. She had known all along that it would be.

"I live in 6B," she said flatly, returning her gaze to the ball of soiled tissues.

She felt the policemen exchange glances. She closed her eyes, shoving the tissues into the pocket of her jacket and wrapping her arms more tightly around her body. She was shivering, she realized, and the little clicking noise resonating inside her head had to be the chattering of her teeth.

"You'd better come along inside and get warm."

She forced herself to look at the sergeant. "What's happened to Karen?"

"There's been an accident," he replied, his voice gruff. His two younger colleagues shuffled their feet and stared over her shoulder. They were worried, poor things. Worried about how a law-abiding citizen was going to take this shocking intrusion of violence into her life. It wasn't true that cops had no emotions. Liz had found that out in Seattle. The first time, when Brian died, they'd all been very sympathetic.

This time, once they knew the truth, they weren't likely to waste much time on sympathy. Some bright-eyed cop, eager for promotion, would check with the authorities in Seattle, and Liz would instantaneously be transformed from victim into suspect. Being a suspect was no fun at all. She'd found that out when Jill killed herself, only four short weeks after Brian.

She needed to know the worst about Karen, to have the horror confirmed. "Is my roommate dead?" she asked brusquely.

The sergeant made soothing noises, avoiding her eyes. He put a hand beneath her elbow, guiding her toward the rear entrance of the apartment building. "I think we should talk about this inside, where it's a bit warmer. Lousy weather for May, isn't it? But that's Denver for you. Swimsuit temperatures one day and a blizzard the next. If you'll follow me, I'll ask the apartment manager to make you a cup of coffee."

Liz allowed herself to be led in through the service lobby and down to the basement where the superintendent had his apartment. She sat meekly at the appointed table and waited in silence while one of the policemen brought her a cup of coffee.

Dear God, Karen is dead. Dead. The awful word echoed in a bleak rhythm with her chattering teeth.

The policemen didn't ask how she wanted her coffee served, and presented it already laced with milk and sugar. The oily liquid tasted revolting enough to jerk her into renewed awareness of her surroundings. The sergeant had disappeared, to be replaced by a tall man, wearing a raincoat that was a fraction too tight. A homicide detective: she'd learned to recognize the breed. She wondered how long he'd been standing on the other side of the Formica-topped table, staring at her.

"I'm Lieutenant Rodriguez," he said, flashing a badge and a small smile. Three months ago, she would have found the smile reassuring. Now she knew better. She blinked her eyelids, the only part of her that seemed capable of movement.

"I'm sorry you had to find out about your roommate this way."

"She's dead," Liz said flatly. "Isn't she?"

"I'm afraid so. If it's any consolation, Miss Meacham, I'm sure your roommate died instantly."

Instantly. Ten seconds after she hit the ground? Twenty? A minute? Liz blinked again, then glanced at the lieutenant. He doesn't look Hispanic, she thought. She stirred her mud-gray coffee, wondering how he knew her name. Perhaps the superintendent had told him. She could have asked, but it was too difficult to form the question. Shock always seemed to reduce her brain to a scattershot incoherence of half thoughts. Maybe she should carry a sign: Sharing an Apartment with Liz Meacham is Terminally Hazardous to Your Health. Horrifyingly, she found that she wanted to laugh.

She took another sip of coffee, swallowing the laughter along with the disgusting brew. The lieutenant's chair scraped over the thin carpet as he sat down. Gradually she became aware of the acrid smell of stale cigarette smoke. Her senses, numb ever since she turned the corner from the bus stop, were beginning to function once again. The cigarette smoke, now that she could smell it, made her stomach roil. All in all, it might have been better if her body had stayed numb.

"There's a few questions I need to ask you, Miss Meacham. I'm sorry, but there's nobody else we can ask."

Liz avoided the lieutenant's eyes. She stared into the kitchen, where she could see the police sergeant talking on the phone. The apartment manager was at the sink, filling his percolator. She shuddered, then dragged her gaze back to the lieutenant.

"Have you told Karen's parents yet? They live somewhere near Detroit, in one of the suburbs. I guess their phone number is on the bulletin board in Karen's bedroom."

"We found it, and we're working on notifying the parents. Have you shared an apartment with the deceased for long, Miss Meacham?"

The deceased. Karen probably hadn't been dead more than a couple of hours, and already she had been transformed from a human being to an item of official jargon. Liz wished she could switch off her awareness of Karen's humanity as easily as the detective. She ran her index finger around the rim of her mug. "I moved in with Karen six weeks ago."

"I see. And did you know her before that, Miss Meacham?"

"No. I only moved to Denver recently." Liz spoke rapidly, giving the lieutenant no time to interject awkward questions. "I met Karen at a party a couple of days after I arrived in town. She was looking for a roommate, and I was looking for somewhere to live. We were glad to find each other."

The lieutenant wrote painstakingly in his notebook. Unlike TV cops, who never seemed to take notes about anything, Liz had learned that real-life policemen wrote everything down. The lieutenant turned the page. Did it take that long to write "Deceased met roommate at a party"?

"Just for the record, Miss Meacham, would you tell us where you lived before you moved in with the deceased?"

Liz's fingers closed around her mug. So there it was, the question she had been dreading. The innocuous-sounding question she had known would come up sooner or later. She wished it hadn't come up quite so soon.

She cleared her throat. "I lived in Seattle."

Lieutenant Rodriguez was not a fool. He obviously heard the tension in her voice, although she'd tried hard to smooth it out. Damn it, she wasn't responsible for Karen's decision to jump out of their apartment window. She wasn't some freakish, latter-day version of Typhoid Mary. Despite what had happened to Brian and then to Jill, the rational part of Liz's brain still insisted that suicide was one of the few deadly diseases you couldn't catch from your roommate.

"Seattle is a big city, Miss Meacham. Could we have an address, please? Just for the record, of course."

Of course, she thought with silent irony. Nevertheless, she gave him what he was asking for. "755 West Arbor Avenue. Apartment 14D."

Jill's address. No point in saying she'd lived there less than a month before Jill had been found splattered on the pavement outside their living-room window. No point in explaining that Brian had committed suicide a month before Liz moved in with Jill. On the other hand, there was no point in lying. Her name alone would be enough to pull up all the facts on the Seattle police computers.

"Do you know where the deceased was employed, Miss Meacham?"

She should have been more alert to Karen's moods, Liz berated herself. Karen had seemed uptight these past few days, ever since Liz had returned from Mexico. But Liz had deliberately refrained from inquiring, deliberately kept her distance. Since Brian died, she hadn't wanted too much emotional closeness—

"Miss Meacham?"

With considerable effort, Liz focused her attention on the detective. "I'm sorry, I didn't hear your question."

"The deceased, Karen Zeit. Do you know where she was employed?"

"She worked for Dexter Rand. She was the senior secretary in his Denver office."

Lieutenant Rodriguez finally showed a degree of surprise. "Dexter Rand? You mean the senator?"

"Yes." Liz didn't—couldn't—elaborate on the stark response.

"Oh, brother, the media are going to love this," the lieutenant muttered under his breath, scribbling in his notebook. "Was the deceased interested in politics?"

"Not that I know of. I think she just enjoyed the hectic pace of Dexter's office."

Something in her voice must have betrayed her. Or perhaps it was her slip in using Dexter's first name. The lieutenant looked up quickly. "Nothing personal in their relationship?"

"Not that I know of."

"Would you have known?"

The look Liz gave him was cool. "Probably not."

The lieutenant changed the subject. "And you, Miss Meacham? Where do you work?"

"I'm in charge of market research at Peperito's. You probably know them. They're headquartered near the airport."

"Peperito's? The Mexican-food company?"

"Yes."

The lieutenant smiled, a genuine smile this time. "My wife always buys their *salsa*. She says it's the best."

"Thanks. We really work hard to keep up the quality. We import all the spices from Mexico."

"Is that so?" The lieutenant flipped through his notes, his moment of informality over. "Well, back to the matter at hand. Did the deceased give any indication that she was depressed, Miss Meacham? Did she have any reason to take her own life? Any arguments with men friends...colleagues...the senator...that sort of thing?"

"I don't know much about Karen's personal life," Liz said. "I travel a lot with my job and I don't suppose Karen and I spent ten evenings together in six weeks. I just came back from an extended business trip to Mexico."

"Is that why you shared an apartment, because of the travel? You and Miss Zeit could both have afforded your own place, I guess. Rents in Denver aren't that high."

"It was one of the reasons. I need to keep expenses down. My mother's in a private nursing home." Liz clasped her hands on the table and stared at her thumbs. Her nail polish was chipped, she realized. Karen would never have left the office with chipped nail polish. Karen had been the most immaculately groomed woman Liz had ever met.

Too immaculate to contemplate ending her life smashed to smithereens on a driveway overlooked by two large trash Dumpsters.

The thought sprang unbidden to the forefront of Liz's mind, then lodged there, obstinately refusing to go away. "Are you sure it was suicide?" she asked the lieutenant. "Couldn't it have been an accident or—or something?"

Why in the world had she said that? Good God, was she actually trying to suggest to the police that Karen's death might not be suicide? Hadn't she had enough trouble as a murder suspect in Seattle? Liz clamped her lips tightly shut, before she could make any more disastrous suggestions.

Rodriguez, thank heaven, didn't pick up on any undertones to her question. He shrugged. "An accident's not likely. There's a kitchen chair pulled up to the living-room window and an open bottle of Scotch standing next to the chair. The bathroom sink has aspirin spilled into it. I guess she might have taken aspirin for a headache, then decided to clean the windows and drink neat Scotch at the same time." The lieutenant's tone suggested that after several years on the city police force, he'd learned to accept any act of human folly as possible. "I'd say everything points to a straightforward suicide, except she didn't leave a note, and suicides usually do. The autopsy will tell us more."

Brian and Jill hadn't left notes, either. Brian had shot himself in front of an open window. Then, four scant weeks later, Jill had filled herself with prescription tranquilizers and pushed herself out headfirst from the fourteenth floor of their Seattle apartment. How many more variations could be worked on the theme of suicide victims spread-eagled on the sidewalk?

Three bloody, crumpled blobs, waiting to greet Liz, waiting to torment her with the knowledge that she had been totally insensitive to their problems, totally insensitive to the edge of desperation that must have crept into their lives.

Unless they hadn't committed suicide.

Brian's suicide had seemed tragic but within the bounds of possibility, given his recurring black moods. Jill's suicide a few weeks later had seemed a terrible, malignant coincidence. But Karen's suicide strained the limits of Liz's credulity. Three roommates tumbling to their deaths within three months just didn't make any kind of sense.

Unless they had been murdered.

Liz sprang up from the table, hearing her chair crash behind her as she groped blindly toward the bathroom. She stumbled into a closet and a bedroom before she found the right door. The light was on. The room was empty. She leaned over the sink and turned on the hot water full force. She heaved for a few seconds but, thank God, she didn't throw up. Her stomach had nothing left to vomit except two sips of coffee.

She was still sluicing her cheeks in zombielike repetition when the lieutenant appeared in the doorway.

"Feeling better?" he asked.

Liz raised her head from the sink. "I feel one hundred percent lousy."

"We'd like to ask a few more questions."

"No." She shook her head. The police were going to find out about her past sooner or later, but tonight she was too tired and too scared to face up to any more of Lieutenant Rodriguez. "I want to go to a hotel," she said abruptly.

"If you wait another half hour until the technicians have finished upstairs, you can go into your apartment and pack a suitcase."

"I don't want to go into my apartment." Liz fought to keep her voice calm. "I can't hang around any longer. I'll buy a toothbrush at the drugstore. I want to get out of here, Lieutenant. Now."

Surprisingly, he didn't protest. Perhaps he was afraid she might faint, bang her head on the tile floor and then sue the city for harassment. God knows, and she knew, having glimpsed herself in the bathroom mirror, she looked rotten enough to give anybody cause for alarm. She'd lost weight steadily since Brian died, and she'd begun to appear skeletal even with makeup on and her clothes in order. Tonight, with every trace of color drained from her face, she looked like a death's-head.

Liz pushed her way out of the bathroom, ignoring a final question from the lieutenant. She grabbed her purse from the table as she passed by. "I'll be in the airport

Hilton,'' she said tersely, knowing Rodriguez had no grounds to detain her. Not yet. Not until he contacted his counterparts in Seattle. Then Lieutenant Rodriguez was going to start asking himself how many coincidences he wanted to believe. How many dead roommates could a law-abiding citizen explain away?

''Do you need a ride, Miss Meacham?''

''No thanks. My car's right in the parking lot. I took the bus this morning because the roads were so icy, but it's not freezing anymore.''

''Still, you want to drive carefully, Miss Meacham. We don't need any more accidents tonight.''

Liz smiled bitterly. ''I don't seem accident-prone, Lieutenant. At least not personally.''

''You're lucky,'' Rodriguez said, but she felt his gaze follow her as she left the room.

Chapter Two

The traffic light flicked from amber to red and Liz drew her Honda to an obedient halt. When the light turned green thirty seconds later, she gazed at it blankly until the irate honking of several horns reminded her that green meant Go.

But go where? She drove across the intersection and stared into the darkness, trying to discover where she was. Alameda Avenue, according to the signpost. Alameda, heading west toward the mountains.

How did I end up here? she wondered. Her mind felt thick and slow-moving, and her hands sat clumsily on the steering wheel, alien attachments at the end of her arms. The simple act of guiding the car through traffic demanded intense concentration. She'd intended to drive straight to the airport Hilton. Instead, here she was on the fringe of some of Denver's most prestigious real estate. The Denver Country Club was only a few blocks away. The Polo Club was even closer.

So was Dexter Rand's Denver home.

The thought came and went without making any particular impact. Liz waited at another traffic light, then turned left. Dexter's house loomed ahead of her at the end of the cul-de-sac. With a shiver of anticipation, she recognized that she'd intended to drive here all along.

She parked the car against the only free stretch of sidewalk and stared at the high brick wall surrounding Dexter's home. As if offering her a welcome, the lights from the upper windows gleamed through the dark evergreens that lined the driveway. Liz grimaced. A false impression, if ever she'd seen one.

The house was a handsome brick-and-timber affair, vaguely Tudor in style, with a spectacular yard designed for summer entertaining. Liz knew all this because she'd tempted fate once before, dropping Karen off for work one morning. But she wasn't sure why she had come here, tonight of all nights, or what she expected to accomplish. Dexter Rand was the last man in the world she wanted to ask for help or comfort.

I'll tell him about Karen before the police get to him. Maybe I owe him that much.

That simple decision exhausted Liz's mental capabilities. She got out of the car, locked it and pocketed the keys, feeling vaguely pleased that she hadn't done something dumb like leaving them in the ignition.

She wrapped her woolly scarf around her chin to shut out the biting wind, and walked up the driveway. *I'll just tell him about Karen, nothing more,* she reassured herself, listening to her boots crunch on the icy path. *I won't mention Seattle, or murder, or anything like that.* She needed to formulate her thoughts into simple instructions, or she knew her control would vanish into a shapeless fog of fear.

She rang the bell. A maid opened the door, and a muted babble of voices and laughter greeted Liz as soon as she stepped inside. Her heart sank. Of course! Dexter was giving a party. That was the reason for the welcoming lights and for all the cars parked along Pinewood Road. She should have recognized the signs. Dexter Rand, national hero, U.S. senator, former Air Force test pilot, and all-around important person, never came home from Washington without entertaining. His house was probably crammed with local VIPs, not to mention aspiring VIPs and the inevitable hangers-on who came for the free cocktails. It had been crazy to drive over here. It had been even crazier to imagine she'd actually get to talk privately with Dexter.

"Good evening, ma'am. May I take your coat?"

Liz blinked and stared at the maid. Her coat. The maid expected her to stay and socialize. It was really funny, if you stopped to think about it.

"Er...no, thanks," Liz mumbled. "I don't think I'm staying." She attempted a smile. "I'm sorry. Wrong party."

Her smile was not much of a success. The maid's welcoming glance faded into a look of downright suspicion, and she glanced over her shoulder, obviously searching for a security guard, or at least a hefty male waiter. Liz didn't want to be thrown out. She turned to go, fumbling for the handle of the front door.

A sudden tension at the base of her spine caused her to look over her shoulder, so that she and the maid saw Dexter at almost the same moment. The maid greeted him with evident relief. Liz stared at him in numb silence. All she could think of was that he looked even better in real life than he did on television. His six-feet-two-inch body was still perfectly proportioned, and his dark, coarse hair remained indecently thick, with no more than the occasional thread of gray to mark the passing of the last nine years. On him, even the crow's-feet around his eyes looked good. She wished he'd gone bald or developed a beer belly. Except, of course, that Dexter Rand never drank anything as plebeian as beer.

"This young lady was just leaving," the maid said.

"But not before I've had a chance to say hello, I hope...." Dexter's professionally warm voice trailed away into stunned silence. "Liz?" he asked hoarsely. "Liz, what in the world are you doing here?"

"Karen's dead."

She hadn't meant to drop the news with such a devastating lack of finesse. If she had been in full control of her actions, she would never have come near Dexter Rand. They had successfully avoided each other for nine years, and this was hardly the ideal time to choose for a reunion.

"Karen? You mean Karen Zeit, my secretary? What in the world happened?" For a moment, but only for a moment, Dexter looked blank. Then his usual capacity for quick thinking under pressure reasserted itself. It was a skill that had made him invaluable as a test pilot. Liz had seen him use it to even greater effect when facing inquisitive reporters on the Hill. Whatever he was feeling, Liz knew he would reveal none of it.

"This is terrible news," he said, his voice tinged with just the right amount of sorrow. "A terrible shock, too. Karen seemed so healthy when she left here this afternoon. Was it...? It must have been a car accident?"

The old, destructive desire to prick Dexter's damnable self-control stirred among the debris of Liz's emotions. She spoke without giving herself time for second thoughts. "No, not a car accident. They found her dead on the sidewalk outside her apartment building. The police think she jumped."

"She killed herself? Oh, my God!" For an instant Liz saw stark horror in Dexter's eyes, then he reached out and drew her further into the foyer, away from the front door. Control once again masked his expression.

"Poor Karen," Dexter said. "I'm sorry, so very sorry. I knew something was on her mind, and now I'm kicking myself for missing the signs that things were getting desperate." His gaze flicked over the name printed on the maid's fancy apron. "Gwen, could you help us out by finding Evan Howard, and asking him to come to my study as soon as possible?"

"I would, sir, but I don't know what Mr. Howard looks like."

"Blond, short, thirtyish. Slender build. Anybody on my staff can point him out to you."

"Certainly, sir. I'll find him right away. You want him in your study, you said?"

Dexter nodded, and Gwen, seeming reassured by Dexter's calm, take-charge tone of voice, walked off briskly in the direction of the main reception rooms. Liz wanted to mock the maid for being so gullible, so susceptible to Dexter's aura of control, but she couldn't. Why had she herself come here, if not to let Dexter take charge? In the last resort, wasn't that what she'd always wanted Dexter to do? Hadn't she always expected him to walk behind her, picking up the disorganized pieces of her life and rearranging them into some neat new pattern?

The thought was shocking in its novel perception of their relationship, and she shoved it angrily aside. Good grief, she must be closer to the edge than she'd realized if she was actually finding excuses for Dexter. Dexter, the inhuman superachiever. The man had exploited her from the day they first met.

"Let go of my arm," she said through her teeth. The anger felt good. Much better than the numb fear that had preceded it. "I'm leaving, Dexter."

"No, you're not. We need to talk." He gave a passing guest one of his patented thousand-watt smiles, slipped his arm around Liz's waist, and propelled her with iron force through the foyer, skillfully eluding the half-dozen people who tried to engage him in conversation. He finally stopped at a heavy oaken door and punched an electronic key code into the pad above the lock. He opened the door and stood back to let Liz pass. His manners always had been impeccable, she thought with a twist of irony. That was only one of the reasons she had found their constant fights so unendurable. She had screamed and yelled like a demented banshee, while Dexter politely—condescendingly—explained the error of her ways.

Even the distant memory of those painful times was enough to make Liz boil inside, a vulnerable nineteen-year-old again instead of a mature woman approaching thirty. She glanced around the room in an effort to calm her unruly emotions.

For anybody who knew Dexter well, the study contained few surprises. The room looked almost the same as the study Dexter had furnished in their Frankfurt apartment: comfortable and efficient, without any particular hint of luxury. The money in Dexter's family had been rattling around so long, he never felt any need to remind people that he had it. Nothing of the nouveau riche about good old Dex. Liz watched, fighting an unwelcome sensation of being transported back in time, as he opened a concealed cupboard in the paneling and revealed a small bar. He poured two brandies.

"Here," he said, offering one to Liz. "I need this, even if you don't."

"I don't drink in a crisis," she said, finally managing to look straight at him. "I learned not to."

He grinned, damn him, his gray eyes cruelly mocking. "Good lesson," he said, downing his own brandy in a single swallow. "You must've had a smart teacher."

"Experience. The best one of all."

For a split second, she felt the tension arc between them, and she knew her words had gotten to him. But when he turned around from the bar he displayed no emotion other than polite concern. He wasn't about to rehash old arguments, a fact for which she ought to be grateful.

"Let's sit down," he said, gesturing toward the sofa. "Damn it, I still can't believe she's dead! We spent two hours together this afternoon going over a speech, and she didn't give a hint of being desperate enough to walk out of here and kill herself. What happened?"

"The police think she threw herself out of the living-room window. I guess she must have...done it...right after she got home from work."

Dexter's eyes were shadowed with pain and a hint of some other emotion Liz couldn't identify. "That's terrible, almost unbelievable." He frowned. "Maybe I just don't want to believe it because I feel so guilty. How could she sit and chat about her plans for the weekend, when she intended to do this to herself a couple of hours later? How could I have missed all her signals of despair? Hell, she must have given me a dozen of them, if I'd been looking."

"Maybe not. Maybe something happened after she got home. A devastating phone call or something."

"I sure would like to think so." Dexter looked up, a new question obviously occurring to him. "How do you know all this, Liz? Come to think of that, how did you know Karen? She never mentioned your name to me."

Liz avoided his eyes. "She was—my roommate."

"You were sharing an apartment with my personal secretary?"

"Yes. Is that illegal or something?"

The pause before he replied was almost undetectable. "Not illegal. Surprising. Did she know about—us?"

"No."

"Odd that she never spoke about you."

"We'd been sharing the apartment less than two months. She probably had no reason to mention me. Why would she?"

He shrugged. "Things like that usually come up in conversation, although Karen never did talk much about her friends."

"I wasn't a friend, only a roommate. We didn't know each other at all well."

She spoke with more vehemence than the subject demanded, and Dexter scrutinized her intently for a moment before taking another sip of brandy. From his perspective, it must be hard to believe that Liz hadn't anticipated a meeting between the two of them from the moment she moved in with Karen. With an unwelcome flash of self-knowledge, Liz realized he was right to be suspicious. At some deeply buried level of her subconscious she had known that living with Karen would eventually bring her smack into the middle of Dexter's orbit. Thankfully, he asked her another question before she had time to pursue this uncomfortable new insight.

"What are you doing here in Denver, Liz? When we parted company, I didn't think anything would tear you away from life in the Big Apple."

If only he knew, Liz thought ruefully. If only he knew how grateful she'd been five years ago to find an obscure job in an obscure corner of southern Ohio. Better that he should never know. Pride made a great substitute for other emotions. She smiled brightly.

"It was tough leaving New York, but you know what companies are like these days. If you want a promotion, you have to be prepared to relocate, and I was tired of the entertainment industry."

"Why didn't you go back to skating, not even to teach?"

She pushed her fingers through her hair, her smile brighter than ever. "I doubt if anyone on the Olympic team would have me, and I'm not interested in anything else. There's nothing more pathetic than a second-rate athlete trying to eke out a living on the fringes of the sports world."

"You aren't a second-rate athlete, Liz, and we both know it. You went to pieces during that last championship, although God knows why. No skater spends years in training and then walks out onto the ice for an Olympic contest with her mind obviously elsewhere. I've always suspected your sister had something to do with it."

"Alison?" He was so far off the mark that it was almost funny. "Poor Alison. You never did like her, did you?"

"The fact that she was your twin didn't make her your friend, Liz. You never would understand that simple fact."

Liz laughed harshly. "Funny thing," she said. "Nine years and nothing changes. Isn't this about where our last conversation ended?"

Dexter stared into his empty glass. "You're right, and this isn't the moment for hashing over the past. We should be thinking about Karen. Did you discover... ? Are you the one who discovered her?"

"No." Liz drew in a deep breath. "When I came home tonight, she was already dead. They'd already moved her. All I saw was the outline of her body on the pavement. . . ."

Dexter put a hand over hers. "I'm sorry, Liz. Really sorry. That must have been a hellish sight to come home to."

She stared at his hand, fighting a ridiculous urge to give way to tears. The strength of his fingers had always fascinated her, especially the way he used that strength so considerately when he made love. In bed, Dexter had not been the cool, self-possessed man of his public facade. In bed, she had always been able to make him lose control. When they made love, she had glimpsed facets of another, more vulnerable man. In bed, she had sometimes thought that Dexter loved her.

He continued to cradle her hand in his clasp. "Why don't you think Karen committed suicide?" he asked softly. "Why do you think the police have got it all wrong?"

Liz jerked up her head and tugged her hand away, anger and a strange relief combining in an explosive mixture. "Damn you, Dexter! Why don't you ever ask the same questions anybody else would ask?"

"Because you don't want me to ask the standard questions. You came here for a reason, Liz, and that must be connected with Karen's death. If you believed she'd committed suicide, you wouldn't have come. Only something really important would reconcile you to seeing me again. We didn't exactly part friends, and I imagine my marriage to Susan only made things worse."

She sprang up from the sofa, turning her back on him. "I'm sorry about your wife," she said abruptly. "Nowadays you don't expect a woman as young as Susan to die of heart disease."

"Statistically it happens, but I guess we never anticipate people we love becoming part of the statistics." There was a tiny pause, and Dexter's voice roughened. "Amanda has found it really difficult to accept her mother's death."

Liz swallowed hard. "How old is Amanda now?"

"She's almost eight, and in my totally unprejudiced opinion, she's gorgeous." Liz could almost hear Dexter smiling. "She was born exactly a year after Susan and I got married. A great anniversary gift for both of us."

Nothing he said was news to Liz, but she'd felt obligated to get the topic of his wife and daughter out of the way. She heard the warmth, the gentle caring that crept into his voice when he spoke their names. Now she knew exactly how he sounded when he loved someone without reservation—and she wished she didn't.

"But you aren't here to discuss Amanda," Dexter said. "Why did you come, Liz? What's bothering you so much about Karen Zeit's death that you were prepared to talk to me face-to-face?"

As soon as he asked the question, Liz realized that she planned to tell him the whole truth, at least insofar as she could call her pathetic smattering of suspicions *truth*. She wasn't entirely comfortable with her decision, and walked over to the windows, keeping her back toward him when she finally spoke.

"I think Karen was murdered."

Silence. She was grateful that he didn't protest, or tell her in polite euphemisms that she was crazy. After a second or two, he simply walked over to where she was standing, turned her around and looked at her assessingly with those cool gray eyes of his. He asked only one question. "Why?"

"Karen isn't my first roommate to die. I was working in Seattle until I moved to Denver at the beginning of March. I shared apartments with two other people there, and both of them died almost the same way as Karen. Either a few weeks of living with me is enough to drive sane people crazy, or somebody is systematically killing off my roommates." She tried a smile, without much success. "Nice alternatives, huh? Liz the Witch, or Liz the Intended Victim."

"Not nice alternatives at all, and both of them hard to believe. First question, if you're the intended victim of a plot, why is somebody killing off your roommates? Why not murder you directly?"

"Maybe the killer makes mistakes?"

"You mean he's murdering by remote control, and the wrong person keeps ending up dead?"

"Something like that."

"Three times? Come on, Liz, even a psychopath would do a better job of fine-tuning his methods than that."

"Then how can it be murder, Dex?" The old nickname slipped out almost unnoticed. "Three unconnected suicides may be hard to believe, but three unconnected murders belong to the land of paranoid fantasy."

He put an arm around her and drew her back to the sofa. "We reach an obvious conclusion: the deaths aren't unconnected."

She held her body very straight against the cushions. "You mean I'm the connecting link?"

"You have to be. That's the only logical explanation."

"But Dex, I'd never even met Karen Zeit until two days before I moved in with her! And she had no links to either Brian or Jill. She came from a different part of the country, her work was different. All their work was different—"

"What did your other roommates do?"

"Brian was a university professor, and Jill was a social worker. Jill was in her twenties, Brian was forty-five and Karen was thirty-something. Dex, they have nothing in common."

"But they do. We just established that. They all shared an apartment with you."

"Which brings us right back to where we started. It makes no sense, Dex. Nobody has a reason to kill off my roommates."

"On the contrary," he said neutrally. "If you're the person doing the killing, everything makes perfectly good sense."

Liz felt herself turn cold with horror. "You think... you believe I murdered my roommates?"

"It seems—unlikely."

"Thanks for the ringing vote of confidence." Liz dug her fingers into the cushion. "Dex, for God's sake, I didn't murder those people. Don't you know me well enough to realize I could never kill anybody? Particularly not by pushing them out of a window?"

"I don't think we know each other at all," Dexter said. "Not nine years ago and certainly not now. But that's beside the point, I guess. I was simply suggesting that there must be logical explanations for three roommates of yours getting themselves murdered. I pointed out the most obvious one."

The chilling fear that had been clawing at Liz for hours began to take on a sharper reality. "The police are going to arrest me," she said, her voice shaking. "Somebody's going to contact the police in Seattle and then it will all be over. I'm going to be arrested, Dex."

His grasp on her hands tightened reassuringly. "Not if I can avoid it."

"How can you keep me out of jail when you don't even believe I'm innocent?"

"I didn't say that, Liz. I simply suggested that we don't know each other very well." His gaze became unexpectedly sympathetic. "You're freezing, Liz. Let me pour you another brandy, strictly for medicinal purposes."

He was right about one thing: she was freezing, inside and out. And if she was headed for a jail cell, she might as well make the most of her remaining few hours of freedom. "All right, thanks. I think I could use some of your vintage cognac."

Dexter walked to the bar and reached for clean glasses. "Aside from the fact that you can't believe the coincidence of three roommates committing suicide within three months, do you have any other reason for thinking Karen and the others might have been murdered?"

She shook her head. "Not a thing, unless you count my feeling that they weren't suicidal sorts of people."

"Did you know them well enough to judge?"

"Not Karen, maybe. But the other two. Jill and I had been acquainted with each other for a couple of years. We belonged to the same health club. And Brian...I guess you could say we knew each other pretty well."

Carefully, Dexter returned the stopper to the brandy bottle. "Were you and Brian lovers?" he asked.

"We'd talked about getting engaged. We were living together."

"That doesn't answer my question, Liz."

"I think it does. If it's any of your business."

Before Dexter could say anything more, a perfunctory knock at the door was followed by the sound of the lock clicking open. A slender man with pale blond hair and a perspiring forehead erupted into the room, trailing an aura of generalized disaster.

"Dexter! Thank God you're here!"

"Hello, Evan. I'm glad Gwen managed to find you."

"Gwen? Who's she?" Without waiting for an answer, Evan rushed on. "Dexter, what in blazes are you doing hiding away in here? Holy hell's breaking loose out there, and nobody can find you. I just had a call from the police. Karen's been found dead outside her apartment, and the reporters are already swarming—" Evan broke off abruptly, as he suddenly realized Dexter wasn't alone. He drew himself up, mopping his forehead with a silk handkerchief pulled from his breast pocket. In the blink of an eye he transformed himself into a dapper, deferential assistant.

"Oh, I'm sorry, Senator. I didn't know you were entertaining. When you've given your guest her drink, perhaps you could spare me a moment? In private? There are a couple of administrative matters that need your attention. When you've finished with your guest, of course."

"Let me introduce you two to each other," Dexter said, a definite note of wry humor in his voice. "Liz, this is my public-relations aide, Evan Howard. Evan, this is my former wife—Liz Meacham."

"Your ex-wife?" Evan looked as if he might faint. "How do you do, Ms. Meacham. I thought you lived in New York."

"Somebody hasn't been keeping your files up-to-date, Mr. Howard. I haven't lived in New York for more than five years."

"Liz lives in Denver," Dexter supplied. "She shared an apartment with Karen Zeit."

Evan dropped his handkerchief. "Holy hell," he said.

Dexter smiled. "Now that you've mentioned it, Evan, I guess that's pretty much what I was thinking."

Evan bent to pick up his handkerchief, and Dexter turned to hand Liz her brandy. For a split second their gazes locked in rueful, shared amusement. The unexpected moment of intimacy made Liz profoundly uncomfortable. She and Dexter Rand did not operate on the same mental wavelength. She didn't want to operate on the same mental wavelength as Dexter Rand. That was one of the illusions that had led her into trouble before.

Taking things calmly was obviously not one of the skills Evan had been hired for. "The media are gonna crucify you, Dex. Holy moly, what have I ever done to deserve this?"

"Signed on to my staff?" Dexter suggested mildly.

Evan ignored this remark. His eyes narrowed in acute concentration. "There's no way we can keep her name out of the paper," he muttered, staring at Liz without really seeing her. "They're bound to find out she was married to you—she's listed on all your official bios. World Champion Figure Skater, Liz Meacham." He nibbled his lower lip. "There must be some angle we could come up with. How about you approached Liz to teach the orphans in that school you sponsor? We'll tie it into the Olympic program somehow. Make it sound patriotic. Overcoming personal differences for the good of your country."

"Why in the world would I approach Liz? There are a dozen world-class skaters active in Colorado, and everybody in the skating business knows Liz hasn't been near an ice rink since she left Germany."

"You're right. Skating stinks." A gleam lighted Evan's eyes. "How about a reconciliation? Now there's an idea. You and Liz are getting together again. Remarriage in the air, and all that good stuff."

"No," Liz said flatly. "No. We'd never be able to pull it off. And how would a story like that help? It would just fan the gossip flames."

"How about telling the truth?" Dexter suggested. "There's a radical new approach for you to consider, Evan. You could tell the reporters that I had no idea Liz was living in the same apartment as my personal secretary, and that until tonight we hadn't spoken to each other in nine years."

Evan's expression turned sour. "Damn it, Dexter, nobody's gonna believe a dumb story like that! Your ex-wife lives with your personal secretary, who commits suicide for no apparent reason. Even you must see the scandal sheets will have the three of you locked up in some sort of bizarre triangular love nest before the first edition hits the streets."

Liz stood up. "I'm sorry, Dexter. I've really done you a bad turn by coming here. I've only been in Denver a few weeks, and half that time I've been out of the country on business trips. If I'd stayed away, we could have played down our past connection. After all, we both know it has absolutely nothing to do with this case. Isn't there some back way I could get out of here and avoid all the reporters who are probably lying in wait out front?"

Evan beamed his approval. "An excellent suggestion, Ms. Meacham. I'll let you out through the kitchen and arrange for one of the catering people to drive you home."

"But my own car's parked out front on Pinewood Road. How will I get it back?"

"Don't give your car another moment's thought, Ms. Meacham. If you'll let me have the keys, I'll see that somebody gets it home to you tomorrow, inconspicuously. What sort of car do you drive?"

"A Hond—"

"It doesn't matter what she drives," Dexter said. "You surely don't think we're going to smuggle her out of this house without causing comment, after at least twenty guests saw me walk down the hallway with her? I'll bet there are already at least a half-dozen rumors making the rounds about the 'mystery woman' I escorted into my study."

"Then what do you suggest? That we take her out front and introduce her as your ex-wife? Just when the story about Karen is breaking? Damn it, Dexter, you can't afford a breath of scandal with the crucial hearings before the Armed Services Committee about to resume. And this sure ain't a breath, it's a gale!"

"I suggest that we don't have much choice except to ride it out. My feeling is that Liz should spend the night here, so that we can work on our stories while you hold the reporters at bay. Then Liz and I'll meet the press together, tomorrow morning. Is that okay with you, Liz?"

It seemed slightly less okay than spending the night in a cage with a hungry tiger. The only thing that might possibly be worse was the prospect of driving to a hotel room and spending the night alone with her imagination and her suddenly overactive memories. She looked at Evan Howard. "Dexter's right," she said quietly. "I think maybe it would be best if I stayed here."

Evan's horrified gasp gave Liz a perverse twinge of satisfaction. She had met dozens of men like Evan during her skating career, and despised most of them. There was some consolation in the knowledge that if Evan

Howard didn't like the idea of her spending the night in Dexter's house, then her decision to stay couldn't be all bad.

She thought she detected the merest flicker of surprise in Dexter's expression when he heard her response, but all he said was, "Handle the press for me, will you, Evan? Liz and I are going to put our heads together and see if we can come up with a few reasons why Karen Zeit might have been murdered."

"Murdered!" Evan's already pale complexion turned faintly green. Then he swung quickly on his heel. "Don't tell me," he said, "I don't want to know what you're talking about a minute before I have to. I'll do the best job I can with those reporters, but I'm warning both of you. You'd better come up with a damn good story."

"Don't worry." For the first time, Liz could hear a note of bitterness in Dexter's voice. "We're experts. We've done all this before."

Chapter Three

For once, Amanda's antics were not absorbing all of Dexter's attentions. He held her hand, relishing the contact of baby-soft skin against his palm, but answered her nonstop barrage of questions with only half his attention.

He had suspected a leakage of classified information from his Washington office for at least six months. An undercover FBI operative had been working secretly on Dexter's staff for the last two. So far, the investigation had been spectacular for its lack of success. As far as Dexter was concerned, Karen's death threw a whole new light on the situation. Was it possible that the leaks had originated in Denver, rather than Washington? Was that why none of the carefully planted red herrings were turning up anywhere?

Guiltily, Dexter acknowledged he was worried less about Karen's death than the part his ex-wife might have played in it. If Karen had been something more than the dedicated office worker she seemed, could Liz possibly be as bewildered and innocent as she had sounded the previous night? He didn't think so. There were limits as to how far he was prepared to stretch the long arm of coincidence.

One fact was irritatingly clear. Liz's unexpected arrival on his doorstep had thrown him for a loop, not least because of the impact her physical presence had upon him. Until last night, Dexter had assumed that his old, tumultuous feelings about Liz had all been resolved. It was a shock, and not a pleasant one, to discover she still exerted the same sexual fascination that had almost destroyed him the first time around.

The sun cast brilliant light but little heat and Dexter scowled, feeling the chill of the morning air now that he had finished his daily three-mile run. "What's the matter, Dad?" Amanda demanded, seeing his frown.

He heard the anxiety in her voice and quickly smoothed his expression. "Nothing's wrong," he said, squeezing her hand. "How could anything be wrong when you're out here playing with me?"

"We're not playing, just walking. I wish the snow hadn't gone away. We could've built a fort."

"We did that already this year. May is too late for snow. In a couple of weeks you'll be asking to go swimming."

"I like swimming. So does Spot." Amanda patted the Labrador who trotted patiently at her side.

"I know Spot likes swimming—he likes it too well! This year we're going to train him not to jump into the pool when we have guests."

She giggled. "Maybe. Spot likes swimming with lots of people, though."

"Unfortunately, most of my guests don't return the compliment." Dexter glanced at his watch. "We have five more minutes, honey, and then we have to go inside. What game do you want to play?"

"Catch."

"Okay." Dexter took a chewed-up tennis ball from his daughter and threw it toward a far corner of the backyard. Amanda and the dog bounded after it in hot competition. Spot—his daughter had insisted on the name, despite the fact that the Labrador's sleek black body bore not a single mark—was the inevitable winner. He obligingly fell over his front paws and allowed the ball to trickle out of his mouth into Amanda's waiting hands.

"I got it, Dad! I won!" She buried her nose between the Labrador's ears, hugging him tight before throwing the ball back toward her father. This time Spot wasn't prepared to be generous. Outstripping his mistress, he snatched the ball with all the skill of his retriever heritage and bounded off toward his favorite hidey-hole in the bushes. Panting, Amanda ran up and skidded to a halt alongside her father.

"He won't come back for ages. Play baseball with me?" She reached into the pocket of her oversize sweater. "I've got another ball."

"I wish we could, sweetheart," Dexter said regretfully. "But I have a meeting early this morning, and I need to change my clothes. There's no time for baseball."

"You always have meetings."

"I guess it seems that way sometimes." He rumpled her hair, loving the feel of curls tickling his fingers. "But the work I do is important, honey. Unfortunately, there just aren't enough people in Congress who really understand military technology, and I do. There are some decisions our government has to take where my opinion can really make a difference."

"'Cos you were a pilot?"

"Mmm, sort of. And because I'm an engineer."

"If it's so important, why can't I come to your meeting? Maybe I oughta learn about airplanes and things instead of dumb old math at school."

Dexter grinned. "Good try, honey, but you know the answer. The meeting's important for me, school's important for you. And if we don't hurry and get back inside, you won't have time to wash the dirt off your hands before your ride gets here. Then I'll be in trouble with Mrs. Morton again."

She gave one of the gurgles of laughter that always made his heart ache. "Don't be silly, Dad. Mrs. Morton can't be mad at you. You're a grown-up and she works for you."

"And you think that makes me safe from Mrs. Morton's wrath? Young lady, you have a lot to learn!"

Amanda chuckled again, understanding the teasing tone of his voice, if nothing else. "Do you have to go back to Washington next week, Dad? I wish you didn't."

"I'm afraid I do, honey." They had reached the kitchen door and he gave her a quick hug, trying not to let her wistful look get to him. Most of his colleagues in the senate couldn't understand why he spent every spare minute that wasn't devoted to the defense budget campaigning for adequate, federally funded day-care centers. But then, most of his colleagues weren't single parents and didn't understand the burden of guilt mothers and fathers felt when forced to spend long hours away from their children. He gave Amanda another kiss. "Have a good day in school and I'll see you tonight. That's a promise."

Dexter left his daughter washing her hands under Mrs. Morton's eagle-eyed inspection. He crossed the hallway at a brisk pace, wondering just how rational his plans for the upcoming press conference actually were. In the cool light of morning, he was beginning to see a dozen problems that hadn't been apparent the night before.

Face it, he told himself wryly. You were functioning strictly on the no-brain, multihormone level last night. You were so busy feeling furious about the past and horny about the present that you'd have agreed the moon was made of green cheese, if she'd suggested it.

The realization that Liz still retained the power to make him act like an idiot wasn't calculated to sweeten Dexter's mood. Once this press conference was over, he'd make damn sure he didn't see her again. If she needed help, he'd pass her over to Evan. Evan would have no trouble finding her a good private investigator or a first-class lawyer, and that was about all the personal attention he owed her.

Dexter took the stairs two at a time, stopping with great reluctance when he heard Evan's voice. "Senator, I'm so glad you're back from your morning walk with your daughter. You have somebody waiting to see you, Senator."

Not only did Evan sound twice as pompous as usual, he also wore one of his gloomiest and most official faces. Dexter's spirits sank a notch. "If it's a reporter, Evan, you know I don't have time for any personal interviews this morning."

"It's not a reporter, it's the police. A Detective Rodriguez. He wants to see you right now, Senator. He says it's urgent."

Dexter glanced down at his watch. When Evan called him "Senator" three times in as many sentences, it meant big trouble. "I have twenty minutes to shower, shave and change for the press conference we called. That means I can give your detective five minutes—unless he cares to wait until after the press conference."

A tall, slightly overweight figure in a raincoat appeared in the foyer behind Evan. "Five minutes would make a good start, Senator. There are a couple of facts in connection with Karen Zeit's death that I need to go over with you. I'm Lieutenant Rodriguez, by the way, with the Denver Police Department."

Dexter concealed his racing thoughts beneath a polite smile. "Good to meet you, Lieutenant, although the circumstances certainly aren't very pleasant. Why don't we go into my study? That seems as good a place as any for us to talk."

"I'll see that we have coffee and rolls set out for the press conference," Evan said. "Unless you need me to stay with you, Senator?"

"At this hour of the morning, if we want the reporters to act like human beings, coffee should definitely be your first priority." Dexter kept his response light, although he had already picked up the tension—hostility?—emanating from the lieutenant. "And check that Amanda gets off to school okay, will you, Evan?"

"Certainly, Senator. I'll be expecting you in five minutes. I'm sure Lieutenant Rodriguez understands how busy your schedule is this morning and will limit himself accordingly."

What the devil had the detective been saying to Evan? Dexter wondered. His aide rarely kept up the "deferential servant" act for more than a few minutes at a time, but this morning he was behaving like a bad imitation of Jeeves.

"You have news about Karen's death?" he said to the lieutenant, shutting the study door. "Have you discovered something that sheds light on why she committed suicide?"

The detective didn't answer directly. "That's a fancy lock you have there, Senator."

"I frequently have confidential papers in here," Dexter replied shortly. "We had a burglary some six months ago, and the security company suggested electronic locks. What was it you wanted to tell me about Karen?"

"Well, Senator, we've discovered several rather interesting things. First of all, I think you should know that we don't believe Karen Zeit committed suicide."

"You mean her death was accidental?" Dexter asked, knowing damn well that the lieutenant meant nothing of the sort.

Rodriguez looked at him without expression. "Karen Zeit contacted an agent with the Colorado Bureau of Investigations last week. She insisted that her life was in danger. She said somebody was planning to murder her."

"What?" Dexter made no effort to conceal his shock. He ran his hands through his sweat-stiffened hair, his mind racing. What in God's name had his seemingly quiet and unassuming secretary been involved with after hours? "I guess it's absurd to say that the idea of anybody wanting to kill Karen strikes me as ridiculous."

"Hardly ridiculous, considering that she *is* dead. I'm sure you realize, Senator, that the Bureau gets crazies coming in every day, telling us their life is in danger. Half of them think they're in communication with aliens from another planet, and most of the rest are borderline psychotics. Karen Zeit didn't quite fit the pattern, although she was too frightened to tell the agent exactly why her life was at risk. She wanted police protection, but wasn't prepared to say more than that somebody in a position of power was out to kill her."

"So did you give her protection?"

There was a tiny pause. "No, we didn't," Rodriguez admitted. "CBI funding doesn't stretch to looking after citizens who won't say who's threatening them, or why their lives might be in danger. It's all they can do to take care of the people who are obviously at risk."

"I think at the minimum I should have been notified of her concerns."

"Yes, that was an oversight."

"I have a suspicion, Lieutenant, that the people at the Bureau are taking Karen's worries much more seriously this week than they were last."

"Death does have an amazing tendency to concentrate the mind," the lieutenant agreed mildly. "Particularly when the death is murder."

"And you're sure Karen was murdered?"

"Our preliminary investigations have disclosed some interesting facts about Ms. Zeit's death. The pathologist has found evidence of bruising around her mouth and wrists. This bruising occurred some time before death, and not when she fell out of her apartment window. The pathologist suggests that the marks are consistent with the deceased being forcibly restrained and compelled to swallow something—sleeping pills and whiskey, perhaps? With the combination of drugs and alcohol found in her system, she would have been unconscious within ten minutes. Think how easy it would have been for a murderer to push her from the window of her apartment and quietly disappear into the shadows."

"But God in heaven, man, what reason would anybody have for killing Karen? She was a pleasant, efficient secretary, but she always struck me as completely—ordinary."

"In some lines of work, Senator, the ordinary sort of person is the most dangerous."

"If that's what you're thinking, Lieutenant, I recommend that you speak with Agent Waterman at the FBI. He's been rerunning some of the background checks on members of my staff."

"Has he indeed?" Lieutenant Rodriguez scribbled furiously in his notebook. "There is one other point, Senator. Did the deceased have any men friends that you're aware of?"

"She had one or two friends who were male. No steady boyfriend, as far as I know."

"No boyfriend, eh? Interesting you should say that, Senator, because Karen Zeit was nine weeks pregnant when she died."

Dexter felt a fresh surge of astonishment. "But how in the world could she have gotten herself pregnant?"

Rodriguez actually smiled. "The same way as any other woman, Senator. She was sexually intimate with a man."

"I understand the biology," Dexter responded impatiently. "But Karen was thirty-three years old and reasonably sophisticated. Why would she make a mistake like that? We're not talking about some high-school kid who's never heard of birth control."

"Why do you assume Ms. Zeit made a mistake? Perhaps she was in love with the father. Maybe she wanted to get pregnant, to force his hand in some way."

"But who was the father, for heaven's sake? Who could he have been? One way and another, Karen spent nearly sixty hours a week with me. That doesn't leave much time for an outside social life, especially one she's keeping secret."

The lieutenant's voice was very dry. "An excellent point, Senator."

Dexter's head shot up. "Oh no, Rodriguez. You're barking up the wrong tree. Karen Zeit was my secretary, and that's all she was. Quite apart from the fact that I would never have an affair with a member of my staff, Karen just wasn't my type."

"Strange you should say that, Senator. The first thing that struck me was how much she looked like your wife."

"Like Liz?" Dexter shoved his hands into the pockets of his sweats. "Oh, I see. You mean like Susan."

"You seem confused, Senator. What's so confusing about Karen Zeit's appearance? Either she looked like your wife or she didn't."

"I've been married twice," Dexter said curtly. "I suppose Karen looked a bit like my second wife, although their personalities were very different."

"I didn't know you'd been divorced, Senator."

"Then you must be one of the few people in the United States who doesn't know all the gory details, Lieutenant. My first wife and I practically got divorced on television."

"And your first wife's name was?"

"Elizabeth Meacham."

"Elizabeth Meacham!"

Dexter felt obscurely satisfied in having finally shaken Rodriguez's cast-iron calm. "Before you say anything more, Lieutenant, I know that my former wife was sharing an apartment with Karen Zeit. I also know that I have to be at a press conference in precisely eight minutes. Regretfully, our time together has just run out." Dexter walked over to the desk and pressed a button on the intercom system. Evan responded instantly.

"Yes, Senator?"

"I have to shower and dress. Maybe you could answer any other questions Lieutenant Rodriguez might have."

"I'll be right there, Senator."

Dexter turned to the detective. "If there's anything else you feel we ought to discuss, perhaps you could phone me some time this afternoon."

"A phone call won't be necessary, Senator. You've given me several useful leads to work on, and I'm sure if I have any more questions, we'll be able to fit a face-to-face meeting somewhere into your busy schedule."

The look Dexter gave the detective was hard with challenge. "I'm not planning to leave town, Lieutenant, at least for the next couple of days."

"That's very cooperative of you, Senator."

"No. I merely have several important meetings scheduled in Colorado. Good morning to you, Lieutenant."

Evan appeared in the doorway and Dexter turned abruptly on his heel, leaving the study without saying another word.

LIZ GLANCED AT HER WATCH. The press conference was scheduled to begin in five minutes, and Dexter hadn't been anywhere near her since he said a courteous good-night at ten o'clock the previous evening.

She certainly couldn't complain that her comfort had been ignored. Her bathroom was stocked with every toiletry she might need, including a new toothbrush. Her clothes had been whisked away last night and returned early this morning, cleaned and pressed by an expert hand. Promptly at eight, a delicious breakfast had been brought to her bedroom, and Evan Howard had stopped by no less than three times, ostensibly to ensure that she was keeping to schedule, but in reality to make sure she had the details of the agreed story fixed firmly in her mind. Evan didn't like wild cards in his neatly ordered system, and had made it abundantly clear that he considered Liz the wildest of the wildest. Considering her decorous life-style over the past few years, she found his opinion of her almost funny. Almost, but not quite. Today nothing seemed really funny.

Liz coiled her hair into a smooth knot and pinned it swiftly in place. She peered at her reflection in the brightly lighted bathroom mirror, grimacing at what she saw. Years of appearing before the public had left her an expert with makeup, and she had managed to transform her unkempt appearance of the night before into a neat, expressionless mask. Understated pink lips, understated pink cheeks, discreetly darkened lashes. Evan and Dexter would both be thrilled, she thought cynically. The doll-like woman in the mirror looked like the perfect appendage for a politician.

Only her eyes betrayed her. Blue and turbulent, they revealed far too much of what she was feeling. They stared back at her from the mirror, disturbing reminders of a passionate child-woman who no longer existed, except in dreams. Liz closed her eyes. When she opened them again, the blue-gray depths were wiped satisfyingly clean of expression. Now her lifeless eyes matched the porcelain texture of the rest of her face.

When Dexter came to the door two minutes later, she was able to greet him with a polite detachment that would have been impossible during their marriage. She inquired if he'd slept well, if Amanda had gotten off to school on time, if all the arrangements for the press conference had gone smoothly. Meaningless conversation that covered over the horrors of silence. Some things, she discovered, did get better with the passage of time.

Dexter waited for her to finish spouting conversational gambits, then assessed her appearance with the faintest of smiles. "You look well armored against the fiends of the press."

"I figured I might need to be."

"With luck, you'll be able to get away with saying no more than how sorry you are that Karen's dead."

"That's the plan," she agreed.

"Liz, there's no time to talk now, and we need to. Can you spare fifteen minutes after the conference?"

"If you think it's necessary. My office isn't expecting me until lunchtime." She looked at the stairs, which provided a convenient excuse for not looking at him. "Dexter, I owe you an apology. I shouldn't have come here last night. The last thing I want is for you to feel obliged to help me. In fact, there's nothing for you to help me with. Three of my roommates have committed suicide. It's a terrible coincidence, but one I'll have to learn to live with."

"There've been some developments you should know about—oh hell, there's Evan, and he's got the *Boulder Post* editor with him. Smile, Liz. We're on."

She had to admire the way Dexter handled the editor, with just the right mix of friendliness and reserve. He introduced Liz by name, without mentioning their previous relationship. The editor showed not a flicker of recognition.

All four of them walked into the main reception room together, and the buzz of voices from the assembled journalists faded into immediate silence.

Evan had been much too smart to set up anything as formal as a podium and microphone. Dexter walked to the center of the small space that had been left at one end of the room and faced the dozen or so reporters and three TV camera crews. Liz was surprised that so many media people had turned out on what surely must be a fairly routine sort of story. Unfortunately, this was a situation in which Dexter's unusually high profile didn't work well for him.

"I'm sorry that the occasion for our get-together this morning is such a sad one," Dexter said without preamble. "Karen Zeit had been my personal secretary for the past year. She worked long hours with tireless efficiency, and kept my personal and business schedules untangled with almost magical skill. She will be sorely missed in my office, and by her colleagues. I like to think that we had become friends, as well as employer and employee, so that her loss is a double blow for me. I think most of your questions can be answered far better by the police department than they can by me, but I'll do my best to respond to anything relevant."

Six reporters were on their feet. Dexter nodded to one of them. "Joan."

"You say Karen was your personal secretary, Senator. What exactly were her duties, and did you often work out of your home?"

Dexter accepted the question with a bland smile, far too old a hand to allow the sleazy subtext of her question to bother him. Liz almost felt sorry for the reporter when Dexter launched into a long, dry explanation of how his office was organized. Karen's duties, it seemed, had consisted chiefly of coordinating his schedule, serving as liaison with his office in Washington, and helping him with fund-raisers and charitable events. "She was kept very busy, but she had nothing to do with any of my Senate committee work," Dexter concluded. "We try to channel most of that through my Washington office. Since I'm on the Armed Services Committee, a lot of my work is classified and therefore off limits for Karen.

She'd never received official security clearance, which all of my staff in DC has."

That's one in the eye for you, Joan. Liz watched the disgruntled reporter sit down, and allowed herself to relax very marginally. With luck and a bit more of Dexter's skill, they were going to get through this conference with flying colors. Perhaps she wouldn't even have to speak.

She had allowed herself to relax too soon. A reporter from one of the TV stations spoke up next. "I was talking to the superintendent at Karen Zeit's apartment building this morning, and it turns out that she was sharing her apartment with a young woman called Elizabeth Meacham. It's not such a unique name, of course, but you were once married to a member of our U.S. Olympic figure skating team, and her name was also Elizabeth Meacham. Is this just a strange coincidence, Senator, or is it possible that your secretary was sharing an apartment with your ex-wife?"

Dexter's grin was a masterpiece of rueful, good-natured resignation. "It's no coincidence, Harry, as I'm sure you realized." Dexter turned and smiled toward Liz. "We anticipated that this item of news would set all your journalistic noses twitching, so my former wife very kindly volunteered to join us here this morning. Liz."

Dexter held out his hand in a casual, welcoming gesture. Liz rose to her feet, stretched her neat pink-glossed lips into a smile and walked across the room to Dexter's side. The ten feet of padded carpet seemed to take so long to cross that they might as well have been ten miles of icy tundra. It had been a while since she last faced a roomful of journalists, but not long enough to forget how easily they could savage you.

"Karen and I met at a party a couple of months ago," she said. Her voice sounded husky and she cleared her throat, angry at the appearance of nervousness. Behind her, the silent strength of Dexter's presence gave her a burst of confidence. "We talked about sharing an apartment. When I found out who Karen worked for, I explained that Dexter and I had once been married. Neither Karen nor I thought that had any bearing on our decision to share an apartment, so I moved in."

The faces of the journalists blurred into a single, avid mob, all shouting questions at her. Deafened by the bombardment, she forced herself to maintain her inner calm. A question from one of the TV journalists caught her attention.

"Hard feelings toward the senator?" she said with a casual smile. "Oh, no. Dexter and I reconciled our differences a long time ago. We're both ten years older now, and events have taken on a whole different perspective." If she'd been a kid, she'd have had her hands behind her back crossing her fingers when she uttered that whopper.

The editor from the *Boulder Post* was on his feet. "Senator, I understand from sources inside the police department that the CBI is working on this case. I also understand that the autopsy results suggest that Karen Zeit didn't commit suicide. As of now, the police are treating this as a case of homicide. Do you have any comment on that?"

Liz plastered the noncommittal look onto her face so firmly that she was afraid it might never come off. Dear heaven, how long had the police suspected Karen had been murdered? She looked up at Dexter, marveling that he could appear so calm. At nineteen, she had never bothered to look below that surface calm. Now—instinctively—she recognized how much effort it was costing him to appear unconcerned.

"If the police autopsy suggests that Karen Zeit was murdered, then I certainly would have no grounds or expertise for disputing their verdict," Dexter said. "If it does turn out that she was murdered, I hope very much that her killer is found quickly and brought to justice."

Some sixth sense retained from her years under a constant publicity spotlight alerted Liz to the fact that the *Post* editor was disappointed with Dexter's reply. Her intuition warned her that the man had come here meaning to make a killing. In the split second pause as the reporter formulated his next question, she saw him coil for attack. "So you have no fears, Senator, that this investigation is going to touch close to home?"

"Karen was my personal secretary. Obviously I'm extremely interested in finding out how she died."

"And how about the note she left, Senator?"

"What note?"

"The one claiming you're the father of her baby and that you refused to marry her."

Chapter Four

Dexter never lost his cool amid the hubbub of the aggressive questions that followed. But despite his most skillful efforts, it took him almost half an hour to get rid of the clamoring journalists. Only the promise that he would issue another statement within forty-eight hours finally persuaded the reporters to sheath their pencils, pack up their equipment and leave.

From the evidence of their avid expressions as they rushed herdlike for the doors, Liz had no problem inferring that the phone wire would soon be vibrating with not-quite-libelous accounts of the thrilling story. She could already visualize the headlines. "Senator's Triangular Love Nest Explodes" would be one of the milder versions.

Evan turned out to be almost more difficult to pacify than the journalists. He paced up and down the study, his self-control obviously shot, trying—with a singular lack of success—to invent some way to put an acceptable public relations gloss on the sordid facts.

Liz watched Dexter soothe his aide, and reflected how much her ex-husband must have changed to employ someone like Evan. In the old days, Dexter's indifference to the press had been monumental, and he'd often been impatient with Liz's efforts to placate the powerful TV sportscasters. She was surprised to discover that she hoped he hadn't changed too much. Oddly enough, Dexter the Arrogant was far more acceptable to her than Dexter the Media Manipulator.

He finally handed the sweating and swearing Evan a glass of club soda. "Look Evan," he said, putting his arm around the distraught publicist's shoulder. "We have to face reality, tell the truth, and move on from there."

"Truth and reality never won any election I heard about."

"I'm still fighting you on that," Dexter said wryly. "In the meantime, you have to accept there's no way to turn Karen's death into a public relations coup for me. All we can do is control the worst of the damage by saying as little as possible and making damn sure that everything we say is true. Stop trying to achieve anything more, or you'll give yourself an ulcer."

"I already have an ulcer. I shouldn't be drinking this carbonated junk. Gas bubbles are murder on my stomach."

"Then let's work on saving you from ulcer number two." Dexter's jaw tensed slightly. It was the only sign of impatience he allowed himself. "We're all agreed that being suspected of murder makes lousy publicity for a U.S. senator, so stop sweating it."

"Why did she have to leave a note, for God's sake?"

"You heard what Rodriguez said. He thinks the note was part of an unmailed letter to me."

"Why did she need to write, for heaven's sake? She saw you every day!"

Dexter's smile was hard. "You didn't ask the more important question, Evan. Why did she write something that wasn't true?"

Evan remained silent, and Liz thought she detected a brief flash of hurt in Dexter's gaze. When he spoke, however, his voice was crisp and businesslike. "For what it's worth," he said, "I would like you to know there isn't a word of truth in Karen's note. If it isn't a forgery, she was fantasizing."

Evan's head shot up, and Liz thought she saw genuine astonishment in his eyes. "You're sure of that? You didn't get her pregnant? You're saying you two weren't—you know—intimate?"

There was a hint of weariness in Dexter's reply. "No, we weren't intimate. You're taking Lieutenant Rodriguez too seriously, Evan."

"No." Evan's voice was quiet now. "The truth is, Dexter, Karen told me in confidence that the two of you were lovers. You know, after that weekend you went up to Aspen together. She was...um...hoping to marry you. I told her not to count on it." He cast a worried glance in Liz's direction, then plunged ahead. "I warned her that you hadn't been taking your women . . . um . . . seriously since Susan. . . ."

When had Dexter ever taken his women seriously? Liz thought cynically. Certainly not during his marriage to her.

"You repeated all this to Lieutenant Rodriguez?" Dexter asked.

Evan hung his head. "I had to. He kept on asking all these questions about Karen and you. I had to tell the truth, Dexter, you can see that."

Liz could barely refrain from asking why truth suddenly ranked so high on Evan's list of priorities. Dexter merely shrugged. "Whatever Karen may have said to you, I wasn't her lover and I didn't get her pregnant. Damn it, I never even kissed the woman, much less had sex with her! We had rooms on separate floors of the hotel, and worked on the final draft of a speech to the League of Women Voters that weekend in Aspen."

"Sure, Dexter, if you say so, but remember the police'll probably be able to run paternity tests on the fetus—"

Dexter cast a single, hard glance at his publicist. "That's good news."

Evan reddened. "Yeah, I guess it is. I'm sure their tests will prove the baby couldn't have been yours, of course."

"Of course." Dexter didn't bother to disguise the heavy irony in his reply. "If the lieutenant asks, tell him I'd be delighted to give a blood sample for comparative testing. Think positively, Evan. Count your blessings that it's two years until I'm up for reelection."

Evan visibly brightened. It was becoming clear to Liz that facts as concrete entities scarcely existed for him—how things would appear in the media made up his personal version of reality. "That's true. Two and a half years, actually. Hell, we have plenty of time to come up with a convincing explanation for everything."

Liz spoke for the first time. For some reason, she found Evan's lack of faith in his employer distinctly annoying. "There's even the faint hope that the police might have discovered what truly happened by then. In which case, you might not need to invent any stories about anything."

"I guess." Evan clearly placed about as much hope in the possibility of the police solving the mystery as he had faith in his employer's innocence. "What do you want me to do, Dexter? Should I work on a statement for you to make to the press tomorrow?"

"Right now we don't seem to have any clear ideas about what I should say, so that seems like an exercise in futility. Why don't you make an appointment to consult with Needinger?"

"Your lawyer? That's a great idea." Evan cheered up again. "Needinger has lots of clout at the police department. He can talk to Lieutenant Rodriguez and make sure we get all the up-to-date information. We don't want reporters springing any more surprises on us. That clunker from the *Boulder Post* this morning was enough for a lifetime. What are you going to do for the rest of the day, Senator? Do you plan to stick to your original timetable? You have a dinner scheduled with the governor, remember?"

"You might cancel that, with my profound apologies. I'm sure he'll be relieved not to have to make polite conversation while we both sit and wonder how likely I am to be arrested before dessert is served."

Evan winced. "Bite your tongue, Senator. How about the rest of your schedule?"

Dexter glanced at the calendar spread open on his desk. "I'm planning to spend the next hour or so talking to Liz. Seems to me we have some useful information to share, she and I."

Evan viewed Liz with distinct lack of favor. "If you really think that's wise, Senator—"

"I think it's very wise," Dexter said firmly. "I'll keep the afternoon appointments. And could you call the agency for a temporary secretary? Bonnie's never going to cope on her own."

"Very well, Senator." From the number of times he'd said "Senator" in the past two minutes, Liz decided Evan once again felt in control of the situation. He gave a smooth smile. "I'll see you after lunch, when I've had a chance to check things out with Needinger."

"If he needs to see you, you know my schedule."

"Yes, Senator." Evan nodded his head toward Liz. "Goodbye Ms. Meacham. It's been a . . . um . . . pleasure meeting you."

She actually felt her mouth twist into a small smile. "I hope your pleasures aren't always so traumatic, Mr. Howard."

Her reply seemed to disconcert him. He smiled nervously, then hurried from the room with a final word of acknowledgment to his employer. Liz waited until the door closed. "For your sake, I hope he's better at his job than he seems," she said dryly. She flushed. "I'm sorry. That remark was uncalled-for."

Dexter seemed amused rather than offended. "He's actually damn good at his job. He has a knack for turning complex policy positions into easy-to-grasp, easy-to-read statements, and he can charm a mob of hungry journalists better than anybody I know."

Liz thought back and realized Dexter was right. Evan Howard had shown no sign of being traumatized until they'd been alone in the study. "Nursing him through a nervous breakdown every time there's a crisis seems like a stiff price to pay."

"He's not usually this upset. He's always a worrier, but I must say Karen's death seems to have thrown him for a total loop. He normally panics for ten minutes, then has the whole situation under control ten minutes later."

"Maybe he's thrown because he thinks you killed her."

Her words fell into a little pool of silence. Dexter stopped riffling through the pages of his calendar and looked up at her. "What about you, Liz? Do you think I killed Karen?"

She gave an odd little laugh. "I wish I could say yes. After the debacle of our marriage, I rather like the idea of you groveling in the courts over a messy crime of passion. It would make you seem semihuman."

"Translated, does that mean you don't believe I murdered my secretary?"

She smiled wryly. "Crazy, isn't it? The evidence all points to you, but somehow I don't believe you did it."

"Why not?"

"Maybe because I can't imagine you ever feeling passionate enough about a woman to kill her."

He looked away. "You're wrong," he said quietly. "I've felt that passionate—and that desperate. But not over Karen."

Susan, Liz thought, and was aware of a sharp little twist of pain in her stomach. Why had he felt so desperate about Susan? Was he implying that his second wife had been unfaithful to him? Surely not, although Liz considered it a splendid irony of fate if she had. The adulterer finally stung by his wife's adultery.

"You're very quiet," he said. "Does that mean you're wondering if I'm guilty, after all?"

"No, I guess I'm quite sure you didn't kill her."

"Should I be flattered?"

"Maybe. Or perhaps I can't believe you're guilty because the evidence is too convincing."

"When there's a bullet-ridden body on the floor and the only other person in the room holds a smoking gun, it's reasonable to conclude that the person holding the gun had something to do with the bullet-ridden body."

"Are you trying to convince me you killed her, Dexter?"

"I'm trying to discover why on earth you believe I didn't. Knowing your opinion of my character, I can't believe it's a burning faith in my integrity."

"Let's just say I have a perverse intuition that this time the guy with the smoking gun didn't pull the trigger."

"You know who the police are going to suspect if they ever give up on me, don't you?"

"Yes. I know I ought to run to Rodriguez screaming that you did it. Because if you didn't kill Karen, that surely puts me right at the top of the police list of likely murderers. Except I know I didn't kill her, or my other two roommates. So maybe you didn't kill her either, despite all the evidence."

"Or get her pregnant?"

She glanced down at her hands. "I—don't know about that."

His voice sounded harsh. "I suppose I should be grateful for small mercies. I guess it's better to have your ex-wife consider you a lecher who's fooling around with the office staff than to have her think you might be a murderer."

Liz dug her nails into her palms. "You . . . were unfaithful while we were married. How do I know what your sexual morals might be nowadays?"

"I was never unfaithful to you," Dexter said, sounding suddenly tired. "But let's not open that old can of worms. I don't think we can have a single thing left to say on the subject of our marriage. God knows, we said it all nine years ago, and most of it in front of a TV camera."

"I still have nightmares about that night." Liz had no idea why she suddenly made the admission that pride had kept inside for so many years.

"Which part of the night?" Dexter asked quietly. "The medal you'd just lost, or the public disintegration of our marriage?"

She hesitated before admitting the truth. "Both."

Dexter was silent even longer than she had been. "With the proper training, you could have come back in time for the world championship," he said finally. "You were a brilliant skater."

"The psychological moment had passed, I guess." Liz shrugged off the lingering regret that could still grab her by the throat when she gave it the chance. "At least the tabloids aren't interested in me anymore. That must be one of the few compensations for getting old and out of shape!"

Dexter's gaze flicked over her. "You don't look out of shape to me," he commented. "Your body's as spectacular as ever." He continued without giving her a chance to respond. "Look, Liz, why don't we make a deal? I'll agree that you're an innocent victim in the deaths of all three of your roommates, if you'll agree to give me the benefit of the doubt about Karen and her pregnancy."

"Does it matter if we believe each other?"

"I think maybe it does. The police aren't going to look very far for their murderer when they have you and me as such convenient suspects, and I'd like to find out what I'm being set up for. Because I sure as hell don't think it's coincidence that my secretary got herself murdered while she just happened to be living with my ex-wife."

"You think I'm setting you up?"

"No, but it's a possibility. A remote one, but I've learned not to discount possibilities. Shall we talk about it?"

"For heaven's sake, why in the world would I bother to set you up?"

"Revenge?"

"Good grief, Dexter! Quite apart from the fact that killing three people seems a somewhat excessive revenge, I'm not neurotic enough or obsessed enough to have spent nine years waiting to get back at you because you're a terminal louse and we had a rotten divorce."

"I see." He grinned faintly. "You mean, a plot to castrate me would meet with your approval, but setting me up for murder goes too far?"

To her surprise, she found herself answering his grin. "Something like that," she agreed. "Although now that you mention it, I can't think why I didn't come up with the castration idea years ago."

"No creative imagination," he said promptly. "Your creativity all goes into your skating."

She smiled, then sighed, feeling a sudden sadness. "Nine years later, and we still come around to the same old topics, don't we? Dexter, I haven't skated in nine years. Wherever my creativity is going these days, it's not into the ice."

He closed the desk calendar with a snap. "You're right. We should stick to Karen's murder and not waste time rehashing the past. Would you be willing to help me come up with some ideas as to who might have killed her?"

"Surely that's something we should leave to the police."

"Unfortunately, I think the police will soon decide that they have all the ideas they need."

"You think they'll arrest you? Or me?"

"How about both of us?"

It was at moments such as these that Liz understood why people smoked. Her hands desperately needed something to do before the rest of her exploded. Dexter seemed to sense her panic. He emerged from behind the desk and crossed the room to sit beside her on the sofa.

"Liz, if we put our heads together, I think we can come up with several insights the police won't have. You see, we know quite a lot that they don't. For example, I know that Karen wasn't pregnant with my baby and that we didn't have an affair. You know that you didn't kill her or your other two roommates."

"Okay, but where do we go from there?"

"At a minimum, it gives us a couple of avenues to explore. Who was the father of Karen's baby, and why were your roommates killed? Those aren't going to be burning questions on the police investigation."

"But Dexter, that brings us back to where we started out last night. I haven't the faintest, remotest idea why my roommates were killed. I've spent the past day and a half trying to imagine any possible connecting link between the three of them. Believe me, there isn't one."

"Were they friends? Acquaintances?"

"Of course they weren't!"

"How do you know?"

"Because they never mentioned each other! Because they moved in completely different circles! Because there's no *reason* for them to have been friends!"

"We don't know of any reason for them to have been murdered, but they were. Okay, maybe they weren't bosom buddies, but are you sure that they'd never met?"

She stared at him, eyes wide with the shock of realization. "No, I don't know that they'd never met," she murmured. "Not for sure. But when I moved in with Karen I told her that I'd been living with a woman called Jill Skinner, who'd died. If Karen knew Jill, why wouldn't she have said so?"

"Liz, stop reacting and start thinking. If Karen and Brian and Jill shared some secret that got all three of them murdered, do you think any of them were going to worry about a little secret like not telling you that they knew one another?"

"Are you saying that they conspired to trick me into moving in with them for some deep, dark purpose we know nothing about?" Even to her own ears, her voice sounded distinctly breathless.

"I'm saying you should consider the possibility. And they didn't have to share a deep, dark purpose. People conceal information for all sorts of reasons. After all, you never told Karen that you'd been married to me."

"That was different. There was no reason to mention a relationship that didn't—doesn't—exist anymore."

"How do you know your roommates didn't have a similar sort of reason? Maybe Brian had been married to Jill. Or Karen."

"No! He'd been single for years. He told me his marriage ended right after grad school. . . ." Her passionate denial trailed away into unconvincing silence.

"You see?" Dexter said softly. "You never checked up on Brian's story, did you?"

"People usually tell each other the truth—"

"But not always." Dexter got up and walked over to his desk. Depressing a button, he spoke into the intercom. "Mrs. Morton, could you please make us a pot of coffee and a couple of sandwiches? Thanks." Turning back to Liz, he looked at her thoughtfully. "Who first suggested that you should move into Karen's apartment?"

Liz cast her mind back, trying to visualize the crowded room at the party where she had first met Karen. "I did," she said. "I'm almost sure of it. Karen asked me all the usual questions, like how long I had been in Denver, where I was working, that sort of thing. I told her I'd just started a new job at Peperito's, and that I was looking for a roommate. She told me that by coincidence her roommate had just moved out—"

"As far as I know, Karen never had a roommate. The subject came up once, and she specifically told me she lived alone." Dexter must have caught some fleeting change in Liz's expression because his eyes flashed dark with irritation. "We were talking about a spate of burglaries in her neighborhood, Liz, not a prospective seduction."

"Maybe it was the burglaries that changed her mind."

"Could be. Who was giving this party? Whoever it was, must be a friend of Karen's."

"Pieter Ullmann."

"The skater?"

"Yes, he won the gold at the last Olympics."

"I detect a tinge of acid in your voice. Didn't he deserve his gold?"

"Sure he did. He's probably the best male skater since Scott Hamilton. I'm just tired of athletes who think an Olympic gold is the master key to unlock every woman's bedroom door. Pieter skates like an angel and has a mind like a sewer. Unfortunately, when I'm around him, I keep forgetting the angelic part and smelling the sewer."

Dexter laughed. "So why did you go to his party?"

"Mikhail invited me to go with him. Pieter was—is—his star pupil at the moment."

"Of course, I should've remembered. There was enough press coverage of them both during the winter games." Dexter's voice was carefully neutral. "How is Mikhail these days? I haven't seen him since he first arrived in the States after his defection, but I heard lots of good things about his teaching program, even before Pieter carried off the gold."

"Mikhail's the best figure-skating coach in the United States," Liz said, smiling affectionately as she thought of her brother-in-law. Now that Alison was dead, and their mother barely aware of her surroundings, Mikhail was Liz's closest substitute for a family.

"He's never tried to persuade you back onto the ice?"

"We don't have any sort of professional relationship. Mikhail always admired Alison's skating style much more than mine. That's what first attracted him to her."

"Technical perfection over fire and heart?"

"Alison was a magnificent skater!"

"You always said so," Dexter agreed. An odd note of hesitancy crept into his voice. "Are you thinking of marrying him, Liz?"

She could justifiably have told Dexter it was none of his business, that he'd lost the right to pry into her affairs years ago, but somehow she found herself confiding the truth. "No, never," she said. "He was Alison's husband. Alison was my twin, and the two of us had always been so close, at least until you and I got married. I could never think of Mikhail as anything except a brother."

A light tap at the door heralded the arrival of Mrs. Morton with a carafe of steaming coffee and a plate of smoked-salmon-and-cucumber sandwiches. As soon as the housekeeper left the room, Liz took a generous bite of sandwich and grinned across at Dexter.

"There are a few advantages to being filthy rich," she said, leaning back against the sofa pillows. "In my next life I'm going to reincarnate as somebody who presses buttons and makes sandwiches appear."

"Take care that the masters of the universe aren't listening, or you may come back as a music-hall conjurer."

She laughed, then sobered abruptly, the sandwich losing its appeal. "Smoked salmon was Karen's favorite, too. Oh God, Dexter, she didn't deserve to end up splattered on a parking-lot pavement."

"No, she didn't. Nobody deserves to die that way. But at this point, we can't do anything to help her except try to find her killer. Which I guess brings us right back to your decision to move in with Karen. With all the advantage of hindsight, would you say that it's possible you were maneuvered into sharing an apartment with her?"

"Of course it's possible—"

"But not probable, you think?"

"I don't know!" Liz's voice faded into silence while she tried to remember the exact chain of events. "I don't know about Karen," she said finally. "But if it'll make you feel better, I can be more positive about my decision to move in with Jill Skinner. That wasn't my decision, it was Jill's. I was numb after Brian died, and she virtually made the move for me. At that point, I was so shattered I'd have moved in with Dracula if he'd been prepared to pack my suitcases and hire the U-Haul. So if you want to suspect some vast conspiracy with me as the helpless pawn, the person to start with is Jill Skinner."

"Tell me about her," Dexter suggested. "And about Brian."

It was easier to discuss Jill, so she did that first. "Like I told you last night, Jill and I knew each other for at least two years, but we weren't close friends. We went to the same health club and sweated through the advanced aerobics class, then commiserated about our aching muscles over fruit juice in the locker room. We saw each other three times a week, but until we shared an apartment, I don't think I knew anything more about her than that she had a terrific body, she was around my age, and had a job as a social worker."

"And once you moved in with her?"

"I found out that she was neat, a vegetarian, a sympathetic listener, and that she took care never to intrude into my space. She had a lot of friends, but she socialized with them in restaurants, not in the apartment. Dex, what can I say? She was a great roommate, but we weren't bosom buddies."

"What about her friends?"

"As I said, she had lots of them. Male and female. She was out most nights."

"Did you like her friends?"

Once again, Liz fell silent. "I don't think I ever met any of them," she admitted finally. "Except maybe to say hi at the door."

"In fact, if you added up everything you know about Jill, you just might be able to fill two sides of a small piece of paper."

Liz felt a chill ripple down her spine. "That's an underestimation, but not by much."

"What about Brian? Did you know him any better?"

"Of course I did! I was living with him, for heaven's sake!"

"You were living with Jill and Karen, too."

"No, I was sharing an apartment. It's different."

"Is it? Aside from what he was like in bed, do you know any more about Brian than you do about Jill and Karen?"

"Yes," she said, through gritted teeth. "Unlike some people, I don't hop into bed with anybody who looks good in a pair of pants."

"Well, bully for you." Dexter's smile was lethal. "So what intimate details do you know about our friend Brian?"

"He was a professor at the university," she replied. "He had a doctoral degree in electrical engineering. He was forty-five, and a wonderfully calm, considerate human being. He'd been married once when he was a student, but the marriage only lasted a few months before his wife left him for another man." She smiled grimly. "As you can see, we had a lot in common."

"Failed marriages, or chips on your shoulders?" Dexter inquired with excessive politeness.

She wished she could think of some brilliant, scathing retort that would reduce him to dust. Of course, she couldn't. "Brian had a very well-balanced personality," was the best she could come up with.

"I'm so sorry," Dexter pretended sympathy. "Was he boring in bed, too?"

He had been incredibly boring in bed, but Liz had no intention of stepping into that particular nest of vipers. Not with Dexter, of all people. She got to her feet, carrying her plate and cup over to the heavy silver tray Mrs. Morton had left on a side table. She smiled with freezing politeness.

"I've just noticed it's noon already. I have to get to work. My boss isn't too understanding when it comes to taking time off to cope with personal crises. Murder or no murder, he's going to want my latest market-research figures charted and on his desk."

Dexter reached out and captured her hand. He exerted almost no pressure, but somehow she felt incapable of walking away. "Liz, I'm sorry. I owe you an apology. We left a lot of things unresolved between us when we split up, and I think we've both been carrying around some excess emotional baggage, but that's no excuse for what I just said."

"It's been a tough morning," she said, not looking at him.

"Things are likely to get tougher, not easier. This isn't the moment for me to start hurling insults."

"No, I guess it's not. Maybe we should both try to count to ten before we speak to each other."

He broke a moment of silence. "Where are you going to stay tonight?"

She blinked, dismayed by the question. Where was she going to stay? Dear God, she hadn't given that problem a moment's thought. One thing was for sure: she couldn't go back to her apartment, wherever else she went. At the moment, she felt she would never be able to live in an apartment—any apartment—again.

"I hadn't thought about it," she admitted. "But it should be easy enough to find a room near the office. There are dozens of motels around the airport."

"You could stay here," he said. "We have plenty of room."

"Thank you very much for the offer, but I don't think—"

"Liz, we could help each other, if you'd only spend some time with me. We haven't even started to work out a list of Karen's friends—"

"Dexter, we already agreed that I know almost nothing about Karen, and even less about her friends."

He put a finger against her lips, gently silencing her. "I'll bet you don't know half of what you know," he said lightly. "Liz, please consider it. For both our sakes."

She closed her eyes, cursing silently. She never had been able to resist Dexter when he gave her one of his tender, sincere looks. She'd grown up a lot in the last nine years, but the extra maturity didn't seem to have done a darn thing for her susceptibility to Dexter. She had more self-control these days than she'd had when she was nineteen, but his offer was still incredibly tempting—

partly because she didn't want to spend the next few nights pacing up and down a lonely motel room with the specters of Karen and Lieutenant Rodriguez looming over her shoulder.

"All right," she said, drawing in a deep breath. "If you really think it would be helpful, I'll pack a suitcase after work and join you later on this evening."

"Wonderful." Dexter's smile was warm, happy, intimate—and made her want to scream in protest at its devastating effect on her hormones. Why couldn't he have developed sagging jowls and a belly to match? She held her body stiff as he gave her a quick, friendly hug.

"See you tonight, Liz. I'll be waiting for you."

Chapter Five

Liz barely survived her afternoon at the office. The combination of an overloaded desk and colleagues consumed by curiosity proved as exhausting as the morning's press conference. Since she'd only recently started work at Peperito's, her colleagues had not yet become friends, and their fascination with her sudden notoriety inevitably came across as prying. Even her boss, a middle-aged workaholic, took ten minutes off from studying his sales charts to bludgeon her with questions. He seemed to have a tough time deciding which part of the breaking news story was most deplorable: Liz's past career as a—failed—skater; her short-lived marriage to the famous Senator Rand; or her involvement in a juicy murder that was clearly destined to remain on the front pages of Colorado's newspapers for several weeks.

Liz was literally shaking with fatigue by the time she turned the key in the lock of her apartment door and pushed it open. The sight of Pieter Ullmann lounging in Karen's favorite armchair proved the final straw to her self-control.

"What the blazes are you doing here?" she demanded. "Who let you in?"

"And I'm thrilled to see you, too, darling." Pieter switched off the television set, jumped gracefully to his feet and bounded across the room to drop a kiss on her cheek. She turned her head just in time, and his kiss landed on her ear.

"Knock it off," she said wearily. "Who let you in, Pieter?"

"Your superintendent's wife," he said cheerily. "I gave her my autograph, and she was thrilled. Her granddaughter sleeps with my picture under her pillow."

"How touching. However, I don't sleep with your picture under my pillow and I already have your autograph, so I'd be grateful if you'd leave. I have a bunch of things to do tonight."

"I came to offer you my sympathy," he said, sounding mortally wounded by her curt rejection. "And my help."

"Thanks. The sympathy's accepted, the help isn't needed. Goodbye."

He winced. "Liz, darling, try to show a few social graces."

She threw her coat onto the nearest available chair. "I'm too tired to be socially gracious. Go home, Pieter."

"Being the generous person that I am, I'll ignore your hostility and invite you to come back to my apartment. What do you say, Liz? I'll call the caterers and we can have a quiet dinner, just the two of us. Champagne. Lobster. Whatever you want."

"And then a quiet little night in bed? Just the two of us?"

Pieter smiled. "Darling, my bedmates are much too ecstatic to be quiet. If you'd only allow yourself to let go now and again, you'd know that my performance in the bedroom is even more spectacular than on the ice. So you know how wonderful that must be."

Liz freed herself from his arms and made her way to the kitchen. "The trouble is, Pieter, I'm old-fashioned enough to think the bedroom is a place to make love, not take part in a performance."

"Darling Liz, you can't be that old!"

Against her will she laughed, and the laughter turned into a yawn. "Believe me, I'm that old. And tired, as well." She opened the fridge, realizing as she peered inside that she was almost grateful to Pieter. Finding him in the apartment had taken some of the sting out of her return.

"If you don't want to go and pursue more promising quarry, you could stay and have a drink. It looks like you can have white wine, soda or orange juice."

He sighed. "I'd better say orange juice, since Mikhail is your brother-in-law and you'll probably report back to him. You two are like Siamese twins."

"Good grief, Pieter, I'm not that much of a witch! Besides, despite all your weary man-of-the-world act, I know damn well that you keep to your training program, whether Mikhail's on your back or not. You can't fool me. I know what it takes to reach Olympic standard as a figure skater."

He took a swallow of orange juice and grimaced. "Liz, darling, I can see that this is one of your nights for being a bore."

"I agree, so why are you staying? Pieter, I mean it when I say I'm not coming back to your apartment."

"Dearest Liz, if you don't want to have the best night of your life, that's your business. My sole purpose at this moment is to make you happy. If you want me to hang around drinking orange juice, that's what I'll do. It's creepy to think of you being here alone. Karen was really inconsiderate to get herself murdered in your apartment."

"Gee, you're right!" Liz loaded her words with sarcasm. "If she'd had a smidgen of good taste, she'd surely have asked her murderer to search around and find some other window to push her out of. Murderers are always so cooperative about that sort of thing."

Pieter stirred an ice cube into his juice with a finger. "You're not going to spend the night here alone, are you, Liz?"

"No," she said, a little surprised by his sudden seriousness. "I'm not staying here. I'm going to a friend's house."

"Whose?"

"Nobody you know. We...um...work together." She silently apologized for the lie, but had no intention of telling gossipy Pieter where she was really going. "I just stopped by to pack a suitcase. In fact, I have to get started on my packing right now." She picked up her diet soda and walked toward the narrow hallway of the apartment.

Pieter followed her into her bedroom without bothering to ask permission. Bedrooms and the ice rink were his natural habitat, and he obviously felt equally at home in both. He kicked off his shoes and stretched out comfortably on her bed.

"Am I in the way, Liz darling?"

"No more than usual." She opened a drawer and dumped a pile of sweaters onto his stomach. "Here, choose me a couple, would you?"

Pieter obligingly began sorting through sweaters. "Liz," he said with determined casualness. "Did you see much of Karen over the past few weeks?"

"Not much. I was in Mexico City meeting with Peperito's suppliers until Friday."

"Oh. Did she say anything to you about—um—anything?"

Liz belatedly remembered it was at one of Pieter's parties that she had first met Karen. She straightened from her search through the bottom of the closet for a missing sneaker, and turned around to face Pieter.

"How well did you know Karen Zeit?" she asked quietly.

He stared at one of her turquoise sweaters as if he'd never seen such a mesmerizing garment. "Not well. I scarcely knew her at all, in fact."

"Well enough to take her to bed?"

A flash of Pieter's usual brittle manner reappeared momentarily. "Dearest Liz, even you should realize it's the people you don't know that you go to bed with. With someone you know, you might have to talk afterward."

Liz's gaze remained cool. "I take it that means you and Karen were bedmates?"

"Then you take it wrong." Pieter got off the bed and handed Liz two pink sweaters. "Here, pack these. You look like death warmed over. You could use some color in your clothes, because you sure as hell don't have any in your cheeks."

"Thank you." Liz took the sweaters, her voice softening. "Pieter, are you sure you're not the father of Karen's baby?"

"Yes, damn it, I'm sure! The baby wasn't mine! It couldn't have been, because we never slept together."

"Then why are you yelling?"

"Because she came on to me like gangbusters, and a whole bunch of my friends know that."

"I didn't know you ever turned down a willing female, Pieter."

"You don't know a hell of a lot," Pieter said tightly. "About me, or about your roommate. From the way Karen approached me, I'd guess half the men in Denver could have been the father of her baby. But whoever the father was, it wasn't me." Pieter swallowed the last of his orange juice, muttered an obscene epithet and pushed himself off the bed. "Damn Mikhail and his training schedule. I'm planning to go out and party."

"Pieter, don't go for a minute! Have you told the police what you know about Karen?"

"I don't know anything about Karen."

"You know she came on to you."

He laughed harshly. "Are you crazy? In the first place, I don't know a thing about her general behavior. All I know is how she behaved with me. And in the second place, don't you think I have enough problems with the media without asking for trouble? I've already got two teenagers suing me in paternity suits, and I swear to God I've never set eyes on either of them."

"The police think Dex—Senator Rand is the father of Karen's child."

"That's their problem. Or his. Anyway, it sure isn't mine." Pieter zipped up his jacket and strode out of the bedroom. Liz hurried after him.

"Pieter!"

He stopped but didn't turn. "Yeah?"

She swallowed, surprised at the words that came out. "Take a cab home from the party if you drink too much."

"I could do that." He swung around and looked at her, his eyes shadowed. "Have you thought about taking a vacation, Liz? Somewhere a long way away from Denver?"

"I only just moved here, for heaven's sake!"

"Looks like now would be a real good time to move on."

"Pieter, what are you trying to tell me?"

He shrugged, reaching for the door. Liz had the feeling he was regretting having come, regretting even more having spoken so freely. "Nothing, babe. I guess I'm just running off at the mouth. See you around, huh?" He left the apartment, slamming the door loudly behind him.

LIZ'S PACKING still didn't go as quickly as she'd hoped, even after Pieter left. She was interrupted by two phone calls. One came from the nursing home in Durango where her mother was being cared for. The ostensible purpose of the call was for the head nurse to reassure Liz that Mrs. Meacham remained unaware of her surroundings and was therefore not at all worried by the news stories that had been blasting forth all day on the lounge TV. But Liz couldn't help suspecting that the real purpose of the call was to find out if she'd been arrested.

The second call came from a journalist offering Liz five thousand dollars for "the inside story on your affair with Senator Rand."

It had been so long since she'd needed to field this sort of call that Liz let the journalist rattle on while she stared at the receiver, literally bereft of words. Finally she gathered her wits together sufficiently to respond.

"The senator and I are not currently having an affair. We did not have an affair in the past, nor do we plan to have an affair in the future. That's my exclusive inside story and you're welcome to it. For free." She banged down the receiver. "I hope that broke your eardrum," she muttered.

Her suitcase finally packed, she was almost at the front door of the apartment when the phone rang again. She hesitated, not wanting to confront another journalist—or Lieutenant Rodriguez, for that matter. When the phone continued to ring, the conviction grew that it was Dexter, calling to say he'd changed his mind about having her stay with him. Reluctantly she snatched the receiver from the cradle and barked, "Hello!"

"You sound horribly fierce, Lizushka. What is all this that I hear is going on up there in Denver?"

"Mikhail!" With a sigh of relief, she sank into the chair alongside the phone. Mikhail had married Alison just as Liz's own marriage to Dexter was going down in flames. He had defected from the Soviet Union during the world figure-skating championships five years ago, shortly after Alison had died in an Aeroflot plane crash. Drawn together by shared grief, he had been Liz's closest friend and confidant ever since his arrival in America. The warm sound of his accented voice made her smile, and she felt herself relax for the first time in hours.

"I'm sorry I sounded so aggressive. I expected you to be a reporter."

"Ah! That explains everything," he said with a laugh. "You and the reporters are never friends, yes?"

"No, we sure aren't. This morning's session with the wolf pack reminded me how much I love obscurity."

"I was at the rink all day and I didn't hear the news until I came home and turned on the TV while I cooked supper. Lizushka, this is terrible. Another of your roommates is dead, and you have been seeing Dexter Rand? What in the world have you gotten yourself into?"

"I don't know, Mikhail. I just absolutely and completely have no idea."

"But how did you get mixed up again with that monster Dexter? I know how bitter you felt after your divorce, and rightly so."

"Karen Zeit worked for him."

"And you never knew this? In all the weeks you shared an apartment with her, you never discussed her job?"

Liz felt herself blush. "I knew Karen worked for Dexter," she admitted.

Mikhail said nothing, but she could feel the silence gradually fill with his concern. "I thought we were friends," he said at last. "Good friends. Why didn't you tell me about Karen's job?"

"It... there was nothing to tell."

"Are you sure, *dorogoya*?" He spoke the Russian endearment softly. "I don't want you to get hurt again. Are you quite certain that the smiles you exchanged with the senator on the TV were just for the reporters?"

"I'm a hundred percent positive! That news conference didn't mean a thing in terms of our personal relationship. We just decided that it would look better for both of us if we joined forces to meet the press, that's all."

"With you and Dexter, things are not likely to be so simple, Lizzie. I hoped you'd finally gotten over your hang-ups for this ex-husband of yours."

"I have!" she declared vehemently. "Don't you see, Mikhail, it's because he means nothing to me that I was determined not to move out of Karen's apartment. I never planned to see Dexter, or speak to him, so what difference did it make who she worked for?"

A rueful note crept into Mikhail's voice. "As it turned out, *dorogoya*, rather a lot."

"But I had no way of knowing Karen would be killed. No way of knowing that I'd be thrust into Dexter's orbit again. Besides, this will all blow over. Believe me, I have no intention of staying within his striking range."

There was another worried silence before Mikhail spoke again. "Liz, do you not think it is time to tell the police about what has happened to your last two roommates? They already believe Karen was murdered. How is it going to look when they find out you were living with two other people who both died by falling out of windows?"

"Brian shot himself first," she said, as if that made the situation somehow less suspicious.

"Shot himself—or was shot? Do you not realize that the police will soon ask you this very question?"

"But I haven't done anything," she protested. "Eventually they'll find the people who are responsible, and in the meantime, I refuse to worry. In this country people are innocent until they're proven guilty."

"The United States is a wonderful place, Lizushka, the best in the world. But in this country the police want to write SOLVED across their file covers, just like in Russia." His voice was husky, his accent strong enough to add a beguiling touch of emphasis to his vowels. Liz felt a familiar rush of affection.

"Mikhail, you worry far too much about me. I'm not nearly as vulnerable as you think."

"I do not think you are vulnerable. But you are my sister, the twin of my Alison. Of course I must worry. How can I remain calm while the police bumble around, searching for a solution? How do we know that the murderer will not turn his attention to you while the police plod through their 'routine investigations'?"

She shivered, then said staunchly, "If somebody wanted to kill me, Mikhail, they would surely have done it by now."

"Who knows what this crazy murderer's motivations might be?"

Her control wavered, perilously close to breaking. "Oh God, Mikhail, don't you realize it's the pointlessness of all this that's driving me crazy?"

Mikhail backtracked immediately, obviously upset that his concern for Liz's welfare had made him add to her worries. "I am a fool," he said softly. "You are right not to concern yourself about a problem that cannot have anything to do with you. There is no reason for anybody to wish to kill you."

She made an effort to laugh. "It's not as if I'm going to leave somebody a trillion dollars when I die."

"And you live like a nun, so it cannot be a crime of passion. *Dorogoya*, let us stop talking about this horrible situation and turn to more pleasant subjects. I did not call to alarm you, but to issue an invitation. You will not want to be alone tonight, so I will drive up to Denver and bring you home to my house. You can spend the night with me in Colorado Springs and take my car into work tomorrow. The drive will be a little long for you, but we shall have dinner together tonight and enjoy each other's company over a glass of wine, so that you will say the long commute was worth it. You know you can stay with me for as many days as you wish. Forever, if you would only agree to it."

His generous offer produced an immediate wave of guilt in Liz. During the past twenty-four hours she had scarcely given Mikhail a thought, so exclusively had her attention been focused on Karen's death and her own meeting with Dexter. The obsession with Karen's death might be understandable, but the obsession with her ex-husband was not. Why in the world hadn't she remembered Mikhail when she'd been trying to come up with an alternative to checking into an hotel? Why had she so meekly agreed to spend another night with Dexter?

"Mikhail, I would love to come to Colorado Springs," she apologized. "But I've already agreed to go to..." She let her words trail off, as reluctant as she had been with Pieter to admit where she was going. Mikhail wouldn't gossip, but he would call her a fool—which she probably was—and right now she didn't feel strong enough to face another brotherly lecture.

"I've already promised to spend the night somewhere else," she amended. "With a friend from work." She blushed at the lie.

"Well, I'm glad you've found a place to stay. Is this new friend male or female?"

She could hear the hurt behind the cheerful words and felt like a worm. It seemed more important than ever not to let Mikhail find out where she was going. He simply wouldn't understand that her decision to spend the night at Dexter's house was entirely practical, based on her need to find an answer to the mystery of Karen's death. Mikhail had known her well at the time of her marriage breakup, and would never accept that she was cured of her infatuation. Knowing that she was spending a second night in her ex-husband's house, he would read all sorts of false significance into the arrangement.

"A married man with a child," she said finally, sticking as closely to the truth as she could. "Pieter Ullmann was pestering me to spend the night at his apartment, and since I didn't feel in the mood to become his bedtime bunny of the week, I accepted an invitation from a...from a colleague."

"Has Pieter been bothering you?" Mikhail's voice was sharp. "That boy is a great skater, but he's about as mature emotionally as a two-year-old."

"The poor guy's only twenty, isn't he?"

"Twenty-one, going on fifteen."

Liz laughed, chiefly from relief that her brother-in-law wasn't pursuing the question of precisely where she planned to spend the night. "I learned to handle the Pieters of this world a long time ago," she said. "You forget how many young men I met who were dazzled by their own Olympic medals and thought I ought to be dazzled, too."

He joined in her laughter. "You're right. You have worked so hard at becoming the efficient woman executive that I forget you were once poetry on ice, and everybody's heartthrob. Well, *dorogoya*, since you are determined to desert me, I shall eat my Stroganoff alone. Think of all that sour cream and fresh paprika and weep."

"I will for sure! It'll probably be hamburgers and French fries for me, if I'm lucky."

"Serves you right for abandoning me. Will you come down to the Springs on Saturday? We will share our favorite meal."

"It's a date," she said, relief flooding her because she had brushed through this difficult conversation without mortally wounding Mikhail's sensitive Russian soul.

"Goodbye, Lizushka."

She was halfway to Dexter's house before it dawned on her that her arrangement to spend the night with her ex-husband had been a somewhat casual thing—scarcely a commitment graven in stone. To avoid hurting Mikhail's feelings, all she had needed to do was call Dexter and explain politely that she no longer wished to accept his invitation.

Liz wondered why this obvious solution had not occurred to her earlier.

It required very few minutes' reflection to decide it would be wiser not to inquire too deeply into the workings of her psyche.

THE MEETING with Igor, his contact from the embassy in Washington, D.C., didn't go as well as he had hoped. He'd noticed that their meetings in Denver nearly always ended on a sour note, and he wondered if Denver's high altitude gave Igor a headache. Certainly, tonight had been one of their less pleasant sessions, despite the fact that Karen had been so successfully taken care of.

Everything had started off well enough, although he'd been too smart to relax and rest on his laurels. Igor was notorious for his habit of lulling his minions into a false sense of security before letting fly with brutal criticisms.

He had set the right tone for the meeting by providing Igor's favorite food. The KGB man had beamed at the generous supply of greasy packages set out on the table, and had selected a jumbo-size box of French fries and a double hamburger.

He himself didn't eat such poisonous foods, of course. He merely watched as Igor squirted ketchup onto the fries, making swirls of bright red sauce. He reflected cynically that Igor couldn't have been allowed to do enough finger painting when he was young. Soviet nursery schools had always been big on patriotic songs and notoriously indifferent to child psychology.

After several minutes of munching, Igor looked up from his earnest consumption of French fries. "So, Karen Zeit is dead. It was time. Past time. She was becoming nervous, I think." Igor had an annoying habit of stating the obvious.

"Yes, Comrade Secretary. As I told you, she feared the FBI investigation authorized by Senator Rand would blow her cover. There is an FBI agent working in the senator's Washington office, and unfortunately, our operatives haven't yet identified him. Karen was very worried. As you know, her past wouldn't stand up to detailed scrutiny."

"I am all too aware of the limitations of the identity we provided. With this murder investigation going ahead full steam, we work under time pressure." Igor munched through a mouthful of burger. "At least the main part of our mission proceeds according to plan. The trap has been satisfactorily set. The senator is already receiving some very unfavorable press."

"Yes, Comrade. And the press conference with his ex-wife can only work to our advantage."

"Ah yes! The former wife of the senator. I am glad that you yourself bring up the subject of Ms. Meacham." Igor licked up a drop of ketchup with a long, pink tongue, closing his eyes in appreciation of the exquisite flavor. "If Congress would only stop trying to sell democracy to the third world and concentrate on hamburgers, the Americans would be invincible."

He smiled, as he was supposed to. Igor liked to be thought of as a humorist. "I expect Congress wishes to export both hamburgers and democracy, Comrade Secretary."

Igor wiped his fingers delicately on a paper napkin. "Hamburgers transplant better than democracy. But, to return to the subject of Ms. Meacham. I hope you have that situation firmly in hand? She is the high-risk element of our operation. She must be seen in public with the senator, but she cannot become too close to him."

"I understand, Comrade Secretary. Ms. Meacham is completely under control."

"Hmm." Igor managed to express a great deal of doubt in a small grunt. "It is one thing for Ms. Meacham to appear at a press conference with her former husband. It would be an entirely different matter if the two of them should start to become—intimate. You have assured me that the hatred between Elizabeth Meacham and Dexter Rand makes any exchange of information extremely unlikely. I trust you have not miscalculated."

He was beginning to sweat, and surreptitiously wiped his palms on the edge of the tablecloth. "Believe me, Comrade Secretary, there is no chance of that. Elizabeth Meacham despises the senator after the way he treated her at the time of their divorce. I have heard this same story repeated on all sides."

"And your own observation?"

"Agrees completely with what I've heard."

"I expected her to be with you tonight. Where is she?"

"I invited her to have dinner with me, but she refused. However, there is no cause for alarm. She's spending the night with one of her colleagues."

"If she is not precisely where we want her to be, then there is cause for alarm. Your much-vaunted success with other women is of no value to us if you cannot attract Ms. Meacham sufficiently to control her movements."

He couldn't stop his gaze sliding disparagingly over Igor's bulging waistline and clumsy, peasantlike hands, then immediately realized it was a mistake to have allowed his disdain to show.

"Comrade Champion," Igor said softly. "My duty to the motherland does not require that I should have a desirable body. My duty requires only that my wits remain sharp and that I possess a profound understanding of the American political system. It is clear that I am fulfilling my duties. Are you fulfilling yours?"

"Yes, yes, of course, Comrade Secretary. Is Karen Zeit not dead? Is Senator Rand not in trouble?" He decided it might be smart to make no further mention of Liz Meacham.

"Who was the father of Karen Zeit's baby?" The question was slashed across the table with the sting of a whip.

He made the fatal mistake of lying. "Senator Rand—"

"Would never take his secretary to bed. He is the model of bourgeois propriety. You are the father of her baby, Comrade. Is that not so?"

Regretfully, he realized he had little choice but to tell the truth. "It isn't certain, Comrade Secretary, but the child could be mine. Karen fell hopelessly in love with me, and her infatuation jeopardized the safety of our operation. I had sex with her only to keep her content. Naturally, I had no idea that she would be so careless as to allow herself to become pregnant."

Igor banged his fist on the table, and the little packets of ketchup jumped with the force of the blow. "You play me for a fool, Comrade Champion. Do you expect me to believe that Karen never told you she carried your child? What reason could she have had to become pregnant, if she did not want you to marry her?"

Thank God, he had murdered Karen. Now she would never be able to contradict his story. He lifted wide, innocent eyes to meet Igor's accusing gaze. It was a blessing that he had always had such marvelously honest eyes. "Comrade Secretary, I swear to you that Karen never once mentioned to me the fact that she was pregnant. Perhaps she knew the child wasn't mine."

Igor grunted. He was a past master of the expressive grunt. This one conveyed scorn, disbelief and indifference in almost equal measure. "We have more important problems to worry about at this moment, I suppose. Our government is running out of time. Our secret lobbying against the new F-19B fighter jet has not been as successful as we hoped. This is an effective weapon, Comrade, and by some miracle, many U.S. senators on the Defense Appropriations Committee understand that fact."

"The new president isn't much in favor of expensive weapons development."

"But on this occasion, there is rare bipartisan support for the project. Except for one or two die-hard pacifists, the F-19B has met with nothing but approval. It is undetectable by radar. It is faster than any other plane now flying. It can carry conventional arms as well as nuclear warheads, and it can come in low to pinpoint a target. Possession of such a plane would give the United States an enormous strategic advantage. Therefore we cannot allow it to go into production. And unless we can convince Dexter Rand to campaign actively against it, the Senate Appropriations Committee is likely to vote funds for production of the plane within a few weeks."

"I understand, Comrade Secretary. I realize that Dexter Rand must be made to declare publicly against the plane. We need to control his vote. His chairmanship of this senate committee has already proven disastrous to the interests of the Soviet Union."

Igor gave another of his grunts. "From our point of view, he does far too good a job of separating useful military technology from projects that are never going to work. Who would have thought the senators would be smart enough to select a military expert to chair their armaments committee?''

He didn't bother to answer what was clearly a rhetorical question. Senator Rand's appointment to the Appropriations Committee had been causing gray hairs in Moscow ever since it was first announced. He spoke reassuringly. "The details of our plan to control the senator have been meticulously worked out, Comrade. With luck, Dexter Rand will soon be a useful tool in our hands instead of a thorn in our sides.''

"Luck doesn't factor in our government's planning, Comrade. I trust that you have left no part of this operation to luck.''

Inwardly he cursed the aggravating old buzzard. Outwardly he smiled. "The plans have been perfected to the last tiny detail, Comrade Secretary. We will deal with the senator and with Elizabeth Meacham before the end of the week.'' He paused for a moment, then pressed ahead with the question that was at the forefront of his mind. "Have the necessary personnel arrived from Moscow?''

Igor's response was curt. "She is already in the embassy.''

"There is—a message for me?''

"She looks forward to seeing you soon.''

He would have liked to ask more questions, but knew that Igor would delight in withholding information. "Do you want me to review the details of our plan for the abduction, and for Elizabeth Meacham's murder?''

"No.'' Igor rose to his feet. "I am well aware of your plans. Have you forgotten that I approved them in the first place? I am spending the next few days collating the evidence that will prove that Senator Rand murdered Ms.

Meacham. Just be sure that your own part of the operation is carried out with similar efficiency."

"It is all taken care of, Comrade Secretary. We shall need the photographs when the senator goes to Washington."

The damned old buzzard grunted again. "A word of warning, Comrade Champion. Neither the senator nor Elizabeth Meacham is a fool. Each of them knows that they did not commit murder. Take care that their efforts to save themselves do not unravel our plans."

"Their efforts to extricate themselves from the trap cannot succeed," he said, with a touch more confidence than he actually felt. "There are no trails for them to follow. We've made sure that whatever line of investigation anybody pursues, they will find only dead ends."

"Very dead, I trust." Igor put on his jacket. "Dead is highly desirable."

He wasn't sure he'd understood. "I'm sorry, Comrade Secretary? If you would be so good as to clarify..."

"One of your collaborators is no longer useful to us, and unfortunately he knows too much. Take care of him, Comrade. Take care of him soon, before his nerves get us all into trouble."

He rose to his feet, relieved that the interview had ended on a relatively positive note. Killing was easy. "I understand, Comrade Secretary. The matter will be taken care of expertly. I will kill him myself."

"No more windows, Comrade. I'm getting tired of windows."

"Certainly, Comrade. There are many other ways. I think perhaps a knife."

Igor grunted.

Chapter Six

Dinner was long over by the time Liz finally returned to Dexter's house. The housekeeper answered the door and directed her to a family room overlooking the backyard, where Dexter and his daughter were engaged in a game of dominoes. From the fierce frown of concentration wrinkling Amanda's forehead, Liz concluded that the game was being taken very seriously by at least one of the participants.

"Your visitor, Senator Rand. Miss Meacham's here."

"Thanks, Mrs. Morton." Dexter stood up and came across the room to greet Liz, and the housekeeper left, insisting on carrying Liz's case up to the guest room.

"Glad you made it back. Amanda and I were beginning to wonder what had happened to you."

"I'm sorry. I was delayed at the office and then I couldn't decide what I needed to pack. But I should have phoned."

"Don't worry about it. You had other things on your mind. Do you need dinner?"

"No, thanks. I stopped at Burger King on the way over."

He grinned. "Shush, don't let Amanda hear those magic words. She had to suffer through chicken breasts, mushrooms and fresh fruit salad. She tells me I'm the meanest dad in the world to keep ordering such yucky meals."

Liz's smile was only a touch strained. "Sounds like you're bringing up a deprived child, Dex. Don't you know that too much nutritious food damages the psyche?"

His eyes softened as he glanced over at the table, where his daughter was occupied in building a long, low wall of dominoes. "She's gorgeous," he said simply. "Not a hint of damage so far. Come and meet her."

Liz gripped her purse a little tighter. "Does she... um... does she know we were married?" she asked, trying to think up some reasonable excuse for hanging back. She couldn't very well say *I hated her mother so much, I don't want to meet her*.

"I told her, but she doesn't seem to find the information relevant. As soon as she realized you weren't about to become her stepmother, she lost interest in our relationship."

Liz followed Dexter across the room, curiosity to meet Susan's child still mixed with a confused grab bag of other emotions. Her stomach knotted painfully when Dexter rumpled Amanda's hair in a casual gesture that spoke volumes about his love.

"Hey, honey, I'm sorry about our game. This is Elizabeth Meacham. She's the friend of mine I told you about, and she'll be staying with us for a few days."

Somebody had obviously taught Amanda very good manners. Or maybe, Liz thought with a touch of bitterness, courtesy to inferiors was bred into the genes of people like Dexter and Susan—part of their birthright, along with their infuriating self-possession. Amanda hopped off her chair, dark curls bouncing. *Susan's curls.*

Susan's green eyes. But Dexter's arrogant, stubborn chin. Amanda held out her hand. "Hello, Mrs. Meacham. It's nice to have you here."

Liz took the tiny hand into her own. It felt warm, a little bit sticky and oddly trusting. She swallowed hard, resisting the craziest impulse to reach down and sweep the child into her arms. Surely she was imagining the vulnerability she saw in those stunning green eyes? "Hello, Amanda." She sought for something to say that was both suitable and honest. Her gaze fell on the dominoes. "Who's winning?"

"It's kind of a draw at the moment." Amanda squinted up at her father. "Will you have time to finish the game, Dad?"

He glanced down at his watch. "It's past your bedtime already, young lady."

"But it's Friday. So there's no school tomorrow."

Dexter sat down at the table with a mock sigh. "I guess we'll have to finish, then, or you'll claim you won."

She giggled. "No, I wouldn't. I have to let you win at dominoes, 'cos I always beat you so bad at Nintendo."

Dexter shot a rueful glance in Liz's direction. "Don't let this child get you in front of a TV set with a joystick. Believe me, it's a totally humiliating experience."

The jealousy Liz felt as she watched Dexter joke with his daughter was intense and shocking. She realized that she resented Susan's success in carrying Dexter's child to term more than anything else. Nowadays she almost never thought about the possibility of becoming a mother herself, and yet for a moment, she felt a pang of loss so sharp that her miscarriage might have occurred nine days instead of nine years ago.

Dexter glanced up, his eyes darkening with sudden concern. "Liz, are you sure you're okay? You look awfully pale."

"I'll be fine." She flashed a determined smile, something she seemed to be doing a lot of lately. "But I might go and beg a cup of tea from Mrs. Morton, if she's still in the kitchen."

"She's probably gone to her room. If so, help yourself to whatever you want."

"Thanks." Liz's main purpose wasn't to drink or to eat; it was to escape from the unbearably cozy scene of domestic intimacy. "Good night, Amanda, I'm glad to have met you. See you tomorrow, Dexter."

"Night, Mrs. Meacham."

"I'll join you in the kitchen as soon as we've finished our game."

"There's no need—"

"We have things to talk about," Dexter said quietly. "For one thing, we need to decide what we should do tomorrow. Also, Lieutenant Rodriguez came to see me again this afternoon."

She swung around, looking at him inquiringly. "He's been checking our alibis," he said. Glancing at his daughter, he added, "I'll talk to you later."

"You need a six, Dad," Amanda interjected.

Dexter laid down a domino with a triumphant flourish. "Ha-ha! Now you need a six, too, and I don't think you have one."

Liz left the room. She doubted if either Dexter or his daughter noticed her departure.

THE DOMINO GAME lasted less time than she would have expected. Dexter came into the kitchen just as she finished pouring out her cup of orange-and-cinnamon tea.

"Would you like some?" She gestured to the pot.

"Thanks, but you sit down. I'll get it." He searched in a couple of cupboards until he found a cup and saucer—he evidently didn't spend much time in the kitchen—then sat next to her at the polished wooden table. "Rough day?" he asked softly. "You look beat."

She stirred her tea with great concentration, although she never took sugar. "No worse than yours, I expect."

He smiled grimly. "That leaves plenty of scope for rough. How were things at the office?"

"Busy. Awful."

His smile relaxed slightly. "Rarely have two small words conveyed such a wealth of information. That sums up my day perfectly." He took a sip of tea. "As far as I can tell, the police have moved us up from being run-of-the-mill suspicious characters into being prime suspects. The preliminary pathology results show that Karen died around four-thirty. The highly efficient Lieutenant Rodriguez has checked our schedules and determined that neither of us have alibis. He clearly suspects us of working in collusion to do away with poor Karen."

"He thinks we were working together?"

"He's convinced of it. We were planning to marry again, you see, only Karen inconveniently became pregnant and wouldn't have an abortion. Since U.S. senators from Colorado can't hope to get elected with sex scandals featuring prominently in their résumés, you and I hatched this plan to toss Karen from a window and make it look like suicide."

The scenario was so preposterous that she would have laughed if she hadn't been so scared. "That's pretty far-fetched as a motive for you to commit murder. It's flat out ridiculous for me. What in the world am I supposed to get out of all this?"

"Me. And my money." He caught her look and his mouth twisted into a wry grimace. "My dear Liz, the lieutenant can't be expected to understand that you wouldn't take me if I came gift-wrapped in million-dollar bills."

She had the oddest impression that she could hear pain beneath his flippant words. "For a double layer of packaging I might consider it," she said.

He looked at her long and hard. "That's a considerable improvement over the situation nine years ago. My lawyer said the sound of my name was enough to make you turn green by the time our divorce case hit the courts."

She looked away. "I was very young then."

"Yes." He hesitated. "So was I, you know. Not in years, perhaps, but in experience."

Liz turned around and stared at him in astonishment. "How can you say that? You were the most sophisticated man I'd ever met! You'd already traveled half across the world. You were the Air Force's ace test pilot. You were a millionaire—"

"And I knew no more about falling in love and being married than you did," he interjected quietly. "Aside from acute hormonal spasms when I was in my teens, I'd never been in love until I met you. A lot of the time we were together, my emotions were..."

He didn't finish his sentence and she prompted him. "Yes?"

"Out of control is the best way to describe it, I guess."

She twirled her teacup on its saucer. It was Dresden porcelain, she noticed, antique and beautiful. Probably imported into the States by Dexter's grandfather, who had once been American's ambassador to Germany. It was Germany where Liz had competed in her last, disastrous skating championship. She cradled the delicate china in her hands, as if by doing so she could contain her memories of that awful time.

"What are you thinking about?"

"The Olympics," she replied honestly.

He didn't have to ask which Olympics. They both knew. "That was a bad night for you," he said. "For both of us."

"I was six weeks pregnant," she said suddenly. "I'd torn a ligament in my ankle and I felt so sick I thought I was going to throw up every time I turned my head."

His body stiffened with shock. "Pregnant! Liz, my God! Why didn't you tell me?"

She traced the thin gold rim of the cup with her thumb. "I was . . . afraid you'd be mad at me. Because you said you didn't want children and you thought I was taking birth-control pills."

"And you weren't taking pills?"

She shook her head, then laughed, mocking her younger self. "I wanted to trap you into staying married," she admitted. "So I used the oldest trick in the world. And then, when I found out I really was expecting a baby, I was too scared to tell you. Not to mention telling my coach, who'd have thrown a fit at the prospect of his star athlete going on maternity leave." Her mouth twisted into a painful smile. "I'd worked out the perfect trap, except I was afraid to spring it."

"What happened to the baby, Liz?"

"I miscarried a couple of months later."

"And you still didn't tell me? Good God, was I really such a monster?"

She finally looked up at him. "I don't know. By that time, I couldn't see you clearly anymore. Susan was always in the way, blocking my view."

He stretched out a hand, then allowed it to fall back into his lap without touching her. She realized now—as she never would have nine years earlier—that he was afraid of offending her, afraid of her rejection. His voice when he spoke was tight, not with impatience as she would once have thought, but with regret. "I never was unfaithful to you during our marriage, Liz. Whatever Ali... Whatever anyone may have told you, Susan and I never made love until after you'd divorced me."

"Alison never suggested you and Susan were lovers," she said. "Susan told me herself."

Silence descended, thick, heavy and fraught with tension. "If Susan told you we were lovers during the time you and I were married, then she lied," Dexter said at last. "I'm sorry, Liz. I must have been doing a lousy job of handling my relationships for them to have gotten so screwed up."

"It was a long time ago," she said, and suddenly the trite words were true. She pushed the cup of tea away, leaning back in the chair to ease cramped muscles. "A long time ago, in a faraway place, with people who've changed so much they're hardly the same."

"You've changed," he agreed. "You're softer. More beautiful."

"Thank you." She was shocked by the intensity of pleasure his comment provoked. She got up from the table, carrying the teapot over to the sink so that she could hide the sudden color staining her cheeks. "We'd better get this conversation back to the present, Dexter, or the lieutenant will be pounding on the door to arrest us and we'll have done nothing except trade compliments about how mature we've gotten since we savaged each other in the divorce courts."

"I wish that sounded funny. The bit about the lieutenant coming to arrest us, I mean. But the fact is, I have no alibi. I left a meeting with the manager of Stapleton Airport at three forty-five. I should have arrived here about twenty minutes later. I actually arrived home at five o'clock."

"What happened?" she asked, returning to her chair.

"I went to the library," he said wryly. "The main one, downtown. The meeting with the airport manager had finished a half hour earlier than we expected, and I've been wanting to double-check some facts in a book on Denver's old, ethnic neighborhoods. Nobody was waiting for me, so I grabbed the chance."

"Did you check the book out? There might be a time on the computer."

"No, the book's for reference only. And before you ask, no, I didn't speak to any of the librarians. I knew where the book was shelved and I went straight there."

"It's a lousy alibi, Dex. Don't you have a research staff to double-check facts for you? Important senators don't visit the library unless it's an official visit."

"Liz, honey, you're singing the lieutenant's song. But you're no better off than I am. Rodriguez claims you left your office at the crucial time without telling anybody where you were going."

"Of course I didn't say where I was going!" Liz protested. "That was the whole point of the exercise. The darn phone hadn't stopped ringing all day, so I hid in one of the typists' offices, trying to catch up on my paperwork."

"Where was the typist?"

"Out sick with the flu."

"Well, good luck telling that one to the lieutenant."

Liz laughed, then sobered abruptly. "When I'm with you, I forget to take the situation seriously. Then, as soon as I'm alone, all the reasons why I should be panic-stricken come rushing back. I mean, we could end up in the electric chair, Dex."

"In Colorado they use the gas chamber."

"Gosh and golly, now I feel much better!"

He smiled, reaching out to clasp her hand. Her stomach danced a little jig. "We're going to find out what's behind this, long before things reach that stage, Liz."

Several seconds passed before she gathered her wits sufficiently to move her hand. "Pieter Ullmann was at my apartment tonight," she said, breaking the momentary silence. "From the remarks he dropped about Karen, I guess several people could have been the father of her baby."

"He'd had an affair with her?"

"He said not. But he also claimed she came on to him in a big way."

Dexter frowned. "Odd, isn't it, how we get to know people in such a one-dimensional fashion? I can't even picture Karen as a sexually active woman, let alone a sexually aggressive one. Now that it's too late, I'm feeling guilty because I spent so little time thinking about her as a person. Maybe if I'd been more attentive to her needs, none of this would have happened."

"You're being too hard on yourself. She was an employee, Dexter, not a close friend."

"She was a damn good administrative assistant, that's for sure. We always seemed to exchange the usual chit-chat about our personal lives, and yet once the lieutenant started questioning me, I realized I knew almost nothing about her. Not even trivial things like whether she preferred Beethoven or Bruce Springsteen."

"Rodriguez thinks you're concealing information."

"Of course he does. Unfortunately I'm not. In fact, I wish I knew something—anything—that would give us a starting point to unravel what was going on in Karen's life. I suppose you haven't come up with any wonderful new insights since this morning?"

"Nothing wonderful. But I've been thinking a lot about what you said last night. About how my roommates must have had something in common, something that linked them."

"And you thought of a link?"

"I'm not sure. It's so tenuous, you may think it's silly to mention it."

"At this point, nothing's too silly to mention."

"Well, like I told you, Brian was an engineer and Jill was a social worker, and Karen's basic training was secretarial. But in a weird sort of way, all three of them worked for the government, although their jobs were so different it almost doesn't coun—"

"Explain their connection to the government," Dexter interrupted, his body radiating a sudden tension.

She was startled by his intensity. "Karen's link is obvious. She was your personal assistant, and you're a U.S. senator."

"Go on. What about Jill?"

"She worked as a civilian employee for the navy. The naval shipyards in Bremerton are so huge, they basically employ the whole town, so I never gave her employer a second thought when you asked me last night. She worked in the personnel-management division."

"And Brian?"

"He was a professor of electrical engineering at the university, but he didn't do much teaching, and I think his recent research was in the field of electronics. Almost all his income came from projects funded by the government, and a lot of his work was secret, I do know that."

"Have you any idea what he was working on when he died?"

"Not specifically. Even if it hadn't been secret, I wouldn't have understood what he was doing. Electronic microcircuitry isn't exactly my area of expertise. He mentioned once that he was part of the design team for a new fighter jet that was on order for the Air Force. He was brilliant at his work, everybody agreed on that."

"A new fighter jet," Dexter muttered. He stared abstractedly into the middle distance, then finally rose to his feet. "I need to make a phone call to Washington," he said. "Come into the study, will you? Liz, I think—just possibly—you may be onto something."

"Mind telling me what? You think it's significant that all my roommates worked for the government?"

"Yes, I do, although at the moment I don't see precisely how. What we need is information, and I should get that from my phone call."

Dexter opened the door to his study, shut it behind them, then pressed a section of wall paneling next to the bar. A small, concealed door sprang open to reveal a scarlet telephone. Dexter punched in a long series of numbers, gestured to indicate that Liz should take a seat on the sofa, and waited in patient silence for about thirty seconds.

"This is Senator Rand," he said finally. "I want to speak with Agent Harry Cooper. Patch me through, please."

Liz glanced at her watch. It was ten o'clock in Denver, midnight already in Washington, DC. Agent Cooper either kept late office hours or slept with his scarlet phone next to the pillow. She leaned back against the cushions of the sofa, listening to Dexter identify himself again, first by name and then by a series of numbers.

She wondered why she felt so little surprise at Dexter's active response to her suggestion of a job link among her dead roommates. Perhaps the unreality of her situation was beginning to affect her. From the day Brian died, she had felt distanced from her everyday life, as if she could only react to events, not take charge of them. Three days earlier, for example, she would have said that being alone with Dexter was as unlikely as the possibility that Karen Zeit would be murdered. Now Karen was incontrovertibly dead, and she was spending the second night in a row with her ex-husband. Her world had lost it familiar boundaries.

"Professor Brian Jensen," she heard Dexter say. "An electrical engineer. Full professor. Possibly working on the F-19B fighter jet project. The control panel for all the F-19s came out of Seattle. I want you to find out anything and everything you can about him. He supposedly committed suicide four months ago."

There was a short silence, followed by Dexter's reply. "In Seattle. He shot himself, then fell out of his apartment window. There must have been a police investigation."

Another pause, much longer this time, then Dexter's reply. "I need this information, Cooper. I need it soon. I'm asking as a personal favor. I'll beg, if you want me to."

Silence. "Thanks, Cooper. I owe you one. By the way, I'm beginning to wonder if the leak is from Denver, and not from DC. You might want to talk to your chief about that. Maybe we have the undercover operative in the wrong place, which would explain our lack of progress.

If we do, Karen's death gives us the perfect excuse to introduce somebody at this end. I'm going to need a new assistant.''

Another pause. ''Fine. But please, just make sure she can type and knows something about party politics.'' A final brief moment of silence, and then Dexter said goodnight, hanging up the phone and closing the wall cabinet.

''Is that a secret phone?'' Liz asked, not sure whether to be impressed or amused.

''Not very secret. Everybody who has access to this room knows about it. But it's supposedly 'safe.' The signal's scrambled, so it's protected against wiretaps.''

''Do all senators get a safe red phone?''

''Not all of them. A lot depends on their committee assignments. I chair the Senate Committee on Defense Appropriations, so a great deal of top-secret material comes into my hands. Not only secret because of policy decisions, but because the technology is new.''

''And that's why you got the phone?''

''Part of the reason.'' Dexter came and sat beside her on the sofa. Their knees touched, and she carefully moved away.

''I feel like I'm dragging out your teeth without benefit of anesthesia,'' she said. ''Can you tell me what that phone call was all about?''

''There have been leaks of classified information from my Washington office,'' Dexter said slowly. ''Nothing too important until a couple of months ago, when the specifications for a section of the new F-19B fighter jet turned up for sale on the international black market.''

''But how do you know all this? Presumably black-market arms dealers don't go around shouting to the world about their sale item of the week.''

"I can't answer your question, Liz. I've already revealed far more than I officially should. Let's just say certain government agencies manage to keep effective tabs on who's selling what to whom."

"Are you allowed to tell me why those government agencies decided the black-market specifications came from your office?"

"Top-secret documents have an extremely limited distribution, and each copy is marked with identifying data. The specifications that turned up on the black market were obviously photocopies of material that had come from my office."

"If you haven't found out who was responsible for the original leak, how do you stop future ones?"

"Liz, I know I sound like a bad actor in a thirties movie, but the answer is: *We have our ways.*"

"Do your ways work?"

"Hopefully. So far they seem to be working."

"It's certainly a strange coincidence that Brian should have been working on the F-19 plane when he died."

"Very strange. Which is why I've asked my contact at the FBI to run a comprehensive check on Brian Jensen's background."

"Couldn't you ask the FBI to run checks on Karen Zeit, as well?"

"You heard my conversation with Harry Cooper. The FBI is short of money and staff, and they're already expending too much of both on my office. I had to beg to get anything done on Brian Jensen. Unless the Colorado law-enforcement authorities ask for FBI assistance, we haven't a hope of persuading the Bureau to run two background checks simultaneously. Besides, Karen lived with you and worked with me. Between the two of us, surely we ought to be able to come up with some information about her, once we start digging."

"I brought her address book with me." Liz searched in her purse, then produced the slender maroon notebook with a flourish. "There aren't too many names in it, which should make it easier to track people down."

Dexter took the book and quickly thumbed through the pages. "The lieutenant slipped up, didn't he? Why didn't he take this away with him?"

"Karen kept it with her recipe books in the kitchen. I guess the police passed right over it."

"Hmm. Your name's here with a work phone number, so is mine with a DC address and number. Here's Evan Howard's home address and phone number." Dexter flicked over the pages. "Home addresses and numbers for all the people in my Colorado office. Phone numbers for the hairdresser, the doctor and the dentist. An address for Pieter Ullmann. No phone number. And there are a dozen names I don't recognize. How about you?"

Liz leaned over so that she could see the pages as Dexter turned them. Her body was pressed against his from shoulder to thigh, and suddenly, over the chasm of nine years' separation, she felt the achingly familiar rush of sexual awareness. She couldn't move away without drawing attention to her reaction—which Dexter had given no sign of sharing—so she drew in a deep breath and reminded herself that she was a mature woman of twenty-eight, not a hormone-flooded teenager of nineteen.

"Rachel Landers is a woman Karen took gourmet cooking lessons with each Saturday. They went somewhere in Colorado Springs." Liz was delighted to hear that her voice sounded cool, crisp and businesslike. Unfortunately, the rest of her wasn't doing so well. She drew in another deep breath. "Bev Dixon and Rita Kominsky are tennis partners. I don't know any of the others. They all seem to be men."

"Did you notice something odd, though?" Dexter's voice was a little husky and he coughed to clear it.

"They're all Denver or Colorado Springs addresses," Liz said, wondering why he didn't move away, now that they'd finished looking at the address book. "Is that what you mean?"

"Yes." Dexter's voice was still husky. "Karen only came to Colorado from Kansas City two years ago. You'd think she'd have one or two friends from Kansas that she kept in touch with."

"Maybe she filed those addresses somewhere else."

"Maybe." Dexter closed the notebook with a snap and got purposefully to his feet. Liz tried hard not to feel bereft.

"Anyway," he said, "it seems to me our Saturday morning is mapped out for us. We have to try to talk to everybody on this list, starting with the people whose names neither of us recognize."

"Sounds good. What about Amanda, though? Won't she resent it if we leave her alone all day?"

"Mrs. Morton takes her to karate class in the morning—"

"Karate! I thought little girls were supposed to dream about ballet and pink tutus."

He grinned. "Amanda seems to prefer white trousers and stinging chops to the head. Anyway, she always brings a couple of friends over for lunch afterward, so she won't miss me. But I have promised to spend the evening with her."

"That works out well, because I've agreed to have dinner with Mikhail."

"Are you planning to spend the night with him?" Dexter's question was a miracle of neutrality. "Just so as I know whether to lock up the house or not," he added.

Liz looked at him steadily. "No," she said. "I'm not planning to spend the night with Mikhail tomorrow, although I often do."

Dexter turned away, his movement abrupt. "Would you like a nightcap? A brandy? A diet soda?"

"No thanks. But you're right, we should get to bed."

Her words fell like stones into the sudden silence, weighted with a meaning she had never intended to give them. Dexter shoved his hands into the pockets of his pants, as if he didn't know what else to do with them.

"It's still there, isn't it?" he said quietly. "For both of us."

"I don't know what you me..." The lie died away, unfinished. "Yes," she admitted, meeting Dexter's gaze. "It's still there. But I realize now that people don't have to...to get involved just because they're attracted to each other."

Dexter came and stood in front of her. His dark brows lifted, giving him a sardonic, almost derisive air. "You think now we've talked about it, we'll be able to ignore the tension between us and get on with more important things?"

"We should be able to. We're mature adults."

"How adult?" he murmured, pulling her into his arms and holding her lightly against his lean, hard strength. Liz tried to ignore the shiver of delight that coursed through her, but she didn't move away.

His head bent slowly toward her, his breath warm against her skin. Against her will, her eyes drifted closed, so she didn't see the moment when his mouth covered hers, but she felt his touch with every fiber of her being.

With a quiver almost of despair, Liz melted into his arms. Why did Dexter's kiss turn her to fire, where other men's attempts at lovemaking left her cool and faintly bored? The years of separation hadn't dulled her memory of what it was like to share Dexter's bed, and when he trailed tiny, seeking kisses around the edge of her mouth, she had a brief moment of madness when she wondered what depth of pleasure would be in store, if she allowed herself to follow him up the stairs into the welcome darkness of his room.

His hands left her shoulders and slid into the tight knot of her hair, pulling out the pins so that he could run his hands through the silken strands. For a single insane minute she allowed herself to be drawn unreservedly into the kiss, until the heat flooding her body triggered some primitive warning that soon she would leave herself with no choice but to surrender.

Panting, shaking, she drew herself away. "No!" she whispered. "Please, Dex, don't make me feel this way. . . ."

As soon as she had spoken, she realized just how much those few words revealed. Dexter, thank God, didn't challenge her. Instead, he lightly touched a forefinger to her lips.

"You taste even better now you've grown up," he said.

Chapter Seven

The first part of Saturday morning taught Liz how frustrating—not to mention exhausting—a supposedly simple investigation could be. She and Dexter called first on Karen's tennis partners, who agreed that Karen played tennis regularly and well. None of them had any idea who her other friends might be, or what she did when she wasn't playing tennis.

Dexter suggested that their next move should be to check out the men on the list. Six of the dozen men listed in Karen's notebook weren't home. Another had moved out of state, leaving no forwarding address. Four were at home and willing to answer questions, but had nothing more to say than that they'd met Karen only recently and didn't know her very well.

The last person on their Most Wanted list turned out to be an airline steward, who'd just flown back to Denver from Hong Kong. The news of Karen's death clearly came as an unpleasant shock to him, since he hadn't read any American newspapers for a couple of days. His surprise might have contributed to his willingness to talk but he—like all the others—denied being a close friend of the dead woman.

"Karen was just somebody I met at a party, if you know what I mean."

"Yes, I know what you mean," Dexter responded neutrally. "Did she spend more than one night with you?"

"How d'you know she spent the night?" The steward's voice contained a heavy touch of belligerence. "I never said anything about taking her home, and I sure didn't get her pregnant."

"Karen mentioned something once...." Liz carefully didn't specify what her roommate had mentioned, and the steward jumped in.

"Hey, whatever she said, it wasn't any great love affair between us, you know. She was feeling lonely and upset about some guy or other who'd dumped on her, and I offered her a few hours of fun. To take her mind off things, you know? We only met a couple of times after that first night."

Dexter spoke quickly. "Did she tell you anything about the man who'd been treating her so badly? His name, perhaps, or where he lived?"

The steward gave a reminiscent smile and winked. "Hey, she might have done, if you know what I mean. I guess I never paid too much attention to what Karen said. That little lady was some bundle of fire, a regular crackerjack in bed. We were really something together." He caught Liz's eye and saw that his kiss-and-tell boasting wasn't going over too well.

"Maybe I do remember one thing," he amended. "This guy who'd dumped on her—she mentioned once that she worked for him. Like he was her boss, if you know what I mean, and he was taking advantage."

Dexter's face revealed nothing of what he was thinking. "Yes," he said. "We know exactly what you mean."

Liz quickly asked another question, but the rest of their conversation revealed little more than that the steward remained very impressed with his own skill in the bedroom.

"He and Pieter Ullmann sound like soul mates," Liz commented as they returned to the car. "We should introduce them to each other."

"He certainly seems like a bad choice of companion, if Karen was feeling unsure of herself," Dexter agreed. He clicked the seat belt closed, not looking at Liz when he spoke again. "Feel free to report what we just learned to Lieutenant Rodriguez. In fact, it's probably your civic duty to report everything the man said."

Liz stared out of the window, although she didn't really see either the budding trees or the sunny stretch of suburban road. Despite the steward's damning words, she had the strongest conviction that Dexter wasn't the father of Karen's baby. She wondered if she was a complete fool to continue believing in his innocence. Nine years ago, she had allowed sexual attraction to overcome her common sense and even her own self-interest. Was she doing the same thing again?

Dexter's voice broke into her reverie. "For what it's worth, Liz, I'll repeat that Karen and I were never lovers, so I can't be the father of the child she was carrying. Although, God knows, after what that steward said, there's no reason for you to believe me."

"Actually there is." Liz's thoughts became clearer in her own mind as she spoke. "In the first place, I don't think you'd ever get involved with somebody working in your office. Why would you bother when you have so many other choices? Washington is full of eligible women who'd love to be the mistress of a young, powerful senator, and you like being a senator too much to risk your job over a love affair with one of your staff.''

He smiled ruefully. ''I'm not sure if that's a flattering assessment of my character or not. Anyway, it's something of a moot point, because I don't think most people would buy your reasoning. Elected officials have affairs all the time with partners who are flagrantly unsuitable. Despite all the aggressive journalists dogging their footsteps, they always assume they'll be able to keep the details of their personal lives hidden.''

''You may be right. But there's a more important reason why I don't believe you killed Karen. I've seen you with Amanda and I'm sure you'd never murder a woman who was carrying your baby. If Karen had been pregnant with your child, you'd have married her—even if only to have a fighting chance of claiming custody.''

''Rodriguez would say Karen might not have told me she was pregnant.''

''He can't have it both ways. If you didn't know she was pregnant, you had no reason to kill her.''

Dexter sent her one of the smiles that always made her heart turn over. Damn him. ''Thanks, Liz,'' he said simply. ''I appreciate the vote of confidence.'' He turned on the ignition. ''Well, if you're not bound and determined to head for the nearest police station, we have an interesting question to resolve. If Karen didn't mean me when she referred to her boss, who did she mean?''

''An old boss from Kansas City?''

''Could be.''

''Why did she leave her last job?''

He frowned in concentration. ''She'd worked on somebody's political campaign, and they'd lost, if I'm remembering correctly.''

''Who checked her references?''

"Evan Howard does all the screening of candidates for my Colorado offices. I'll ask him to check the personnel files and get back to me with some names and addresses." He gestured to the notebook lying on Liz's lap. "Do we have any other hot leads in Denver?"

"Except for the people who are out of town, there are no more men left on our list."

"Then let's go visit one of the women. Unless you're hungry?"

She shook her head. "Not at all."

"Then how about visiting some of the people from my office? Maybe she indulged in heart-to-hearts over the watercooler."

"We could try them. But Rachel Landers's home is much closer than anybody who works for you. She has an apartment on Havana, and that's only ten minutes from here."

"Okay." Dexter headed the car west. "Rachel Landers? Wasn't she the woman Karen took cooking classes with?"

"Yes. They went to some retired master chef in Colorado Springs. If Karen ever mentioned the chef's name, I've forgotten it, but he's obviously darn good. Karen always came back to Denver with the most delicious food. I never accepted invitations to eat out on Saturday nights."

"She never invited you to go with her to cooking class?"

"She was too smart for that. You know me and kitchens."

"Still?"

"Still." She smiled. "Not many people have my astonishing level of skill, you know. There can't be many adult females in the world routinely able to scorch water."

Dexter's grin changed to a frown. "You know, I could have sworn Karen didn't enjoy cooking, although I can't remember why I have that impression."

"You must be mistaken. Nobody could prepare food like we ate on Saturdays, unless they enjoyed cooking. Karen was a real expert, Dex." She peered out of the window. "Here's Rachel's building. Her apartment number's 304."

Rachel Landers, a plain woman of about thirty-five, eyes almost invisible behind pebble-lensed glasses, was at home and more than willing to cooperate. Delighted to be entertaining a United States senator and a former world figure-skating champion—even if the morning newspaper had implied they might well be guilty of murder—she insisted on serving them freshly brewed coffee and homemade pastries.

"I can see you put your gourmet cookery classes to wonderful use," Liz said, finishing a mouthful of flaky, raspberry-filled turnover.

Rachel blushed with pleasure. "When you punch numbers in a bank all day, it's nice to do something creative on the weekend. I made those pastries last night. They're quite simple, once you learn how to manipulate the Greek phyllo dough."

Liz suddenly realized how surprising it was that they had found Rachel at home. "Has your class been canceled for this morning?" she asked.

"Oh no, but it'll take me a while to find another ride." She pointed to her glasses. "I see quite well close up, but I'm not safe behind the wheel of a car. Chef Robert is the best teacher in the Rocky Mountain region, and Karen made his class possible for me. I was very grateful to her. I shall miss her a lot. For the ride and for the company."

Liz savored her last bite of pastry. "That was wonderful, Rachel. You're an even better cook than Karen was."

"Thank you." A hot red blush crept up Rachel's neck. Not a flush of pleasure, Liz realized, but of acute embarrassment.

"Did you and Karen meet at a cooking class?" she asked, wondering what could possibly have upset Rachel in such an innocuous compliment.

"No." The blush receded. "I do a little bit of catering on the side, and a customer recommended me to that nice young man who won the Olympic medal for figure skating. Oh, you probably know him, since you're in that line of work yourself. Pieter Ullmann. He was so young to be hosting a party, but he'd just won his gold medal and he was celebrating."

Liz felt a little leap of excitement. "You met Karen at Pieter's house? That must have been over a year ago."

"Yes, like I said, it was just after Pieter had come back from the Winter Olympics."

Liz wasn't sure whether to be excited or disappointed. On the one hand, it was interesting to learn that Karen's acquaintance with Pieter stretched much farther back than he'd been willing to admit. On the other hand, she'd been half hoping that Rachel would reveal some entirely new name and set of relationships. She smothered a small sigh of frustration, recognizing that she and Dexter were clutching at straws. There was no good reason for a casual acquaintance like Rachel to have any deep insight into Karen's personality and friends.

Dexter returned his coffee cup to the tray. "How many of Chef Robert's classes had Karen actually attended with you, Miss Landers?"

Again the ugly red flush stained Rachel's neck and pushed into her cheeks. She sat down hard on a nearby chair. "I don't know what to say, Senator," she mumbled, flashing a wary glance from Dexter to Liz. "You see, I read in the papers that she was pregnant."

"What has Karen's pregnancy got to do with her cooking lessons?" Dexter asked. "Was she having an affair with the chef?"

Rachel stared fixedly at her sensible, low-heeled shoes. The flush had now crept up to the tips of her ears. "The cookery classes were just a cover," she whispered. "Karen never attended them."

Liz stared in surprise. "Never attended? But who cooked all that wonderful food she brought home?"

Rachel hung her head even lower. "I did. Karen paid me for everything she took home. There's only me, you see, and I can't eat everything I prepare."

Dexter leaned forward, and although his voice remained calm and soothing, Liz could see tension in every line of his body. She reflected that nine years earlier she would have heard the calm and totally missed the inner tension. Odd how she had been married to Dexter and perceived him less clearly than she did now, when they were mere acquaintances.

"Why did Karen bother to set up such an elaborate pretense?" Dexter asked. "Do you know why she wanted everyone to think she was attending cookery school, when she wasn't?"

Rachel looked away, blinking rapidly behind her pebble glasses. "Yes, I know. She was—having an affair."

"With a married man, you mean?"

"That's what I assumed. Why else would she have to sneak around and hide what she was doing? I sometimes wondered if her lover was in an important public position, as well as being married, you know?'' Rachel threw an embarrassed, inquiring look in Dexter's direction.

''I'm not married,'' he said quietly. ''I admired Karen as an employee, but that was the extent of our relationship, and we never had an affair.''

''Oh, of course not! I never meant...I don't want you to think, Senator...I'm sure you wouldn't dream...''

Liz took pity on Rachel's floundering efforts at a disclaimer. ''Karen never mentioned the name of her lover to you, Miss Landers?''

''Oh no, she never said anything specific about him. Just how much she loved him and then, toward the end, how he wouldn't treat their relationship seriously. How he'd taken advantage of her loyalty.'' She looked up, her expression apologetic and more than a little guilty. ''I know I shouldn't have covered up for Karen. Some poor wife probably spent her Saturday mornings wondering what her husband was up to. But Chef Robert is such a wonderful instructor, and he teaches the business side of catering as well as the food presentation. It's my dream to set up a full-time catering service....'' Once again her voice trailed away.

''I doubt if Karen would have ended her affair, even if you'd refused to cover for her, Miss Landers. She'd have found another alibi. I don't think you need carry around too big a burden of guilty conscience.''

Dexter's words seemed to cheer Rachel, and she perked up enough to insist on pouring them another cup of coffee and boxing a chocolate torte for them to take home.

''I'll call on you when my daughter needs her next birthday cake,'' Dexter promised, and Rachel's answering smile was so gratified that her plain face became almost attractive.

"Do you want to chat with some of your employees now?" Liz asked when they had said their farewells and returned to the car.

"You don't sound thrilled at the prospect."

"I just think we're going to hear more of the same stuff we've been hearing all day. You might as well save yourself the hassle of driving all over Denver, and talk with them on Monday." Liz got into the car and waited while Dexter filtered into the stream of traffic. "Surely if one of your employees knew anything really startling about Karen, they'd have told you by now."

"I'm sure they would. It's getting late anyway, so we may as well head for home."

Liz muttered in exasperation. "Dex, have you noticed that Karen never said a word about her love life to you or to me, but she seemed willing to reveal her deepest emotional problems to virtually everyone else? People who were barely acquaintances."

"I did notice. I also noticed that she may have talked a lot, but she never seemed to give people any practical details about her lover. Was he old or young? Handsome or ugly? Rich or poor? Where did he work? Where did he live?"

"Presumably he lived in Colorado Springs. That's where she went every Saturday."

"Maybe. Or maybe not. It's only a forty-five-minute drive from the southern suburbs of Denver to the Springs, and there are a dozen motels along the highway."

"We know that he was married, and that Karen claimed he was her boss," Liz pointed out.

"Do we? I'd say those are conclusions people drew, which might tell us more about the people drawing the conclusions than they do about Karen. The fact is, we've spoken to eight people this morning, and not one of them really knew anything about her or her lover. In fact, nobody seems to know anything more about her than you and I."

"But why would she be so secretive?"

Dexter shrugged. "The obvious answer is that she had something to hide."

"You mean she was scared to reveal the name of her lover?"

"Something like that. It seems to me that either Karen or her lover stood to lose a lot if their affair became public knowledge."

"Nowadays, it's difficult to imagine how any affair could be that threatening."

"I may have become paranoid in the last two days," Dexter remarked, "but I keep thinking that if Karen had wanted to set me up as her murderer, she couldn't have done a better job. All this rushing around town, muttering dire things about her cruel boss and her broken heart. Naturally everyone concluded she was talking about me."

"I agree, but she couldn't have known she would be murdered, so she couldn't have been setting you up, even if she had some obscure motive for revenge."

"She couldn't have been setting me up for murder," Dexter agreed, "but how about for a paternity suit?"

"And the murderer just took advantage of the groundwork Karen had laid, so to speak?"

"It sounds possible, don't you think?"

"Except that Karen was an intelligent, educated woman. She must have known that blood tests today can determine paternity with ninety-nine percent accuracy. And if you weren't the father, how could she set you up?"

Dexter frowned as he turned the car off Alameda and headed toward his home. "Maybe she was just going to *threaten* me with a paternity suit, unless I paid her and her lover lots of money."

"That's it!" Liz squirmed around inside her seat belt so that she could look at Dexter. "Of course, that's it, Dex! She hoped you would pay up to avoid the bad publicity. She knew all the voters would say 'there's no smoke without a fire,' and that half of them would read about the lawsuit but never get around to reading the verdict, when you were proven not to be the father. Sometimes an accusation doesn't have to be true for it to cause a heck of a lot of damage."

"I guess that's possible," Dexter agreed slowly. "Except that sort of scheming doesn't fit the efficient, bland Karen I knew."

"But then it seems you didn't know her very well. Neither did I."

"True. She's the last woman I'd ever have suspected of being promiscuous. I feel like I'm watching a character in a play, who's repressed Miss Prim-and-Proper in Act One. Then in Act Two she fixes her hair, rips off her glasses and bingo!—she's a sultry bombshell."

"I guess this morning's investigations have taught us something," Liz said. "For whatever reason, Karen was playing a part with both of us. And she lied a lot."

He grimaced. "Great return for seven hours of running around town. Damn, but I wish we could come up with a few more names to check out. At least then I'd have the illusion we were achieving something."

"Remember five or six of the men listed in Karen's address book weren't home."

"I'll try to reach some of them by phone early this evening, or first thing tomorrow." He glanced at his watch. "Probably tomorrow. Today's pretty well shot. Normally I'd ask Evan, but he's worked two eighteen-hour stints back-to-back. He deserves the rest of the weekend to himself."

Liz glanced at her own watch. "I hadn't realized how late it is. I'll have to hurry if I'm going to be in Colorado Springs by six-thirty."

Dexter made a smooth turn into the long driveway leading to his house. "I have a dinner meeting tonight with a dozen or so suburban mayors, and it would be wonderful if you could join me."

"I'm sorry," she said. "I've already accepted another invitation. Didn't I mention that I was having dinner with Mikhail?"

"Possibly. I don't remember." Dexter's voice was cool. "Are you sure I can't persuade you to change your plans? Take pity on the poor journalists. Think how exciting they could make their Sunday editions, if we turned up together at the same function."

Liz felt a wave of frustrated irritation, an unpleasant reminder of feelings that had been all too common in the days of her marriage. "No, you can't persuade me to change my mind," she said, her voice as cool as his. "Offering myself up as journalistic fodder isn't my idea of Saturday-night fun. Besides, I've not seen Mikhail since Karen died, and I'm looking forward to relaxing with him for a couple of hours."

"He's done some outstanding work for the Special Olympics Committee," Dexter said. The praise seemed torn from him, as if it hurt to admit any good points about Liz's brother-in-law. For some reason, Mikhail—along with Alison—had always been high on Dexter's list of nonapproved persons. For the first time, Liz thought to question why.

"What in the world has Mikhail done to make you despise him, Dexter?"

"Nothing," he said curtly. He punched the button on the remote-controlled garage-door opener, then broke a momentary silence by turning to her and giving a rueful smile.

"Sorry," he said. "I'm being a pain in the neck. The fact is that I don't like Mikhail, and I've no reason to dislike him. It makes me feel guilty, which is why I snap every time someone mentions his name."

Liz didn't reply for several seconds, then she turned and met Dexter's gaze with a dawning sense of wonderment. "Do you know, Dex, that's the first time in our entire relationship that you've ever admitted to possessing a single irrational feeling?"

"You sound as if you think that's good."

"It's more than good. It's marvelous! I feel like breaking into a rousing rendition of the 'Hallelujah' chorus."

His eyes gleamed. "Feel free," he said, drawing the car to a halt inside the garage. "As I remember, you have a lovely voice. Although I never recall hearing you sing *The Messiah*."

Against her will, Liz felt her cheeks flame with heat. She had a tuneful but oddly throaty voice, which imparted a sensual promise to even the most innocuous of tunes. Dexter had once told her that she could make "Yankee Doodle Dandy" sound like a love song. Liz had only ever sung for him in the privacy of their bedroom, and her songs had almost never reached the end. They would both be lying on the bed, tugging at each other's zippers and buttons, long before the final verse.

"Dexter, we don't have time for chitchat," she said, avoiding his gaze. "It's over an hour's drive from here to Mikhail's house, and I still have to shower and change."

Dexter wasn't to be deterred from his line of questioning, although he led the way out of the garage into the rear hallway. "Do you still play the guitar?" he asked.

"Not in the past few months," she said. "I haven't felt much like playing since Brian died."

Dexter halted his swift progress along the corridor and turned to face her. His hands lightly touched her shoulders. "I'm sorry, Liz," he said softly. "I have this urge to catch up on what's been happening in your life, and I keep forgetting this is the third time within a few months that you've lost a friend."

The warmth of his hands felt almost like a caress. The sensation was strangely comforting. "The odd thing is," she admitted, "now that I know there's a chance my roommates were all murdered, I actually feel better. I've felt so unbearably guilty from the moment Brian died. You know, going over and over in my mind if there had been any clues that should have warned me he was in trouble."

"And were there?" Somehow she found herself held in a loose embrace, while one of Dexter's hands stroked gently up and down her back.

"He'd been irritable on occasion and he apologized by saying his research wasn't going well. But if he didn't commit suicide, then his mood can't be important, can it?"

Dexter's arms tightened around her. "Probably not, but—"

"Senator!" Evan Howard appeared at the end of the corridor, noticed that his boss was not alone, and gave Liz a halfhearted nod. Without haste, Dexter released Liz from his grasp and returned Evan's frazzled greeting with a friendly smile.

"You look as if this hasn't been a good day, Evan."

"It's been an awful day. Karen's file is missing from our personnel records, and some squirt of a police sergeant virtually accused me of destroying it to protect you. Then Lieutenant Rodriguez came around and when he found out you weren't home, he acted like you'd caught the first available flight to South America."

"He must have been reassured when you told him we'd only gone to Aurora."

"Hell, Dexter, how can you joke at a time like this? Do you know what the lieutenant has discovered? There are no records for Karen prior to the time she arrived in Denver. Her name and social-security number were fakes. Or at least they were stolen. They belonged to some baby who died in a car accident."

"Fakes!" Liz exclaimed. "So we don't even know Karen's real name?"

"Nothing. We don't know anything about her."

Liz subsided into stunned silence, while Dexter stared abstractedly into the distance, his expression unreadable. Evan began to look calmer, now that his revelations had produced a suitably amazed response. He shepherded the unresisting Liz and Dexter into the living room.

"What about our reference checks?" Dexter queried. "We always run a routine credit check, and call at least two work references. How can we have done that for someone who has no past?"

"Of course she had a past when I checked on her!" Evan almost exploded. "Damn it, I spoke to Harry Spinkoff's campaign manager. A guy called John Booth. I even remember the name, because I thought how odd it was for parents to inflict the same name as Lincoln's assassin on their kids."

Dexter cut into what was obviously becoming an endless flow of aggrieved reminiscence. "And you gave all this information to the police?"

"I told them she passed our investigation with flying colors. Banks, doctors, credit bureau, security—the whole caboodle. Everything checked out. Except they don't seem to believe I did any of it, because I can't find the darn file. How could it possibly go missing right at this crucial point? We never lose paperwork."

"Of course it isn't missing," Dexter said with a touch of impatience. "It's been stolen." He got up and walked to the door, seeming to remember Liz's and Evan's presence only at the last minute.

"I have to make a couple of phone calls," he said, and left the room without any further attempt at an explanation.

Evan pulled out his handkerchief and patted his forehead. "Why doesn't he just admit the darn baby was his and have done with it?" he muttered.

Liz looked at him coldly. "Possibly because it wasn't."

"Then who took the file? He's the only person with access to those cabinets apart from me."

Her temper flared, chiefly because she was furious with herself for defending Dexter. Why was it that after only a couple of sweet smiles, she was ready to jump through the hoop for the darn man?

"He's the only person with legitimate access, Mr. Howard. Hasn't it occurred to you yet that somebody is trying very hard to set Dexter Rand up for murder?"

Chapter Eight

After coping with Evan Howard, not to mention all the other frustrations of the day, it was a relief to turn into Mikhail's neat, flower-bordered driveway. Over the past few years, since his escape from Soviet Russia, Mikhail had become more than a brother-in-law to Liz; he had become her closest friend. She had moved to Colorado at his urging, and even before her move, when she had been living in Ohio and then in Seattle, they had seen each other frequently. Their shared interest in skating and their mutual love of Alison gave strong roots to their friendship.

Mikhail already had the door open by the time she parked the car. "The caviar's on ice!" he called out. "So's the vodka."

She grinned, appreciating the familiar routine in a world suddenly adrift. "Those slimy fish eggs are all yours, Mikhail, and you know it. Where's my fried chicken?"

He made a comical face of disgust, tossing his brown, windblown hair out of his eyes. "Your grease-and-cholesterol snack is warming in the oven. You can smell it right out here."

"Mmm-mmm. Yummy. Thank heaven you're not my trainer, you old grouch." She brushed her cheek against his in greeting. "Pieter is welcome to you, slave driver, gold medal and all."

"Pieter never breaks his training," Mikhail responded tranquilly. "That's part of the reason he won at the Olympics. Your trainer wasn't strict enough with you."

"So you keep telling me." Liz walked into the family room that led off the kitchen and curled up in her favorite armchair. "Ease up, old codger! I'm not in training for anything anymore."

"Except a heart attack," he muttered in mock disapproval. "And old codger, what means this?"

"A term of affection," she said, her eyes bright as she glanced up at him. "Oh, Mikhail, I'm glad to be here. These past few days have been hell."

"Now you are here you can relax." He poured her a vodka and tonic, adding a slice of fresh lime before handing her the glass. He took his own vodka neat, Russian-style, without ice. That, apparently, didn't offend his health consciousness. He put a platter of dip and raw vegetables on a coffee table comfortably within reach of Liz's chair, then took his own seat nearby. "Do you want to talk about things, Lizushka?"

She was surprised to find that she did. She launched into a detailed account of finding Karen's body, trying her best to share with Mikhail the horror she had felt in experiencing the same terrible trauma three times within four months. She described as honestly as she could the strain of the press conference and the frustration of her unproductive investigations with Dexter. The only element missing from her story was the unexpected ambivalence of her personal feelings toward her ex-husband.

Since she wasn't ready to admit those feelings even to herself, she saw no reason to expose her idiocy to Mikhail's brotherly scorn.

When she finally ran out of steam, he took her glass and insisted on refilling it. "Your first drink barely smelled the vodka bottle," he said, when she reminded him that she had to drive back to town. "Besides, what is this nonsense, *dorogoya*? You don't have to drive anywhere, you can stay here. You should stay here. Why must you rush back to Denver?"

She blushed, knowing that Mikhail didn't approve of Dexter any more than Dexter liked Mikhail. "I need to look in at the office tomorrow and clear up my mountain of paperwork." It wasn't precisely a lie. She had every intention of spending the morning in the office.

Mikhail frowned, and she tried to gloss over a tight little silence. "How a company as small as Peperito's can generate so many internal memos, I'll never know."

"Too many desktop computers," Mikhail said, banishing his scowl. "Once everybody finds out how to make columns on their screens, they feel compelled to invent figures to go inside their columns." He tossed off his glass of vodka in a single swallow. "You haven't told me the whole story, have you, Liz? You're not just going back to Denver. You're staying with that monster of an ex-husband, aren't you?"

She swished the lime around in her drink. "Yes. How did you know?"

His smile was rueful. "Lizushka, you are the world's worst liar. Your nose turns pink with embarrassment if you try to tell the smallest fib."

"Right at the moment, he isn't being much of a monster, Mikhail. He's too busy trying to find out what was going on in Karen's life."

"*Dorogoya*, you are not only the world's worst liar, you are also the world's most softhearted fool. Your miserable ex-husband knows exactly what was going on with Karen. He was having an affair with her and got her pregnant. Can you not read the newspapers, Liz? Have you not heard the police detective interviewed on TV? What is his name, this lieutenant?"

"Rodriguez," she said absently. "Mikhail, I know the evidence looks damning. But when the lieutenant finds out about my other two roommates, he's going to think I'm involved in something, too. And Lord knows, nobody could understand less about what's going on than me."

"And because you are guilty of nothing, you assume Dexter is equally innocent? *Dorogoya*, you should move to the Soviet Union. My former government needs citizens like you."

She laughed, more than a little embarrassed by her apparent gullibility. "Most people would say you're right, Mikhail, I'm sure. But in my heart of hearts, I know Dexter isn't any more guilty than I am. Dexter is too smart to plan a crime and leave himself such an obvious suspect. Someone is setting him up."

The oven pinged and Mikhail rose to his feet. "And just who do you think is setting up the great Senator Rand? Who could possibly plan such a thing? They would need to know that Karen was pregnant, for one thing—"

"Half the town seems to have known that," Liz said. "In fact, I had moments today when I wondered if Dexter and I were the only people in Denver who didn't know Karen was having an affair with a married man."

Mikhail smiled sympathetically, wrinkling his nose as he handed Liz her plate of reheated chicken and biscuits. "Well, perhaps you are right, and anyway, it is not of great importance to us whether or not your ex-husband seduced his secrétary. While we eat, let us talk of more cheerful subjects. I have happy news to report to you, Lizushka."

A tiny break in his voice caused Liz to look up. "Mikhail?" she asked. "It isn't—is it your mother?"

He nodded, stretching his mouth into a huge grin as he reached behind the cushion to produce a letter written on heavy, embossed paper. "You have guessed it," he said. "Read what I have received from the embassy."

Liz laughed, sharing his happiness. "Mikhail, I don't read Russian."

"I forgot. Alison, you know, had begun to learn." For once, the mention of his dead wife brought no sadness to Mikhail's eyes. "In brief, the letter says that my mother has completed all the necessary paperwork, and that regional approval has been given to her request for an exit visa."

"Thank God for *glasnost*," Liz breathed. "Oh, Mikhail, what wonderful news!"

"I do not become too excited," he cautioned. "But my mother requires only one more step, this one from the ministry in Moscow."

Liz had spent five years following Mikhail's tortured efforts to secure an exit visa for his elderly mother. Their hopes had been high on several occasions in the past, so she knew better than to assume "one more stamp" would be a trivial detail in the endless progression of setbacks and false hopes. "How long do you think the final approval might take?" she asked cautiously.

"One day is sufficient for my mother to travel to Moscow, if she receives permission to buy an airline ticket." He shrugged with Slavic resignation. "If the authorities decide to be difficult, then we may still be talking of years."

Liz sought for something comforting to say, and found little. Her faith in Soviet officialdom was no deeper than Mikhail's. "Surely the embassy wouldn't have written the letter unless things were looking good?"

Mikhail smiled sadly. "Lizushka, you know better than that. But I allow myself a little bit of hope and today—yes, today I am truly optimistic. I do not allow myself to think that tomorrow I may again be in the depths of despair. Now eat up. Your chicken gets cold, and I have more good news. I spoke yesterday on the phone with my mother."

"But that's great! The authorities allowed your call to go through without any hassle?"

"They did. And she sounds in excellent health, most cheerful. She has been receiving the money I send, and has bought a new cooking stove." Mikhail chuckled. "She is the envy of the neighborhood, and very pleased with herself."

Liz swallowed hard over the sudden lump in her throat. "Mikhail, you know I'm counting the days for you."

He gave her hand a grateful squeeze. "I know, *dorogoya*. And since we are talking of mothers, what is the latest news from Durango?"

"The head nurse called the other day, and I visited with Mom two weeks ago. Nothing much seemed to have changed."

"She doesn't recognize you at all?"

Liz shook her head. "Nothing. The doctor commented recently that her type of memory loss is very rare. She can remember the names of public figures, like the president, for example, but she has to keep being reminded of the names of her nurses."

"It's as if her personal life doesn't exist."

"Exactly, and of course that's the most painful thing of all. When I call her Mom, she looks right through me. At least she doesn't have to mourn Alison, although I often wonder if there's a psychological component to her memory loss."

"The doctors insist that her symptoms are entirely physical, don't they?"

"Of course. They can see the brain damage on their machines. Why would they bother considering that the machines don't tell the whole story?"

Mikhail patted her gently on the arm. "You hope for miracles, Lizushka. Could you not try to remember only the good times before your mother's stroke, and forget about yearning for the impossible?"

"Most of the time, that's what I do. The rational part of me has accepted that she's never going to be cured. The stroke after Alison's death destroyed the part of her brain that stores family memories."

"Certainly she is content with the life she leads, and her physical problems do not become worse. I was down south to judge a skating contest last month, you know, and I paid a quick visit to the nursing home. Really quick, though. It was little more than in the front door and out the back, with just time to say hello as I walked through her room."

"You're too good to us, Mikhail," Liz said impulsively. "Most sons-in-law have to be nagged into tolerating the occasional family get-together. You pay half my mother's nursing home expenses, and then visit her as well, even though she doesn't recognize you. You know how much I appreciate your caring, don't you?"

He grinned. "*Dorogoya*, you thank me a minimum of three times per visit. How could I not know? But your thanks are unnecessary. Your mother is also the mother of Alison, who was my wife, and in Russia we hold such relationships close to our hearts. The great American capitalist system has made me rich, simply because I can teach people how to skate and win competitions. How else should I spend my money, if not on the mother of my wife?"

Liz pushed away the remainder of her chicken, assailed by a sudden memory. "The anniversary of Alison's death was last week. With everything that happened, I'd forgotten. I'm sorry, Mikhail."

"After five years, I have discovered that the pain fades, and all that is left are happy memories. Now when I think of Alison, I recall her beauty on the ice and her warmth in my arms. Believe me, I do not dwell in my thoughts on the crash that took her from me."

"If the grief is finally fading, maybe it's time for you to think of marrying again."

He put his hand to his heart, rolling his eyes in pretended passion. "Liz, my love, you wound me with your careless words. I think of marriage all the time, but you will not have me, so what am I to do?"

She smiled. "I was serious, Mikhail. Don't you want to find yourself some nice American girl and produce dozens of little Olympic champions?"

"One day," he said, sobering. "But the right woman has not yet appeared. Alison is not an easy woman to replace, as you will realize. In the meantime, I hope it won't offend your sisterly ears if I confess that even though I have not yet found the mother of my children, I do not spend every night alone in an empty bed."

Liz just managed to conceal her start of surprise. Intellectually she had never expected Mikhail to remain celibate. In addition to being one of the best-looking men she knew, he had a tempting athletic body and an appealing gleam in his dark gray eyes. Moreover he worked in a glamorous job that kept him surrounded by beautiful, lissome females. Emotionally, however, she was shocked by his admission, mostly because Mikhail had always kept his sexual activities screened from her view.

"You are blushing again, Lizushka." Mikhail's voice was warm and faintly quizzical. "I did not think American women knew how."

She laughed. "I've been cursing my pale skin since high school. You know I turn scarlet for every reason under the sun—and sometimes for no reason at all."

"I know," he said softly. "And you know that my love for Alison will always be buried deep in my heart—"

"But you can't love only a memory," Liz interjected. "You can't and you shouldn't. There's no reason in the world to apologize because you enjoy feminine company, Mikhail."

The doorbell rang, breaking the slight tension between the two of them. "One of your luscious lovelies?" Liz queried lightly.

He pulled a face as he walked to the door. "More likely an angry mother whose child I refused to take on as a student. I think sometimes to buy a guard dog." He opened the door. "Pieter! I wasn't expecting you tonight. Nothing's wrong, I hope? No pulled muscles or sprained wrists?"

Pieter's voice came low and urgent. "Mikhail, I'm in big trouble. The police came to see me. They found a letter in Karen's papers—"

"You'd better come in and calm down, Pieter. Liz is here."

"Hell, Mikhail, you don't understand. The police have found this letter, and it looks like my writing. The police expert swears it is my writing. Hell, man, that letter is big trouble for both of us."

Mikhail's voice took on the cool authority of trainer to athlete. "Pieter, come inside and sit down. We'll talk about this when you stop pacing on my doorstep like a caged tiger. This is America, not Russia. The police do not jump to conclusions without proof."

"This letter is proof, man." But Pieter sounded calmer, and he greeted Liz with some of his usual cockiness. "Hello, beautiful."

"Hello, Pieter. Forgotten my name?" she queried dryly.

He looked at her blankly, and Mikhail thrust a small shot glass into his hand. "Here, drink this. Trainer's orders."

Pieter took a tiny sip of the vodka, then put the glass aside, glancing at Liz almost defiantly. "I'm okay now," he said to Mikhail, holding out his hands. "See, steady as a rock and I'm sitting down like a good boy."

He's embarrassed, Liz thought, finding this sudden reminder of Pieter's youth almost endearing. *He's still young enough to be embarrassed because he doesn't like hard liquor.*

"So tell us what caused this visit from the police," Mikhail said, settling into his own chair.

"They found a letter, shoved inside one of Karen's journals. Man, it's trouble. It reads like I'd been involved in blood doping before the last Olympics, and Karen was trying to blackmail me."

Liz gave an exclamation of concern. "But Pieter, didn't you explain to the police that blood doping's only useful to endurance athletes? There would be no point in you trying to boost your blood supply for a figure-skating competition."

"That is irrelevant," Mikhail said impatiently. "Pieter claims he didn't write the letter, so what we must do is contact our lawyer and insist on having a copy submitted to an independent graphologist." He banged his fist on the counter and muttered some obscure Russian curse. "This whole stupid mess over Karen is becoming ridiculous. She was a boring woman, who could not remain alone in her own bed for fear of what she would discover about herself. And now Liz and Pieter are drawn into her silly problems."

"You think the...um...what's-it—what you said..." Pieter's vocabulary ran to nine different translations of *Let's make love, beautiful woman,* but few English words longer than two syllables, Liz reflected.

"You mean the graphologist."

"Yeah. Will he be able to prove I didn't write the letter?" Pieter asked hopefully.

"I am sure. Come, we will phone the lawyer right away and you will find there is no problem."

Liz admired the ring of confidence Mikhail was able to inject into his voice. She didn't know all that much about graphology, but she had the impression it was an inexact science and that handwriting experts often showed an alarming tendency to disagree on whether or not documents had been forged. Mikhail, however, obviously knew his student well. Under his trainer's calming influence, Pieter looked a different man from the frightened young person who had appeared on the doorstep ten minutes earlier.

"I'll clear up in here while you phone," Liz offered, carrying the debris of her chicken into the kitchen.

"Thanks," Mikhail responded, his mind clearly with the lawyer.

Liz covered the remains of the caviar with plastic wrap, returning it and the vodka to the fridge. She had stacked the plates in the dishwasher, wiped down the counters and plumped up all the cushions before Mikhail and Pieter reappeared.

"The lawyer's coming right over," Mikhail said briefly.

"Great. In that case, I'm going to leave you guys to it," she said. "I've been a bit short on sleep these past few days, and an early night would be welcome."

Both Mikhail and Pieter protested that there was no reason for her to go, but she felt their secret relief when she insisted that she needed to get back to Denver. She knew Mikhail well enough to guess that he was a great deal more worried than he cared to admit. Quite apart from any problems Pieter might face, Mikhail could not possibly afford to have the rumor getting around that his athletes indulged in illicit practices in order to win.

She gave Mikhail a hug as he walked her to her car. "Don't worry," she said. "The letter's obviously ridiculous, and anybody who knows anything about figure skating will be able to tell the police that. It must be a forgery."

"You are so swift to rush to everyone's defense," Mikhail said, his smile wistful. "Even Pieter, whom you do not like. *Dorogoya*, did it never cross your mind even for an instant that Pieter is so nervous because the letter is his?"

"And true, you mean?" Liz couldn't disguise her bewilderment. "Are you saying that you suspect Pieter did infuse himself with extra blood?"

Mikhail hesitated. "I... shall be very careful not to ask," he replied slowly.

Liz drew in a deep breath. "I'm not naive," she insisted. "But why would he do such a dangerous thing for such a minuscule advantage?"

"You were once in the finals of the Olympics, Lizushka. If you had thought that an extra dose of your own blood might—just might—give you the chance to win, can you swear you would not have taken the chance?"

"Yes, I can swear," she said. "Oh, don't get me wrong. Not because I'm so superethical, although I like to think I am. But I'd have been in such dread of discovery by the Olympics Committee that any possible edge I might have gained by injecting the blood would have been wiped out by nerves."

"Pieter, I think, does not share your sensitivities. If he wished to deceive the Olympic Committee, he would believe he could do so, and get away unpunished. I do not say that he blood-doped. I say only that it is possible. And to anybody except you, of course, I will swear that the very idea is nonsense. We are so free with our discussions, Lizushka, that sometimes I forget that I should not burden you with the truth of my thoughts. I have, perhaps, given Pieter's career into your hands. I ask that you do not voice my doubts to the police, although I shall understand if you feel you must speak."

"The police already know about the letter," Liz said. "They have graphologists they can consult. My opinion as to whether or not Pieter might have blood-doped is irrelevant."

"Thank you," Mikhail said. "I had better not leave Pieter alone any longer, or his nerve may once again fail him. Drive safely, Liz."

"I'll call you tomorrow to find out what the lawyer said."

"Fine. And by next weekend, let us hope the police have made an arrest, so that we can put all this nonsense behind us."

LIZ WAS BONE-WEARY by the time she pulled the car into the garage at Dexter's house. The fatigue, she realized, was mental far more than physical, the result of too many questions chasing too few answers around and around her brain.

Dexter had given her a set of house keys, and she opened the door leading from the garage to the kitchen, stopping abruptly when she realized she wasn't alone. Dexter sat at the table, his face lined with a weariness that matched her own. The stubble of the day's beard made a dark shadow across his face. His tie hung loose, and his shirt buttons were unfastened. Perversely, he didn't look rumpled, merely devastatingly sexy and more than a touch vulnerable, she had to admit. Liz mentally armored herself. Dexter was at his most dangerous on those rare occasions when he allowed himself to appear vulnerable.

"You're home early," he said. "I'm surprised Mikhail didn't barricade you in his spare bedroom, rather than let you come back to my house."

"It's been a long day," she said, ignoring his taunt. "Several long days, in fact. I wanted an early night. How was your dinner?"

He rattled the ice cubes in his glass. "The dinner was murder, if you must know." He laughed harshly. "No pun intended."

"The suburban mayors insisted on talking about Karen?"

"No." He looked up, his eyes veiled and hard to read. "They wanted to talk about us. About you and me."

"There is no *us*, for heaven's sake!"

"Try telling that to the suburban mayors. I ought never to have suggested you should stay with me, Liz. Evan was right when he said the reporters would find out you were here and put their own construction on the facts."

"You're not responsible for my choices, Dex. You didn't bind and gag me."

"But I've exposed you to the worst sort of media gossip, and I know how much you hate that."

"I'm older now, and not at all famous. Journalists bother me less." She walked over to the fridge and poured herself a glass of chilled water. "What precisely were the suburban mayors accusing us of?"

"Precisely isn't quite the word. 'Vague but all-encompassing' would be more appropriate. They seemed to have two main schools of thought. Most of them believe that you and I are passionately in love and killed Karen because we found out she was pregnant with my child."

"Didn't it occur to them that it would have been simpler for us to pay Karen to keep quiet?"

"*Simple* isn't a favorite mayoral concept," he replied dryly. "If you'd ever read an official town-zoning plan, you'd know that mayors aren't noted for their common-sense approach to life's everyday problems."

"And most of the mayors believe you and I were dumb enough to commit a murder where we were the most likely suspects?"

"Seems so. Or else they believe—"

"Am I going to like this theory any better?"

"I doubt it."

She sighed. "I may as well hear the worst. Tell me anyway."

"You and I are passionately in love, and Karen committed suicide when she found out about our relationship."

She frowned in exasperation. "This is crazy, Dexter! Why would you have been impregnating Karen, if the two of us are passionately in love?"

"That interesting question doesn't seem to have occurred to the mayors. Or their spouses."

She sipped her water, avoiding his eyes. "Why are they so set on the passionately-in-love part of the story?"

He shrugged. "We were married once before. Now you've reappeared in my life, they refuse to believe we're just good friends."

"Would they believe wary acquaintances?"

"Is that what we are?" he asked quietly.

"I don't know." That was true. "I haven't thought about it." That was a lie.

It was his turn to stare with great concentration into his glass of melting ice cubes. "I had a phone call this evening from the chairman of the Reelect Dexter Rand Committee."

"Let me guess," Liz said flippantly, wanting to move the conversation from ground that seemed suddenly treacherous to her emotions. "He asked you please not to murder any more secretaries before next November. Right?"

"No. He asked me to get married. To you."

All at once, Liz's hands were ice-cold. "I see," she said carefully. "Did you tell him we already tried that once? With spectacularly disastrous results?"

"He knew already. He'd like us to try again."

"What did you say?"

"No comment."

"A political career sure does demand sacrifices," she said, determined to keep her tone light. "Are you thinking that you might be willing to get remarried to me, simply to keep your voters happy?"

"I would never marry anyone, least of all you, for such an inadequate reason."

She lifted her head and met his gaze head-on. "You still hate me that much, huh?"

"I don't hate you, Liz. I never did."

"Gee!" she said with heavy sarcasm. "At last I understand. You've been suffering from unrequited love. All those months when you damn near froze me to death with your icy looks and frosty behavior were because you needed to mask the real you, and your burning fire of uncontrollable passion."

"Yes," he said simply. "That's exactly what happened."

Inwardly she was shaking, but all she said was a flippant. "Give me a break, Dexter."

"I'm telling you the truth. Finally."

"Your love for me was so overwhelming it left you tongue-tied? Come on, Dexter. Are you forgetting about the pilots who elected you Stud Supreme of the Frankfurt military base?"

"For heaven's sake, Liz, there's a difference between acquiring an asinine reputation as a stud, and being a man who's mature enough to handle a complex relationship with a woman."

"And when you married Susan you were suddenly mature?"

He was silent for a long time. Eventually he pushed his chair away from the table and stood up, turning his back on her. "I never loved Susan," he said. "That made a big difference."

"It's easier to be married to someone you don't love?"

"Maybe." Slowly he turned around to face her again. "Susan was a wonderful mother and the perfect political hostess. We were good friends, who respected each other's life-styles. I would say our marriage was as happy as most others."

Dex was describing the sort of marriage she might have had with Brian, Liz realized. In retrospect, she could scarcely believe she had almost let herself be sucked into such a cold, bloodless relationship.

"Would you want another marriage like that?" she asked.

His eyes strayed to her mouth and remained there, causing her entire body to flood with heat. "Last week I would have said yes."

She could guess—perhaps—what had caused him to change his mind, but didn't ask for confirmation. She didn't want to hear again that he shared her own unwilling sexual awareness. Dexter was a perfectionist, and given the mess they had made of their marriage, she understood how he might feel the need to rewrite their joint past by entering into a new, more mature relationship in the present. Unfortunately, she also knew—God, how she knew!—that she couldn't afford to risk getting too close to Dexter. While he might end up feeling more comfortable, she would end up badly burned.

His gaze lingered on her mouth, causing her tongue to thicken and her planned answer to die unspoken somewhere deep in her throat. Her instinct for self-preservation seemed to have taken a holiday, because she didn't run screaming for safety when he closed the small gap between their bodies and wrapped her in his arms.

"God, I missed you, Liz," he murmured, and the hesitancy in his voice touched off a response that no amount of aggressive male confidence could have provoked. Her knees felt shaky, blood pumped thickly through her veins, and her body ached with a sweet, familiar pain. She closed her eyes, knowing what would inevitably follow, but wanting him too much to care.

Their kiss was like every other kiss they had ever shared, and yet it was utterly different. Her body still ignited with the same, immediate force. Her veins still ran hot with fire, and her stomach still knotted tight with desire. But something in his touch was different, just as her response was different from everything that had gone between them in the past. This time, his lips moved over hers with supplication as well as expertise, and her response lacked the old humiliating element of helplessness. Her body's reaction was primitive, fierce, elemental, but it was a reaction given of her own free will.

They couldn't continue a kiss of such intensity for long without progressing to a stage of lovemaking Liz wasn't ready to contemplate. Reluctantly she pulled her mouth away, turning her head to one side. His body pulsed against hers, and for a moment his lips hardened demandingly. Then she felt him relax, and he rested his forehead against hers for a fleeting moment before stepping away.

"Maybe you should go upstairs first," he said. "And you might want to consider locking your door."

She tried to laugh, but it came out as a breathy, husky sound, not at all what she had intended. "Dex, you're long past the stage of finding yourself swept away by overmastering passion."

"Am I?" he asked. "Funny, I was just thinking that I hadn't felt such a strong urge to push a woman to the floor and fall on top of her since . . ."

"Since?" she prompted, knowing that if she'd been smart, she'd have remained silent.

"Since the only time I ever did it before," he said. "In Frankfurt. With you."

Liz wondered how many fingers she would need to burn before she finally realized she was too close to the fire. She drew in a deep breath and from some hidden corner of her soul extracted a remaining shred or two of willpower.

"Good night, Dexter," she said with convincing firmness, then spoiled the whole effect by turning tail and running from the kitchen as if her life depended on it.

Chapter Nine

The office was blissfully empty on Sunday morning. Liz worked assiduously on her paper mountain and succeeded in reducing it to a modest-sized hill. Wanting a break before tackling the fine print of the latest market-research report, she contemplated the rival merits of McDonald's and the local health-food bar. She had just reluctantly decided that the health-food bar was the winner, when the phone rang.

"Elizabeth Meacham," she said absently, wondering if there was any way to convince her taste buds that bean sprouts were more enjoyable than French fries.

"Liz, this is Evan Howard."

The PR man's voice came low and urgent over the phone, and Liz's attention snapped back with a jerk.

"Evan? Is something wrong? What's happened?"

"I need to see you urgently. At my house. We'll be safe there. I have something important to tell you."

The muted roar on the line was pierced by the distinctive beep of a car horn. "Are you calling from a phone booth?" she asked. "I can scarcely hear you."

"Yes, but I'm going home right now. Liz, you have to come and see me." His voice sounded frankly desperate, although she knew enough to take his desperation with a grain of salt. Evan was not a man notable for his calm disposition.

"I don't know where you live," she said. "And what about calling Dexter—?"

"No!" His command was sharp, instantaneous. "No! Don't say a word about this meeting to Dexter. It would be dangerous for both of us."

"Evan, you have to tell me what this melodrama is all about. If it's connected with Karen's death—"

"My address is 244 South Clark," he interrupted. "Clark intersects with University. Be there as soon as you can." The hum of an empty wire warned Liz that Evan had hung up.

She grabbed her purse and dashed for the parking lot. Despite Evan's penchant for self-dramatization, she had detected a note of true fear in his voice, and she had an uncomfortable conviction that what he was about to tell her was something important—and quite possibly something she didn't want to hear. About Dexter? As far as she knew, she and Evan had no other mutual friends.

She drove too far south, and it took her longer than it should have done to find Clark. The street, part of a pleasant residential neighborhood, was Sunday-morning quiet, but the sunshine and peace didn't reassure her. Oppressed by a sudden sense of urgency, Liz parked the car haphazardly against the sidewalk and dashed up the steps leading to number 244.

The house was a typical Denver bungalow, recently restored. The door had been carved into the sort of artsy-craftsy look Liz would have expected from Evan, and she had to search to find the doorbell, which was nestled against the stem of an opulent bunch of cast-iron grapes. An electric buzzer sounded loudly within the house when she pressed the bell, but elicited no response. For a man who had been so insistent in his request that Liz come calling, Evan didn't exactly seem to be panting by the front door for her arrival.

She pressed the button a second time, her sense of urgency dissipating into the more familiar irritation Evan usually provoked. The buzzer once again faded into silence. The street remained empty and somnolent. Infuriated by her wasted trip, she searched around for a note or some other sign that Evan had been expecting her. Again nothing.

"Next time I'll know better than to come tearing out to meet you," she muttered, straightening from her foray into the flowerpots. She blew a stray strand of hair off her forehead, gave the bell another halfhearted push and surveyed the door one final time.

She had no idea what impelled her to test the handle, except maybe a generalized feeling of frustration. To her astonishment, it gave under her fingers, and when she pushed, the door swung open.

Feeling a bit like Goldilocks, Liz stepped into the narrow hall. "Evan?" she called. "Are you home? Is everything okay?"

She took two or three cautious steps into the hallway, and then two or three more. Nothing greeted her save the echo of her own footsteps. Staring around, she saw a series of half-open doors leading into silent rooms.

Belatedly it dawned on Liz that she was not terribly smart to be walking into an unknown house in response to a phone call from a man she scarcely knew. In fact, in retrospect she realized she couldn't even be entirely sure that it was Evan who had called her. The connection crackled, the caller had spoken softly, and the noise of passing traffic had drowned many subtleties of inflection.

With the sudden conviction that at any moment Karen's murderer was going to burst out of the hall closet and bop her on the head, she swung around and ran back down the hallway.

She had almost covered the short distance to the front door, when a slight, almost inaudible sound caused her to glance to her left. Coming back along the hall, her angle of sight into each of the rooms was different. For the first time, she noticed a foot, encased in a black leather loafer, poking around the edge of the living-room door.

Liz stopped, her breathing shallow and her stomach churning with dread. Instinctively tiptoeing, she crept into the living room.

Evan lay on his back, his face drained of color, his eyes closed, one hand resting limply around the knife handle protruding from his rib cage.

"Oh God! Dear God, no!" Liz whispered in agonized supplication. She fell on her knees alongside Evan's body, ripping open the neckline of his shirt, desperately seeking the pulse she was certain she wouldn't feel.

When he groaned, she jumped with shock, her hand slipping into the patch of blood that was congealing around the knife. His eyes flickered briefly open, then closed.

"A doctor," she instructed herself, wiping her hand on her skirt. "I must call the doctor." She half rose to her feet, pausing when Evan opened his eyes again.

"Liz..." Her name was no more than a breath of sound, and she leaned over him in order to hear, bracing herself on the floor above his shoulder to prevent her weight from resting on his blood-seeping wound.

"It's all right," she murmured. "Everything's going to be okay, Evan, I'm here."

"Liz?"

"Yes, I'm Liz. I'm here, and I'm going to get a doctor."

His eyes blurred, and although he stared straight at her, she wasn't sure he knew to whom he spoke. "They will have to kill you. . . ." he said. He made a horrible gurgling sound, which Liz realized was meant to be a laugh. "I didn't know. . . . I was a fool. . . . I loved her so much. I did it for her."

"Who did you love?" she asked urgently. "Was it Karen?"

He didn't answer. "Evan," she said. "Oh God, Evan, who did this to you?"

His thoughts seemed to follow their own track, or perhaps he hadn't even heard Liz's question. "He is . . . so beautiful . . . and so danger—" His eyes rolled upward and he fell silent.

"No!" she protested. "No, damn it, you're not going to die!" She cupped his lips under her mouth, trying to force air into his lungs. Only when she was panting and dizzy with exhaustion did she stop the hopeless task.

She leaned back, pushing her sweat-soaked hair away from her forehead, and in that moment became aware of the dried blood coating her hands. She stared hypnotized at the ugly red splotches, her body gripped by an uncontrollable shuddering. A groan of horror pushed its way out of her throat, but she didn't—couldn't—move. She was still kneeling beside Evan's body, bloody hands wavering in front of her eyes, when the door to the living room banged open.

DEXTER HAD A PREMONITION of disaster as soon as he arrived at Evan's house and found the front door unlocked, but no sign of a police squad car. *A setup, then?*

Maybe. But then again, maybe not. He had the feeling that whatever was going on, his enemies very much wanted him to remain alive.

Careful not to make any sound that would betray his presence, he slipped into the narrow hallway. His body tensed reflexively, alert for any hint of danger as he looked around. There was no sign of Evan, and nothing seemed disturbed, but the house was much too quiet. The silence vibrated with a special kind of menace, and the hallway smelled of death.

No sound came from the living room, but he would stake his life on the suspicion that someone was in there. His life, perhaps, was what he would be staking. With infinite care, he edged toward the living-room door. He knew better than to attempt any form of unarmed combat when he was out of training, but his old skill at moving noiselessly hadn't been lost. So far he wasn't taking much of a risk.

He paused before making the final, dangerous move past the half-open door of the living room. If somebody was lying in wait behind that door, he would be virtually without defense. As he paused, he heard someone groan. A woman. He would swear it was a woman. He would swear it was Liz.

Dexter reached out and banged the door open, adrenaline surging as his body fell automatically into the attack mode. The door crashed against the wall, telling him nobody was concealed behind it. He took a single step into the room, then froze.

Liz, her face and hands smeared with blood, was three feet away from him, crouched over Evan's—obviously dead—body.

For a moment she didn't seem aware of his presence, then her head jerked up, and she stared at him from terrified blue-gray eyes. Eyes that had haunted his dreams for the past nine years. Even now, as his pulse calmed and reason took over, he recognized his instinctive, involuntary response to her beauty.

"What happened?" he asked. The question came out brusquely, not only because of Evan's death, but because he was tired of remembering, tired of yearning for the unattainable, tired of wanting a mental rapport with Liz that would match their physical awareness.

She didn't say anything, but her eyes widened in panic. Her mouth opened, then closed again, and he realized that she was literally incapable of speech.

He walked to her side, a brief glance at Evan confirming that there was no need to rush for a doctor. Dexter had seen violent death too often during his years as a fighter pilot, and he felt a wave of bitter anger against the person who had so brutally ended Evan's life. He controlled the anger and the accompanying grief. At this moment he needed facts, not emotion.

"What happened?" he asked Liz again, more gently this time. He knelt down to brush his thumbs swiftly across Evan's eyes, restoring a tiny measure of dignity to the sprawling body. Then he put his arm around Liz and helped her to her feet.

She flinched at his touch, as if she couldn't bear the warmth of human contact so close to violent death, but he was relieved to see some of the wildness leave her eyes. "I didn't do it," she said. "Dexter, I didn't kill him."

"I never thought you did." He spoke the truth. Despite the compromising situation in which he'd found her, he knew Liz hadn't killed Evan. Like many athletes, she was indifferent to her own physical pain, but she'd always been squeamish about other people's. There might be some facets of Liz's character that remained mysterious to him, but he knew she could never have thrust a knife into a man's chest and then knelt beside him to watch him die. He smoothed a hand along her spine, calming her as he would have Amanda. "How did you get in? Was the front door open?"

"Yes. I j-just w-walked in."

"Did you see anything suspicious?"

"No. The house was empty. . . . Evan was—like that—when I found him."

She had always been a hopeless liar, and he knew at once that she wasn't telling the truth. Evan might have been at the point of death when she entered the living room, but he hadn't been dead. That was why she was covered in blood. She'd tried to save him.

"What did Evan say to you before he died?" Dexter asked quietly.

She looked at him with renewed horror, as if she couldn't bear to hear the question, and he saw full-blown panic return to her face. "The police," she muttered. "Oh God, the police!"

She tore herself out of Dexter's arms and dashed blindly down the hall, bumping into an ornamental stand and sending a china vase crashing to the floor. He doubted if she even heard the vase fall.

He followed her into the kitchen, his most immediate concern to calm her down before he called the police. She rammed the faucet full on and splashed steaming water onto her face, scrubbing with a ferocity that suggested she wanted to wash away not only Evan's blood, but all memory of the scene in the living room.

"Did you call a doctor?" he asked. If she had, they needed to worry about the imminent arrival of somebody who was going to ask a series of very awkward questions.

"No, I didn't call anybody. I've got to get out of here! You should go, too." Liz was clearly hanging on to her self-control by the merest thread. "Did you touch anything?" she demanded. "We have to get rid of our fingerprints." She elbowed past him without waiting for a reply, a roll of paper towels clutched in her hand.

"Liz, stop! Talk to me for God's sake! You can't dash around wiping off fingerprints!"

"Watch me!"

He caught hold of her arm. "Sit down, calm down, and tell me what happened."

"Sit down! Calm down!" She laughed, and began rubbing feverishly at the front door handle. "I'm getting out of here, Dexter, just as soon as I've cleaned off my prints. If the police find me anywhere near Evan's body, they're going to have me handcuffed and in a squad car as soon as they can spit out a Miranda warning. I don't blame them, either. If I were in Lieutenant Rodriguez's shoes, I'd arrest the pair of us."

Despite her panic, Dexter knew she had a point. His lawyers weren't likely to leave him lingering in jail longer than a couple of hours, but did he really want to subject himself to all the publicity an arrest would cause? On the other hand, he and Liz had discovered a crime and had a duty to report it. Sometimes, he thought wryly, duty was a damn nuisance.

"Nothing's going to bring Evan back to life," Liz said, almost as if she had read his thoughts. "And since I can't help him, I don't see any point in getting myself arrested."

She was right, Dexter conceded. Moreover, he suspected he might be playing straight into the murderer's hands if he and Liz were found here, hovering over Evan's body. Like the audience that is distracted by the conjurer's dazzling display of silk scarves, so that the crucial card can be slipped up his sleeve, Dexter had the feeling that the police and the FBI were having their attention directed to the murders of Evan Howard and Karen Zeit, while some much more complex evil was being plotted elsewhere.

"Where do you plan to go?" he asked.

"To the airport. To some place faraway."

"Is Boston far enough?" he asked, coming to a decision. "I planned to take Amanda to stay with her grandparents, anyway. If we left this afternoon, I'd just be moving things up a couple of days."

"I couldn't possibly impose on your parents—"

"Please come," he said, not even sure himself why her company seemed so important. "We have a lot to discuss, a lot of information to share, and there's no time now."

She was suddenly very still, and he knew that he had touched a sensitive nerve. It occurred to him for the first time that she probably suspected him of being involved in Evan's death. Her question confirmed it.

"Why did you come here?" she asked. "I thought you planned to spend the morning with Amanda."

"I did. But somebody called, claiming to be a police officer, and said Evan had found Karen's missing personnel file. He asked me to come over here right away. Since there's no sign of a policeman or a file, I guess we can safely assume the call was a fake. What brought you?"

"A phone call. Evan insisted he had something very important to tell me." She looked away. "He also told me it would be dangerous to get in touch with you."

"Dangerous?" Dexter tried without success to fit this piece of information into the puzzle. "Who was it dangerous for? Did he say?"

She hesitated for a second or two. "For me. For Evan. Not for you. At least, I don't think for you."

"I see." In fact, he saw a lot more than he wanted to. Like the reason for her panic at the sight of him. "Liz, I didn't kill Evan."

The color had once again completely faded from her face. "That's what you said about Karen, too."

"You're right," he replied quietly. "It looks suspicious, doesn't it?"

"Yes." Her reply was no more than a whisper.

"You told me you didn't murder Karen, though she was your third roommate to die. And you told me you didn't kill Evan, though I found you hunched over his body, covered in blood."

"I was trying to give him mouth-to-mouth resuscitation."

"I believe you."

He let the words fall into the sudden silence of the nallway. He thought she was about to speak, when the blare of a police siren shattered the quiet. Liz tensed, her entire body going ramrod stiff.

"Do you think they're coming here?"

"Doesn't sound like it, the direction's wrong. But we'd better leave, just in case. There's a back entrance. Let's take it." He didn't point out that if they'd been set up, somebody would have notified the police, for sure. For once, he was grateful for the fact that response time to emergency calls was less than wonderful.

She hesitated, momentarily irresolute. "Afraid you're aiding and abetting a murderer, Liz?" he queried softly.

"Just—afraid."

He sensed her continuing resistance and her doubt, but there was no time for explanations, even if he could have provided them. He took her hand and pulled her along the hall toward the kitchen. "Liz, we don't have time for any more protestations of innocence. We've got to get out of here."

She obviously agreed with that, if not with his innocence. "My car's in front," she said, as they emerged into Evan's backyard.

He stopped and listened for a moment before taking her hand. "No police around that I can hear," he said, guiding her down the narrow path to the front of the house. "Drive your car to the airport and leave it in long-term parking. That's as good a place to get rid of it as any. Then book us three one-way tickets on the next flight to Boston. Do you have money?"

"A credit card."

"Good. I'll meet you at the departures gate."

"My clothes . . ." she said. "The blood—"

"Stop off at one of the big discount stores on the way to the airport. Change in their ladies' room and throw away the skirt you're wearing. And I'll pack a suitcase for you at the house."

The sound of another siren sliced through the air, and this time it didn't conveniently fade into the distance. Dexter sprinted toward his car. "I'll pick up Amanda," he said. "Give me one hour. Get moving, Liz! You don't have time to stand around thinking!"

HE WAITED until he was safely home before placing the call to Igor. For some reason, he felt the need for familiar surroundings before he confessed what had happened. Anyway, his home phone was as safe as a phone booth, and a lot quieter. They sent in professionals to sweep the phone line regularly, and he himself was expert at checking for bugs. Not that anybody suspected him, so there was no reason in the world to anticipate a bug. Even Igor—who was paranoid about security—had agreed that he could make sensitive calls from his home in perfect safety.

It wasn't easy to dial the number. His fingers, poised over the buttons, shook. Igor did not tolerate mistakes on the part of his underlings, nor did he believe in effete capitalist notions like forgiveness. Igor eliminated his mistakes, thus preserving his reputation and saving the Soviet state a great deal of money in pension benefits.

He wondered if this was a mistake he could cover up. Damn Elizabeth Meacham to hell! She'd always seemed such an asexual creature, he'd been sure the senator wouldn't have a chance of getting close to her. Particularly since their divorce had been so bitter. But Evan had sworn he'd seen them kissing—in the kitchen, of all places, and it hadn't been a friendly peck on the cheek. Thank God, he'd been instructed to kill Evan Howard. It was one thing to admit that Elizabeth Meacham seemed closer to the senator than was desirable. It was another thing to admit they had been observed locked in a passionate kiss. That was a piece of information he'd make sure never filtered back up to Igor. It was grotesque to think of Liz responding to Dexter Rand, after the number of times she'd turned him down!

He put the receiver back into its cradle and drew in a series of short, deep breaths. An old trick learned in competition, but it calmed him, just as it had done before the Olympics.

No point in delaying this call any longer. He drew in one final, cleansing breath and punched out the numbers quickly, before he could lose his nerve. After all, he had a success to report along with the failure. Evan was dead. Quickly and cleanly dead, although there had been that split second when his hand had wavered. He wasn't quite sure why that had happened. He couldn't possibly be losing his nerve for simple things like killing. Not now. Not when their plans were so close to success. Not when the intolerable wait was almost over.

"Yes." Igor always answered the phone himself on the first ring. It was a small, chilling example of his efficiency.

"Evan Howard has been taken care of in accordance with your instructions," he said. His voice, he was pleased to note, sounded strong and confident. "You were correct, as always, Comrade Secretary. He was no longer reliable. He threatened to tell the police that Elizabeth Meacham was in danger."

"Did he know the Meacham woman is to be killed?"

"I'm sure Evan knew nothing." He hoped to God that was the truth. "Karen Zeit was immensely effective in bending her lovers to her will, Comrade Secretary, but I'm afraid that—toward the end—she was not always discreet." Because she had developed this insane obsession that they should marry. How many people had she blabbed to before he silenced her? "Evan should never have known my name," he added. "Karen was totally unprofessional in revealing it."

"You chose Zeit. You ran her. You should have controlled her. If you hadn't impregnated her, she might have been more reliable."

"Yes, indeed, Comrade. But no harm has been done. Neither Karen Zeit nor Evan Howard knew why Elizabeth Meacham must be killed. In fact, I doubt if Evan knew much more than the fact that Karen wished very much for a job on the senator's staff. It was the order to destroy Karen's personnel file that disturbed him. As you suspected, he was beginning to think far too much about what was going on."

"Karen Zeit and Evan Howard are now part of the past. We are concerned with the present and the future. Our visitor from Moscow is now fully prepared for her task. The final stage of our plan may be set in motion. I assume Senator Rand is being followed?"

"Yes, Comrade."

"Where is he? Is he implicated as ordered in Evan Howard's death?"

He drew in a deep breath. "The police, unfortunately, did not arrive in time to find him in Evan's house. I have been informed that he is now at home."

Igor grunted. "This is your official order to set the next stage of operation in motion."

"Yes, Comrade Secretary." Should he admit that Liz had been at Evan's house? Should he drop a hint that maybe—just maybe—Liz and the senator were becoming more intimate than was desirable? If he spoke up, the plan could be amended, if necessary. If he remained silent, life would be easier now, but might be impossible later. He wiped away the sweat that was beading on his forehead.

"There is one more thing, Comrade."

"Yes?"

"Elizabeth Meacham and the senator..."

"Yes?"

"They have spent a great deal of time together over the past few days. It seems that our assumption that they would be mutually hostile and avoid each other was not entirely correct."

"Our assumption?" Igor asked softly. "My plan was based on your assessment of Elizabeth Meacham's likely behavior, Comrade Champion. Are you telling me that I must revise my plan?"

"I suggest only that you keep in mind that the senator has seen the Meacham woman quite frequently over the past few days."

Igor grunted. "I will ensure that my plans cover all eventualities. Your task is so simple, Comrade Champion, that I hope sincerely you will not screw up."

The American slang was so unexpected that for a moment he couldn't reply. He swallowed and said finally, "The kidnapping will proceed on schedule."

Igor hung up without speaking again.

Chapter Ten

Most of the passengers had already boarded the plane for Boston when Liz spotted Dexter and Amanda hurrying along the moving walkway to the flight gate. Dexter held an oversize panda, presumably because Amanda's arms were already filled with a scruffy teddy bear and a neon-yellow stuffed rabbit. An Easter gift that had been unexpectedly successful, Liz guessed, eyeing the creature's virulent pink satin ears with disbelief.

Even from a distance of fifty yards or so, she could see that Amanda was hopping with excitement, and that Dexter was smiling down at her, the hard lines of his jaw softened into tenderness, every angle of his body speaking of love and the urge to protect. When they reached the end of the walkway, he clutched the panda in his teeth, freeing a hand to help his daughter onto firm ground.

In that moment, Liz knew—without logic, but with utter, unshakable conviction—that Dexter was no killer. Evan's dying words might mean a multitude of different things, but she would never accept that Evan had intended to accuse his employer of murder. She had decided days ago that Dexter would never kill a woman to rid himself of the threat of a paternity suit. Today, witnessing the agony of Evan's death, she had lost her mental bearings for a while. She had spent the past two hours wondering why she was waiting to board a plane with a man who could well be a murderer. Now she realized that Evan's stumbling words had temporarily distorted her understanding of Dexter's character. Watching him with his daughter, she knew that her instincts were a safer guide to the truth than a dying man's semiconscious ramblings.

"Time to board?" Dexter asked as he approached.

"Yes, it's a DC-10. We're all together. Nonsmoking." She glanced toward the suddenly silent child. "Hi, Amanda. Would you like me to hold one of your animals?"

"No, thank you, Ms. Meacham. I can hold them myself." Her response was exquisitely polite—and totally lacking in warmth.

"Please call me Liz. 'Ms. Meacham' makes me feel like your teacher."

"You're nothing like any of my teachers," Amanda said positively.

Liz decided not to explore the precise meaning of that statement. Dexter, she noted, was looking faintly amused by his daughter's covert hostility. She wondered why. "We'd better get moving," she said brightly. "We don't want the plane to leave without us."

"I like going to Grandma's house." Amanda threw down the words more as a challenge than as a statement. Eyeing Liz with a hint of speculation, she added, "Grandpa's fun, too. We go fishing. Only him and me."

"How nice for you," Liz said and smiled, somehow refraining from pointing out that "fun" was just about the last word she would have used to describe the dour, fastidious Mr. Rand, Sr. Dexter's prim and proper parents, with their old-fashioned, aristocratic attitudes, had been one of the greater tribulations of her brief marriage.

Amanda took the window seat, Dexter squeezed his long legs into the cramped center position, and Liz took the aisle. "Sorry," she apologized. "None of my credit cards would stand first-class fares. You're flying as *Mr. Meacham*, by the way."

"Good idea. It might throw the journalistic hounds off the scent for a while."

"Not to mention the police."

"I'm not sure that we can avoid the police," Dexter said. "I told my housekeeper where we're going. I didn't want to create the impression that we were running away."

"I thought running away was exactly what we were doing."

He grinned. "Good grief, no! Just beating a strategic retreat."

"Translated into plain English, that sounds to me a heck of a lot like running away."

"Who's running away, Daddy?" Amanda's childish treble floated with appalling clarity across the hum of the engines and the clatter of the meal carts. "Is it Ms. Meacham?"

"Nobody's running away," Dexter replied. "Not literally. Here, have a lollipop." He pulled the candy out of a plastic bag tucked into his briefcase. "My emergency kit," he murmured to Liz. "Before Amanda was born, I wondered why parents ever gave their children candy or cookies. Then I wised up to the real world."

"Why is Ms. Meacham coming to Boston?" Amanda asked, licking her lollipop.

"Because I asked her to. I want her company."

Amanda digested this information in silence. "Is she going with you to Washington?"

This time her comment was overtly unfriendly, and Liz wondered what had prompted the change in Amanda's attitude. When they'd first met a couple of nights ago, the child had been more than ready to be friendly.

"I hope Liz will come with me." Dexter didn't rebuke his daughter for her rudeness, but he gave subtle emphasis to his use of Liz's name. "You know, Liz is a very good friend of mine, and I hope she'll be a friend of yours, too, one day."

Amanda scowled. Without replying, she leaned down and pulled a coloring book out of her carry-on bag. Dexter watched her for a second or two, then turned back to face Liz and spoke softly. "Her best friend at school took her aside yesterday and gave her a long lecture, during which she apparently pointed out that stepmothers are always mean and wicked. Amanda has converted overnight from wanting me to marry again into wanting me to remain single forever."

Liz spoke quickly. "She certainly has no reason to view me as a threat."

He hesitated for an instant. "We've spent a lot of time together the past few days, you and I. Naturally, she doesn't understand why."

Amanda thrust her picture under Dexter's nose. "Look, Daddy," she said. "What color shall I do the house?"

After that, Dexter devoted most of his attention to entertaining his daughter, and the tedium of the four-hour flight was interrupted only when the flight attendant arrived to serve cocktails and dinner. Liz normally avoided meals on planes, but realizing she had eaten nothing all day, she chose something optimistically called chicken cacciatore. Dexter and Amanda chose beef bourguignonne. The attendant seemed to have considerable difficulty in deciding what each tray contained, which wasn't surprising, since both the beef and the chicken were smothered in an identical dark red sauce. Happily, Liz discovered she was too hungry to care which dinner she got.

Darkness had long since descended when Dexter finally drove the rental car into the maple-lined driveway of the centuries-old Rand family home. Amanda, wedged between Liz and her father on the front seat of the car, fought a valiant battle against dozing off. With a visible effort, she would straighten up and demand attention every time Dexter addressed a remark to Liz.

Strangely enough, Liz found this typical childlike need for attention and reassurance more endearing than the polite self-possession Amanda had displayed on the first occasion they met. A couple of times she had to restrain herself from putting an arm around the child and saying, "It's okay. Relax. I'm not going to take him from you. I couldn't, even if I tried."

Dexter's parents caused an even stranger reaction within Liz. Either time and a grandchild had mellowed them out of all recognition, or her perspective was vastly different from the tension-filled days of her marriage.

They greeted her with the polite, formal reserve she expected. Her reaction to their cool courtesy, however, was neither irritation nor a burning sense of her own inadequacy. It was merely relief. One of the advantages of centuries of selective breeding, she reflected wryly, was that proper Bostonians seemed to have a repertoire of polite conversation for every occasion. Meeting a divorced former daughter-in-law, who had recently shared an apartment with their son's murdered-possible-mistress, seemed to present no special problems.

"How are you, Elizabeth? You look very well. I hope the flight wasn't too tiresome. I asked the housekeeper to put you in the blue bedroom. I'm sure you will find it comfortable."

Liz had nothing to do except mumble platitudes—a soothing end to a traumatic day.

By contrast, their welcome to Amanda showed just how far off the mark Liz had always been in assuming that neither Mr. nor Mrs. Rand was capable of deep emotion. They welcomed their granddaughter with a brief kiss on the cheek rather than the exuberant hugs and kisses traditional in some families, but love shone in their eyes, and their voices were warm with the intensity of their feelings.

What was more, Amanda clearly understood that she was the apple of her grandparents' eyes, and basked in the glow of their devotion. The adults shared coffee and liqueurs, while a maid brought in a tray of hot chocolate and cookies especially for Amanda. Curled up between Mr. and Mrs. Rand on the sofa, she displayed her drawings with the entirely accurate expectation that they would be rapturously received. Leonardo da Vinci could not have had his early sketches examined with more attention or greater enthusiasm, Liz reflected in silent amusement. If only Mr. Rand's colleagues at the bank could see him oohing and aahing over Amanda's purple house, their impression of his personality might undergo a radical change.

Amanda's artistic treasures had finally been laid to one side as she drooped more and more wearily against her grandmother's shoulder. "We'll talk tomorrow," Mr. Rand said to Dexter. "No, my boy, don't hurry your brandy. Stay here with Elizabeth. I'm sure you need some time to yourselves right now."

"Thanks. I'll just get Amanda to bed—"

"Indeed you won't." Mrs. Rand rose gracefully to her feet, demonstrating that it was possible to interrupt with every appearance of perfect manners. "Amanda and I have a special story to read tonight. We've been saving it since last time she was here, haven't we, dear?"

"Yes. It's called *The Secret Garden*, and now I'm big enough to read it to Grandma."

"If I may, I'll come along and listen, too." Mr. Rand put his brandy snifter on the tray. "I seem to remember that was always one of my favorite stories."

Mrs. Rand looked across at her son. "You'll show Elizabeth where the blue room is, Dexter?"

"Of course. Good night, Mother."

The masculine Rands exchanged handshakes. Mrs. Rand gave her son a brief peck on the cheek, but Liz noticed, as she wouldn't have done nine years earlier, that the older woman's eyes were bright with unshed tears. "I'm glad to have you home, Dexter," she murmured. "If there's any way we can help..."

"You've helped already," he said. "Just being with you and Dad puts things into better perspective." Hunkering down, he held Amanda close. "Sleep tight, poppet. I'll see you in the morning."

She clung to his neck for a few moments, then turned quite happily to take her grandmother's hand. "Good night, Ms. Meacham," she said pointedly.

There was no doubt about it, Liz thought ruefully. The Rand family genes got to work early, teaching little junior Rands how to annihilate their enemies with politeness. On the brink of returning an equally cool good-night, she astonished herself by bending down and gathering Amanda into a swift hug.

"My name's Liz," she said softly. "It would be awfully nice if you could call me that. Sleep tight, Amanda. Give Rabbit a kiss from me."

Amanda didn't return Liz's hug, but neither did she reject it, which seemed a step in the right direction. Although why she felt this pressing need to be accepted by Dexter's daughter, Liz couldn't quite decide.

When Amanda and her grandparents left the room, a silence descended that was less than comfortable. "What I want more than anything in the world is a shower," Liz said.

"Me, too. I'll show you to your room."

"You don't have to bother. Just give me directions."

"The second door on the right as you go up the staircase. There's a connecting bathroom."

"Fine. Well, thanks for everything, Dexter. I'll see you in the morning."

"I should be thanking you," he said quietly. "But you're right. We'll do better if we talk in the morning. You must be exhausted, and by coming here, we've bought ourselves some time to relax."

"Yes. It was a pretty miserable day." She didn't move, and neither did Dexter. "Well," she said at last. "I guess I'd better be on my way. Second room on the right, wasn't it?"

"Yes." Dexter was noted as a brilliant conversationalist. At the moment, however, he seemed to be having as much difficulty as Liz in finding anything coherent, let alone brilliant, to say.

"Um . . . good night," she managed finally.

"Er . . . Sleep well."

His voice sounded as tense as she felt—which was like a tightly tuned guitar string, waiting to be strummed. Unfortunately, this sort of tension had become very familiar to Liz over the past few days. She felt it anytime she was with Dexter, but when they were alone together, it became almost unbearable. Her body screamed out the message that if she stepped forward into Dexter's arms, her tension would be wonderfully, blissfully, released. Her mind, meanwhile, sent out frantic reminders about what had happened the last time she allowed her physical desires to control her response to her former husband.

For once in her life, Liz got smart. Without trying to explain her actions, she turned abruptly on her heel and hurried from the room. Too many more minutes of staring at Dexter, and she might have done something totally crazy. Like telling him what was on her mind. And at that precise moment it surely wasn't murder.

NO BATH, not even after a grueling competition, had ever felt so good. Liz shampooed her hair and scrubbed every inch of her body with imported English lavender soap. She couldn't expunge the morning's horrific memories, but the hot water helped to rinse away at least some of her guilt at leaving Denver. Evan had been long past mortal help when she and Dexter abandoned him, and yet she was having difficulty in smothering the sharp prick of her conscience. She had been the last person to see Evan alive. Therefore she felt an obligation to report everything she had heard and seen to the police. Somewhere in her childhood civics classes she had obviously absorbed the lesson that policemen were good guys, and anybody who evaded them was bad. Liz felt bad, as if she deserved to be arrested.

She stepped out of the claw-footed tub, which was no decorator touch but had been there, she was sure, since "modern" plumbing was installed in the Rand mansion at the turn of the century. She wrapped her damp hair in a hand towel and her body in a bath towel, which was fluffy, but not overlarge. Yawning, she pushed open the door and stepped into her bedroom.

Dexter, clad in a T-shirt and faded jeans, sat on the bed. Her bed. "We need to talk," he said. His voice sounded low and oddly thick.

She tightened the towel above her breasts, although it was already so tight that breathing seemed difficult. "Now? This minute? I thought we decided everything could wait until the morning."

"Not this." He stood up and came toward her. "Precisely what happened that day in Frankfurt?" he asked.

"In Frankfurt? At the Olympics?" She was so astonished that she forgot to hold onto her towel. He caught it for her and handed her the ends, but not before his gaze had made a swift, burning assessment of everything the towel was supposed to conceal.

"Thank you," she said, her voice husky.

"You're welcome." His gaze rose slowly from the swell of her breasts to the curve of her lips, and stayed there. Fire exploded in her veins and raced throughout her body.

Don't look at me! she wanted to shout. But another part of her yearned to throw the towel to the floor and yell, *Yes, look at me! Look at what you've been missing for the last nine years!*

In the end, it seemed simplest not to say anything. Besides, she needed all her concentration. Her fingers were trembling so much that she couldn't complete the simple task of tucking one end of the towel into the other.

"Here, let me," he said. His hands, cool against the blazing heat of her skin, traced the swell of her breasts and then slowly, with infinite care, tucked in the ends of the towel together. "What happened that night in Frankfurt?" he asked quietly.

Defiance shaped her reply. "I messed up," she said, the old defensive mechanisms rushing into action. "I threw away a first-place standing and robbed America of its guaranteed gold. Didn't you read the newspapers?"

"I'm all grown-up, Liz, and I've learned not to believe everything I read."

"You were there. You saw for yourself."

"I don't think I saw the truth."

She turned away, shaking with the pain of remembering. "It doesn't matter now. It's a long time ago. I was winning at the end of the short program. I skated terribly in the final segment of the contest. I lost. There's nothing else to say."

His hands were on her shoulders, his callused thumbs circling in a hypnotic massage. "I always blamed Alison," he said. "I assumed that somehow she messed up your concentration. But it wasn't Alison, was it? It was Susan. If it had been Alison, you'd have talked to me afterward."

She drew in a long, sharp breath. "Yes," she agreed, her voice scarcely more than a whisper. "It was Susan." Honesty compelled her to add, "And it was me, too. In the last resort, Susan didn't have the power to make me lose. It was entirely my own fault. Champions like Pieter Ullmann can block absolutely everything out of their minds except what they need to do to win. Alison had that same capacity, although her artistic skills were never quite strong enough to take her to the absolute top. My problem was the opposite. Technique and artistry weren't hard for me, but my coach warned me that my mental discipline was never up to scratch. I always allowed my feelings to affect my skating."

"That's why you were so damn brilliant," Dexter said, an odd hint of anger in his voice. "Your coach was wrong to try to train the emotion out of you. When you had a really good day, you weren't just a superb skater, you were fire and passion captured on ice."

She twisted in his arms, suddenly needing to see his face. "I didn't know you were so impressed by my skating," she said.

He gazed down at her, eyes hooded. "I never once saw the end of your long program, because I couldn't stand the emotional tension you generated. That was why I had to choose my seat so damn carefully, so that you wouldn't notice when I stopped watching."

"Why didn't you ever tell me any of this before?"

His shoulders lifted in a self-mocking shrug. "I was young. I was intimidated by your talent."

"Intimidated! You? Good grief, Dexter, you were the most arrogant, self-assured man I'd ever met—"

"In my own area of expertise, maybe. You showed me that there was a whole creative side to the universe that I'd never even suspected. A lot of the time when I was with you I felt hopelessly... inadequate."

"And I felt inadequate because I couldn't be controlled and efficient like you." She wanted to laugh, or perhaps to cry, with the frustration of so many months when they had totally failed to understand each other. "Why didn't you tell me what you felt?" she asked.

"Because I was a fool. And because I was a combat pilot, working in a brutally masculine environment, testing supersonic jet fighters. I'd spent years being trained not to express my feelings. It needed to be that way, or we'd have gone to pieces every time a test plane showed up with problems. Nerves over my wife's skating performance didn't fit too well with my macho self-image. How the hell could I talk to you about the way I felt, when I couldn't even admit the truth to myself?''

She felt a wave of regret, not for her lost Olympic medal, a loss she'd long since learned to live with, but for the foolishness of two people who'd thrown away a marriage because they were too scared to admit that they were less than totally competent, less than a hundred percent perfect. She smiled sadly. ''Wouldn't it be nice if there was some way to prevent people getting married until they're mature enough to handle it?''

His answering smile was wry. ''Heck, half of us would never pass the test.'' He ran his hand slowly down her side, shaping the narrowness of her waist and the delicate flare of her hips. ''I wish I'd known you were pregnant,'' he said.

''Alison was the only person I told. I was so sure you'd be angry. I didn't want you to be tied in to a marriage that you regretted.''

He didn't answer her directly. ''I saw Alison hand you a glass of something to drink, right before you went out on the ice. You know, all these years I assumed she'd put some sort of drug in it.''

''Dexter, she gave me Gatorade! And I took maybe two sips maximum! Why in the world did you suspect Alison of doing something so horrible?''

''Because she was jealous of you—''

''You mean, you thought she was jealous of me.''

''No, I haven't changed my opinion about Alison. I may not have assessed my other relationships too clearly, but I always understood Alison. She hated the fact that you skated so much better than she did. You were her twin—"

"But not an identical twin," Liz protested. "We were no more alike than any other set of sisters who happened to be the same age. It's not surprising our ability levels were different."

"Believe me, Alison didn't see it that way. She envied your talent."

Liz looked away. "She's dead now, so we can never resolve this disagreement. Besides, that night in Frankfurt, she had nothing to do with what happened. I'd pulled a tendon in my ankle during practice and I was pumped full of Novocain and painkillers. That was a big part of the problem. But it was Susan who destroyed my concentration, not Alison. Although in the last resort I don't blame anyone but myself. I should never have let Susan get to me."

"What did she say, Liz?"

"Does it matter? I accepted a while ago that she was so far removed from the world of competitive skating that I truly don't think she understood the damage she caused by talking about my failing marriage an hour before I was due to go out on the ice. The whole incident's over, Dexter. We have no reason to discuss it."

"It's not over," Dexter said. "How can it be over, when what she said affected our lives for the past nine years? Tell me, Liz. I need to know."

She stared abstractedly into the distance, seeing the cavernous entrance to the ice rink as if it were yesterday. "Susan told me she was in love with you," she replied slowly. "That was no surprise. Everyone on base knew she'd been in love with you for years."

"And that threw you enough to destroy your concentration?"

"No. But she pointed out that her father was your commanding officer, and that she was the perfect wife for you."

"I'd known her for five years," Dexter interjected impatiently. "Didn't it occur to you that if I'd wanted to marry her, I could have done that years before I ever met you?"

Liz lifted her eyes to meet his. "She told me that you finally realized you should have married her, not me. That you bitterly regretted our marriage, and that our life-styles were totally incompatible. Given the fact that you and I couldn't be in the same room without starting to fight, what she said seemed to make a lot of sense."

"Given the fact that we couldn't be in the same room without tearing each other's clothes off and making passionate love, what she said made no sense at all."

Liz's mouth twisted painfully. "I didn't know our sexual relationship was anything special—"

"Dear God, Liz, you can't have been that naive!"

"Whatever you felt for me, it seemed pretty easily transferable. You married Susan a month after our divorce was final."

"Because I was so damn torn apart, I didn't care anymore! I wanted peace and quiet and calm and stability. And..."

"And?"

"I'm ashamed to admit it, but I wanted you to think I didn't give a damn. I didn't want you to know that I was bleeding inside and grieving for what we'd shared. No siree, I wasn't going to have people feeling sorry for me. Hell, if I married Susan fast enough, everybody would think I'd had another woman lined up and waiting all along, and that suited me just fine." He flushed slightly. "You deserved better. For that matter, so did Susan. She wasn't vindictive, you know. Just entirely, totally without imagination. She thought you were an unsuitable wife for me. She saw how tempestuous our marriage was. She concluded that I would be happier married to her. She told you her conclusion. Logically, as far as she was concerned."

"Unfortunately, the rest of the world isn't made up of imitation Mr. Spocks."

"Thank God for that!" His hands skimmed back up her body to rest on her shoulder. "You're shivering," he said.

"This bath towel's damp. It doesn't make the best cover."

"Then take it off."

"No!" Her mouth spoke the word with suitable vehemence, but her treacherous body was already leaning toward him in silent longing. Dear God, but she wanted him to make love to her!

He cupped her face in his hands and brushed a thumb tenderly across her mouth. "I want to love you," he said huskily. "I've been aching to feel myself inside you every minute of the past three days. But I'm not falling into the old, destructive patterns again. If you say no, Liz, I'm going to accept what you say. I had my fill of playing caveman when we were married."

He bent his head and kissed her, a long kiss, full of hunger and adult need. "Come to bed with me, Liz," he said, when the embrace finally ended. "Come willingly. Let me know that for once you want me with your heart and mind, as well as your body."

It was a simple request, but one she wouldn't have been able to fulfill nine years earlier. Now, however, she was many years wiser, as well as older. Her gaze never leaving Dexter's face, she let her arms drop to her sides. The towel slipped down her body and fell into a soft heap at her feet.

"I want you in all the ways there are," she said huskily. "All the ways a woman can want a man. Make love to me, Dex. Remind me of what I've been missing."

For all the passion they had shared during their brief marriage, it was the first time Liz had ever admitted she wanted Dex before she was so fully aroused that she had no choice but to beg for completion. He had obviously not been prepared for her openness, and for a moment she felt him go still, as if he couldn't quite believe what he had heard. Then, with a small, incredulous sigh, he reached out and pulled her into his arms, crushing her mouth beneath his and holding her tight against his hips.

"You feel so right in my arms," he murmured. "God, how did I ever let you go?" His fingers stroked over her breasts, dancing a trail of fire down to her thighs.

"With difficulty. Like me letting you go." Her hands reached for the zipper of his jeans. With an incoherent groan, he took her fingers and guided them in a swift downward movement, opening her hand over himself as he stepped out of the jeans. His lips reclaimed hers with something akin to desperation, and his tongue thrust into her mouth, sparking a thousand pleasure points deep within her.

She clung to him, her body molten, but her mind sharp and clear with the knowledge that she wanted to be held by this man, that she wanted him to caress her, and that his possession would be total only because she willingly gave herself to him.

Dexter swept her into his arms, carrying her to the bed in a gesture familiar from a hundred previous occasions. But this time her response was different from everything she had experienced before. This time she was mature enough to recognize that he didn't take her to bed as an act of domination, so she didn't cling to him in anguished resentment that her body had once again taken charge of her will.

Instead she curled against his chest, reveling in the sensation of hard muscles rippling beneath her cheek. As soon as they reached the bed, she pulled his head down to her mouth, actively seeking the pleasures of his kiss. At last, after nine years of growing up, she realized that Dexter was not the conqueror and herself the conquered. They were equal partners, each wholly dependent on the other for fulfillment.

"I want you so much," she whispered, her fingers tangling in his dark, springy hair. The wonderment in his eyes made her realize how rarely in the past she had consciously expressed her needs.

"Show me how you want me," he commanded, his voice hoarse.

"Like this." She arched her hips upward in explicit invitation. His answering penetration was swift, deep and total. She felt his possession in every cell of her body, and his name sprang in a reflexive cry to her lips.

"Liz," he groaned. "Liz, my love, never go away again. Don't leave me."

How could she risk a second relationship with Dex? On the other hand, how could she ever leave him? For a moment Liz was filled with panic. To stay with Dex opened her to the chance of endless pain, but to leave him again would be to condemn herself to a future of bitter regret. Then the icy coldness of her worry vanished, unable to survive in the burning heat of her passion. Her body shook with the rapturous beginnings of climax, and her thoughts spiraled away into darkness.

Clinging to him, murmuring his name, Liz surrendered herself to the ecstasy of ultimate union with the man she loved.

Chapter Eleven

It was still pitch-dark when Liz awoke out of a bone-deep sleep. Fear clutched at her throat and chilled her limbs. She rolled over onto her back, staring up at the ghostly glow of the high ceiling, deriving comfort from the warm feeling of Dexter's legs intertwined with her own. Whatever caused her to wake had been terrifying.

She listened carefully to the late-night sounds of the house. All she heard was the rustle of the May breeze in the bushes, the sigh of Dexter's breathing, and the creak of two-hundred-year-old wood settling a fraction of an inch deeper into the ground. Nothing very scary. Nothing to bring her panting and sweating out of a deep sleep.

Slowly the realization dawned that it had been her own dreams that had jerked her so abruptly into consciousness. Liz closed her eyes, trying to return to the drowsy state in which dreams could be remembered. A memory teased at the corner of her mind, and she frowned in fierce concentration. Evan. It had been something about Evan. Something he had said just before he died.

Suddenly, with the brilliance of a spotlight shining behind a flimsy curtain, she realized precisely what it was that had brought her awake. She leaned over and shook

Dexter's shoulder. With the instincts of a longtime combat pilot, he sat up, instantly awake and alert.

"What is it?"

"Evan—when he was dying. He said some things, and I didn't tell you. Dex, I'm scared."

He didn't waste time inquiring why she hadn't told him earlier, or even why Evan's remarks had suddenly become urgent at four in the morning. He folded his pillows into a backrest. "What did Evan say that's worrying you?"

"He said somebody would have to kill me."

"What? And you've only just now decided to mention this? For God's sake, Liz, who's going to kill you? Or didn't Evan mention that trivial detail?"

"He just said *they*. And he said several other things at the same time," Liz added defensively.

"They must have been damned exciting if you forgot you were slated as the next murder victim!"

"Not exciting. Frightening. I guess my brain overloaded and stopped processing information logically. At the time I convinced myself he hadn't recognized me—"

"You think that's possible?" Dexter interjected. "You think somebody else may be at risk rather than you?"

"No, I don't. My subconscious obviously treated his words more seriously than the rest of me. Once I fell asleep, and my mind had time to sort out its impressions, I guess my subconscious decided that Evan had definitely meant me, and that I was at risk."

"Did he speak to you by name? Give any sign that he'd recognized you?"

"He called me Liz a couple of times. And remember, he'd phoned my office asking me to come around to the house, so he was expecting to see me. Presumably when he went to the door and let in the murderer, he thought it was me. So all in all, it seems like Evan knew exactly who he was speaking to, and tried to warn me."

Dexter took her hands and pulled her against his chest, stroking her hair with gentle fingers. "I won't let it happen, Liz. I swear to you, I won't let it happen. Now we know you're at risk, there are all sorts of things we can do to protect you."

Rationally she knew that even Dexter couldn't stop a truly determined killer, otherwise presidents and princes would never be assassinated, but the passionate concern in his voice soothed the ache of her fear. Hope replaced the knot of dread that lay coiled in waiting at the pit of her stomach. "Should we call the police?" she asked.

"I have a better idea than that; we can contact the FBI. I'll explain more later. First I need to know what else Evan said before he died."

She looked up at him, without moving from the warm circle of his arms. Even in the darkness, the angles of his face seemed hard, uncompromising—and starkly honest. Nestled against his chest, her body still soft with the imprint of his lovemaking, it was difficult to remember that yesterday, however briefly, she had suspected him of murder.

"What else did Evan say?" She organized her thoughts. "Well, he admitted that he'd been in love with Karen."

Dexter didn't seem surprised. "I wondered if the baby was his," he said quietly. "Once or twice, Evan let slip remarks that indicated he cared about Karen. I never noticed them at the time, only in retrospect, when my twenty-twenty hindsight vision started to operate."

"Why didn't you say anything to the police?"

He shrugged. "I didn't have anything constructive to say. There were already enough groundless suspicions bubbling in the police cauldron without adding mine to the stew. I pointed out to Rodriguez that Evan was solely responsible for personnel records in my Colorado office, and that was as far as I could go."

"You think Evan deliberately lost Karen's file?"

"I suspected it all along."

"But why?"

"Evan screens every applicant for employment. He checks all the references. He would be the first person to know if Karen's records didn't quite tie together. Either he recommended her for hiring, knowing her references didn't check out. Or, more likely, he became suspicious later on, double-checked and then destroyed the file, knowing her records wouldn't stand up to scrutiny."

"It fits," Liz admitted. "He said that he'd been a fool, and that he'd done it all for her. The odd thing is, Dex, I still don't believe Evan was the father of Karen's baby."

This time, Dexter appeared startled. "Did he actually say that? For a dying man, he seems to have said an awful lot."

"That's just it. He only mumbled a few half sentences, and all the rest is conjecture on my part. But he did make specific reference to another man. It was almost as if discovering Karen was pregnant had finally made him accept the truth. 'He is so beautiful and so dangerous.' Those were the last words Evan spoke before he died."

Dexter smiled grimly. "Well, that takes us a giant step farther forward in unraveling the puzzle. Now we know there was a mystery man in Karen's life who exerted a great deal of influence over her. We knew that four days ago."

"We also know that somebody must have wanted to introduce Karen onto your staff really badly, to go to all the trouble of compromising Evan Howard."

"You're right. Which makes me more convinced than ever that those security leaks from my Washington office were somehow engineered from Denver by Karen."

"But she had no clearance to handle secret documents, did she?"

"None. She didn't need it as my administrative coordinator. She handled party political matters, not government material. But the reality is that people become lax about security, particularly with colleagues they know well. By the time Karen made her sixth or seventh trip to my DC office, she might have been able to gain access to a supposedly off-limits area. She was probably trained to find ways of doing just that."

Liz shivered, her fear returning with renewed intensity. "But I don't understand what this has to do with me! Why am I going to be killed? Dexter, for heaven's sake, what connection have I got with secret documents missing from your office? I sell *picante* sauce, for heaven's sake, not missiles!"

"Blueprints for part of a fighter jet," he corrected absently. "That's what went missing." He fell silent for a moment. "I wonder if we've been approaching this whole situation from totally the wrong direction," he said at last. "We've been trying to work out ways your roommates might be connected to each other. We've been trying to find out details about Karen's hidden past. Let's look at the puzzle differently. Let's assume *you* are the center of what's going on, not an inconvenient intruder who keeps bobbing up at the edges."

Liz resisted the urge to break into wild, frustrated laughter. "But Dexter, I am an intruder! How can I be at the center of something when I've not the faintest idea in the world what's going on?''

He looked at her, his expression coolly assessing, but his eyes conveying warmth and support. ''If you're intended as the next murder victim, you don't need to know what's going on. Maybe your death is the crux of the plot. Whatever that plot is.''

She refused to give way to the hysteria that threatened to engulf her. Wrapping her arms around her waist, she fought against a wave of sickness by forcing herself to respond logically. ''We already know of four people who've been killed. Three of my roommates and Evan Howard. At the same time, your office has been traced as the source for some top-secret blueprints that have turned up on the international arms market. Do I have it right so far?''

''You're making a link between two separate sets of events, but I think the link's justified. We're also guessing that Karen and Evan were at least marginally involved in the theft of top-secret papers from my office.''

''But none of this *leads* anywhere!'' Liz exclaimed. ''So let's say, for argument's sake, that I'm the next victim on the list. What happens then? Does it become easier to steal more secrets? No! Does it protect the master criminal? No! I've no idea who he is! I couldn't reveal a thing about him, because I don't know anything. So someone who knows nothing about anything at all is going to die. Big deal.''

''Perhaps they're afraid you might discover who the murderer is?''

''Then they could as logically kill you or Rodriguez. Why me?'' Liz jumped out of bed and began pacing. ''Maybe Evan didn't recognize me, after all. Maybe I'm not going to be killed. I think we've got this all wrong, Dex."

"Unless," he commented slowly, "unless they want a specific person to be accused of your murder."

Liz's head jerked up and she stopped her pacing. "You?"

"Don't you get the feeling that somebody out there is working very hard to set me up?"

Liz gave a small, scared laugh. "I'm real anxious to frustrate them, Dex. Tell me how."

Dexter stared silently into the darkness for several seconds. His decision reached, he flung back the bedclothes and reached for his jeans. "We'll do what I suggested in the first place. We'll get the FBI to take you into protective custody."

"They'll agree to do that?"

"If I tell them they must," he said, with unconscious arrogance. "Whether or not I'm being set up, you seem to be on line as the next victim. I'll contact Harry Cooper at the FBI. . . ." His voice died away. "Damn! We're not at home. I can't contact him from here, except by calling the Bureau and leaving a message with the switchboard operator. Maybe I'm becoming paranoid, but I don't want to do that." He pulled on his T-shirt, then resumed. "Would you be willing to come to Washington with me on the early flight? Most of the emergency safe houses are in the DC area, so you'd be flying to the right place. If we take the first flight out from Logan, we can be talking to Harry in his office by nine o'clock."

"If I have to fly to Washington in order to stay alive, I vote in favor," Liz said dryly. "I've decided recently that I'm amazingly interested in staying alive."

He walked around the bed and kissed her hard on the lips. "You'd better believe I'm not going to let you die," he said. "We have nine years of catching up to do. Last night just made me hungry for more."

Hungry for what? Liz wondered. For more sex, or a deeper, more meaningful relationship? From prudence or cowardice, she chose not to inquire.

DEXTER'S PARENTS ACCEPTED their son's departure with the same equanimity with which they had greeted his unexpected arrival the night before. Amanda, however, was hopping mad that her father and Liz were once again taking off together.

"I went into your room this morning and you weren't there," she told her father accusingly.

"I expect I was in the shower."

"You were in *her* room." Amanda pointed her finger accusingly. "I saw you come out. You like her better than me."

Liz felt herself blushing, but felt obligated to make some sort of explanation. "Your daddy doesn't love you less, just because he and I are friends," Liz said, bending down so that she was at eye level with Amanda.

The child glared at her. "I hate you!" she said and burst into tears.

With less patience that she had ever seen him demonstrate, Dexter took out his handkerchief and dried his daughter's eyes. "Amanda, you're being silly," he said crisply. "You're also being extremely rude to someone who would like to be your friend."

"I want to come to Washington with you!"

"Honey, you can't. I'm sorry. Grandma and Grandpa have agreed to bring you down at the weekend. I'll look forward to seeing you then. In the meantime, please try not to believe all the stories your friends tell you. Stepmothers are often wonderful people, who make the children in their families very happy.''

Amanda buried her nose in her grandmother's skirts, ignoring her father's outstretched hand.

''Don't worry, Dexter,'' Mrs. Rand said with her usual patrician calm. ''Amanda will soon settle down with us, and we'll see you on Saturday morning at National, if you'll come to pick us up. We'll take the usual flight.''

''Of course. I'll be there.''

Liz was concerned about Amanda's escalating dislike for her, but she had little time to mull over the problem. Dexter plied her with questions all the way to the airport, making her recount Evan's dying words in painstaking detail, and then analyzing every possible meaning that they could come up with for the enigmatic phrases. By the time their plane landed in Washington, Liz felt that her brain had been sucked dry, and the only firm conclusion she and Dexter had reached was that some beautiful and dangerous man, clearly not Evan, must be the father of Karen's baby.

''How do we define beautiful and dangerous?'' Dexter queried ruefully. ''That airline steward we interviewed was damn good-looking in a meaty kind of way, but do you think he could be termed dangerous?''

''Lethally boring,'' Liz commented. ''And the kind of bedmate who likes to find out if you can do it suspended from the chandelier. But I doubt if that's what Evan meant.''

''With all his international travel, an airline steward might be able to set up the contacts to make a sale of stolen documents, though. It's a possibility, however remote.''

''He didn't seem bright enough,'' Liz said.

"How do we know that wasn't a brilliant facade?" Dexter's face showed a hint of weariness. "Damn, but I have the feeling we're running awfully hard just to remain in the same place."

The morning didn't improve. Murphy's Law was in full operation, and when they arrived at the FBI building they learned that Agent Harry Cooper was in Seattle until the next day. "Probably checking on Brian for me," Dexter commented ruefully to Liz.

Drawing on all the clout he could muster as a United States senator, Dexter asked to see the director of the Bureau. The director, he was informed with icy politeness, was giving a briefing at the White House and then was flying by Air Force One direct to Texas. The receptionist, conveying the impression that she was granting an undeserved audience with a divine being, suggested that a deputy chief would be able to speak with the senator at three-thirty that afternoon. "He will have to cancel another appointment in order to see you, Senator," she added reprovingly. "A very important appointment."

"My business with the director does happen to be a matter of vital national security," Dexter said, his own voice biting.

The receptionist looked offended. "National security is what the Bureau deals in, Senator. All our business is of the highest importance."

"You're losing your touch," Liz said teasingly as they emerged from the FBI building. "A few years ago, she'd have been eating out of your hand."

"A few years ago I wasn't old and impatient—and you weren't in danger of being murdered."

His clipped words caused a chill to ripple along Liz's spine. Her steps faltered and she almost slipped. Dexter reached out, steadying her, and she quickly regained her balance. In an unthinking, reflex reaction, she glanced around to see if anybody had noticed her clumsiness.

A thin, middle-aged man, fifteen yards or so to their rear, was pocketing something that looked suspiciously like a camera. She groaned. "Damn! Dex, I think there's a reporter on our tail."

Dexter swung around in the direction she had indicated, reaching the reporter in a few athletic strides. Liz could see that his body was stiff with frustration. "I don't want anyone to know I'm in Washington," he said to the man, his voice low and hard. "I'd appreciate it if you'd not publish any of those pictures you've just taken."

The reporter's expression was difficult to read, but Liz could have sworn she saw fright, as much as anything else. How strange, she reflected. Fear wasn't an emotion she associated with photojournalists on the prowl.

"I'm free-lance," the man jerked out. "I can't afford to waste a morning's work."

Dexter pushed a bundle of notes into the man's hand, his mouth twisting with distaste. "Here. That's enough to buy the whole damn camera. I'd like the film, please."

The reporter stared blankly at Dexter, and Liz gained a fleeting impression that, like a cornered animal, the man was poised between fight and flight. With a sudden nervous gesture, he pulled the camera out of his pocket and flipped open the back. He unrolled the film and waved it back and forth in the weak sunlight.

"There," he said. "Now you know for sure I'm not gonna publish these anywhere." He thrust the ruined film into Dexter's hands, snapped the camera closed, and took off at a brisk walk toward the nearby subway.

"Unpleasant little reptile," Dexter remarked. "What next?"

"Don't you need to go to your office?"

"Would you mind waiting there with me until it's time for our appointment with the deputy director?"

"If you like. Or I could check into a hotel—"

"No hotels," he said flatly. "Look, we've decided there's a good chance that someone's going to try to kill you, and then frame me. The best way to protect both of us is to make sure you're always in a group of at least three people. That way I can't be framed, so presumably you won't be killed."

"I hate to cast doubts on such a comforting theory, but what if we're only half right? What if somebody wants to kill me and doesn't care about setting you up? Then your scenario doesn't work."

"Yes, it does," he said, directing her toward his offices on Capitol Hill. "If you're never without three or four people around you, then you can't get killed."

"Unless the three or four people are all in this crazy plot together."

"Liz, after those blueprints went missing, the employees in my DC office were checked out so carefully that we almost know the last time each of them went to the bathroom. I suppose I can just imagine the possibility that one of them might have slipped through the screening net, but three? Take my word for it, the people in my DC office are clean."

"Don't you ever go to the movies, Dex? It's always the guy who's Mr. Clean personified that ends up being the villain in chief."

"Liz, honey, this isn't the movies. This is real life."

Liz, honey. The words sounded sweet, and Liz allowed herself to relax. After all, she only had to survive until three-thirty that afternoon, and then her problems would be over. Despite all the horror stories in the press about government incompetence, Liz retained an optimistic faith in the ability of the FBI to protect U.S. citizens. The deputy director would listen to her story, wave his magic wand and whisk her away to a safe house. The very name of the place suggested that once there, the risk of being murdered would vanish. While she stayed safe in her safe house, Dexter and Agent Harry Cooper would then busy themselves with the investigation, and before long, some master criminal would be revealed.

A niggling doubt surfaced as Liz contemplated the fact that she had no idea who the master criminal might be, and even less idea of what he was up to. She banished the doubt to a far corner of her mind. What was the FBI for, if not for flushing out master criminals and uncovering dastardly plots?

Whether Dexter shared her sudden lightheartedness, or whether he disguised his true feelings in order not to depress her, Liz wasn't sure. Superficially, however, their mood as they entered his suite of offices was surprisingly carefree. Dexter made brief introductions, and then took Liz into his private office, asking a secretary and two research assistants to join them.

While Dexter busied himself reviewing a forthcoming speech on Air Force overspending, Liz quietly retreated to a corner of the room and made herself useful by tidying the small library of books and softcover publications dealing with Colorado. She was in the midst of arranging a tasteful display of travel magazines trumpeting the beauties of the Rocky Mountains, when the phone rang. It was the sixth or seventh call put through to Dexter already, and Liz had no idea why she suddenly straightened from her magazines, her mouth dry with irrational fear.

One of the research assistants picked up the phone. "A personal call for you on line three, Senator."

Dexter took the phone and listened in silence for about a minute. Without placing his hand over the mouthpiece, he looked at his three staff members and nodded politely toward the door. "I'm sorry, this call may take a few minutes. Would you mind leaving me?"

Liz stepped forward. "Dexter, no! Remember what we agreed."

He looked in her direction, but Liz had the feeling he scarcely saw her. He turned back toward his assistants without acknowledging her in any way. "Would you start work on those amendments, please? Right away."

The young man and the two women trooped obediently from the room. Liz hurried forward and leaned against the desk. "Dexter, for God's sake, what is it?"

He spoke into the phone as if he had no awareness of her existence. "I am alone now."

The voice at the other end of the line echoed in the sudden, suffocating silence of the office. "Amanda has a message for you, Senator. She says please cancel your appointment with the deputy director of the FBI."

A child gave an anguished cry. "Daddy, where are you?"

"Don't leave your office, Senator, and keep Ms. Meacham with you. We'll be in touch."

The line went dead.

Chapter Twelve

Dexter returned the phone to the cradle with infinite care. "I was mad at her," he said. "When we left Boston this morning, Amanda knew I was mad at her."

Liz swallowed hard over the horror that had lodged like a physical object in her throat. She reached out and touched him very gently on the back of his hand. He was ice-cold.

"We have to call your parents, Dex. Maybe...maybe Amanda's at home with them. Maybe the call was just some horrible, sick joke."

"You know it wasn't." He pressed a hand against his eyes, as if willing himself to think rationally. "My parents' number is in the Rolodex," he said, and she realized his mind had temporarily blanked out. He couldn't remember his own parents' phone number.

She searched swiftly through the card index, then dialed with shaking hands. It was a personal line, and Mrs. Rand answered the phone with a bright "Hello."

"This is Liz. Liz Meacham. We've run into a bit of a problem here." She refrained from any further explanation, not wanting to worry Dexter's parents, if by any chance the threatening phone call turned out to be a hoax. "Could you please hold on for a moment while I pass you over to Dex?"

She put the phone into Dexter's hand, and he gripped it so tightly that his entire fist went white.

"Where's Amanda?" he asked without any preliminaries.

"Heaven's, you sound fierce," Mrs. Rand replied cheerily. "Amanda's on her way. Your secretary didn't expect to be in Washington until five at the earliest."

"My secretary? You sent Amanda here, to Washington? With my secretary?"

"Well, that's what you asked us to do! And I must say, Dexter dear, your father and I don't agree with giving in to Amanda like this, just because she had a temper tantrum this morning. With all that journalistic fuss over Evan Howard's death, she'd have been much better off staying with us until the weekend. Have you seen the papers this morning—?"

"My secretary came to your house to collect Amanda? Is that what happened, Mother?"

"But of course it is. You should know, for goodness' sake, she was following your instructions. Judy came, that nice young woman from your Washington office that I always speak to." Mrs. Rand's voice was no longer cheery, but choked with the beginnings of fear. "She gave me your note, Judy I mean, and said that she and Amanda would have to hurry to catch the next flight. I packed her suitcase.... Dexter, dear heaven, has the plane crashed or something?"

"No, Mother. Nothing's crashed." Liz could see the monumental effort with which Dexter pulled himself together. The veins stood out on his forehead as he gritted his teeth, using sheer force of will to lower his voice into a semblance of its normal tone. "I'm glad Judy decided to try for the earlier plane. I'm sorry, Mother, I didn't realize she and Amanda had already left Boston. I didn't mean to alarm you."

"But Dexter, you *have* alarmed me! Two minutes ago you didn't seem to know what I was talking about. Are you sure everything's just as it should be?"

"Of course, everything's fine."

"Dexter, you sound—strange. Promise me nothing's happened to Amanda. Did we do the right thing in allowing her to go with your secretary?"

The vein in Dexter's forehead throbbed, but by some miracle of control he kept his voice steady. "Yes, Mother, please don't worry. You did exactly what I wanted. Liz and I—" He swallowed hard. "Liz and I both felt that Amanda was getting far too upset about our relationship. It seemed better to have her here with us."

"I've never understood this modern obsession with having one's children approve of one's adult relationships." Mrs. Rand spoke with some of her normal tartness, and Dexter's grip on the phone relaxed marginally.

"Mother, I have three separate people making urgent hand signals at me. I must go. Will you and Dad still come down to DC this weekend?"

"Probably not. Just make sure you bring Amanda to stay with us as soon as school's finally out. In fact, we were thinking of taking her on vacation to—"

"Mother, I'm now fielding four sets of hand signals. I'll talk to you and Dad later. Bye now."

He hung up the phone, his face drained of every trace of color. "I couldn't tell her," he said. "She and my father wouldn't understand. They'd think it was just a question of paying the ransom, and I don't believe money is what these kidnappers are after. My parents would want to contact the police, and I know Amanda will die as soon as we do that."

It didn't seem like a good idea to allow Dexter to focus his attention on the frightening unknown of what Amanda's kidnappers planned to do. Liz decided to direct his thoughts to the few areas where they might be able to come up with answers. "Is Judy really your secretary?" she asked.

"Yes, one of them."

"Is she in the office today?"

Dexter blinked, focusing his thoughts on the mundane question with obvious difficulty. "I believe I saw her as we came in."

He depressed a button on his intercom and a pleasant voice answered, "Yes, Senator?"

"Judy, have you ever met my mother? In person, I mean?"

"Why no, Senator. Although we've spoken several times over the phone, when she's been trying to track you down."

"Thank you. And I guess you've never met my father, either?"

"No, Senator. He attended a Christmas party once, but I had the flu and didn't get to meet him."

"Thanks, Judy. By the way, screen all my calls, will you? I only want to take personal ones." Dexter flipped off the intercom and leaned back in his chair. "They knew exactly whose name to use," he said bitterly. "I suppose we have Karen to thank for that."

"They took a big risk, though, didn't they? Assuming your mother wouldn't recognize the difference between the impersonator and the real Judy?"

"Not much of a risk. Judy has a pleasant, medium-pitched voice, and as close to a standard American accent as you can get. How distinctive would that be? She introduces herself as my secretary, produces a note from me—"

"And how did they get that, do you suppose?"

He shrugged. "Easily, if they have access to samples of my writing. Not to mention a supply of stationery probably stolen by Karen. Provided the handwriting was close to mine, it would pass muster. My mother isn't likely to submit the damn note to a graphologist before letting Amanda go."

Something prickled at the back of Liz's mind. *Graphologist.* Why did that word make her uncomfortable? The connection clicked into place. *Pieter Ullmann.* His defense on the blood-doping charges would rest largely on the evidence of a graphologist. Odd that the irrelevant connection should have flashed into her mind at such a tense time.

Dexter's fist crashed onto the desk, sending papers flying. "Damn it, Liz, I can't just sit here waiting! I'll go mad. Why don't they tell me what they want me to do? God knows, I'm willing!"

"Perhaps we should ask one of your secretaries to cancel our appointment with the deputy director of the FBI? Maybe they're waiting to hear that you've obeyed that instruction before they give you the next one."

Dexter closed his eyes for a second. "Thank God you're here, Liz. At least one of us is thinking like a sane human being." He pressed his intercom again. "Judy, please contact the FBI urgently and tell them that I won't be able to keep my appointment with the deputy director at three-thirty this afternoon. Make all the necessary apologies, won't you?"

"Certainly, Senator. Should I give any special reason?"

Dexter's mouth tightened. "You could say an unexpected emergency."

"I'll call right away, Senator."

Liz walked over to the window and stared down at the crowds hurrying toward the Capitol building. The day was warm, and the men had doffed their jackets, while the women mostly wore bright summer dresses, their arms bare to the sun. The beautiful spring day didn't seem a good moment for contemplating the end of life, either her own or Amanda's, but Liz was very much afraid that her death was the next item on someone's agenda. And by canceling her appointment with the deputy director, she had lost her best chance of safety.

In his inevitable concern for his daughter, Dexter didn't seem to have registered the significance of the demand that Liz should remain in the office. She hoped that the kidnappers simply wanted to prevent her from making contact with law enforcement officials. She feared that they wanted to keep tabs on her for some infinitely more gruesome reason.

Far beneath her, a family grouped itself on a flight of marble steps, posing for a picture. Even at this distance, she could see that the two children were prancing around in excitement, and the parents were attempting to keep them still with fond exasperation. Amanda should be prancing like that, Liz thought. Instead, she was probably bound and gagged in a dark room.... Shuddering, she snapped her mind closed on the unbearable images.

She sensed Dexter come up behind her. "Liz, I'm sorry," he said, putting his arms around her waist. "I went to pieces for a while, but I'm back together again now."

She turned in the circle of his arms, and saw that he spoke the truth. His face was still a stark white, but his eyes were sharply focused and fierce with intelligence. His fear for Amanda had been leashed by his habitual iron control.

"No father could hear that his daughter had been kidnapped and carry on as if nothing had happened," she said. "I understood."

"I've only just realized that it was your safety I put at risk by canceling our appointment with the deputy director. I had absolutely no right to ask you to make that sacrifice."

"You didn't ask," she reminded him. "I suggested that you should make the call."

"And I'm truly grateful, Liz." He drew in a deep breath. "If it'll make you feel any better, I think the kidnappers have already made their first mistake."

She looked up eagerly. "What's that?"

"If they hoped that keeping me in suspense would soften me up, they've miscalculated. Badly. My first reaction to that phone call was as a parent. Whatever they'd asked me to do to get back Amanda, I'd have done it. Now I'm reacting with my head as well as my heart. We may not have much time, Liz, so the first thing I want you to do is memorize a phone number." He picked up a pen and scrawled a series of eleven digits across the back of her hand. "That's what you might call a high-powered emergency number," he said. "Dial it anytime, and you can summon pretty much whatever help you need."

"Why don't you call it now and ask for a commando squad to rescue Amanda?"

"They have some highly trained specialists available at the other end of that number, but they're not miracle workers. We have no idea where Amanda is. Where would a commando squad start looking? It's much better if we wait for the next phone call, so that we at least have a chance to find out what's at stake in this hideous game."

She cleared her throat. "Dexter, in view of your position in the Senate... Have you considered...? I mean, what are you going to do if they ask for another top-secret weapons blueprint in exchange for Amanda?"

He was silent for a while. "I'm going to pray a lot," he said at last. "And then try to fool them. I have convincing fakes—blueprints and specifications—for all the systems currently being considered by our committee. Agent Cooper insisted on getting them when we first tried to track down the source of the leak in my office. All the plans and papers have been produced by government experts and should fool anybody except a top-notch weapons specialist. The errors had to be pointed out to me, and I've had a lot of intensive technical training. With luck, I should be able to get Amanda back before her kidnappers realize they've been cheated."

Liz had no idea how realistic Dexter's hopes were, although she derived some reassurance from the knowledge that he was talking about expert fakes, prepared at leisure, not some botched job rushed through in response to the crisis of Amanda's kidnapping. And it wasn't certain, of course, that the kidnappers wanted blueprints. They might yet astonish both Dexter and Liz by demanding a straightforward cash payment.

The phone rang before she could say anything. "A personal call for you on line three," Judy announced. "Do you want to take it, Senator? The caller wouldn't give her name."

Liz and Dexter exchanged glances. *A woman?* Dexter picked up the phone, his deliberate movements showing the strain placed on his control, she thought. "Put her through, please."

"Dexter, darling, this is Jeanette." He recognized the low, husky and stunningly sexy voice immediately. "I wasn't sure whether you were in Denver or DC this weekend. I'm going sailing, and I wondered if you were up for a little rest and recreation."

"I'll have to take a rain check this weekend. But thanks, anyway, Jeanette. I'll look forward to seeing you soon." Dexter hung up the phone.

"I think you just ruined a beautiful friendship," Liz said, trying to lower the level of tension and disappointment. "I'd guess that's the last time Jeanette's going to offer you the full facilities of her boat."

"We're just good friends," Dexter replied impatiently. "Hell, I wish they'd call!"

"Just good friends," Liz repeated, the phrase triggering another memory. This seemed to be her day for making odd connections. "Dexter, do you remember that reporter we met outside the FBI building? In retrospect, does it occur to you that he looked a heck of a lot more like a private detective than an aggressive photojournalist?"

"You may be right, although how a P.I. fits into this—" The phone rang again and he snatched up the receiver.

"A personal call for you on line three, Senator. The caller preferred not to give her name."

Dexter's shoulders slumped. "Put her through," he said wearily.

"Good afternoon, Senator." The voice was crisp, businesslike, and strangely flattened, as if it echoed through some sort of synthesizer. "Please depress the red button on the right of your phone, thus scrambling our conversation and making it impossible to trace."

Dexter pressed the button. "I have done what you asked."

"Please wait a moment, Senator, while I check the accuracy of your statement."

The pause lasted about thirty seconds. "I am delighted to see that you are prepared to cooperate, Senator. It bodes well for our future negotiations."

"I want my daughter back. Where is she?"

"Your daughter is well and reasonably happy, although she misses your company. She will continue to be well if you follow some simple instructions. Please listen carefully, Senator, since I don't plan to repeat this information. Within the next half hour, your office will receive a delivery from the Golden Slipper Boutique. The delivery will be made by an employee of the store and will consist of evening clothes and accessories for Elizabeth Meacham. You will pay cash on delivery for these purchases. We know that you, Senator, keep a spare tuxedo in your office. You and Ms. Meacham will dress for the evening in the clothes I have indicated. At six o'clock, having said a cheerful good-night to any of your staffers still lingering in the office, you will summon a cab. You and Ms. Meacham will drive directly to the French Embassy, where a reception for the new ambassador from Chad is being given. Your office, I'm sure, received an invitation. You will be contacted again later this evening."

The voice stopped abruptly and was followed by an echoing silence.

"Amanda!" Dexter yelled the name desperately. "Amanda! Let me talk to my daughter!"

The silence of the phone was absolute. Dexter dropped the receiver into the cradle and turned to look at Liz. "I wish they'd let Amanda speak to me." Despite all his efforts, his voice shook.

"Next time they probably will. Dexter, she'll be all right. They need to keep her well, so that they have something to bargain with. The kidnappers know you aren't going to do a deal unless you have proof that she's alive and unharmed." The platitudes seemed unavoidable, even though they were patently false. She wished that Dexter were a little bit less clear-sighted, a little bit better at the art of self-deception. Kneeling beside him, she clasped his hands and pulled them gently against her breasts. "What in the world do all those bizarre instructions mean, do you think?"

Once again her ploy worked. The practical question brought his emotions back under a semblance of control. "Probably no more than a test to see if we're willing to follow their directions."

"And are we? Is it smart to go partying at the French Embassy because some brutal kidnappers told us to?"

"Yes," he said. "It's smart, because it's the only way we're going to get more instructions." His face became remote, harder than ever. "Liz, I wish I could pretend that I'm offering you a choice, but I'm not. I need you at this reception."

"I'm willing to come with you."

He freed his hands from her clasp, so that he could frame her face. His thumbs stroked a gentle caress across her lips. "Liz, I truly believe that you would be more at risk if you tried to contact the police than if you come with me. But my beliefs may not be a reliable guide at the moment. I have tunnel vision, and Amanda is at the end of the tunnel."

"I wouldn't expect it to be any other way."

His expression didn't soften at all. He bent his head and took her mouth in a quick, hard kiss. "I love you, Liz," he said. "I love you like hell."

A tap at the door was followed by the appearance of a young woman's head, poking uncertainly around the corner. "Sorry to interrupt, Senator, but a delivery boy is here from the Golden Slipper Boutique. He says you're expecting him, and that you owe him six hundred and ninety-three dollars."

"I'll be right out," Dexter said. "Thanks, Bobbie."

LIZ EXPERIENCED a definite sense of unreality as she showered in the small bathroom attached to Dexter's office, then dressed herself for the reception. The gown the kidnappers had sent from the Golden Slipper was black, sleek, low cut and elegant. The price tag hanging from the zipper indicated $495 in discreet gold figures. A bargain for some society matrons, perhaps, Liz thought, but for herself, whose clothes usually came from a discount warehouse, there was an undeniable pleasure in the soft swish of heavy silk against the new designer underwear that had come with the gown.

Putting on her makeup, she wondered if French aristocrats on their way to the guillotine had felt something like she did now: a curious mixture of anticipation, defiance and a fear too great to be acknowledged. Why did it seem so important that she should look good for the delectation of a bunch of kidnappers? She could find no answer. But as she twisted the final pin into her long blond hair, she knew that tonight of all nights, she was determined to look her best.

She stepped into high-heeled, diamanté-buckled evening shoes, and pushed her wallet and a few cosmetics into the matching purse also thoughtfully provided by the kidnappers. A final glance into the mirror revealed a sophisticated, attractive woman whom Liz scarcely recognized. With a twinge of sadness, Liz realized that this particular style of dress reminded her of her sister Alison. Alison had loved the dramatic combination of black and silver, choosing the combination for most of her skating outfits.

Liz couldn't allow herself the luxury of such bittersweet, distant memories. At the moment she had more pressing matters to worry about. Like finding Amanda. And keeping herself alive.

THE FRENCH EMBASSY was located opposite Georgetown University Hospital. During the cab ride from his office, Dexter tried to warn Liz of what was in store for her but, lacking any experience of the Washington cocktail party circuit, she was still unprepared for the barrage of attention that was directed toward her.

Washington's inner power elite throve on gossip. A scandal involving one of their own provided meat and drink for the endless round of formal functions that had to be endured. A double murder involving a popular senator rated almost a ten on Washington's ecstasy scale.

"The French ambassador ought to send you a personal thank-you note," Liz muttered after a particularly bruising encounter. "You've obviously made his night. Do you think *anyone* remembers this reception is supposed to be in honor of the ambassador from Chad?"

"Nobody," Dexter replied promptly. "Probably not even the ambassador from Chad."

"When do you think we can leave?"

His expression became momentarily bleak. "I don't know. Can you hold out for another half hour?"

She took some champagne from the tray of a passing waiter. "Another glass or two of this, and I might even make forty minutes."

"Miss Meacham, I believe?" The voice was soft, insinuating, and Liz felt the blood freeze in her veins. Somehow she forced herself to turn around and face her questioner.

"I'm Elizabeth Meacham, yes."

The woman was pushing sixty, with teeth and skin yellowed by smoking. "It's a pleasure to welcome you to our nation's capital, Miss Meacham. I'm sure it was wise of you to take a holiday from Colorado. Do you and the senator have any statement you'd like to make for my column?"

Liz expelled her breath in a rush that left her limp. A journalist. The woman was a darned journalist! Liz wasn't sure whether to scream with frustration or laugh with relief. She was still trying to make up her mind when Dexter intervened.

"If I give you an exclusive, Betty, will you go away and leave us in peace?"

The reporter's eyes gleamed. "You betcha."

"Miss Meacham and I recently became engaged and are planning our wedding shortly. There, you owe me one, lady. Coming at this particular time, that announcement is going to make your column the talk of the town tomorrow morning."

"You and Miss Meacham were married before, and the marriage only lasted nine months. Any reason to expect a longer relationship this time?"

"Don't push your luck, Betty. You can say, quote: 'The senator commented that this time he was older and wiser. A hell of a lot older and hopefully a hell of a lot wiser.' End quote." Dexter turned and looked down at Liz, his eyes darkening as if he meant every word he said. "Off the record, our marriage is going to work this time, because we're even more in love. At least, I am."

Although she knew he'd only invented the story in order to get rid of the reporter, Liz's whole body responded to the lie. She felt the heat rise in a deep flush from the pit of her stomach, and her cheeks flamed. With seeming indifference to Betty's avid eyes and flapping ears, Dexter carried Liz's hands to his mouth and dropped the lightest kisses against her knuckles. "You're always beautiful," he said huskily, "but tonight you're positively stunning. I love you, Liz."

Her heart hammered wildly in her chest. When he looked at her like that, she couldn't quite convince herself that this was all a charade. She was so lost in the fantasy world Dexter had created that she jumped when Betty's voice intruded. "Too much sentiment makes me nauseous," she said. "I'll see you two lovebirds later. Like you said, Senator, I owe you one."

They lingered another half hour at the reception, but no one approached them with cryptic messages or whispered instructions. The crowd had thinned to a mere handful of guests when Liz and Dexter finally took their leave.

"Your limousine, monsieur?" the doorman asked.

"We'd like a cab, please," Dexter responded.

The doorman whistled one up, accepting Dexter's tip with the smoothness of vast experience. "Your destination, monsieur? I will tell the driver."

Dexter and Liz exchanged helpless glances. "To my apartment, I guess," he said. "Tell him The Fountains, in Chevy Chase."

"Certainly, monsieur." The cab door was slammed, and Liz leaned back against the tattered leather of the seat, trying to think of something she could say that might make Dexter feel better.

"Perhaps they couldn't approach us because there were too many people around."

"They could have made the opportunity if they'd wanted to. Betty Stone managed to get us alone, and we weren't even cooperating with her."

Liz developed a sudden fascination with the beading of her purse. "Couldn't you think of any other way to be rid of Betty? Is that why you told her we were getting married again?"

"No. I was a low, underhand conniving schemer. I told her we were engaged because I hoped it might—" He broke off as the cab swerved violently to the right, cresting the sidewalk but continuing to move.

"What the devil?" Dexter demanded, just as an ambulance with lights flashing and siren howling roared out of the Georgetown hospital driveway and catapulted in front of the cab. The cabdriver braked immediately and swung around in his seat, leveling an extremely menacing gun straight at Liz's head.

"Either of you move and she gets it," he said.

The two doors closest to the sidewalk were wrenched open. "He has a gun!" Liz screamed in warning.

It was all she said. A leather-gloved hand was clamped over her mouth and she was hauled from the cab. For a crucial second she failed to struggle, thinking that her abductor might be intent upon rescuing her from the gun-toting cabbie. In the two seconds it took to realize her mistake, all chance to scream and attract attention had been lost. With one hand still clapped over her mouth, her captor pulled her arms behind her back with brutal efficiency and bundled her face first onto the floor of the ambulance. The driver didn't even wait for the doors to be slammed behind her before he released the brake and set the ambulance shooting forward into the narrow Georgetown street.

The fist pressing her down to the ground relaxed its pressure. "You can sit up now, *dorogoya*."

She lifted her head, too stunned to move the rest of her body. "Mikhail?" she whispered. *"Mikhail?"*

He smiled the warm, familiar smile she knew so well. "Hello, Lizushka. Welcome to Washington."

Chapter Thirteen

He couldn't do a damn thing, because they had him covered by two guns: the cabbie's .45 Magnum and the 9-millimeter Soviet Makarov pistol aimed square between his eyes by the squat, balding man who'd just climbed into the front passenger seat.

Dexter silently cursed his helplessness. Dear God! Now they—whoever they were—had not only Amanda, but Liz, as well! He writhed under the knowledge that he had brought Liz into this danger. He was the one who'd insisted they follow instructions and attend the reception at the embassy. He was the one who'd insisted on canceling their appointment at the FBI.

The sick knot of guilt in Dexter's guts hardened into a bitter determination to frustrate his opponents or die trying. And right at this moment, he reflected grimly, it looked as if he was going to die for sure.

The gunman in the passenger seat steadied his aim with brisk professionalism. Not a good sign. "Good evening, Senator Rand. My name is Igor. It is certainly my pleasure to meet you."

Dexter stared ahead in stony silence.

Igor sighed. "It would help your situation, Senator, if you would cooperate. The driver of this cab is about to put his gun away and resume driving. We do not wish to attract the attention of a cruising police vehicle by remaining parked. You will clasp your hands behind your neck, please. If you do not, you will be shot in the knee."

Igor meant what he said, Dexter was sure of it, and a broken kneecap would make escape virtually impossible. Without breaking his silence, Dexter did as Igor instructed. He stared out of the front window, not deigning to meet the eyes of either of his captors. With a despairing lurch of his stomach, he saw the ambulance containing Liz hurtle off into the darkness, its emergency beacons flashing. An old trick for hurrying from the scene of a crime, but nonetheless damnably effective, he reflected wryly.

Schooling his features into blankness, Dexter held his hands unmoving behind his neck. He carried no concealed weapons, and therefore cherished no hope of outshooting his captors. Any attempt at escape would have to wait.

Igor gave a curt nod to the cabbie, who returned his .45 to the inside pocket of his jacket and immediately set the cab in motion. Dexter had hoped Igor might try to frisk him, but the man was obviously too seasoned a veteran to attempt something so dangerous. Igor knew—unfortunately—that in the close confines of the cab, it would be easy for Dexter to grab Igor's gun and turn the tables on his attackers.

"We are taking you to a house in the country," Igor announced. His tone of voice suggested that Dexter should be appreciative of this rare treat. "Miss Meacham will be joining us there."

Dexter tried to show no reaction to this piece of news. He willed himself to remain silent, but lost the battle.

"Where's Amanda?" he asked, the words torn from him. "What have you done with my daughter?" By a superhuman effort, he managed to bite back the need to ask anything more about Liz. It might give him some infinitesimal advantage, if Igor and his crew thought him indifferent to Liz's fate.

"Amanda is already at home with her grandparents, Senator Rand. When we arrive at our destination, I will permit you to make a phone call confirming her safety. You may dial the number yourself, so that you will know there are no tricks, and you may ask any questions that come into your head to ensure that she is indeed at home and unharmed."

"How can I believe you? Why would you—?" Dexter cut off his question. Since he expected nothing but lies in answer, he wouldn't demean himself by asking.

"Ah! You wish, perhaps, to know why we have released your daughter? The answer is simple. We took her to demonstrate our power. We have released her as a gesture of goodwill, Senator Rand. We want you to see that cooperating with us is not a difficult business. It was never part of our plan to harm your daughter. We Russians are sentimental about little children."

"May I lower my hands?" Dexter asked curtly. "My arms ache."

Igor curled his finger around the trigger of the gun. "No, Senator Rand. You may not lower your hands."

Dexter leaned back against the seat and stared out of the cab window. He recognized exactly where they were. Ironically, for all the good it would do him, they were driving past Langley, headquarters of the CIA in suburban Virginia. Now that he had time to reflect on his situation, he found the fact that he wasn't blindfolded deeply depressing. He could think of several reasons why his captors wouldn't have bothered with a blindfold. All of them were unpleasant.

The roads were relatively clear of traffic as they drove through Tyson's Corner, but the cabdriver seemed in no hurry, or perhaps he was avoiding the risk of a ticket for speeding. Their journey continued through Reston until, after about an hour, the cab stopped outside a pleasant-looking house in a semirural setting. Dexter recognized the area as one much favored for weekend trysts by Washington's "in" crowd.

Igor's method of removing his prisoner from the cab once again demonstrated his experience. At a nod from Igor, the driver, .45 in hand, pulled Dexter from the cab with sufficient force to send him sprawling on the gravel driveway. With a foot in the small of Dexter's back, the driver expertly searched him for weapons.

"He's clean, boss."

Igor exited from the cab and grunted. "Stand up, if you please, Senator Rand. I would remind you that the more quickly you walk into the house and demonstrate some signs of cooperation, the more quickly you will be permitted to telephone your daughter."

They knew precisely which carrot to dangle in front of his nose, Dexter reflected. Unfortunately, the knowledge that he was being manipulated didn't prevent the ploy from working. At this moment, he wanted to hear Amanda's voice with an intensity that overrode all other considerations.

The cabbie dug the .45 into the base of his spine. Unresisting—not that he could have resisted in any way that would have left him alive, he reflected—Dexter allowed himself to be led up to the front door and into the comfortably furnished living room.

"Sit," Igor commanded.

He sat down on the cream leather sofa the man indicated. Later, he cautioned himself. Later you can try the heroics. "I'm ready to phone my daughter," he said, his tone curt.

Igor smiled, displaying a gold tooth. "I see you are a practical man, Senator, who believes in dealing with first things first. I am glad that my superiors, in selecting you for our purposes, did not underestimate your common sense." Igor gestured with his gun to indicate a phone on the glass-topped coffee table. "Please feel free to call your parents' home, Senator."

Dexter picked up the phone and examined it carefully, pulling off the base and unscrewing the mouthpiece. It looked like standard phone-company issue. He could see no sign that it had been tampered with, and Agent Cooper had recently given him a refresher course in methods of bugging and otherwise distorting normal phone service. Dexter screwed the phone together again.

"I want to dial Information," he said curtly.

"Please, Senator, be my guest. You are welcome to test for yourself that this is simply a normal phone. You do realize, of course, what will happen to your daughter, should you attempt to communicate with anybody we deem . . . undesirable."

"I want to check that the phone isn't rigged to go through to one certain number, manned by your personnel, whatever digits I dial."

"I repeat, Senator. Feel free."

Dexter called Information in New York, and asked for the number of an old friend from his Air Force academy days. The woman responding sounded bored enough to be the genuine phone-company article. He even heard her gum snap as she connected him to the computer, which provided the correct number.

Feeling more confident that the phone hadn't been rigged, he then dialed his parents' home. His father answered with a crisp "Hello."

"Hi, Dad, this is Dex. Sorry to bother you at this hour, but is Amanda there?"

"Yes, she is, but she's on her way to bed. What in the world's gotten into you, Dexter? Dragging her off to Washington, and then turning around and telling your secretary to bring her back again to us! The poor child's exhausted from all that useless flying."

Dexter gripped the phone and willed himself to stay calm. "Let me talk to Amanda, Dad. And could you save the lectures until tomorrow? One way and another, this has been a helluva day."

"Here's Amanda," Mr. Rand said, his tone still disapproving. "It seems she wants to talk to you."

"Hi, Daddy! Why didn't you come to see me when I was in your secretary's apartment? Judy was pretty nice, but I didn't like being there with her. She told me you were too busy to come and see me."

Dexter drew in a long, shaky breath. "Hello, sweetheart, it's great to hear your voice. I'm sorry we missed each other today. Was Judy—? What did Judy give you for lunch?"

"Hot dogs, and she let me have two slices of chocolate cake." Amanda sounded less than interested in Judy. "Why didn't you come to see me, Dad? Why did I have to fly to Washington if you're too busy to come and see me? I felt sick on the plane coming back to Boston, and my ears popped."

"Judy and I had a bit of a mix-up in our communications, sweetheart. I didn't actually know you'd arrived in Washington. I'll explain to you what happened another time. In fact, I didn't really want you to leave Grandma and Grandpa's house, so if anyone else comes to get you, anyone at all, you just stay put with Gran and Gramps, okay?"

"Okay. When are you coming to see me?"

"I don't know exactly, sweetheart, but soon, very soon."

"I miss you, Dad." A small pause. "Is Ms. Meacham with you?"

"Not at the moment." He needed every ounce of discipline he possessed to keep the urgency from his voice and the panic from his expression. "Amanda, promise me you'll stick close to your grandparents, will you? That's very important."

"Okay. Grandpa and I are going fishing tomorrow. And Grandma says I have to go to bed now. It's eleven o'clock and a ridic—ridikolus hour for me to be up."

"Yes, it is late." Dexter's voice thickened. "Good night, Amanda. I love you lots and lots."

"I love you, too." She yawned. "Good night, Dad. Take care."

"I will," Dexter said, holding the receiver long after his daughter had hung up.

"Satisfied, Senator?" Igor asked. "Your daughter, as you heard, is well and happy."

Dexter played back the conversation in his mind. Amanda's chatter had been entirely natural. If there had been kidnappers in the room, coercing her to reply, Dexter knew he would have heard the fear and constraint in her voice. And his father would have been even less capable of pretending cheerfulness than Amanda. There was no way, he decided, that either of them could have been under any sort of duress. Whatever hideous payment Igor might try to exact in exchange for his generosity, Amanda was temporarily safe.

Dexter shifted his position on the sofa and looked straight into Igor's eyes. "Okay," he said. "My daughter's home with her grandparents, and she hasn't been harmed. What do I have to pay to keep her safe?"

AS SHE PULLED HERSELF off the floor of the jolting ambulance, Liz felt no fear. For a crucial few moments, she was aware of nothing save an overwhelming sense of betrayal. "Why, Mikhail?" she asked. "Why are you doing this?"

"Doing what, *dorogoya*?" His warm smile had not changed at all, giving her an unearthly feeling that somehow she must have misunderstood, that somehow she wasn't in danger, that somehow Mikhail was still the same friendly brother-in-law she had known and liked for years.

She shook her head, trying to clear her mind of its dangerous fuzziness. "Mikhail! You've kidnapped me, for God's sake!"

His eyes twinkled in what she now realized was a sickening parody of brotherly teasing. "God, Lizushka, has nothing at all to do with my actions. I follow the orders of my government."

Bile rose in her throat. "Your defection... it wasn't genuine, was it?"

"I am Russian. I will always be Russian. Only you Americans, in your arrogance, would believe that I wished to change my nationality. My defection was a carefully planned move, approved by the leaders of the KGB."

"But why, Mikhail? Why didn't you stay in the Soviet Union? Nobody in America begged you to defect!"

"My government saw an opportunity," Mikhail said. "I willingly took it."

"For your government? The same government that holds your mother hostage—?" Light suddenly dawned in Liz's fuddled brain. "Was that it?" she asked. "Did they promise to get your mother an exit visa if you helped them? Oh Mikhail, you should have known better. They'll never honor their promises, and you'll be in their service forever."

"My mother," he murmured mockingly. "Ah yes, my dear old mother, pining for her exit visa. You are so easy to deceive, Liz, that it almost becomes boring. There is no mother. I haven't seen the woman who bore me since the day she left me on the orphanage steps in Leningrad. What's more, I have no desire to see the old bag, if she still lives. The staff tell me she was an extremely inefficient whore, who was forever getting pregnant. I was the third bastard of hers that the state had to take care of. And who knows how many abortions the workers of Leningrad paid for on her behalf?"

"I thought that the great and glorious Soviet state had abolished whores," Liz said caustically.

"Only high-paid ones," he said. "And with the current political climate, who knows, even the high-priced ones may soon reappear. We like to feel that our motherland has all the amenities of her capitalist rivals."

Despite the fact that the gun in his hand had never once wavered, Liz couldn't bring herself to believe that her images of Mikhail were so totally false. "What about Karen?" she asked. "Was her baby—? Mikhail, was it yours?"

He shrugged. "Probably."

"Did you—kill her?"

"But of course. It was always our plan to compromise Dexter Rand through Karen. Her death was the catalyst designed to set all the other ingredients of our plan bubbling. My dear Liz, please stop bouncing around. You are making the driver nervous. And you know how sensitive I am to other people's nerves."

"On the contrary. It's obvious I know nothing at all about you."

"*Dorogoya*, you have seen me regularly for the last four years."

"Seen you through blinders, I think."

"Not at all. I am the man who enjoys spending Saturday nights drinking vodka and eating caviar with you."

"But you were living a lie, Mikhail!"

"What is truth? Part of me is that man you spent time with in Colorado Springs."

"It's the other parts of you that I'm worried about. What's going on Mikhail? Why have I been kidnapped? How are you hoping to set up Dexter?"

"So you did at least work out that much."

"If you're planing to use me as leverage against Dexter, you're wasting your time."

"Lizushka, I never waste my time. That is how I clawed my way out of the orphanage."

"I would say you've been wasting your time for the past four years. How does it help the Soviet Union to have you train Americans like Pieter Ullmann to become Olympic winners? It was a Russian who got beaten into second place."

Mikhail was silent, and enlightenment dawned. "That was a mistake, wasn't it?" Liz breathed. "Pieter was never supposed to win! You assumed you'd be able to psych him out, to tempt him into breaking training at some crucial point. You didn't realize how rock-bottom determined he was to win the gold."

Mikhail's eyes glittered in the dimness of the ambulance interior, but he said nothing.

"That business about blood doping was all nonsense, wasn't it?" Liz persisted. "Were you so angry with Pieter that you and Karen plotted to get his gold taken away from him?"

"Pieter's been a womanizing fool since he was sixteen!" Mikhail burst out. "How was I to know that where skating is concerned, he is pure dedication and hard work?"

"Two hours watching him on the ice should have given you a hint," Liz taunted. "Maybe you're not quite such an expert judge of character as you think, Mikhail. Your masters can't have been too pleased with you recently. I doubt if they sprang you from the Soviet Union so that you could produce winners for the United States."

Mikhail leaned forward and backhanded her hard across the mouth. She tasted blood, but refused to cry out. He thrust her onto the stretcher bed, propping her against the wall of the ambulance.

"Whatever my mistakes with Pieter, I have read your character well, Lizushka. You share in abundance the two fatal flaws of all Americans: you believe your friends tell you the truth, and you have hope for the future."

"Those aren't flaws, Mikhail, they're strengths."

"You are naive, *dorogoya*. Perhaps it is better so. Perhaps you will be lucky enough to die without suffering the anguish of knowing your death approaches. Even now, even at this moment, I can see that you somehow expect the cavalry to come riding to your rescue. Isn't that how Hollywood promises it will be? In the United States, innocent maidens are never run over by the train."

"If it's naive to believe that good guys win in the end, Mikhail, then I'm proud to be naive. Whatever you're plotting against Dexter Rand, it isn't going to work out."

"There is one small flaw in your reasoning, Lizushka. I believe *I* am the good guy and that my cause is just. I also know that the plan we have for subjugating the senator to our will is foolproof. Dexter Rand will be our man by the end of this night, take my word for it."

"You're wrong!"

"We shall see, Lizushka. Now, we are nearly at our destination and I say only this. Prepare yourself for a shock, little sister. I think you will find that we have a most amusing surprise awaiting you."

When they let her out of the ambulance, Liz saw that they were in the driveway of a typical two-story, upper-income suburban house. Whether they had driven into Maryland or Virginia, she had no idea. Of Dexter there was no sign.

Mikhail had bound her wrists together with surgical strapping tape, and he held his hand tightly over her mouth as they walked up the gravel path to the house. His gun poked into the small of her back, so she didn't even consider screaming, but some absurd, lingering hope of rescue caused her to sneak surreptitious glances to the left and right as she was propelled toward the back door.

There were other houses in the neighborhood, she saw, although they were relatively far away and screened behind trees and bushes. But even if she could somehow make a break for it, she knew she couldn't assume those houses represented safety. The chances were good that they contained enemies rather than friends. Mikhail said something in Russian to the ambulance driver, a young man shaped like a gorilla, carrying a submachine gun that seemed to grow like an extension from his right arm.

Sandwiched between the two men, Liz was taken in through a back door and conducted down a brightly lighted staircase to the basement. Liz barely had time to register that it was furnished in typical suburban style—complete with a Ping-Pong table in the center of the large room—before Mikhail bent forward and murmured in her ear.

"The moment has arrived," he said softly. "There is somebody who has been waiting most anxiously to see you, *dorogoya*."

Liz's heart pounded with sudden, suffocating force and her lungs felt squeezed tight by lack of air. "Who is it?" she asked. "Who wants to see me?"

A rustle of silk whispered behind a Victorian-style screen in the far corner of the room, and Liz's head jerked in that direction, like a puppet's pulled by a string. A slender, fair-haired woman, wearing a scarlet silk robe and a pair of high-heeled black shoes identical to Liz's own, stepped out from behind the screen. Her blue-gray eyes were fringed by long lashes, and her naturally pink lips formed a striking contrast with her pale, almost translucent, complexion.

The pounding of Liz's heart intensified. She felt giddy, nauseous, disoriented. The fear she had held at bay for so long rose up in her throat and emerged in a single giant scream. She gazed at the woman in hypnotized horror. Except for the red silk robe, she was looking at a mirror image of herself.

At the sound of Liz's scream, Mikhail clapped his hand back over her mouth with bruising force, but the woman merely smiled—a cruel, mocking smile that held no hint of sympathy.

"Hello, Lizzie," she said. "It's been a long time, babe."

Chapter Fourteen

The nausea wouldn't go away, neither would the dizzying sense of unreality. Liz clutched at her stomach. "Alison?" she whispered. *"Alison?"*

The woman smiled. "That's who I am, sweetie. Although not for long."

"Wh-what have you done to your hair? And your nose is different." Liz realized belatedly that she was hardly addressing the major issue. "I thought . . . we all thought you were dead."

"You were intended to, sweetie."

"But how could you let us all believe you'd been killed? Good God, Alison, Mom had a stroke when she heard about the plane crash! She's been a helpless invalid ever since, and all over something that never really happened!"

A faint trace of color stained Alison's cheekbones. "Mother had high blood pressure for years, so she was probably headed for a stroke anyway, whatever happened. Besides, she isn't miserable. How can she be, when she doesn't know what's going on? And the Soviet government helps to pay for the best nursing care. I'll bet she's happier than half the people who haven't had a stroke."

Liz stared at her sister in stupefied silence. Alison, she realized in wonderment, truly believed what she was saying. Even as a child, Alison had always been capable of twisting the truth to fit her own personal needs. Apparently that character trait hadn't altered. Liz clenched her fists in an effort to keep herself from screaming.

"What's going on?" she asked tightly. "Why have you suddenly decided to come back from the dead? And why have you changed your hair and your nose to look like me?"

"That, sweetie, should be obvious even to you. Alison Kerachev isn't coming back from the dead. Elizabeth Meacham is merely going to be played by a different person."

"I see." Liz, in fact, saw a hell of a lot more than she wanted to. Like the fact that she was shortly going to be dead. Two Elizabeth Meachams obviously wouldn't fit into anybody's scheme of things. She swung around and sought out Mikhail, who was viewing the encounter from a corner of the room, an amused, proprietary smile flashing occasionally as he looked from one newly identical sister to the other.

"Somebody's gone to a lot of trouble to change Alison's appearance," Liz said. "We both know your government doesn't spend money just to keep its citizens happy, so what's going on, Mikhail?"

"You will know in good time, *dorogoya*."

"Don't call me that!" The endearment lacerated Liz's nerves, and she struggled to regain control of herself. "Something important's at stake here, that much is clear. It must have taken months of surgery and a great deal of money to make so many changes in the way Alison looks."

Alison strolled over to link her arm through Mikhail's. "There wasn't that much to change, sweetie. We weren't identical twins, you and I, but the plastic surgeons tell me our bone structure is remarkably similar. I had to have my nose bobbed, and they did a bit of work on my jaw, which was damn painful and definitely isn't an improvement. I have to tint my hair, because yours has more red in it than mine, but that's easy enough to do, except for the fact that I hate the color. Fortunately our eyes have always been amazingly alike, and they're the most difficult feature to change."

Liz's gaze traveled over her sister's body. "You're thinner. At least in most places."

Alison grinned mockingly, running her hands over her breasts. "You like my new boobs, sweetie? Best quality silicone implants, courtesy of the toiling Soviet masses." She jiggled her bosom with evident satisfaction. "Yes, these almost make up for all the months I spent on a starvation diet, trying to keep pace with your weight loss. Every time Mikhail sent us a new picture and a new set of statistics, you'd lost another couple of pounds and another few inches. What the hell's been going on in your life?"

"My roommates were getting murdered," Liz said dryly. "I have this weird aversion to coming home and finding my friends splattered over the sidewalk. It affects my appetite."

Alison shrugged. "They weren't friends, only acquaintances. Besides, you're so damned stars-and-stripes patriotic, you ought to be glad they're dead. They were all spying for the Soviet Union. Karen didn't even exist except as a creation of the KGB. She was smuggled into the country two years ago, direct from her Siberian training camp."

Liz didn't dispute her sister's statements. There seemed little point. Alison's definitions of patriotism and friendship seemed to have nothing in common with Liz's. "I'm a market-research specialist with a medium-sized Mexican-food company," she said. "What interest could the Soviet government possibly have in me? Why in the world would they spend all this money to replace a junior manager at Peperito's?"

"Nobody cares about your job at Peperito's," Mikhail said curtly. "We are replacing you in your role as the former wife of Dexter Rand. It is the illustrious senator who interests our government."

For a few moments, Liz was shocked enough to forget to be frightened. "You think Dexter won't notice the substitution?" she asked incredulously. "He'll know Alison isn't me, the second she walks into the room."

Alison glanced toward her husband. "I do hope she isn't correct, sweetie."

Tight-lipped, Mikhail replied. "It's unfortunate that your sister has spent so much time with the senator over the past week. Our plans required her to be thrown again into his orbit, which is why she was persuaded to share an apartment with Karen Zeit. However, we didn't anticipate—"

"We?" Alison queried softly.

"I didn't anticipate such an occurrence," Mikhail admitted, scowling at his wife. "Based on your information and the many conversations Liz had with me, it seemed her hatred for Dexter was too great to be overcome, whatever the circumstance. Even so, I am sure he will not detect the substitution."

"And if he does?" Alison persisted.

"In the last resort it doesn't matter—provided the realization doesn't come for a week or two. You know as well as I do that the senator will be forced to comply with our wishes, if he wants to remain alive. Our plan is foolproof."

"But you already kidnapped Amanda!" Liz said. "If the KGB want to force Dexter to do something—anything—you have the perfect method of control!"

"Not at all, sweetie." Alison turned away from a narrow wall mirror where she had been admiring her silhouette. "Kidnapping Amanda gives us only limited control. Either we return her and so lose our hold over Dexter, or we kill her. In which case, once again we have no hold over Dexter. Taking Amanda was nothing more than a device for getting the two of you to the French Embassy, and keeping you away from the FBI."

"You would kidnap a child just to get Dexter and me to the French Embassy?"

"Of course. Why not?"

"Why is Dexter so important to you?" she asked Mikhail. "There must be at least twenty or thirty senators with more political clout than him."

Alison smiled pityingly. "Shall I give her a lesson in world politics, Mikhail?"

"If you wish. Although time marches on, and I see no necessity for explanations."

"That's your Russian background, sweetie. You never think the toiling masses need to know anything. Personally, I'm all in favor of freedom of information."

Mikhail laughed bitterly. "You're not in favor of anything unless it puts power or money into your pocket."

"Are you complaining, sweetie? I've directed quite a lot of those useful commodities your way since we were married, so I suggest you shut up." Alison bestowed a mocking kiss on Mikhail's cheek and walked without haste across the rec room.

She stopped when a few inches still separated her from Liz. For the first time in years, the two sisters were within touching distance. Liz's heart constricted painfully as she looked into her sister's blue-gray eyes and read there the certainty of her own death. The pain wasn't only for her imminent end. She wanted to live—desperately—but at this moment her most profound regret was that Alison could so readily conspire to abet her own sister's murder.

"Why?" Liz asked. "Why are you doing this, Alison? What did I or anyone in our family ever do to make you so full of hate for us?"

Alison gave an odd, defiant little shrug. "How could you understand? You have no idea what it's like to be constantly second best. The apple of Daddy's eye, as long as Lizzie wasn't around to enchant him. Pretty, but not quite as pretty as Lizzie. Smart, but not quite as smart as good old Lizzie. A world-class skater, but not quite as good as the ethereal, passionate Lizzie."

"You're wrong, Alison. Our parents never measured out their love according to how worthy we were. They loved us because we were their children, not because we were pretty or smart, or because we won medals for skating."

Alison totally ignored Liz's remarks. "For a while, I could train harder and win more competitions than you," she said. "But eventually your natural talent showed through. You won the U.S. championship, I bombed out. Then I barely made it into the first round of the Olympics, whereas you were expected to win. And then, to crown it all, there was Dexter—"

"Dexter? What on earth has he got to do with our relationship? You'd fallen in love with Mikhail long before I even knew Dexter."

Alison's mouth twisted into a thin, bitter line. "You never realized how I felt about Dexter, did you? I met him when we first went over to Germany, weeks before you even heard his name. The only snag was, I couldn't get him interested in me, however hard I tried. Finally I persuaded him to come to the rink and watch me skate. Only you were already out on the ice practicing when we arrived. I remember the music that was playing. It was Ravel's *Bolero*, and you were going through a routine that was so erotic that even the cleaners had stopped to watch. So what happened? The same damned thing that always happened to me when you were around. He forgot about me. Dexter saw you and stopped dead in his tracks. The music ended. You looked up. You opened your innocent little eyes wide, smiled your cute, naive little smile, and two minutes later he was at your side, asking you out to dinner."

"Alison, you know my marriage to Dexter was nothing to envy! It was already broken past repair by the time you married Mikhail and left for Moscow."

"And I worked damned hard at breaking it, sweetie. With a little help from Susan, who was almost as naive and gullible as you in her own way."

Liz felt her confused emotions coalesce into a hard ball of pride. She lifted her head. "No, Alison. You didn't destroy my marriage to Dex. You didn't have that power. Nobody has the power to destroy a marriage except the couple themselves."

"Well, if you say so, sweetie, but I sure think I helped things along a little. And now I'm going to have the power to do a whole bunch of exciting things where Dexter's concerned. You see, Lizzie, I'm going to make sure that Dexter's votes in the Senate all go the way the Soviet government wants them to go."

"You're crazy!" Liz breathed. "Even if Dexter thought you were me, he wouldn't vote according to my instructions. Don't you understand anything at all about his character?"

"Sweetie, I know everything about Dexter Rand. As soon as he became a senator, the KGB started to compile a dossier on him. Right from the first, he was targeted as the senator they most wanted to neutralize."

"But why?" All Liz's frustration and bewilderment sounded in her question. "I would have thought the KGB had much bigger problems to worry about than the junior senator from an underpopulated state like Colorado."

"You still don't understand, do you, Lizzie? It's Dexter's expertise in weapons technology that's so worrying. Not only is his vote always technically sound, but other senators recognize his mastery of military hardware and follow his lead. Since Dexter took over the Appropriations Committee, Congress hasn't funded a single useless weapons system, and Dexter's managed to swing financial backing for three breakthrough defensive systems that would never have left the drawing board if not for his support."

So that was it, Liz thought, recognizing the ring of truth in her sister's voice. It was Dexter's years of practical experience in the Air Force, coupled with his outstanding technological training, that made him so dangerous as a senator—and such a valuable target for the KGB. "I still don't see where you come into this, Alison. Do your spy masters plan to have you curl up beside him in bed and seduce him into voting your way? 'Darling Dexter, I love you so much, please vote no on the Phantom X-32 jet fighter aircraft?' Even the KGB can't be dumb enough to think that would work."

Mikhail stepped forward. "Enough," he said. "There is no reason for this conversation to continue. Take off your clothes, Liz. Your sister needs to wear them."

Liz sat down. "Go to hell, Mikhail."

She had known resistance would be useless, but she was tired of surrendering so tamely to her own inevitable destruction. When Mikhail dragged her back onto her feet, she kicked him hard on the shins. His response was a swift, brutal punch to the ribs that knocked the air out of her lungs. As a skater, she had fallen often enough to be quite familiar with physical pain, but she couldn't control her instinctive gag reflex, and for several seconds she fought to draw every breath. When she opened her eyes again, the driver from the ambulance was holding her hands immobile in front of her, and Mikhail was unzipping her gown at the back.

Mikhail gave another Russian command to the driver, who at long last put down his submachine gun. Silently he found the end of the strapping tape and ripped it off Liz's wrist, so that Mikhail could take off the black gown. Once her wrists were free, she struggled to resist being undressed, but achieved nothing except to slow down the process slightly and to receive several stinging slaps from Mikhail and the ambulance driver.

Alison lit a cigarette and puffed on it nervously as Liz's slip was removed and handed to her. Still smoking, she shrugged out of the red silk robe and into the long black slip.

"The damn thing's too tight," she muttered around her cigarette. "Hell, Mikhail, she lost even more weight."

"I think not. Calm down, Allie. You chose the outfit in the first place, remember? You wear the same size as Liz in everything except for the shoes, and you're already wearing the identical pair of shoes." He smoothed the slip over his wife's hips and handed her the dress. "Perfect," he said, closing the zipper.

"She's split the damn seams. Dexter'll notice for sure if he touches me. Why did you let her wriggle around like a stuck pig in a thunderstorm?"

"Split seams are no problem. The senator will expect Liz to have struggled. Here, take her purse. There is makeup inside, and a perfume spray. Do you want me to hold her face still so that you can copy her exact style of makeup?"

Alison grimaced. "Just the eyes. I don't want to go upstairs wearing fresh lipstick and powder."

Liz shivered and bent to pick up her sister's robe. The very thought of being touched by Mikhail—or Alison—made her physically ill. The ambulance driver gestured menacingly with his gun, which he'd picked up again, but he didn't prevent her from slipping into the robe. It smelled of cigarette smoke and Alison's perfume, but Liz felt marginally less vulnerable when Mikhail and his sidekick weren't staring straight at her bra and stockings. Mikhail waited for her to tie the belt, then caught hold of her face and turned it toward Alison. Liz closed her eyes, willing the nausea to go away.

"Very good," Mikhail said softly. "With eyes shut it is easier for Allie to copy your eye shadow."

Liz didn't struggle. When Mikhail finally released her, she turned one final time to look at her sister—the sister who was now a mirror-perfect image of herself. She knew that at any moment she would start to feel fear, but right now, all she felt was anger and sick revulsion, mingled with shame that a member of her own family could contemplate such treachery.

"Alison, don't do this," she pleaded. "Don't betray your own country."

Alison didn't reply at once, and Mikhail jumped in. "Russia is Alison's country now," he said. "Russia has given her power and wealth and a useful task to perform. She owes no loyalty to America, merely because an accident of birth decreed that she would be born here."

"She wasn't just born here. She spent the first nineteen years of her life benefiting from the opportunities that America provid—"

"Try not to sound like such a naive fool, Lizzie, dearest." Alison stubbed out her cigarette. "I'll see you around, little sister. Your ex-husband is upstairs, and I don't want to keep him waiting."

IGOR'S SMILE showed no sign of strain. Positively exuding cordiality, he chuckled at Dexter's grim question. "You are required to pay nothing, Senator Rand. We ask merely for a little cooperation."

"Kidnapping Amanda and abducting Elizabeth Meacham at gunpoint isn't likely to inspire me with feelings of goodwill."

"But Senator, how can you be so unreasonable? Amanda is safely at home with her grandparents. And, as a further gesture of our extreme benevolence, I have somebody else waiting to see you. She comes now." Igor clicked his fingers to the cabdriver, who walked over to the door and pulled it open.

"Dexter!"

At the heartrending cry, he stood up and turned around, just in time to see Liz being half dragged, half carried into the living room. Her arms were held by two men: the cabbie, and another man whom Dexter vaguely recognized but couldn't quite place.

Fighting down his immediate, instinctive impulse to rush to Liz's side, Dexter struggled to remain in control of his reflexes. If he kept his cool, there was a slight chance he might be able to find some weakness in Igor's position that would enable him to bargain for Liz's safety. But if he once allowed himself to start reacting emotionally, it would be all over. Except in the movies, unarmed combat provided no defense against three expert gunmen. If he gave in to his emotions and started throwing punches, he might—with luck—win Liz twenty seconds of freedom before the bullets exploded in her body.

Liz was obviously not doing too well. *Poor kid,* he thought. He could hear the choked little sounds emerging from her throat as she bravely attempted to silence her sobs, and when her two captors finally released her arms, she ran across the room and collapsed helplessly against his chest, repeating his name in an endless, desperate litany.

Overwhelmed by a primitive masculine urge to hold her tight and pour out meaningless words of love and comfort, Dexter strained to remain alert and rational. He couldn't afford to let Igor guess how desperate he felt about Liz. Dexter knew Igor's type of old, and he had no doubt that the man was capable of ordering Liz's fingernails pulled out one by one if that seemed the quickest or surest way to manipulate him. Willing Liz to understand his coldness, he brushed a hand over her hair in a friendly, but somewhat impersonal gesture of reassurance. He tried to imagine how his father would behave with an overwrought, but distant, relative and modeled his own behaviour accordingly.

"Liz, my dear, you must calm down. Hysterics aren't going to help anybody." *That was it,* he told himself on an inner sigh of relief. Just the right mixture of mild affection, tolerance and exasperation. About a hundred light-years away from what he was really feeling.

"Oh Dex, I'm so frightened!"

Her words were little more than a squeak of panic, and something deep within him stiffened in surprise. Why was Liz behaving like this? Of all the women in the world, she was surely the one least likely to crumple into his arms and reveal her fears. He would have expected her to come into the room fighting and spitting out defiance to her captors. What the devil had they been doing to her to provoke such an atypical response?

With gentle hands he pried her away from his chest, so that he could look at her more closely. "What's happened?" he asked softly. "Are you hurt?"

"They hit me," she whispered.

Alarm prickled down Dexter's spine. The antennae that had so often warned him of danger in his fighter-pilot days quivered into alertness. Why was Igor allowing Liz to sob out her ill-treatment in his arms? Why did he have this odd sensation of breathless expectancy—as if everybody in the room were waiting for him to show some reaction to this encounter with Liz?

To buy himself some time, he drew her back into his arms and dropped a light kiss on her forehead before reaching up to stroke her hair again. To his surprise, she wriggled within his clasp and turned up her mouth, asking for a kiss.

It was an invitation even Superman could not have found the strength to refuse. Dexter bent his head and touched his lips to Liz's soft, delicate mouth. She clung to him, her lips parting eagerly, her tongue seeking his. He responded automatically, his mind reeling, waiting for the flame—the inevitable, mind-blowing flame—that always burst into life when he and Liz exchanged kisses.

Nothing. His body didn't harden, his pulse didn't quicken. Nothing.

Dexter slowly raised his head from the kiss, breathing deeply, and simultaneously casting a quick, surreptitious glance around the room. He became aware of three things: Liz smelled of cigarette smoke and a heavy, unfamiliar perfume: Igor was looking like a cat who'd swallowed the cream and the canary; and the man who had dragged Liz into the room two minutes earlier was Mikhail Kerachev.

Mikhail Kerachev. Alison's husband. Alison, who was dead. Liz's brother-in-law.

Dexter rapidly concluded that he would stake his life on the fact that the woman in his arms was not Liz.

Chapter Fifteen

Mikhail pulled roughly at the woman in Dexter's arms, dragging her away with such force that she tumbled to the floor with a bone-jarring crunch. Dexter had trained enough men in unarmed combat to know that Mikhail's roughness hadn't been faked. Looking down at the whimpering woman, he realized he was in the bizarre position of having to pretend concern for her well-being, when every atom in his body was screaming with concern for the real Liz.

He knelt beside the woman, wondering what subtle signals he had picked up to warm him so quickly that she was a fake. A ringer for Liz, maybe, but definitely not the real thing. He examined her covertly for telltale differences. He'd be damned if he could spot any, except perhaps for the eyes. The blue-gray shade was identical to Liz's. The sweeping lashes had the same upward curve and thickness, the eyebrows the same delicate arch. But the mind and soul looking out from the window of these eyes bore no relationship to Liz's passionate, generous nature. This woman was calculating every tear and every whimper—and as far as Dexter was concerned, her calculation showed.

"Liz, my dear, come and sit on the sofa." Turning to Igor, he spoke stiffly, as he would have done if he'd really felt compelled to ask for a favor on Liz's behalf. "She needs water. And can you instruct your minions to behave with a little less brutality?"

"But certainly. Comrade Mikhail, you have heard the senator. Please refrain from exercising your temper on his ladylove."

"She is not my ladylove," Dexter said swiftly. *Too swiftly?* he wondered. He tried once again to adjust his voice to the controlled, strained tones he would have used if Liz had really been curled at his side, nursing her bruises. "If you think I have any special feelings for Liz, you're wrong. She is merely my former wife. You of all people should know that any relationship between us ceased to exist long ago. We hadn't seen one another in nine years until you precipitated our reunion by killing Karen Zeit."

"The reality of your relationship with Ms. Meacham is of little interest to us, Senator Rand. As is so often the case, truth is irrelevant. The appearance of truth is all that concerns us."

"Is that what this is all about?" Dexter asked. "Is there some specific lie you're expecting me to palm off as truth?"

"Such a quick wit," Igor murmured admiringly. "We shall deal well together, Comrade Senator."

"That seems unlikely. And I am not your comrade."

"Not yet, Senator. But wait. You have not heard the terms of my proposition. I hope you will agree they are heavily weighted in your favor—given the circumstances in which you find yourself."

"Just state your terms," Dexter said wearily.

"You will change your *Yea* vote on the F-19B fighter aircraft to a *Nay*. Furthermore, you will campaign actively against the plane in the Senate and in the United States as a whole. The vote is already skintight because—fortunately—most people do not have your expertise in military matters. If you switch your vote and speak against the project, the F-19B will not go into production."

"Which will be very convenient for your government," Dexter said softly. "That plane is the best airborne defensive weapon ever to leave the drawing board."

"Indeed. I acknowledge the truth of your statement. In return for this considerable favor, you, Senator, will be allowed to live. In fact, you will be allowed to live precisely as before, with perfect freedom to vote as you please on most other Senate issues."

"Most other issues?" Dexter queried cynically. "Just how many times will I be required to sell my vote in exchange for my so-called freedom?"

Igor smiled tightly. "Only on military matters, Senator. Whenever a vote comes before your Defense Appropriations Committee, you will wait for instructions as to how you are to cast your vote. Otherwise, feel free to follow the dictates of your conscience."

"How generous you and your government are."

"Indeed, I am glad you appreciate our generosity. Do you agree to our terms, Senator Rand?"

"Yes," Dexter said instantly. "I agree."

The woman seated next to him on the sofa drew in a sharp breath, but Igor simply laughed. "Now, now, Senator. We are not fools, and I must tell you that your prompt agreement fails to carry conviction. As a responsible representative of my government, I have to ensure that you do not pretend to agree with us merely to buy your freedom.''

Dexter's body tensed. ''We should speak bluntly, Igor. I'll tell you frankly that I don't see any way you can force my cooperation, if you allow me to leave here alive.''

''You are wrong, Senator. We have a guaranteed method of ensuring your cooperation. Quite simply, Ms. Meacham will die if you do not vote as we have requested. What is more to the point, you will be accused of her murder.''

''Dexter, don't let them kill me!'' The woman on the sofa clung to his arm, sobbing pitifully.

If anything at all had been needed to clinch Dexter's conviction that this woman was not Liz, her hysterical reaction was it. Careful to conceal his disgust, he bent over her, whispering false words of consolation and encouragement. When he straightened again, he looked at Igor with a scorn he had no need to fake. ''If I vote in favor of funding the F-19B, killing Elizabeth Meacham won't change anything. The plane will still go into production, whether or not I'm accused of her murder. True, I'll have to bear the weight of Liz's death on my conscience, but the aims of your government won't be advanced by one millimeter.''

''Alas, Senator, it seems that you gravely underestimate the wisdom of our planning. The circumstances of your trial will seal the fate of the F-19B.''

''Even if I am found guilty, how does that invalidate my vote on a piece of military hardware?''

Igor's laugh was triumphant. ''Because the FBI and the CIA in a rare moment of cooperation will uncover documentary evidence proving that Ms. Meacham is a Soviet spy, and that she has been working in collusion for many years with her friend Karen Zeit and her brother-in-law Comrade Mikhail Kerachev. We plan to take a series of most compromising photographs tonight, featuring you and Ms. Meacham. This house is already known to the FBI as a trysting place for personnel of the Soviet Embassy. We will have all the documents we need to make it appear that Ms. Meacham has blackmailed you successfully for some months."

"How can you hope to prove that, when it's totally untrue?"

Mikhail walked across the room to stand beside Igor. "In several interesting ways, Senator. For example, the military blueprints missing from your office. The FBI has been searching for some weeks without success to find the culprit. We have proof that you yourself were the person responsible for their theft."

"Karen Zeit stole those documents, I'll stake my life on it."

Mikhail smiled. "The evidence shows otherwise, Senator."

"What's more," Igor interjected smoothly, "the evidence also shows that Elizabeth Meacham coerced your favorable vote on the F-19B and that you then murdered her in desperation to escape from the toils of her blackmail. Tell me, Senator, do you doubt, in such circumstances, that the Senate will reconsider its vote on the new aircraft? I think we can safely guarantee that the Senate will eventually vote against the plane. The only question for you to decide is whether they vote against it before or after Ms. Meacham is killed and you are accused of her murder."

Dexter bought himself time to think by comforting the woman who was once again huddled in his arms. Her capacity for producing crocodile tears was truly remarkable, he reflected. He'd only ever known two women capable of turning on a flood of tears at whim. One was a famous movie actress, now gray-haired and over fifty. The other had been Liz's sister Alison. If Alison hadn't been reported as dead, he would be suspecting... In fact, he was suspecting..

With falsely tender hands, Dexter framed the woman's face and used his thumbs to brush away her tears. The blue-gray eyes stared up at him with barely concealed calculation. *Yes,* he thought grimly. Plane crash or no plane crash, the woman he held in his arms was undoubtedly Alison. Even after nine years, he'd recognize that look of mingled sexual invitation and cold self-interest anywhere.

Igor gave one of his characteristic grunts. "I await your answer with interest, Senator."

Dexter forced himself to stroke his hand soothingly down Alison's back, while his brain raced at a feverish pace, weighing options and calculating odds. "Don't worry, darling, I'll get us out of this mess somehow," he whispered. "You can trust me."

"Oh Dexter, darling, please save me!"

Her lines had a distinctly hackneyed ring to them, Dexter decided cynically. Obviously exile in Moscow hadn't prevented Alison from watching the current crop of corny American TV shows. He nuzzled her hair. "We'll find some way to escape," he murmured. "You'll see, dearest."

Alison gave a pretty little sigh that ended on a delicate little sob. "Oh Dexter, you're so brave."

Barely concealing his distaste as she insinuated her fingers between the pearl studs of his evening shirt and stroked his chest, Dexter looked up at Igor. "If I promise to vote as you wish on the F-19B, how do I know Liz will be safe? How do I know you won't kill her as soon as I walk out of here?"

Igor seemed to recognize the first hint of real concession in Dexter's attitude, and couldn't quite conceal the triumphant twitch of muscles in his cheek. The outcome of this elaborate plot had perhaps not been as certain in his own mind as he liked to pretend.

"Senator Rand, how many times do I have to repeat that we are all of us here men of goodwill? Ms. Meacham will be safe, for the simple reason that we wish for your continued cooperation in halting the insane arms race between our two countries. You are a man of peace. My government is a government of peace. In working with us, you will make the world a better place for everybody. Your vote against the F-19B is valuable to us, yes, but it is nowhere near as valuable to us as a continuing voice in the Senate that reliably reflects our views."

That was undoubtedly true, Dexter reflected. A senator whose vote could be counted on in all matters related to the defense and the military would be a tremendous asset to the Soviet government. But he didn't want to seem to compromise too early, even though he was almost eaten up with the desire to get out of the house so that he could initiate a search for Liz. God damn it, he'd call out the whole U.S. Army if need be, but he'd find her!

Dexter removed Alison's straying fingers from inside his shirt, and kissed her knuckles with what he hoped was a reasonable facsimile of tender sorrow. Still holding Alison's hands, he turned again to the Russian. "Somehow, Igor, your goodwill doesn't strike me as a very reliable form of protection for my ex-wife."

"Senator, our government wishes you to be happy. We don't wish to kill Ms. Meacham unless your actions make her death absolutely necessary. Indeed, we hope that one day soon we may read in the newspapers that Washington society has turned out in force to dance at your wedding to Ms. Meacham."

His wedding to Liz! Like a drumroll underscoring the moment of revelation, Dexter heard the thunderous beat of his heart. Igor, he was sure, had unwittingly revealed the purpose behind the substitution of Alison for Liz. They wanted him to marry her! If Alison became Mrs. Dexter Rand, the KGB would have pulled off the enormous coup of planting one of their agents in the innermost circles of Washington power.

Resisting the impulse to punch her squarely in the jaw, he gazed down at Alison. Soulfully she gazed back up, the picture of suffering womanhood. Her role was obviously to play the terrified victim to the hilt, so that Dexter would be convinced that "Liz's" life was in danger and would comply with Igor's demands.

It was symptomatic of the limitations of KGB planning, Dexter thought, that they could seriously believe he wouldn't detect the substitution of Alison for Liz. Although, looking at the perfect duplicate the KGB had created, he was forced to admit that a month earlier he might have been deceived. If Liz hadn't come to him the night of Karen's death... if their old attraction hadn't instantly flared... if they hadn't spent long hours making love until every cell of her body seemed imprinted on his soul...

But none of that helped one goddamned bit with his major problem, which was how to get out of here in time to rescue Liz. If he could convince Igor that he was safely "turned," there was a chance that Liz could be saved. Dexter wouldn't allow himself to calculate just how slim the odds of saving the real Liz actually were. Some calculations were better not made, if he wanted to preserve his sanity.

Why the blazes didn't Alison stop sniffling? Didn't she understand anything about the way her twin would behave? "Hush, sweetheart," he murmured. "We'll find a way to come out of this in one piece, I promise you."

She lifted her face, eyes glistening jewellike with tears. How the hell did she cry so much without smudging her mascara? he wondered.

"Oh Dexter, how can you save me? You'll never vote against your conscience, I know you won't. You're not that kind of a man, or I wouldn't love you."

The urge to sock her one was getting stronger by the moment. "The F-19B is just a plane," he said, gritting his teeth. "I place more value on human life than on a weapons system. Especially your life, Liz."

Would that do it? he asked himself. Acting wasn't one of his major skills. Did he sound convincingly like a man preparing to compromise his lifelong beliefs to save the woman he loved? He glared at Igor. "But don't think I'm going to vote the way you tell me ever again!" The last wriggle of a man in a noose. Had he pitched his voice more or less right?

Igor grunted with satisfaction, but Mikhail looked uneasy. He muttered something in Russian to Igor, who dismissed his comment with a curt reply and an impatient wave of the hand. Mikhail was obviously more worried than his boss about Dexter's relatively swift surrender. Dexter decided it might be smart to voice a few more doubts.

"I'm still not sure you'll keep Liz safe," he said, draping an arm around Alison's shoulder. "I think you may be stringing me along. What's going to happen to Mikhail, for example? According to your scheme, he's going to be identified as a spy if I don't vote the way you want. Does that mean Mikhail's volunteering to spend the rest of his life in an American jail? That seems unlikely."

"Very unlikely," Mikhail agreed. "But it won't happen, Senator. I leave tomorrow—" He glanced at his watch and corrected himself. "I leave today for Stockholm, and from there I fly immediately to Moscow. My time of exile in America is over. I shall soon be back among my own people, training Russian skaters for the next Olympics."

Igor spoke. "You see, Comrade Senator, we have thought of everything. So may we have your agreement that you will vote *Nay* on the F-19B fighter project?"

Dexter allowed his temper to snap. "Yes, you have my agreement, damn it! You've left me no choice. And I've told you before, I'm not your blasted comrade!"

Igor smiled. Very gently. "But Senator, that is exactly what you have just become."

He crossed to the sofa and hauled Alison roughly to her feet. "And now, Comrade Senator, we come to the most interesting part of the evening. The photographs. Would you start undressing your former wife, please?"

THE AMBULANCE DRIVER turned guard looked bored out of his mind but attentive. Gun clasped firmly in hand, he had stationed himself midway between the chair Liz was tied to and the stairs leading out of the basement. Liz had needed about two and a half seconds to decide that appealing to his better nature was unlikely to produce very positive results. Wisely, she had kept silent.

She had reached several other equally gloomy conclusions, among them one that even if she miraculously managed to overpower the guard, she still wouldn't have a snowball's chance in hell of making it out of the house alive. But since she seemed destined to die anyway, she damn well intended to die escaping, not tied to a chair.

A noise overhead—a sound almost like furniture being moved—caught the guard's attention for a couple of minutes. Liz scooted her chair a vital six inches closer to the wall, the carpet muffling the telltale scraping noises. Her goal was the nail head she had seen sticking out of the paneling. If she could just pierce the surgical tape that kept her hands strapped uselessly behind her back, she would be one step closer to a successful escape.

She poked the nail through the tape and began sawing away, keeping her upper body still so that the guard wouldn't realize what she was doing.

She had a couple of advantages, Liz thought, flexing her wrists within the layers of tape. The guard didn't expect her to try to escape, and he didn't know that she was an expert in self-defense—not the stylized self-defense of karate and judo schools, but the real-life self-defense she had been taught by a women's group in New York. Liz had gone to the class after being mugged and almost raped on a New York subway. If she could somehow get the guard to come up close without arousing his suspicion, Liz thought—hoped—prayed—she would have a chance of overpowering him.

From his frequent glances toward the ceiling, it was obvious that the guard's interests lay on the floor above, where the action—whatever that might be—was actually taking place. For a man with a body like King Kong and a trigger-happy finger, playing keeper to a mere woman presumably wasn't much fun.

Her hands were free! A sizable chunk of skin had been left on the nail, but at least she was now potentially mobile. Liz turned an involuntary crow of triumph into a passable imitation of a sob and huddled pathetically in her chair. The guard glanced indifferently toward her, then went back to stroking his gun.

How the devil was she going to get him to come closer? Displaying several inches of thigh wasn't likely to do it. The guy looked as if his bedmate of choice would be a Sherman tank. Liz waited until his gaze wandered toward the door, then toppled her chair with as much of a crash as she could muster on the carpeted floor. For good measure, she added a strangled shriek that she hoped sounded feminine and flustered. She was careful not to scream too loudly. She didn't want to attract the attention of whoever was moving around overhead.

Blood drumming in her skull, she lay on her side, coiled and ready to spring. She watched the guard stride across the room, his body language hinting at irritation rather than suspicion. With a carelessness that Liz prayed might save her life, he allowed the submachine gun to dangle by his side. He came closer. Liz held her breath. His stance suggested he might be in the habit of relying on his size for protection. If so, he might not know it, but he was extremely vulnerable.

Go for his eyes. The instruction from her defense class remained with her, although Liz wasn't sure she'd be able to carry it out.

Your life depends on it, she told herself. *No wimping out, kiddo. This isn't a trial run. This is for real.*

Muttering angrily, the guard bent over her. She launched herself upward from the balls of her feet, butting her head into his stomach with the full force of her weight. Before he could catch his breath, she stomped on his instep with the steel-shafted heel of her shoe, simultaneously sticking her fingers straight into his eyes. He gave a scream of pain even as he raised his gun. He was too late. Liz lowered her fist in a chop that knocked the weapon from his hand. They both dived for it, but she succeeded in grabbing it. She brought the barrel crashing down on his head. It connected with a sickening thud of metal pounding against bone.

The guard keeled over and lay in a crumpled heap on the floor. Liz stuffed a fist into her mouth. She wanted to cry. She wanted to throw up. She wanted to lean against the wall, shaking and shivering.

But she didn't have time for any of that. Tugging the broad silk belt of Alison's robe from her waist, she tied it around the guard's mouth in a makeshift gag. Panting and puffing, she pulled his wrists behind his back and strapped them together as best she could with the tape left over from the roll he and Mikhail had used on her. Right now the guard looked out for the count, but for all she knew, he might revive in five or ten minutes.

"Sleep well, buster," she murmured, wiping her sweaty palms on the sides of Alison's robe.

The stairway was obviously useless as an escape route. Liz had no doubt she would encounter armed opposition long before she reached the upstairs hallway. However, from what little she had been able to see, the house was a typical upper-income suburban home. Which meant that the narrow door in the far corner of the basement was worth exploring. Chances were good that it led into some sort of furnace or utility room.

Tucking the submachine gun under her arm, Liz ran to the corner and pulled open the door. A utility room lay concealed behind the paneling. Never had a bare concrete floor, a dusty furnace and miscellaneous wispy cobwebs looked so attractive. Smiling, she stepped into the little room.

As soon as the door to the rec room closed behind her, darkness descended. Her heart rapidly sliding into her shoes, Liz fumbled for a light switch. Such complete darkness must mean that the room had no windows. *No windows.* And therefore no way out.

When the naked overhead bulb flicked into life, she hesitated, almost afraid to walk around the tiny eight-by-ten space. What would she do if the basement was entirely below ground level? *You'll start digging, that's what,* Liz told herself grimly.

It took her less than a minute to confirm her worst fears: the furnace room lacked any form of window, even a tiny, single pane.

Liz slumped against the plasterboard wall and stared blindly at the furnace. As if to mock her earlier optimistic thoughts, she saw a small gardening trowel, minus its handle, nestled at the base of the hot-water heater. To dig her way out? She gave a bitter laugh. She had no idea where Alison and Mikhail had gone, but she doubted if she had more than thirty minutes before somebody would come back to check on her. Even if she had two hours—an impossible dream—she couldn't dig her way out of the basement in two hours.

But maybe she could find a hiding place and outwait her captors. Maybe she could squeeze between the furnace and the water heater. Or clamber onto the top of the appliances to reach the ceiling. The acoustical tiles would be easy to remove.

Anything, any hope, was better than surrendering meekly to the fate Mikhail and Alison had in store for her. With renewed energy, she resumed her inspection of the utility room.

She found the grating tucked into an odd position behind the furnace. At this time of year the furnace wasn't operating, so she had only marginal difficulty in squeezing behind the furnace to examine her find more carefully. Clamping down hard on her rising excitement, she peered through the iron latticework at the murky hole behind. She couldn't see all the way to the end, but had the definite impression that there was a faint lessening of the darkness toward the end of the crawl space. A window? *Dear God, let it be a window.*

The grating should have been easy to remove, but rust had welded it stuck and she struggled for almost ten minutes, using the trowel as a lever, before she managed to pry it loose.

Sweating, filthy and triumphant, she rested the grating on top of the furnace, tossed the submachine gun onto the rocky concrete floor of the crawl space, and then heaved herself inside. By lying flat on her stomach and stretching out her hand as far as it would go, she was able to reach the grating and pull it into place behind her.

Surely the crawl space must lead somewhere outside? Wasn't that what they were for—to provide access to water pipes and telephone lines? Liz closed her eyes, willing herself not to hope too fiercely. Squatting, because the rough concrete floor was too painful to crawl on, she waddled and wobbled along the ten feet of dark tunnel. High-heeled evening shoes and a silk robe definitely didn't make the most convenient escape outfit ever invented, she realized.

She was steeling herself for disappointment, so when she found the window she stared at it stupidly, wasting several precious seconds in blank contemplation. It was encrusted with grime and dust, so she scraped at it with the heel of her shoe, trying to detect some sign of an alarm system. As far as she could tell, there wasn't an electronic beam or even an old-fashioned electric wire anywhere in sight.

They can't have been careless enough to leave this entrance to the house unprotected, Liz warned herself. *When you smash this window, all hell's going to break loose.*

But waiting wasn't going to disconnect the alarm system, if there was one. And every minute she delayed made the prospect of pursuit more likely. Drawing in a deep breath, Liz plunged the heel of her sandal through the glass.

Silence. No bells clanged, no sirens hooted, but she knew that meant nothing. Some of the most sophisticated alarm systems flashed silent warnings in every room. In a frenzy of fear, she slashed at the glass with the butt of the gun, indifferent to the shards of glass splattering against her wrists and arms. When the wooden frame was denuded of glass, she pulled herself through, ignoring the ripping of glass fragments on her breast and stomach and legs.

She emerged into a shallow window well, which was slimy with leaf mold and garden debris. Liz peered cautiously over the rim of the well and allowed the night breeze to caress her face with the promise of freedom. She smiled wryly. Cobwebs, crawl spaces, leaf mold, chilly night air. This was her night for finding strange things beautiful.

Body tense, ears straining, she gazed rapidly from one side of the house to the other. She could see most of the front driveway, and it seemed empty. The ambulance must have been driven into the garage, out of sight of any inquisitive neighbors. Abandoning the gun as too heavy to carry, Liz used her upper-body strength to pull herself out of the window well.

She was on her feet, kicking off her high-heeled shoes and running across the damp grass before her conscious mind could scream caution. She ran away from the lighted driveway, away from the front of the house. Like any other frightened night creature, she sought the safety of darkness, and angled through the trees and bushes as she dashed toward the road. At any moment she expected to hear the hue and cry of pursuit. At any moment she expected to hear the hateful softness of Mikhail's laugh. *Dorogoya*. She would never be able to hear that word again without shuddering.

She was on the road now, running along the grass bank at the side. Still no sound of pursuers, only the rasp of her own breath in her lungs and the distant bark of a dog.

The lights of a house loomed ahead. Was it safe to knock on the door and beg for help? Her feet had almost turned into the driveway, when some primitive survival instinct flared to life, reminding her that she had no way of knowing who owned these houses. The owners were as likely to be enemies as friends.

Over the relentless thrumming of blood in her ears, she heard the unmistakable sounds of a car approaching. Instinct once again took over, sending her scurrying for the protection of a clump of shrubbery, thick with spring foliage. Now that she had stopped running, she had time to notice that her teeth were chattering, even though she didn't feel cold. Oh God, she didn't want to die! Not before she had a chance to see Mikhail and Alison in jail. Not before she had a chance to tell Dex how much she loved him.

It wasn't a car she had heard, but a small pizza delivery truck, and it turned into the driveway right next to where Liz was crouching. After her experience with the ambulance, she was no longer trusting enough to believe that a truck saying Poppa Pellini Delivers on its side panels necessarily meant that the truck contained pizzas. Squirming as deeply as she could into the protection of the bushes, she watched the truck draw to a halt.

A young girl in a gingham uniform climbed out of the truck, cardboard carton in hand. If she carried a bomb, Liz could only think it smelled a lot like pepperoni. The girl walked across the grass toward the front door, leaving the engine running and the radio blaring a hit from the top twenty.

Swifter than thought, Liz left the protection of the bushes and ran toward the delivery truck. She threw herself into the driver's seat and let off the hand brake. The truck moved forward. The Fates were on her side, Liz thought, glancing down. It had automatic transmission.

Without a twinge of remorse for having entered the ranks of car thieves and other felons, Liz stepped on the accelerator. Ignoring the anguished shouts of the delivery girl, she gunned the truck out of the driveway.

First she was going to rescue Dexter. Then she was going to eat some stolen pizza.

Chapter Sixteen

Liz found the all-night convenience store about ten minutes down the road at the first intersection she came to. It was obviously a hangout for local teenagers and, despite the fact that it was almost one in the morning, the place was quite crowded.

Liz jumped down down from the truck and headed for the phone. A stack of cracker boxes inside one of the windows turned the glass into a shadowy mirror, and for the first time in hours, she became aware of how she looked—and how little she was wearing.

But there was no time to worry about the red silk robe, now tattered, smeared with leaf mold and flapping beltless in the nighttime breeze; no time to worry about the fact that she wore nothing underneath the robe except a lace teddy, a fancy garter belt and shredded stockings. There was certainly no time to worry about what her face and hair must look like, daubed with dust and festooned with cobwebs.

Pulling the robe firmly around her waist, Liz strode into the convenience store with all the dignity a shoeless, mud-spattered woman could hope to muster.

By some miracle, the phone was not only in working order, but nobody was using it. Ignoring the open-mouthed stares of two teenagers, who obviously felt somewhat resentful that their dyed-feather mohawks and safety-pinned ears couldn't begin to compete with Liz's bizarre outfit, she picked up the phone and reached for some change—only to realize that she had no money. Her body beaded with cold sweat, she wondered if Dexter and Amanda were about to lose their lives for the sake of a quarter. Shaking, she turned to the teenagers.

"Could you please loan me a quarter?" she asked. "I have a really important call to make. Somebody's life is at stake."

His gaze pitying, one of the youngsters reached into his pocket and flipped her a quarter. "You oughta give him up, lady. Ain't no good thinking he'll stop knocking you around, because he won't."

"Thank you. It's not what you think, but I'm really grateful." She dropped the coin into the slot and dialed the FBI emergency number. Her fingers shook so badly that it was a miracle she managed to dial correctly.

The thirty seconds before an FBI operator came on the line seemed endless. The moment the call connected, Liz started speaking.

"I'm calling on behalf of Senator Dexter Rand of the United States Senate," she said. She knew her voice sounded squeaky and uncertain, but she drew in a steadying breath and continued with all the firmness she could muster. "I have a special emergency number I need to reach, and only the FBI can put the call through."

"What number's that, Miss?" The FBI operator sounded bored and irritated, as if she'd already handled more than her share of crank calls that night.

Liz repeated the eleven digits Dexter had compelled her to learn, and sensed an immediate change in the attitude of the woman at the other end of the phone. "I'm connecting you now," the woman said briskly. "Hold on, please. The connection will take about thirty-five seconds."

Precisely thirty-two seconds later, Liz was talking to the commander-in-chief of Washington's Special Forces.

ALISON, clad only in a black satin slip, pretended to cringe and sob as Mikhail positioned her in yet another seductive pose on the cream leather sofa. Dexter wondered how many more tears the woman could shed before his temper frayed completely. Not very many, he suspected. He glanced at his watch. One-thirty a.m. Three hours since he and Liz had been captured. Time to get the hell out of here.

"Enough of these damn fool photographs," he said, picking up Alison's dress and tossing it to her. For once the role he was playing and the reality of his feelings coincided. "Igor, you've made your point. These pictures link me to Elizabeth Meacham. They strengthen the circumstantial evidence of the case you're constructing against me. But nothing you photograph here tonight will compel me to vote against the F-19B. You're going to have to trust my word that I'll vote against the plane, just like I'll have to trust you to set Liz free. It's a standoff, Igor. If both of us acknowledge that fact, maybe we can all go home."

Igor grunted, but whatever reply he might have made was lost as a huge gorilla of a man burst into the room, shielding his bruised and puffy eyes against the overhead lights that had been turned on for the photographs. Waving his arms—seemingly to display a grubby red silk belt—the man burst into a stream of impassioned, apologetic speech in Russian.

Taking advantage of Igor's momentary distraction, Dexter edged toward the arched doorway that connected the living room to the dining room. The overhead light switch was fixed to the connecting wall right by this arch. And the heavy table lamp that provided the only other source of light in the room rested on a nearby coffee table. If he were very lucky he might be able to flip the overhead switch and, in a continuation of the same movement, throw the table lamp at one of his captors. His chosen victim would almost certainly be knocked out, since Dexter's aim was outstanding. And the resulting darkness would provide him with a valuable few moments' head start, if he wanted to make a dash for freedom.

The temptation to go out fighting was great, and yet cool logic warned him that this wasn't a situation that warranted physical action. Pretending to accept Igor's demands was probably a safer, more certain way to extricate himself from Igor's clutches. Unfortunately, for a man of Dexter's training, pretending meekness required more self-discipline than anything else.

Igor and Mikhail were obviously furious at whatever news the newcomer had brought. Shooting a quick glance at Alison, Dexter saw that she, too, was so perturbed that she had temporarily forgotten her role as Liz. She sat on the edge of the sofa, eyes flashing in cold fury as Igor hurled questions at the gorilla man. There was no doubt in Dexter's mind that she understood every word Igor and Mikhail were saying.

If he was going to make a run for it, the dining room would provide his only possible escape route. Dexter turned unobtrusively to scan the room behind him. A very swift survey was sufficient to tell him that it didn't present a realistic prospect of success. Both doors opened onto the main hallway, and he would undoubtedly be caught long before he reached the front entrance.

Dexter allowed himself one more regretful glance around the shadowy dining room. A slight movement caught his eye, and he froze into absolute stillness. Someone was crouched there, half-hidden by the bulk of the china cabinet. His heart leaped.

A black-clad man, face masked with greasepaint, rose slowly to his feet, fingers pressed against his mouth in an urgent signal for Dexter to keep quiet.

"What is going on over there?" Igor demanded suddenly. "What are you doing by the door, Senator Rand?"

"Keeping out of your way," Dexter replied easily, shoving his hands into the pockets of his pants and lounging carelessly against the wall. "Seems like you and your friend Mikhail are seriously upset about something."

Igor hesitated. "A minor administrative matter only," he said coldly. "There has been some small mistake in regard to Comrade Mikhail's airplane ticket for Stockholm."

Right, Dexter thought. *That's why gorilla man looks ready to shoot himself, and the rest of you look mad enough to hand him the gun.* Aloud, he merely said, "A mistake in the ticket, eh? It's amazing how no government seems able to get its clerical system working efficiently, isn't it?"

"I admit that our bureaucracy has not yet attained the degree of socialist efficiency we might wish." Igor sounded considerably more mellow. He was too seasoned a campaigner to allow Dexter more than a glimpse of his anger. "Mikhail, why don't you and Yuri go back downstairs to the basement and search for the missing ticket? I'm sure Yuri has simply mislaid it somewhere."

"Very well, if you think it worthwhile. Personally, I think he must have dropped it outside the house." Mikhail took Yuri's arm and propelled him with considerable force toward the basement stairs. Casting a glance toward the sofa, he said, "Lizushka, my sweet, do you not wish to put on your dress? The Comrade Senator will not be able to take advantage of your charming body tonight. That pleasure must await the vote on the F-19B."

Alison flashed her husband a look of sheer venom, but recalled to a realization of her role, she stood up and struggled into the dress, a fresh set of tears flowing down her cheeks. Dexter thought the woman deserved an entry in the Guinness Book of World Records. Most Crocodile Tears Ever Shed in One Continuous Session.

Mikhail and Yuri disappeared from view. Dexter sincerely hoped they would walk straight into the arms of a pair of waiting commandos. He was becoming more and more optimistic that somehow Liz had managed to escape. How else had the commandos known where to come?

Pretending to refasten the studs on his shirt, he risked another quick look into the dining room. The single black-clad figure had now become four. Dexter let his hand creep up toward the light switch. One of the blackened faces dipped in a brief, authoritative nod of approval.

In a single swift move, Dexter flipped off the overhead switch and leaned forward to grab the table lamp, jerking the cord from the wall socket. In the last moment of light, he took aim at Igor, then threw the lamp with all the force he could muster. He heard the satisfying clunk of lamp hitting flesh, a split second before the four black shadows erupted into the room.

ALISON FINALLY STOPPED CRYING when one of the commandos walked over and slipped her wrists into a pair of handcuffs. "What the *hell* do you think you're doing?" she demanded.

"Arresting you. I have to warn you that anything you say may be taken down and used in evidence at your trial—"

Panic swept over Alison's lovely features. "I don't know what you're thinking of," she said, her voice husky. She looked with desperate appeal toward Dexter, who was talking softly and animatedly to another of the commandos. "Dexter, darling," she called. "Darling, please tell this silly man he's making a dreadful mistake."

Dexter turned slowly, allowing every ounce of his scorn to show. "Why would I do that, Alison? I hope they lock you in jail and throw away the key."

She paled. "A-Alison? Y-you knew I wasn't Liz? All the time?"

"Not all the time. You had me fooled for about five seconds."

"But we're identical!"

Dexter smiled coldly. "You're nothing like Liz. You never have been and you never will be. Liz would no more have sat on that sofa weeping and wailing than she would have flown. Somebody should have told you that silicone implants and a nose job can't change a person's character."

"But you can't let me go to prison!"

"Watch me. You were perfectly willing to have your sister killed. Thank your lucky stars you're in America, and nobody's going to let me be alone with you in a quiet corner of the jail. Otherwise you'd need another nose job."

Alison was weeping again. This time her tears might even have been real. A commando entered the living room. "Ms. Meacham has just arrived, Senator, if you'd like to meet her outside."

Dexter left the room without a backward glance.

HE SAW LIZ as soon as he stepped out of the front door. Spotlighted in the beam of a police floodlight, her entire face shone with joy as he walked toward her.

"Dex!" She ran into his arms, and he held her tight, feeling the softness that was Liz, the warmth and the passion that seemed to flow from every pore of her skin. He stroked his hands up and down her spine, trying to reabsorb the essence of her into his soul.

"The KGB are such fools," he said, lovingly plucking a dead leaf and a wisp of cobweb from her hair. "Imagine thinking I wouldn't know the difference between you and Alison."

She insinuated her fingers underneath his shirt. Wherever she touched, he felt a little explosion of desire. "How could you possibly tell us apart?" she asked. "They made her look just like me."

"They couldn't capture the magic," he said softly, only half teasing. "When she kissed me, I felt empty. My heart didn't start pounding, and my skin didn't feel as if it was on fire."

"Is that how you feel when we kiss?" Liz lifted her face, blue-gray eyes dark with wonder. "I thought it was only me who felt like that."

He hadn't realized how much he loved the eloquence of her eyes until he had seen the coldness of Alison's. "I think that's how I feel,'' he said solemnly. ''But Igor had me captive in there so damn long I've almost forgotten. Can we test it and see?''

She raised her mouth eagerly to meet his. Their lips joined in an explosion of need and pent-up anxiety. She tasted warm and passionate, generous and sexy. She tasted of Liz. She tasted of love. His heart started to pound. His skin felt as if it were on fire. He knew that if they remained together for the next sixty years, she would still retain the power to stimulate and entrance him. He wondered why in the world they had wasted so much time apart.

The spotlight mounted on one of the trucks swung around to focus on the squad of commandos escorting Igor, Mikhail, Alison and four other men to the waiting vans. Liz and Dexter didn't even notice.

She put up her hand to touch his cheek. He caught her fingers, and kissed every spot where he could see a cut or a graze. ''Did they tell you Amanda is safe?'' he asked. ''She's been back home with my parents since early this evening.''

She nodded. ''The commander told me. I'm so glad for you, Dex. My biggest nightmare was that they'd kill her before the Special Forces could get to wherever Mikhail and gang were hiding her.''

''We'll fly home tomorrow and see her,'' he said.

''I'd like that. You won't feel completely secure until you've hugged her.''

''Marry me, Liz,'' he said huskily. ''Live with me and be my love. This time we'll get it right, I know we will.''

She went very still. She was quiet for so long that he forced a laugh. ''I hoped it wouldn't be such a difficult decision.''

She looked up, her expression grave. "Dex, you don't have to feel obligated—"

"Obligated? You think I feel obligated? Are you crazy, woman?" He dragged her hard against his body, moving his hips aggressively so that she could feel the potency of his arousal. "Does that feel like a man who's *obligated*? Liz, where in the world did you get such a crazy notion? I love you. I want to marry you."

She looked away. "My twin sister's going to jail for treason," she said. "Sometimes . . . maybe . . . love isn't enough."

Dexter felt the relief start to seep into his veins. "Love is always enough," he said quietly. "Answer me one question, Liz. Do you love me?"

"Yes, but—"

"There are no buts. Your sister's choices are her responsibility, not yours. And if you're worried about the damage her actions will do to my career in the Senate, there'll be none. Alison and Mikhail will almost certainly be tried *in camera* and Igor, unfortunately, won't be tried at all. He's already shrieking for his lawyer and claiming diplomatic immunity. The most the State Department will be able to do is get him shipped back to Moscow."

The commander slammed the door on the second of the navy-blue unmarked vans, then gave the instruction for the small convoy to move out of the driveway. Two rows of faces peered over the bushes on either side of the property, as two sets of neighbors viewed the fascinating goings-on. Liz and Dexter didn't even hear the engines start up, much less notice that the vans were leaving.

"Even if you don't care about Alison and what she's done, there's still the problem of Amanda. She doesn't like me."

"Darling Liz, I love my daughter to distraction, but that doesn't give her the right to choose my wife."

"How about the right to choose her stepmother?"

"Liz, you're worrying about phantoms. The week before last, Amanda was all in favor of me getting married. Last week she was opposed. Next week she might be all in favor again. It's not that I'm dismissing the importance of her feelings, but she doesn't know what a stepmother is. I'm confident you can show her that stepmothers are wonderful."

"I'd like to try," Liz whispered. "I love you so much, Dex. I think maybe I never stopped loving you."

"I love you, too. Darling Liz, it's so good to have you back."

Liz was only vaguely aware of the commander of the Special Forces, the driver of the commander's car, and two rows of fascinated neighbors watching as Dexter swept her into his arms and demonstrated—with amazing thoroughness—that two human beings can kiss almost indefinitely without any need to come up for air. Then the outside world faded from her consciousness, and nothing was left except Dex: the taste of him in her mouth and the throb of him in her heart.

She returned to reality when the commander, a man not normally noted for his overflowing supply of sentimentality, finally tapped Dexter on the shoulder. "Senator, I'm getting chilly, even if you and Ms. Meacham seem to be doing a damn fine job of setting each other on fire. You might be interested to know that our headquarters contains a most comfortable suite of rooms." He cleared his throat. "With a king-size bed. We could drive you there now, if you and Ms. Meacham are ready to leave. Then you'd be on hand for tomorrow's debriefing."

Dexter grinned. "If your suite has a shower as well as a bed, it's a deal."

"A king-size shower," the commander replied. His men would never have believed it, but Liz could have sworn there was a distinct twinkle in his eye. "There's also a most accommodating Jacuzzi."

Liz looked up at Dexter, her mouth curving into a tiny smile. "The possibilities," she said, "seem almost endless."

Dexter lifted her hands and pressed the tips of her fingers to his lips. "Yes," he agreed. "They do."

In the wild, some species mate for life.
Some men and women are the same way....

MADE IN HEAVEN

Suzanne Simms

1

THE HEAD USHER took a step or two toward Jack Royce as he entered the vestibule of the Scottsdale, Arizona church. "Friend of the bride or groom, sir?" the usher inquired politely.

"The bride," replied Jack.

As he was shown to a pew on the left side of the center aisle, Jack Royce noticed the usher was dressed in traditional black tie: a white dinner jacket, black cummerbund and black trousers. The boutonniere on the man's lapel was pale pink, a small splash of color against an otherwise stark background. The evening wedding was formal, at least by Southwestern standards. Apparently the Quicks had decided to go all out for their youngest daughter.

Looking around at the wedding guests assembled in the church sanctuary, Jack realized that everyone was dressed to the teeth. He was suddenly very glad that he'd worn one of the new suits his tailor had made for him. It was cut from fine, gray Italian silk and fit him like a glove.

He was the first to admit that until a few years ago his sole idea of style had been anything and everything that was comfortable, usually a plain cotton shirt, faded blue jeans and a pair of hiking boots. He'd lacked any real knowledge of business suits, casual sport coats or dinner jackets. He hadn't known, or particularly cared, when it was appropriate to wear black wing tips, or if brown loafers were the better choice, or what was the best cut of jacket for broad shoulders and a narrow waist or whether worsted wool was any less likely to wrinkle than pure new wool. What he *had* known about was what a man should wear while shooting the rapids along the Colorado River, or crawling on his belly through the Amazonian jungle. After all, it had been his business to know—if he'd wanted to survive.

A smile highlighted the strong, handsome lines of Jack's face. Since then, he'd found that the corporate business world could sometimes be a jungle, too, and it was the wise man who knew how to dress appropriately for it.

Taking the seat the usher indicated, Jack tried to make himself comfortable. It was impossible. There were any number of advantages to being more than six feet tall with a thirty-six-inch inseam, but he'd found over the years that there were at least an equal number of disadvantages. Most chairs, sports cars, movie-theater seats, roller coasters and church pews simply weren't large enough to contain his long, muscular body and his equally long, muscular legs.

Depending on a man's point of view, of course, there were other advantages or disadvantages to being tall. He'd had more than one woman stop him on the street, or come up to him at a party, and ask if he was Tom Selleck. He supposed any male standing six-four with dark, curly hair and a mustache got asked that question. The first few times it had happened he'd been amused and a little flattered. Now being mistaken for the well-known TV star was more annoying than anything else.

The woman sitting on his left was beginning to squirm in her seat. Jack could tell she was getting curious about him. Finally she cleared her throat. "Excuse me, but are you . . . ?"

Turning his head, Jack toyed with a sardonic smile. "No. I'm afraid I'm not."

Although the woman appeared to be a well-preserved forty—she was exquisitely groomed, with hair the color of champagne—Jack put her actual age at somewhere between fifty and sixty. She was wearing a silk dress in turquoise with an expensive hammered-silver necklace around her throat. Matching silver earrings dangled from each lobe. Her skin was evenly and perfectly tanned, as if she spent a substantial part of each day stretched out by the backyard pool or on the golf course. She was obviously well-heeled. Her voice had a cultured lilt to it as she attempted to carry on a conversation with him.

"Do you know the family well?"

Jack wrinkled his brow. "The family?"

"The Quicks. Marilyn and Harry and their daughters."

He scowled. "Not as well as I should have."

Jack could see that his answer had the woman puzzled. Should he bother to enlighten her? He decided not to. It was, after all, a long story.

She went on. "I must say Marilyn and Harry have gone all out for Catherine's wedding, haven't they?"

"So it seems."

"Are you going to the reception at the country club afterward?"

"I might drop in for a while," he answered noncommittally.

She glanced down at his ring finger. "Are you married, Mr. . . ?"

"Royce. Jack Royce." He offered her his hand. "And, no, I'm not married."

The woman's face brightened immediately. She made no attempt to be coy. She shook his hand, then said, "In that case, I'd like to introduce you to our daughter later.

I'm Amelia Rinehart, by the way. My husband, Teddy, is at the other end of our pew, and our daughter, Buffy, is sitting beside me."

Jack glanced at the aging sorority girl down the pew from them. "Buffy?"

Amelia Rinehart's laugh was intimate. "That's what the girls at her school nicknamed her. Her real name is Eleanor. Eleanor Stowe Rinehart."

"I see," he murmured.

He wasn't sure he did see, actually. Was the Rinehart name supposed to mean something to him? Or perhaps it was the daughter's middle name the woman was trying to impress him with.

Jack knew as well as anyone that every level of society existed here in the Valley, within the ring of smaller, affluent cities—including Scottsdale, Paradise Valley, Tempe, Glendale and Mesa—that surrounded metropolitan Phoenix. There was abject poverty on one end of the scale and an almost unbelievable amount of wealth on the other. In some neighborhoods Mercedes were more common than houseflies. Swimming pools were standard features of every home. Their predominance had actually raised the humidity in the desert city.

Eleanor Stowe Rinehart? If the name was supposed to have some significance it was wasted on him. Jack wanted to explain that to the woman sitting beside him as he flexed his broad shoulders against the back of the pew.

The organist began to play something by Mozart. Or maybe it was Bach. Jack wasn't sure. Either way, the congregation quieted down. One of the ushers escorted a woman to the front pew on the right; a distinguished-looking man followed behind her. Jack assumed they were the groom's mother and father. Then the head usher came down the aisle with Marilyn Quick on his arm, signaling that the processional would soon start. Two handsome young men, undoubtedly the groom and the best man, took their places before the minister at the chancel steps.

Reaching inside his suit jacket, Jack Royce withdrew the engraved invitation he'd received in the mail a few weeks earlier. He opened it and scanned the printed page.

Mr. and Mrs. Harry Quick
request the honor of your presence
at the marriage of their daughter
Catherine
to
Mr. Eric David Porter
on Friday, the ninth of June
at the Camelback Mountain Church
Scottsdale
and afterward at
the Valley Country Club
Paradise Valley

R.S.V.P.
1500 Buena Vista Drive
Paradise Valley, Arizona

All very formal and proper. And expensive, Jack concluded as he fingered the thick vellum paper. He wondered if Harry Quick ever asked the fates why he'd been blessed with five daughters. Sooner or later those five daughters were going to cost the man a bundle in weddings alone!

With a flourish, the organist went into the opening chords of the traditional *Lohengrin* wedding march. The guests rose and turned toward the rear of the church. The processional was beginning.

The ushers came first, followed by the bridesmaids—in this case, the bridesmaids would be Catherine Quick's four older sisters—then the flower girl and the ring bearer, and finally the bride on her father's arm.

Jack didn't have to crane his neck to see. That was one of the advantages of his height. But never in a million years could he have anticipated what happened next. He was standing there, knowing that at any moment he would see Diana for the first time in more than three years, when he caught a glimpse of her and his heart began to race, faster and faster. He thought it would surely burst out of his chest. He couldn't seem to catch his breath. The wind had been knocked out of him; it was as if someone had slammed their fist into his solar plexus!

Then Diana came into view.

As Jack watched her move down the church aisle, he realized she was still everything and more that her name conjured up in a man's mind. Tall, blond, willowy, coolly chic and utterly beautiful—that had been his Diana at the age of twenty-four. That was *this* Diana at thirty-one.

Jack couldn't take his eyes off her. Lord, she was lovely. As lovely as the first time he'd seen her. She was the same golden goddess he'd fallen head over heels in love with more than seven years ago. The lovely Diana: his wife!

EX-WIFE. And she hadn't seen him, Jack realized as he forced life-sustaining air into his lungs. Ahead of her, the other three sisters—Sloane, Elizabeth and Jayne Ann—filed toward the front of the church, their dresses sweeping down the aisle in a cloud of pale pink silk. Each sister was as lovely in her own right as the eldest, Diana, with hair ranging from palest blond to lightest brown and eyes of various shades of blue and green.

At five feet nine inches, Diana was the tallest, but the others were above average in height, as well. The four of them were followed in the wedding processional by two young cousins acting as the flower girl and the ring bearer. And then the bride, Catherine—Kit to her intimates—and the girls' father.

Harry Quick was the palest of them all, Jack noted. Not that he could blame the man. He wondered if Harry ever found himself feeling overwhelmed, as well as outnumbered, by all that femininity.

On more than one occasion he'd seen his father-in-law with his daughters and his wife, Marilyn, gathered around him. Harry Quick, tall, gray-haired, distinguished, on the quiet side, surrounded by six fair-haired beauties. Individually the Quick women were rare enough, indeed. Taken as a group, they were nothing short of stunning!

Jack's attention was drawn to the front of the church. The processional had stopped, and the bride and groom were taking their places in front of the minister.

The ceremony commenced as the clergyman opened his liturgy and began to recite: "Dearly beloved, we are assembled here in the presence of God, to join this man and this woman in holy marriage; which is instituted of God..."

Jack heard the words, and they took him back to that day in June seven years before when he and Diana had married. No large, fancy church for them but a small chapel just off the Strip in Las Vegas. No family and friends present to hear them exchange their vows, only two strangers: the justice of the peace, who'd performed the ceremony, and his wife, who had stood as their witness. He hadn't even owned a suit to get married in, Jack recalled, shaking his head. In the past couple of years he'd had plenty of time to wonder if that rather inglorious start to their marriage was partly to blame for the fact that he and Diana weren't husband and wife today.

He tuned back in just as the minister was saying, "If either of you know any reason why you may not lawfully be joined together in marriage, you do now confess it . . ."

Jack glanced around the church a moment later and realized the entire congregation was bowing their heads. He quickly put his head down as the minister said a prayer for the young couple.

There was something special about getting married in a church with your friends and family around you. It was the first thing he'd do over with Diana if he ever had the chance. When they'd met, he'd been young and wild and a little unconventional. As a matter of fact, he'd taken great pride in being unconventional. Now that he was thirty-five, the ceremonies of life had come to mean something to him.

He looked up as the minister inquired, "Who giveth this woman to be married to this man?"

His one-time father-in-law stepped forward and placed the hand of his youngest daughter in that of the minister. "I do," he said in a quavering voice that belied his position as president of one of the largest banks in the Southwest. As he stepped back, the usually dignified man wiped a tear from his cheek.

He should have given Harry the chance to give Diana away, to shed a tear or two, Jack realized years too late.

Then the young man standing beside Kit began to recite his wedding vows in a slightly husky baritone, and there was more than one tear shed throughout the congregation.

"I, Eric David, take thee, Catherine, to be my wedded wife. And I do promise and covenant before God and these witnesses to be thy loving and faithful husband, in plenty and in want, in joy and in sorrow, in sickness and in health, as long as we both shall live."

Jack sank his teeth into his bottom lip. That's what he'd promised Diana: to be there in the good times and the bad for as long as they both would live. But he hadn't kept his promise. Oh, he'd been faithful—although he was pretty sure Diana had wondered about that more than once—but he hadn't always been with her during sickness and health. He hadn't always been there when she'd needed him. So she had stopped needing him. Stopped relying on him. Stopped loving him. Jack reached up and touched his face. He was surprised to find his cheeks had a trace of dampness on them.

Then Kit's voice came sweet and clear, sounding so much like Diana's that Jack felt as if he'd somehow traveled back in time to his own wedding day.

"I, Catherine, take thee, Eric David, to be my wedded husband; and I do promise and covenant before God and these witnesses to be thy loving and faithful wife, in plenty and in want, in joy and in sorrow, in sickness and in health, as long as we both shall live."

The young couple exchanged rings, and the minister said yet another prayer and read from the Bible before he went on, "By the authority committed unto me as a Minister of the Church, I declare that Eric and Catherine are now husband and wife, according to the ordinance of God, and the law of the State of Arizona. Whom therefore God hath joined together, let no man put asunder."

Or no lawyer put asunder, Jack thought, the bitter taste of bile rising momentarily in his throat.

Eric and Catherine knelt to receive the final benediction. When they stood, the minister was the first to congratulate them. Then her young husband lifted Kit's veil and kissed her, sweetly, devoutly, eagerly. A collective sigh rose from the congregation as the young couple turned and started up the aisle. Organ music swelled to fill the church from stained-glass window to stained-glass window. It was Mendelssohn's wedding march from *A Midsummer Night's Dream*. The wedding ceremony was to be traditional from beginning to end.

Kit's face was flushed, and her green eyes danced with excitement as arm-in-arm she and her new husband swept along between the rows of smiling, teary-eyed guests. Then came the flower girl and the ring bearer, followed by the bridesmaids, coupled with the best man and the ushers.

Diana was the maid of honor. Or did she consider herself the matron of honor, Jack wondered as he watched her walk toward the pew where he was sitting.

The only sound he could hear then was his own pulse pounding in his ear. Diana Quick had been the best damned thing that had ever happened to him. How could he have allowed her to slip through his fingers? How could he have let her go without a fight, without a single word of protest? He'd been a fool! Worse than a fool, he'd been arrogant and chauvinistic and just plain stupid!

Jack tried to rein in his emotions, to exercise some control over them before they wrested free of him entirely.

That's when he realized Diana had finally seen him. The shock of it was written all over her lovely face. She stumbled, and the handsome man beside her steadied her on his arm. She looked at Jack for an endless moment, then two. There was something in her eyes. Was it surprise? Yes. Bewilderment? Certainly. Curiosity? Anger? Panic? Perhaps. It was pretty obvious he was the last person on earth she'd expected to see at her sister's wedding.

Jack tried to smile at her, but the muscles around his mouth were frozen. Then his lips began to move and he managed to form one word. Diana.

2

JACK!

Diana missed a step and tripped over a nonexistent bump in the carpeting. To keep herself from falling flat on her face, she was forced to hold the best man's arm.

Sweet sanity, could it be Jack? Of course it was Jack. It had to be Jack. It may have been three years, five months and an odd number of days since she'd last seen him, but she recognized her own husband, for heaven's sake. She quickly amended that. *Ex*-husband.

What was he doing here?

Diana nearly laughed out loud. What a perfectly ridiculous thing to ask herself. It was obvious Jack was here for the wedding. Her youngest sister must have exercised her prerogative as the bride and sent him an invitation. Kit had always been Jack's favorite among her sisters. And Kit had adored him as only a young, starry-eyed girl can adore an older brother. A vulnerable fifteen-year-old when Jack Royce had waltzed into their lives, Kit had worshipped him at first sight.

Jack had been a diamond in the rough in those days. Apparently he'd acquired a little polish—and a new wardrobe—in the intervening years, although Diana had only had a quick glimpse of him as she'd walked down the aisle. A quick glimpse or two after all this time . . .

At the thought of the months, the years, that had passed since she'd seen Jack, Diana felt a wave of emotion wash over her. The muscles of her throat contracted. Her breathing became labored. Her heart began to slam against the wall of her ribs, and an ice-cold pain lodged in her chest.

God, how she had once loved the man! More than anyone had ever known, even Jack. She'd loved him with a love that had burned like an eternal flame, hot and pure and unceasing.

Even an eternal flame needed some source of fuel, however, to keep its fire from going out. Something Jack Royce had never comprehended. He'd done just what he'd wanted and assumed she'd always be there for him whenever he was ready to come home to her.

Absence didn't necessarily make the heart grow fonder. That was the heartbreaking lesson Diana had learned in the early months of her marriage. Despite her objections, Jack had taken off for Alaska, specifically Kodiak Island, to hunt the huge, brown bear that bore the island's name. The arrangements for the hunting trip had been made before Jack had met her. She had understood that. What she hadn't understood was why he would still want to go once he was a married man.

In the end, Jack had flown north to Alaska and she'd been left behind in Phoenix, bewildered and hurt by his eagerness, his excitement, his undisguised relief at leaving her.

After the Alaskan trip, there had been one venture after another for him, including acting as guide for a group of anthropological students trekking through the jungle to a Mayan pyramid in Belize, an exploration of the Hoh Rain Forest in northern Washington State, rafting the Bio-Bio in Chile. When all was said and done, Diana's love, even the heat of her once-searing passion for her husband, had flickered and died from neglect, turning into nothing more than cold accusations and even colder ashes.

Sometimes a woman was attracted to a man who was all wrong for her, lending truth to the old cliché that opposites attract. They might attract. They might even marry. But Diana was convinced they didn't *stay* married.

Not that Jack alone was to blame for the failure of their marriage. She'd made plenty of mistakes, too. If only they'd been a little wiser when they'd met, or a little more cynical, she often thought in retrospect. They could have indulged in a wild, passionate love affair and then, by mutual consent, parted company. As it was, their separation and divorce had been somewhat less than amicable. Still, it had been the best thing for both of them. At least that's what Diana liked to believe.

In time, she'd got over Jack and on with her life. Not that it had been easy, Diana admitted to herself as she walked toward the back of the church, her hand firmly resting on Tom Skelly's reliable arm.

Actually, getting over Jack reminded her of when she'd quit smoking: an experience she could still vividly recall as if it were only yesterday. The very first day after she'd thrown her cigarettes away, she'd wanted one constantly. By the end of the week, her craving for a cigarette had been reduced to once or twice an hour. By the end of the first month, she thought about smoking quite regularly. And now, after three years, she still had the urge every once in a while....

Make or break any habit in two weeks! That's what the tabloid headline had screamed while Diana waited in the checkout line yesterday at the supermarket. Perhaps it was true for cigarette smoking, but it would take her longer—much longer—to get over Jack Royce. As the lyric of a hit song from a few years back lamented, he was a hard habit to break.

Suddenly, inexplicably, hot, salty tears began to prick the corners of Diana's eyes.

"Damn!" she muttered under her breath.

She would not cry over the man again. She'd wasted enough years and more than enough tears on him. Putting an unhappy and unsuccessful marriage behind her had been the hardest thing she'd ever had to do, but she'd done it!

And if she occasionally found herself getting sentimental or maudlin over Jack Royce, it was only natural. After all, she was flesh and blood just like everyone else. Jack had been her husband and her lover, if not her best friend. She would probably always feel something for him.

That had been made clear enough to her just last week. That was the day Kit had announced to her four older sisters that she wanted to model her finished wedding gown for them. As her sister pranced around her bedroom in a swirl of hand-beaded satin and lace, Diana had naturally thought back to the simple, beige dress she'd worn on her own wedding day.

Dredging up old memories had proven dangerous. All Diana's regrets had come to roost, and her hard-earned peace of mind had been shattered. While the others were busy oohing and aahing over Kit's gown, she'd had to quickly excuse herself and dash into the bathroom at her parents' home for a good cry. Afterward, as she'd pressed a cold washcloth to her reddened eyes, she had vowed to make that the last time she would cry for Jack, for herself, for what might have been and never could be.

Diana buried her teeth in her bottom lip. She intended to keep that vow. This was her sister's wedding day. She wouldn't dream of ruining it for Kit—or herself. Any tears she shed today would be tears of joy!

"Are you all right?" whispered the man beside her as they reached the rear of the sanctuary.

She looked at Tom Skelly and reassured him with a small, well-intentioned white lie. "Yes. I'm fine. Thanks for catching me back there. The heel of my shoe must have caught on something."

That seemed to satisfy Tom. They joined the rest of the wedding party congregating in a private room off the vestibule. The photographer and his assistant were trying to maintain some semblance of order as the parents of the bride and groom entered the room. Once the churchful of guests had departed, it would be time for the official wedding photographs.

"Diana, dear."

She felt a warm hand on her shoulder, and she turned to see her mother standing beside her. Swallowing hard, she flashed a brave smile. "It was a lovely ceremony, wasn't it, Mother?"

"Yes, it was a lovely ceremony," Marilyn Quick agreed as she gently touched her oldest daughter's cheek, brushing away a solitary tear that had somehow managed to escape.

"Kit makes a beautiful bride," Diana declared proudly as she watched her sister with an almost maternal air.

Further words were unnecessary between the two women. Her mother was perhaps the one person who understood how hard this day was for Diana. They both knew it was bound to unearth painful memories she would prefer to keep buried.

Marilyn Quick was a woman of strong convictions and even stronger maternal love, a woman of rare intelligence, well-bred manners and a grace under pressure that never failed to impress anyone meeting her for the first time. She discreetly drew her daughter aside and, lowering her voice, said, "There's something you need to know, darling."

Diana looked into the clear, blue eyes that were a mirror of her own. "What is it?"

The elegant woman hesitated, touched the Majorcan pearls at her throat, smoothed the skirt of her blue lace tea-length dress and finally went on. "Kit informed your father and me before she did it, but we didn't see any reason to upset you unless it was unavoidable."

"And now it's unavoidable?"

Her mother sighed. "It would seem so." She appeared to brace herself for what she had to say next. "Your sister sent a wedding invitation to Jack. She was absolutely adamant about it. Of course, I don't think at any time any of us believed he would actually accept."

"But he has."

Her mother nodded her head. "Yes. Jack's here. Your father and I spotted him in the congregation as we were leaving the sanctuary just now."

The muscles around Diana's mouth tightened as she repeated, "Jack's here."

"I am sorry, Diana."

She shook off the lethargy that had momentarily claimed her and reassured her mother, "There's no need for you to apologize. It's not your fault."

"We did try to talk your sister out of inviting him. But Kit can be stubborn, as you know. She has more than a little of your father in her," said Marilyn Quick affectionately, but with a touch of exasperation in her voice, as well. "I'm sure she didn't do it to hurt or embarrass you."

Almost to herself, Diana murmured, "Kit was always crazy about Jack."

"And he adored her," Marilyn Quick agreed, as if that were to his credit.

"Naturally Kit would want him to be here for her wedding."

"Or perhaps it was simply that she wanted to let Jack know she was getting married."

Diana shrugged her shoulders. "Maybe she just wanted to see him again."

Blue eyes filled with maternal concern continued to stare at her. "Have you seen him?"

"Yes. As I was walking down the aisle during the recessional. He looks . . ."

"Tall, dark and handsome." It was not altogether an approving remark.

Briefly, unexpectedly, a smile transformed Diana's face. "Jack has always looked tall, dark and handsome, Mother. No, I was going to say that he seems different somehow."

An elegant eyebrow was raised. "It may be the suit he's wearing. It's expensive, tailor-made, undoubtedly Italian silk, if I'm not mistaken."

Marilyn Quick was never mistaken when it came to things like Italian silk. Both women knew that.

A tiny, proud lie sprang from Diana's lips. "I can't say I noticed."

Her mother continued, trying to give her former son-in-law the benefit of the doubt. "Goodness knows Jack never wore a suit in all the time your father and I knew him, but it's been several years since any of us have run into the man. I suppose even Jack could have changed in that time."

The smile was gone. "That's about as likely as a leopard changing its spots," Diana shot back.

"Are you going to be all right?"

"Of course I am. I'll admit at first I was surprised to see Jack—" stunned was more like it, but she'd be damned if she would admit that much even to her mother "—but we're both adults. I'm sure we can handle this whole thing in a civilized manner."

The two women looked up as the photographer requested, "Could I please have the bride and groom and their parents at the front of the sanctuary now?"

"I'm very proud of you. Be brave, darling," said Marilyn Quick as she gave Diana's hand an encouraging squeeze before rejoining her husband.

The church was empty except for the organist, who was still gathering up her music. The guests were already leisurely making their way to the country club for the buffet dinner and reception scheduled for that evening. The wedding party would join them as soon as the picture-taking was over.

"Kit looks beautiful, and happy," Tom Skelly volunteered as they watched the bride and groom take their places.

Diana concurred. "Yes, she does."

"Eric's a lucky man."

"We like to think so." She heaved a great sigh. "They're so young."

"And so in love," Tom added before they were required to enter the next pose.

Diana participated in the photography session with only half a mind to what she was doing. The other half was remembering that she'd been young like Kit once. And so terribly in love. But that wasn't where it had all started. It had started at a party given by Barbara St. John.

IT WAS THE SPRING Diana celebrated her twenty-fourth birthday. There was a faint breeze off the desert that night, stirring the palm trees alongside the lighted swimming pool and garden into a swaying, dancelike movement.

It was one of those perfect April nights that only happen in Arizona: warm and wonderful, with a thousand stars twinkling in the heavens above and the distinctive outline of Camelback Mountain over a distant adobe wall, with the intoxicating scent of red roses and cascading bougainvillea and flowering orange trees perfuming the night air.

Diana was sitting with a group of her friends, laughing and talking and eating. They were nibbling on tortilla chips dipped in chili con queso and guacamole, consuming plates of delicious, spicy enchiladas, washing it all down with ice-cold margaritas. A mariachi band was playing carefree south-of-the-border tunes while a few couples danced on the flagstone patio.

Out of the corner of her eye, Diana spied Barbara St. John strolling onto the terrace with a man on her arm and a smug, cat-that-got-the-mouse smile on her face. She slanted a glance at her friend, but it was the man who immediately caught and held Diana Quick's attention.

He was tall, dark, powerful, with a thick mustache and a day's growth of beard on his face. Dressed in wrinkled khaki, he looked as if he'd just stepped off the plane from some exotic clime—which, it turned out, was precisely the case.

It took some doing, but Diana managed to get an introduction without appearing to want one. Indeed, she wasn't altogether sure she did want to meet the man. He was definitely not her type. Her type was civilized above all else. And if there was one thing Jack Royce wasn't—as she was to find out in the days and weeks ahead—it was civilized. At least not according to her and Noah Webster's definition of the word.

There was a certain sense of destiny, fate, karma, about their first meeting. Jack was the flame—hot, bright, fully capable of burning her badly. Diana was the butterfly, drawn to his light despite the dangers of getting hurt. She thought she was so sophisticated. But it was a sophistication based on how she'd been raised and the schools she'd attended. It wasn't the lasting kind, not the kind that came from learning how to gracefully handle whatever life handed you. That was to come later.

Somehow she found herself alone with Jack in a small grove of orange trees. Romantic music floated across the various levels of the desert lawn that wound around the swimming pool. She looked up and caught him studying her, and she was left tongue-tied. That should have served as a warning. But she was young and daring and invincible, and the world was her oyster.

"What's your name again?" asked Jack without the slightest sign of being embarrassed.

Then and there, Diana nearly labeled Jack Royce an insufferable bore. She was tempted to point out to him that their hostess had introduced them less than ten minutes earlier. After all, she wasn't used to men forgetting her name.

"My name is Diana. Diana Quick," she informed him haughtily, then realized almost instantaneously that the name meant nothing to the man. She relented a bit. "You're not from the Valley, are you, Mr. Royce?"

"No, I'm not. And the name's Jack."

"Where do you come from, Jack?"

"Wisconsin."

"Madison?"

He shook his head and chuckled. "Trust me. You've never heard of it."

"Try me."

One dark eyebrow arched. "Walleye Lake."

She smiled in spite of herself. "You're right. I've never heard of it."

He smiled back, and it was all white teeth against tanned skin. "That's not surprising. Walleye Lake is no more than a pinpoint on the map between Milwaukee and Racine."

Silence fell between them again. Jack Royce was many things, but a dazzling conversationalist apparently wasn't one of them.

He finally resorted to pulling a rabbit out of his hat. "Did you know, Miss Quick, that after one recent tourist season at Yosemite National Park the rangers found, along with all the other debris, sixteen toupees, a World War Two gas-rationing book, a 1931 camera with undeveloped film inside and two church pews complete with cushions?"

Diana put her head back and laughed wholeheartedly. "No, I didn't. And the name is Diana." That seemed to break the ice.

No doubt encouraged by her amused and rapt attention, Jack dove headlong into a dissertation on African beer. "Gala's the best on the whole African continent," he told her, then shrugged and tempered that claim with, "Certainly in Chad, anyway. Often as not it's served at room temperature."

"Which must be one of two ways in Chad—warm and even warmer," Diana correctly surmised, wrinkling her patrician nose at the notion of drinking anything lukewarm. Her personal preference was for chilled champagne any day.

"There's also Kenyan Tusker and Club beer from Liberia. Gazelle and Lion and White Cap and Stork." Jack recited the names as if they were lines of poetry. His conversation opened up a whole new world for Diana and allowed her a peek inside.

And if he was beer and she was champagne, neither of them seemed to mind. Jack was from a family of modest means. He was a hunter, a fisherman, an outdoorsman. Diana was from a wealthy family whose idea of the outdoors was a tennis court.

He was a jack-of-all-trades with a high-school education who had thumbed or worked his way around the world several times by the time he was twenty-five.

She had graduated from an exclusive college, had traveled on the continent, staying in only first-class hotels, and worked for a prestigious Arizona magazine, covering fashion, home interiors and charity benefits. He had a variety of odd jobs. She had a career.

Their two different worlds collided that first night at Barbara St. John's. Their common language was passion, and they both spoke it fluently in each other's presence.

"You aren't married, are you, Diana Quick?" he said, taking her left hand in his. She knew he could feel her pulse racing beneath his fingertips, and she tried to will her heart to slow its frantic pace.

"No." It came out low and husky and unintentionally inviting.

"Engaged?"

She shook her head and thought about drawing her hand away.

"Living with anyone?"

Looking up into his eyes, she answered honestly, "I have my own place." A dark brow arched questioningly. She explained. "After growing up in a household with five girls, I prefer to live alone."

Jack chuckled knowingly. "I used to share a bedroom with my two brothers."

She cocked her head. "If they're both as big as you are, I imagine it got a little crowded."

"They are, and it did." Then he stepped back into the shadows, taking her with him, drawing her into his arms as if they were going to dance. "In Africa when a man and woman dance, it's like making love. Their bodies come together. They begin to move as one. The rhythm becomes faster and faster until at the end they nearly collapse from exhaustion."

Diana attempted to make light of his gambit, trying not to show how much his voice, his words, his touch were affecting her. "I imagine, Jack Royce, that you're an expert on the subject."

"I could be . . . with you," he murmured, brushing his mouth along her slender neck.

Diana looked into his dark, dark eyes then and saw that he wanted her, desired her on a totally primitive level. Plenty of men had wanted her; that wasn't new. The difference was that this time the same desire was reflected in her own eyes. There was no sense in trying to explain it logically. There was nothing logical about her feelings for Jack.

She knew only one thing. She felt a fatal attraction for him from the moment she laid eyes on him. Perhaps what drew her was the sense of adventure that he wore as naturally as some men did a three-piece suit. Perhaps it was because he was different from any man she'd ever known. Perhaps it was because she felt strangely and wonderfully alive when he looked at her, touched her. There was an undercurrent of something dark and dangerous about him, something wild and exciting and forbidden.

They were as different as night and day, yet the chemistry between them ignited into flames, flames that licked around their bodies as they danced there amid the orange trees.

And when he finally kissed her, muttering hot and heavy words in her ear, he rashly confessed, "I want you! God, how I want you, Diana!"

"DIANA, I WANT YOU to step forward an inch or two so we can see your face better."

She was abruptly brought back to the present by the sound of the photographer's voice.

"Is—is this all right?" she stammered, taking the appropriate stance. She could feel the heightened color in her cheeks and was grateful that no one knew why or about whom she'd been daydreaming.

"That's perfect. Now, everyone hold it right there, please." The shutter on the large camera clicked again and again.

Diana went through the motions, confident that no one would notice her preoccupation. This was Kit and Eric's day. They were the center of everyone's attention.

When the photographer was finished, waiting limousines whisked the wedding party from the church to the country club. In the excitement and natural confusion, Diana had the opportunity to ask herself how she really felt about seeing Jack again.

In the past three years she had imagined that moment often enough. Dreamed about it. Dreaded it. Prayed for it. A dozen or two scenarios had been played out in her head, most of them involving Jack down on his knees begging her to come back to him, pleading with her, swearing that his life had ended when she'd walked out.

Not that she'd ever *literally* walked out on the man, Diana mused as she retouched her makeup in the ladies' room at the country club. That satisfaction had been denied her. There had been no histrionics, no melodramatic scenes, no impassioned declarations of love or war for either of them. Their marriage had ended with a whimper, not a lion's roar.

After the perfunctory receiving line and the required number of dances with the best man, the ushers, her father and a few honored guests, Diana was relieved to find herself by the buffet table.

"It's stunning!" declared a woman guest to her husband.

"Must have cost Harry an arm and a leg," the man observed as he heaped another serving of expensive food onto his plate.

It was and it had, Diana thought wryly as she glanced over the elaborate buffet table.

There was a three-tiered wedding cake in the center, surrounded by exquisite ice sculptures flown in from Boston, mounds of fresh shrimp and imported caviar. Perfect, whole strawberries were ready for dipping into a creamy fondue made from Godiva chocolate. There were platters of wafer-thin smoked salmon, cold lobster salad with artichokes and hearts of palm and bowls of sugar-glazed fruits: apricots, pears and kiwi. Beside the tables was a fountain of Moët et Chandon champagne, sparkling like a waterfall of diamonds.

"The chef and his staff have done a wonderful job with the buffet," a family friend commented to Diana. "Of course, how could he do otherwise under your mother's supervision? Marilyn seems to have the knack of getting people to do their best for her, doesn't she?"

Diana smiled. "Yes, she does."

Most of the organization, if not the actual preparation, of the wedding and reception, had, indeed, fallen on Marilyn Quick's capable shoulders. Kit had been too busy completing her senior year at Arizona State University, Tempe, to be of much help. Still, it was a job their mother had been looking forward to for years and had been denied in her own case, Diana recalled with chagrin.

Eloping had been the only choice for her and Jack. But she'd always felt a little guilty about it, Diana admitted to herself as she popped a luscious, chocolate-covered strawberry into her mouth. A sip of cold champagne followed, raising goose bumps on her flesh. The chill passed, but the goose bumps remained.

It was then that she sensed a presence in the room, felt it as surely as the evidence of it existed on her skin. Someone had just walked into the large banquet hall.

Adrenaline shot into her bloodstream, potent, undiluted. Jack Royce was standing in the doorway, that wealth of dark brown hair atop his head clearly visible even from the far side of the room. Those broad shoulders, straining against the confines of his suit jacket, and the masculine physique that bordered on perfection made him stand out from all the others. He was the same, and yet he was different.

Diana shivered at the thought.

All of a sudden she realized she was holding her breath. Her palms were damp, and her heart insisted on thrashing around wildly in her breast. The champagne glass in her hand was frozen in midair, halfway to her mouth.

She exhaled and then took another deep breath. How did she feel about seeing Jack again?

Angry? Yes. Eager? Perhaps. Expectant? Afraid? Furious? Curious? Damn, her emotions were all ajumble! She wasn't sure about anything anymore. She was reminded of that first night at Barbara St. John's, when she'd looked up and spotted the tall, dark, handsome stranger across the crowded terrace.

Surely history wasn't going to repeat itself.

Diana didn't know. Only one thing was abundantly clear to her, she realized as she gulped down the rest of her champagne. She'd wanted Jack Royce then. She wanted Jack Royce now.

3

A COLD BEER. That's what he really wanted, what he really needed about now, thought Jack as he sauntered into the banquet room at the Valley Country Club.

Several well-stocked bars were located around the perimeter of the dance floor. He made a beeline for the nearest one, skirting a fountain of bubbling champagne along the way.

Sure, he'd like to have a beer. He reached up to stroke his jaw in typically masculine fashion. His tastes hadn't changed that much over the years. But he was willing to bet his last dime that they wouldn't be serving beer at a fancy reception like this one. It looked as if Marilyn and Harry had finally gotten their wish to have a formal wedding in the family, complete with all the trimmings.

He wondered how the bridegroom was handling all the formalities and the trimmings. What was the young man's name? Eric David Porter? Yes, that was the name on the wedding invitation, the name he'd heard repeated earlier that evening at the church.

Well, he hoped that Eric Porter proved to be a better husband to Kit than he'd been to Diana. If the guy dared to harm even one hair on sweet Catherine's head...

Jack's mouth twisted into a wry smile. He sounded just like an overly protective father or a big brother, but he was neither to Catherine Quick. He wasn't anything anymore. He'd been quite effectively erased from Kit's life, from Diana's, from the whole damned family's.

He grimaced. It was a hell of a depressing thought. Now he really did need that drink.

At his approach, the bartender glanced up and inquired with a polite smile, "What would you like, sir?"

"Bourbon and water," Jack answered succinctly.

Once he had his glass in hand, Jack took a healthy swallow. The expensive liquor slid down his throat, nice and easy. After a moment or two, he felt its soothing warmth in the pit of his stomach, letting him know that he hadn't eaten since breakfast. He'd have to pay a visit to the buffet table soon, although a drink or two on an empty stomach wouldn't hurt him.

Standing to one side, feet planted aggressively apart, Jack watched the goings-on over the rim of his glass. The reception was already in full swing. There were numerous people gathered at the bars and the buffet. Other guests were sitting in clusters around small, intimate tables, eating and drinking. A sixteen-piece orchestra was playing light rock music interspersed with Broadway show tunes. An appreciative audience had crowded onto the dance floor.

He'd deliberately delayed his own arrival to avoid the formal receiving line, of course. In his opinion it was best for everyone concerned. Why make it any more awkward than was absolutely necessary for either the Quicks or him?

Now he was debating whether he should have shown up at all. There were so many people in attendance, surely Kit would never know whether he was here or not. Especially when he hadn't told anyone he was coming.

It was probably considered an unforgivable faux pas in Marilyn and Harry Quick's social circle, but he'd never sent a formal reply to the wedding invitation, just a gift—

something silver and expensive—with a card expressing his best wishes to the bride and groom.

What was one guest more or less, Jack had asked himself at the time. He hadn't wanted to give a definite yes or no, hadn't wanted to commit himself one way or the other—so he'd simply ignored the R.S.V.P.

Besides, he'd maintained all along that he was going to Phoenix on a business trip, a business trip that happened to coincide with the date of Kit's wedding.

Jack snorted disdainfully. Who in the hell did he think he was kidding? He wasn't here just to see Kit get married, or to wish her well on her wedding day. He wanted—he needed—to see his wife. His *ex*-wife. He wanted to talk to Diana, to get some answers to a few questions that had been bothering him for a long time now. In fact, ever since he'd lain in a delirious state, hovering between life and death, wondering why she wasn't at his bedside.

In the past three years he'd had more than one bad dream about that time in his life, had awakened on more than one occasion to find that Diana wasn't there. She was never there.

And just when he thought he'd finally put the past behind him, the dreams would begin again. They invariably came back to haunt him when he least expected them to . . . vivid images of the Amazon and of a blond-haired angel.

But there was even more behind his current visit than dreams of the jungle and his ex-wife, Jack admitted to himself as he polished off the last of his bourbon and water and headed back to the bar for a refill.

He was afraid. Frightened. Nervous as a bridegroom. Scared. His mouth turned up in a grim caricature of a smile. Scared? There was a way to describe just how scared he was, but the word wasn't permissible in polite society. And the Quicks were very polite society.

It was time he faced the truth. He was afraid, afraid that he might still be in love with Diana.

There was one valuable lesson that Jack had learned a long time ago. The only way to handle fear was to confront it. Look it straight in the eye. Spit in its eye, if necessary. He knew that if he was ever to have any peace of mind, he had to confront his ex-wife and find out how he felt about her.

"Bourbon and water?" recalled the bartender as he refilled Jack's glass.

Jack nodded. "Thanks."

He raised the drink to his mouth. That's when he spotted Amelia Rinehart coming straight toward him with her husband, Teddy, and daughter, Buffy, in tow. Escape entered his mind, but he could see it was already too late to take any evasive action. He was trapped.

"Mr. Royce, I'd like to introduce my husband and daughter," Amelia Rinehart declared.

Giving her one of what he called his charming-as-hell smiles, Jack insisted, "Please, call me by my first name."

The woman beamed at him. "Only if you promise to call me Amelia."

"I promise. Amelia."

She finally remembered her mission. "This is my husband, Teddy." The man Jack recognized from the church stepped forward and shook his hand. "And of course, our daughter, Buffy."

"Hello," the younger woman said with a painful attempt at nonchalance.

Jack's greeting to Buffy was genuine and sympathetic. He tried to put her at ease. "Hello. Do you mind if I call you Eleanor?"

She seemed vastly relieved. "Not at all."

"Where are you from, Jack?" inquired Teddy Rinehart.

"Wisconsin."

"Madison?"

For a moment Jack experienced a strange feeling of déjà vu. "No. I'm from a small town just south of Milwaukee, along Lake Michigan."

"I'm originally from Cedarsburg, Iowa, myself," Teddy Rinehart confided. "When I was a boy the population was three hundred and twenty-five, if you counted all the cats and dogs." At that, he chuckled. "We used to say, 'Don't blink as you drive through Cedarsburg, or you'll miss the whole darned town, including both gas stations.'"

Amused by the man's description of his hometown, Jack heard himself volunteer in a congenial tone, "I'm from Walleye Lake, Wisconsin, population somewhere around a thousand."

Teddy Rinehart laughed. Amelia Rinehart wasn't amused. She seemed determined to guide their conversation down a different avenue altogether. "What brings you to Phoenix, Jack?"

"I'm here on business."

She took a ladylike sip of champagne from the crystal glass in her hand. "Business?"

"We're considering opening a branch of my company here in the Southwest. I flew out to look over some potential locations."

Her ears perked up. "A branch of your company?"

The astute businessman in Jack took over. Amelia Rinehart was curious. He could satisfy that curiosity. It didn't cost him one red cent, and it was always good business. "Yes. I design, manufacture and sell a variety of outdoor wear and sporting equipment—clothing, tents, survival kits, hunting knives."

"What's the name of your company?" Teddy Rinehart inquired amiably.

Jack finished his drink and set the empty glass on the bar behind him. "The Outdoorsman."

"I believe I read an article about you in the business section of the Chicago newspaper not so long ago," the older man recalled, scratching his chin. "I was in the Midwest for a convention. It seems you've made quite a name for yourself in the past couple of years, Royce. If I remember correctly, you're also something of a mountain climber or an explorer, aren't you?"

Jack's quick smile didn't quite reach his eyes. "I used to do a little of each. After all, my customers expect me to know what I'm talking about if I claim a pair of boots is waterproof, or an insulated jacket will keep them warm even on the coldest day in Alaska."

Amelia Rinehart shivered. "My goodness, have you been to Alaska?"

"A couple of times."

Her perfectly made-up eyes widened slightly. "Did you encounter any wild beasts while you were there?"

He bit back an indulgent smile. "A few."

"Have you ever been—attacked?"

Jack realized the woman was serious. "Once. By a seven-foot, man-eating grizzly bear." He dropped the fact at her feet as a house cat would a half-dead mouse.

Horrified, Amelia Rinehart opened her eyes even wider. She clutched her manicured hands to her bosom in an agitated gesture. "Did you escape?"

Teddy Rinehart turned to his wife and declared with a hint of impatience in his voice, "Well, obviously the man escaped, Amelia. He's here, isn't he?" He drained the amber liquid in his glass.

Jack figured he had one of several choices left. He could either continue this innocuous conversation with the Rineharts, or he could ask their daughter to dance. He chose the lesser of two evils.

"Yes, I'd love to dance," she responded, setting her empty glass down on the bar. Apparently she'd had enough of her parents' conversation, as well.

They'd made almost a complete turn around the dance floor before his partner laughed lightly under her breath, looked up at him and wanted to know, "Were you ever really attacked by a six-foot-tall, man-devouring grizzly bear?"

Jack was surprised—and delighted—to discover Eleanor Rinehart had a sense of humor. "It measured a good seven feet," he corrected. "And the damned thing chased me right up a tree."

Her eyes twinkled with amusement. "Did it actually eat anyone that you know of?"

He shrugged his shoulders and then joined in the laughter. The story was funny now. It hadn't been at the time. "There were rumors that a large brown bear had dragged off a dog or two from a nearby Indian village."

They let the subject drop after that. Eleanor filled in the lull in their conversation by reiterating, "So you're from a small town in Wisconsin."

"Born and raised in Walleye Lake. What about you?"

"I was born in Iowa. But my parents moved to the Phoenix area when I was a baby. I've lived here ever since."

"Do you like the Valley?"

"Yes, but . . ."

"But?"

"But sometimes I think I'd like a change of scenery."

Jack knew the feeling. "Sometimes we need to get away from home just so we can come back and say there's no place quite like it."

"Exactly," she agreed.

The orchestra finished one tune and immediately went into another.

As they danced, Jack inquired, "What do you do, Eleanor?"

A tiny crease formed between her eyebrows. "What do I do? I play tennis. I golf. I swim."

"No. I meant what do you do, as in a job?"

Her cheeks turned pink. "Oh. I, ah, work part-time for my father. He's in real estate."

Jack found that interesting. "Do you like working in the real-estate business?"

She nodded and confessed to him, "I'm only allowed to do secretarial work in the office. Although I'd love to get my license and actually sell real estate."

He was curious. "Why don't you, then?"

Eleanor sighed. "My mother thinks I should make a career out of finding a husband. My father believes I'm too much of an introvert to be a success in sales."

"What do you think?"

She put back her head and gazed up at him. "I think I'd be good at selling real estate."

"Then why don't you do it?"

The woman frowned. "It would mean going against my mother and father."

His eyes became cool and assessing. "Sometimes when it comes to other people, we're damned if we do and damned if we don't."

Eleanor Rinehart studied him thoughtfully. "Have you ever gone against your parents' wishes?"

"Dozens of times," he admitted without a scrap of regret.

She didn't say anything for a minute or two. "Somehow it's easier for a man, I think. Perhaps it's because you don't want, or don't need, the parental stamp of approval on your actions the way a woman does. It takes a lot of determination to go against your family."

"And a certain amount of callousness," Jack added, thinking that in some ways Eleanor was a throwback to the last generation. "I'm not sure that comes as naturally to a woman as it does to a man."

"Were you callous with your parents?"

Jack's smile was hard and quick. "I've been callous with just about everyone that ever meant anything to me."

"At least it's gotten you what you wanted," Eleanor Rinehart said wistfully.

Jack was about to tell her he wasn't so sure about that, when he caught sight of a familiar face. A moment later Sloane Quick danced by with her partner. She nodded regally but didn't speak to him.

He stiffened.

Eleanor turned her head and followed the direction of his gaze. "Do you know Sloane?"

His mouth thinned. "Yes."

She hesitated. "Do you know her well?"

"Well enough."

"I see Elizabeth Quick is with that lawyer boyfriend of hers."

Jack tried to relax his shoulders. "Never met the guy."

"You seem to know Sloane and Elizabeth and the other Quick sisters. Not that they're exactly rolling out the red carpet for you." It was an astute observation on her part. Eleanor Rinehart was inching closer and closer to the truth. Maybe it was time to just tell her.

"If I don't seem very popular with the Quick family, there's a good reason. I was once married to Diana," he said bluntly.

Eleanor gave him a funny look. "So you're the mystery man."

Jack hated feeling like a zoo specimen. "Yes."

Her curiosity quickly became admiration. "How very brave of you to show up for Kit's wedding."

"Stupid may be more like it," he grumbled. "I have a strong feeling I'm persona non grata with the Quicks. Not that anyone's actually been rude to me. The Quicks are too polite to be rude. But you may want to run for cover, just in case."

"I'll take my chances," Eleanor declared.

"Brave girl."

"Stupid may be more like it," she said, repeating his comment, and Jack laughed. Spurred on by an appreciative audience, Eleanor Rinehart went a step further. "Let's face it, Harry Quick runs a tight ship."

"A very tight ship," he concurred. "It's a good thing medical science has shown that it's the male who determines the gender of his offspring. Otherwise, I'm sure Harry would have laid the blame for five daughters on Marilyn."

"Well, he shouldn't complain. There isn't a bad apple in the whole bunch," she said admiringly.

Jack almost blurted out that most women in her shoes would have been jealous.

"I mean, take Kit, for instance. She's young and pretty and vivacious. She's just graduated from college and knows exactly what she wants. Then there's Jayne Ann. She's the brains of the outfit. Elizabeth is the social conscience. Sloane seems determined not to make the same mistakes as her oldest sister." Eleanor looked up quickly. "Sorry about that. No offense meant."

"And no offense taken," he reassured her. "What about Diana?" It cost him to ask that question.

"Diana? She's the Virgin Queen, the ice maiden. Won't go near men. I suppose that's your doing." The comment was nonjudgmental. "Of course, she's made quite a career for herself."

Jack thought of Diana's rapid advancement on the magazine she'd worked for during their marriage. "She was always destined for success."

This time it was Eleanor Rinehart who stiffened. "Here come the bride and groom. And they're headed right toward us," she hissed in warning.

They stopped dancing, and Jack turned, opening his arms just as a young woman threw herself at him.

"Jack!" she cried out with pleasure.

His arms went around her in a brotherly embrace as he dropped a light kiss on her cheek. "Hello, Kit."

Catherine Quick—Kit—put her head back and smiled up at him through a veil of happy tears. "I knew you'd come," she declared triumphantly. "I knew you wouldn't miss my wedding. You were there, weren't you, Jack?"

"I was there," he assured her.

The expression on Kit's face was reward enough for him. His being here *did* make a difference to her. Whatever else happened now, his trip to Phoenix could be deemed a success.

Kit hugged him again as they left the dance floor for a private reunion by the patio doors leading from the banquet room.

"The three of you will have to excuse me. I see some old friends I'd like to say hello to," Eleanor Rinehart announced as she made a discreet exit.

"Oh, Jack, I can't believe you're really here!" Kit exclaimed with a radiant smile.

"I wouldn't have missed your wedding for all the tea in China, Kit." Then he added, his voice full, "You make a beautiful bride." Clearing his throat, he turned to the young man at her side and held out his hand. "It's time we introduced ourselves. I'm Jack Royce."

"Eric Porter," the groom responded cordially, shaking his hand. His brow furrowed. "Jack Royce? Aren't you Diana's ex?"

So the good news was getting around, Jack thought wryly. He replied to the question with a simple yes.

"I'm glad to meet you. Kit thinks you're the cat's meow."

Jack gazed down at her affectionately. "Kit has always been an exceptionally intelligent young woman."

"I've wanted you two to meet for such a very long time," she enthused, slipping one arm through her new husband's and the other through one of Jack's. "You have a lot more in common than you may realize."

Eric was the younger of the two men, but he possessed the same self-confidence—and at six feet two inches, the same imposing physical appearance—as Jack Royce. He also had a keen sense of humor. "I think I have you to thank for all of this," he claimed, indicating the large wedding reception.

Jack surprised even himself by laughing. "I was afraid of that. I'm sorry."

"Don't apologize," Kit cut in. "The fact that we're having a big wedding has nothing to do with you. Or Diana. Or your elopement. We both wanted a wedding with all the trappings, didn't we, darling?"

What could Eric Porter say in the face of that declaration from his bride, other than, "Of course we did, sweetheart." His eyes were filled with love as he gazed down into Kit's face.

Jack watched, speechless for a moment. It seemed Kit's "big brother" didn't have to worry about her, after all.

"I'd like to propose a special toast," he said a few minutes later as the three of them were sipping champagne and catching up on each other's news. "To Kit and Eric, may theirs truly be a marriage made in heaven."

The next thing they knew it was time for Kit to change into the clothes she would be wearing for the first leg of their wedding trip. They weren't going far tonight, Eric confided to Jack. Just to the honeymoon suite at a nearby hotel.

"We'd better start saying goodbye to everyone, or we'll be here all night," he said, shaking Jack's hand. "I'm glad we finally met. Kit and I hope to see more of you when we get back from our honeymoon."

"I'd like that," Jack said, and meant it.

As he walked away with his brand-new wife at his side, the younger man threw over his shoulder, "Why don't you get some fresh air? I'd try the patio if I were you."

Jack had to admit a breath of fresh air sounded inviting. A growl of protest came from his empty stomach. He'd go by the buffet table on his way....

IT WAS A WARM NIGHT, even for Phoenix on the ninth of June, Diana realized as she tried to fan herself with a soggy cocktail napkin. She needed a few minutes alone before helping Kit change into the linen suit her sister had chosen as her going-away outfit.

She stood on the edge of the patio, gazing out over the perfectly maintained grounds of the country club, its cascading rose bushes, tropical palm trees and thorny ocotillo outlined by strategically placed spotlights.

Nightscaping. That's what the effect was called here in the desert Southwest.

She supposed the familiar sound of a door opening and closing must have registered in some small corner of her mind, but she didn't think anything of it until a slight chill raced up her spine. She shivered as a second premonitory chill ran up her back and into the hair at her nape.

For a moment she simply *felt* his presence. She couldn't breathe. Her heart seemed to stop beating. The world around her was trapped in suspended animation.

Then her pulse picked up speed, and she began to breathe again. She inhaled, catching a faint whiff of his after-shave: it was subtly masculine and slightly wood-scented.

"Diana."

It had been so long since she'd heard him say her name like that, since she'd heard him say her name at all. The sound of his voice resounded through her flesh right through to her bones. It was that old feeling, that old black magic brought to light. The fine hairs on the back of her neck were standing on end. Like Sleeping Beauty, she was coming strangely and wonderfully alive.

Whatever else happened, Diana realized, there would always be this between them. This immediate reaction, this physical attraction, that neither could control or even begin to explain.

She didn't turn to face him right away. She had her pride. She wasn't the same woman he'd left three years ago when he'd gone off to the Amazon. She would make sure he knew that from the start.

Diana Quick assumed a cool, regal, slightly blasé expression, put her shoulders back and then slowly turned.

"Hello, Jack."

4

HE MADE AN IMPOSING FIGURE, standing there with the light beyond the patio doors behind him, outlining his tall, broad-shouldered form, larger than life, a stranger to her, yet somehow still so familiar.

He didn't say anything. Diana began to wonder if he'd heard her, although the music coming from inside the country club was soft and the sounds of the night air muted. His face was in shadow; she couldn't read his expression. He took another step toward her, moving quietly, stealthily, like the hunter he was. A thought skittered across Diana's mind. This time, was she the prey?

He stopped, and she could see his features clearly now. His expression was as bland and as guarded as her own. It seemed that neither of them was willing to take any chances.

Jack stared at her, unblinking, then finally said, "Hello, Diana."

The moment had finally come, and Diana realized she didn't have the slightest idea what to say to the man.

"You were at Kit's wedding." Inane. Obvious. But it was the best she could do under the circumstances.

He smiled faintly, without humor. "Yes. I was at Kit's wedding. She makes a beautiful bride, doesn't she?"

Diana nodded. It was trite, but it was also true in Kit's case.

Jack went on. "From the few minutes I spent talking with him, I'd say she's married a nice guy."

"Eric is perfect for Kit," she declared.

It was a moment before he added, "They seem very much in love."

She swallowed. "They are."

More safe, standard conversation, Diana realized, relaxing the painfully tense muscles of her neck and shoulders. Perhaps they could be civil to each other, she and Jack, despite the years since they'd seen each other, in spite of everything that had gone on during those years.

Jack stayed where he was. She took a moment to study him. Her mother was right. He was wearing a beautiful, tailor-made Italian silk suit. A man of his size and proportions would never be able to find clothing off the rack that fit so perfectly.

He looked like a prosperous businessman. That surprised her. The Jack Royce she'd known—and loved—had never thought about money and had never had any. He'd been more at home in scruffy blue jeans and a faded shirt, or his perennial favorite, wrinkled khaki. This was the first time she'd seen him in a suit, and the transformation was quite astounding. If possible, he was even better looking than when she'd last seen him, more than three years ago.

In fact, Diana admitted grudgingly, he was gorgeous.

She wanted to deny it, but that's what her former husband was, with that dark, thick, curly head of hair, that prominent, slightly aquiline nose, that sensuous mouth framed by a trim mustache, and those eyes, always those eyes that seemed to peer into her very soul. Broad shoulders and sinewy arms gave an impression of tremendous physical strength. Added to that was a certain attitude, an air of self-confidence, of solidity, of being a man who could take care of himself, who could handle whatever came his way.

Jack had always been a survivor, whether alone in the middle of the scorching desert, climbing the highest mountain or trudging through the jungle. Diana knew that much. Yet she wasn't altogether certain, even now, that he could have survived her world in Phoenix.

Eventually he asked, "How are your parents and sisters?"

She managed to reply. "Fine."

"How have you been?"

Again, "Fine."

A trace of sardonic humor crept into his voice. "I suppose it's kind of ridiculous to ask what you've been doing with yourself since I last saw you."

Taken aback for a moment, Diana mumbled, "I suppose it is."

There was dead silence.

He stood there, staring at her. Then he opened his mouth. Ridiculous or not, he was determined to know. "What *have* you been doing with yourself?"

Diana considered her answer as she watched him raise his glass to his mouth. He took a long drink. His Adam's apple bobbed as the liquid slid down his throat, and she thought of all the times she'd lain beside him in bed, sprawled on her stomach, and had reached up with her fingertip to trace the outline of that small, odd physical difference between them—one of many—wondering at it, almost enchanted by it, pressing her lips to it. . . .

Diana gave her head a reprimanding shake. What had she been doing with herself? What was she willing to tell him? "I've been working, of course."

The slightly upturned smile on Jack's face matched his earlier sardonic tone. "Of course. I hear you're quite successful, too."

"Kit told you?"

He drank from his glass again. "No. Actually, it was a young woman named Eleanor Stowe Rinehart."

"Ah, Buffy." She wasn't surprised. She'd seen the two of them dancing together. "In the market for an heiress this time, Jack?" The comment slipped out before she could do anything to stop it.

The man beside her was very still. "Is she an heiress?"

She'd only been joking. Couldn't he see that? Although Teddy Rinehart's money was anything but a joke.

"Buffy's—Eleanor's father owns half the Valley," she told him. "One day she'll inherit millions."

Jack shrugged. "Doesn't matter. Eleanor is nice enough, I suppose, but she isn't my type." He arched one dark eyebrow. "Don't you agree?"

The question was unexpected. Stumbling over the first reply that popped into her head, Diana said, "I—I don't know. I'm not sure what your type is anymore. I don't think I ever really knew."

Jack's voice was soft and caressing as he leaned toward her and murmured, "I think you know. I think you always have."

Then he moved another step closer and took a deep breath.

It was as if he wanted to inhale the very essence of her: the subtle fragrance of her shampoo, the slightly exotic interaction between the perfume she was wearing and her own body oils, the way the desert night smelled on her skin.

Swaying toward him, Diana closed her eyes for a moment. This was, after all, the man who used to tell her that he would know her anytime, anywhere, simply by her distinctive scent. He'd loved it, couldn't seem to get enough of it—or of her—as he nuzzled her neck and bare shoulders, the vulnerable curve of her ear, his lips on her flesh, tasting, touching and inevitably arousing....

Diana's eyes flew open. She quickly retreated, drawing back from him mentally and physically.

Jack shifted his weight and broke the silence by saying to her, "You haven't changed a bit."

She didn't know if that was meant as a compliment or not. But she followed his comment with, "You've changed."

Jack laughed. "Good thing, huh?"

He *had* changed. For the first time Diana began to realize just how much. The Jack Royce she'd known would never have had the ability, let alone the inclination, to laugh at himself. She had to confess she was intrigued by this unexpected development.

Giving him the once-over, she said, "I see you finally bought a suit."

"I thought it was about time." There was that flash of self-deprecating humor again.

"It looks good on you," she admitted aloud.

He seemed pleased by the compliment. "Times change. Circumstances change. Sometimes people have to change along with them."

But can a leopard change its spots? The question gnawed at the edges of Diana's consciousness.

She turned her head and gazed off into the night. "I suppose you're right. We all have to change, grow up, grow older, perhaps wiser, if we're lucky."

"Not you. Not older, anyway. You look exactly the same," he said carefully.

She didn't want to be reminded of the final days, weeks, months they'd spent together. In fact, she'd expended a great deal of time and energy trying to forget that period of her life. Besides, Jack was wrong. She didn't look the same. She didn't feel the same. She wasn't the same, inside or out.

It was time to change the subject. "Kit must have been happy to see you."

"Yes, she was. I was happy to see her again, too."

"She always was partial to you."

"Unlike some members of the Quick family."

Diana heard the momentary bitterness in Jack's voice and knew she wasn't the only one who had suffered.

She tried to be diplomatic. "Have you seen anyone besides Kit?"

"Do you mean has anybody else in the family condescended to speak to me? The answer is no. Although Sloane did give me the cold shoulder as she danced by. Politely, of course." Jack lost all trace of his former good humor. "Not that I expected to be met with open arms, mind you. Mine is hardly a case of the prodigal son-in-law returning to the fold. I know how your family feels about me, Diana. How they've always felt about me." Jack paused and seemed to consider the direction their conversation was taking. Apparently he didn't care for it any more than she did. He shrugged. "It's all water under the bridge, anyway."

"Yes, it's all water under the bridge now," Diana echoed so softly she could barely hear herself.

They stood there in the soft summer night, silent once again. The strains of a familiar song could be faintly heard coming from inside the country club.

Diana found herself humming along under her breath. She recognized the tune. It was an old love song. "That's 'Where or When' the band's playing, isn't it?" she said, trying to sound nonchalant.

"Yes. It was a big hit for Dion and the Belmonts back in . . . 1960, I believe."

"I see you've kept up with your musical trivia."

He looked at her with a wry smile. "That's what comes from being the youngest brother in a family of early rock-and-roll enthusiasts." He reached behind her and set his glass on a patio table. Then he gazed down into her eyes and murmured, paraphrasing the lyrics of the one-time top-ten hit song, "Haven't we stood and looked at each other in the same way before, Diana Quick?"

Her pulse was becoming slightly erratic, and she gave a short, nervous laugh. "I—I don't know."

"I think we have."

"Perhaps," she allowed.

"You've never remarried, have you? I wonder why." He took her left hand in his and proceeded to examine her ringless fingers.

His hand was warm to the touch, warmer than the desert night surrounding them. His grasp was light but as unyielding as a steel bracelet. Her heart was beginning to pound in her breast, and Diana knew full well that he could feel the frantic pace of her pulse beneath his fingertips.

She took a deep breath and willed her body to relax. "I've had no desire to remarry," she informed him, although she suspected her answer only confirmed what he already knew.

"Are you living with someone?"

She wasn't sure why she answered him. It was really none of his business. "No. I'm not living with anyone," Diana said, frowning. She was almost certain they'd had this conversation before. If only she could remember where and when. To cover up her confusion, she added, "I have a place of my own out in the desert."

"I seem to recall you always preferred living alone," he commented dryly.

They both knew there was more to it than that. She had not only preferred to live alone; she'd often had no choice in the matter.

Seven years ago Jack had assured her that any place he hung his hat was home, so after they were married Diana had kept the downtown condominium that was close to her job; the sleek, Danish modern furniture that was her personal preference; the pink and apple-green accessories that were far too feminine for a married couple, and the impractical wall-to-wall white carpeting. Jack had never said a word to her about redecorating, but she'd always suspected he hated the place from start to finish.

Maybe that had been part of their problem, a lack of communication. The verbal kind. They'd never had a problem communicating on a more primitive physical level.

Suddenly, realizing her former husband was still holding her hand, Diana tried to pull away.

"Don't go." Jack's voice had a raw edge to it.

Astonished, she blurted out, "Why ever not?"

He hesitated, then said in a low and slightly husky baritone, "Because I want you to dance with me."

Her head came up. Their eyes met. She wondered if he could see the panic that was threatening to swamp her. "I can't."

"Surely you aren't afraid of me."

Terrified was more like it. But she'd be damned if she would admit that to Jack.

"It's not that." Another lie added to the growing list of lies she'd been telling herself—and others—all evening. "I have to help Kit change into her going-away outfit," she said, heading toward the patio doors.

"Don't run away from me, Diana." Like an archer's arrows, his pointed words shot across the short distance separating them and hit their target, dead on.

Her back stiffened. "I'm not running away. But the maid of honor does have certain duties to perform."

"I was wondering about that."

She turned. "About my duties?"

"No. Whether you were calling yourself the maid of honor or the matron of honor. Diana Quick or Diana Royce."

She finally found her voice. "I took my maiden name back."

"Will you dance with me, then, Diana Quick?"

Jack didn't wait for an answer. He simply swept her into his arms and began to move around the shadowed patio.

Diana tried to hold herself away from him, refusing to give in that last inch.

"Maybe you *have* changed," he murmured in the vicinity of her ear, his breath a warm, wafting breeze on her bare neck. "You used to like dancing with me."

Her posture was perfect. "As you said yourself: times change, circumstances change, people change. I used to do a lot of things I don't do now."

Jack drew back long enough to glance down at her with a sly smile on his handsome face. "Really? And what kind of things might those be?" His remark was typically arrogant and typically masculine.

A self-conscious blush spread across Diana's cheeks. He'd embarrassed her. She wanted to lash out at him. She wanted to kick the man in the shins. Hard. Only her good breeding prevented her from doing so.

Exhaling an angry breath, she tried to regain control of herself. Why, oh why, did Jack Royce have the ability, the singular talent, of egging her on to the point of emotional frenzy and physical passion? He always could get a rise out of her. And she, him.

She calmed down and glanced up at him, only to see a strange expression flit across his face. He was very quiet. Then he caught his breath; it sounded like a groan.

"Are you all right?"

"Never felt better," he tried to assure her.

She regarded him suspiciously. "Are you . . . tipsy?"

Jack snorted disdainfully. "Me? Tipsy?"

"Yes. You. Tipsy."

"Have you ever heard of a man who stands six-four in his socks and weighs in at nearly two hundred pounds being tipsy?"

She had to admit she hadn't.

"I may have had one glass too many of bourbon," he admitted, "or one strawberry too few, but tipsy . . ."

Jack's voice trailed off as he pulled her closer. He curled an arm around her waist and captured her right hand in his. He settled his chin against her forehead, his slight growth of whiskers an abrasive on her skin. Despite the warm June night, Diana shivered when his mustache grazed the tip of her ear.

"Diana . . ."

Her name came out on a breath that sent a strange quiver down her spine.

As they danced Jack urged her into the natural cradle of his thighs. She could feel his body stirring to life, and for a moment she couldn't stop herself from going soft against him. It was insane, but it felt so good to be held in a man's arms, this man's arms, to know that he wanted her, desired her, was still excited by her.

Her fingers trailed along his broad shoulders and partway down his arm. She could detect the muscles, the inherent strength just beneath the surface of his suit jacket.

It tempted her. It always had, this inexplicable physical attraction he held for her.

Allowing her head to rest on his chest, Diana closed her eyes again and concentrated on the exquisite feel of Jack's body moving against hers. With his fingertips, he traced an erotic pattern along her back. His hand settled in the small indentation at the base of her spine, and he pressed her even closer. She could feel the outline of his semi-arousal, could hear the tortured exhalation through his lips.

Suddenly, Diana realized they'd stopped dancing. She had no recollection of just when.

Trembling, she dropped her arms and stepped away from him. She opened her right hand. The soggy cocktail napkin was wadded into a ball. She turned and dropped it into the empty glass Jack had set on the patio table.

"Diana—"

She turned to face him, sharp, reprimanding words on the tip of her tongue. She was angry with him, angry with herself for being putty in his hands.

The words were never spoken. She studied his face thoughtfully. Was it a fleeting look of regret she saw there?

Jack didn't even blink. "Don't be angry with me, with yourself. We always did have that effect on each other."

She exhaled and said after a time, "I know. I'm not really angry."

"I want to ask you a question," he went on.

There was something in his voice that caught her attention. Her head came up. "What?"

"Why didn't you ever write?"

"Why didn't I ever write?" She bristled. "Why didn't *you* write?"

"I did."

She laughed. The sound rang hollow even to her own ears. "Surely you don't mean that cryptic note telling me in twenty-five words or less that you were back from the Amazon and living in Wisconsin?"

His retaliation was immediate. "At least I wrote it myself."

That stung. "What is that supposed to mean?"

"All I ever got from you was some damn typewritten letter from your divorce lawyer!"

Ten minutes together, and it had started already—the mudslinging, the accusations, the name calling. Some things—some people—simply weren't meant to be.

Diana was breathing hard. "I don't think this is the time or the place to be having this discussion."

Jack hooted. "Discussion? Since when did we ever have a discussion?" He drove an exasperated hand through his hair. "I'm sorry about that. I didn't come out here to pick a fight with you. I just wanted to talk to you."

Could the man actually be apologizing to her? If so, the changes in Jack went far deeper than she'd suspected.

"This isn't the time or place for us to talk, either. I really do have to go help Kit change her clothes."

"Name the time and the place, then," he insisted.

"I don't know." Diana saw the look he gave her and relented. "I guess I could give you my telephone number. Maybe we could arrange some mutually convenient time."

"I'll be glad to call and make an appointment to speak with you," Jack said, the sarcasm in his voice thick enough to cut with a knife.

Diana tried to appear unperturbed. "I, ah, don't have anything to write on." Jack took the soggy cocktail napkin from his glass, tore off a relatively small but dry corner and handed it to her. "I don't have anything to write *with*." He forked over a pen from his breast pocket. "I won't be home tomorrow. I'm staying in town overnight," she added as she jotted down her number.

He put his shoulders back. "I have meetings all day Monday, but I'll try to call in the evening."

"I should be home." She returned his pen. "Thank you."

"You're welcome," Jack replied with the same excruciating politeness.

"I really must go," she said, trying to sound less eager to escape than she was.

With that, Diana turned tail and ran for her life. She didn't dare look back. Not even a quick glance over her shoulder.

In her rush to get away from Jack, she didn't see the expression of longing on his face. She didn't see the look of longing become one of utter determination. And she didn't hear his softly spoken vow as he watched her disappear into the safety of the country club.

"Run as fast as you can, my lovely Diana, and as far as you can. It won't make a damn bit of difference in the end. This time I won't let you get away from me."

HE FOUND THE DIRT ROAD on his third try. Even then it was a lucky guess.

Jack stopped and studied the rough map he'd sketched from Diana's directions last night. The air-conditioning vents were blasting frigid air into the interior of the pale blue Mercedes sedan, ruffling his hair and cooling his frustration.

"Good grief," he grumbled under his breath as he steered the rental car down the unpaved driveway, "talk about going from one extreme to the other." The last he knew, Diana had lived in a high-rise condo. Apparently sometime in the past three years she'd moved out to the boonies.

Not that anything on the north end of Scottsdale stayed the boonies for very long. Here today, gone tomorrow. The old adage certainly applied to what was happening to the natural landscape. Today's desert was tomorrow's golf course, complete with luxury homes on the ninth fairway, although the saguaro cacti—some a century or two old—were carefully preserved. They were protected by law and desired by everyone with a desert lawn.

Jack spotted a house at the end of the dirt lane and pulled up alongside it, shutting off the ignition. The Santa Fe style adobe structure was low to the ground and weathered by wind and sun and the occasional storm. The house melded into the desert as if it had always been there, surrounded by sand and saguaro, jutting boulders and blowing tumbleweeds.

The Four Peaks were visible on the horizon, earth's undying monuments, rising from the blue summer haze. East of the sprawling city of Phoenix were the Superstition Mountains, allegedly the site of the legendary and world-famous Lost Dutchman's Mine. Now that area was part of a designated U.S. Forest Service Wilderness.

He'd always had a hankering to go exploring up in those mountains, Jack daydreamed, thoughtfully rubbing his jaw. Who knew what treasures lay buried beneath a crumbling stone wall, or a plank of wind-weathered wood, or beside bits of colored glass and rusted bric-a-brac? But like everyone else, he'd heard horror stories of naive tourists who had invariably tried hiking through the mountains on their own and gotten lost. Every year a few people were found dazed, suffering from sunstroke and dehydration—or worse. Some were never found at all, of course.

Jack had to admit that he'd be lost right now if he hadn't spotted the name Quick stenciled on the mailbox at the end of the dusty road.

He opened the door on the driver's side of the rented Mercedes and got out. A furnace blast of air hit him squarely in the face. Typical of Arizona in mid-June, it was hotter than Hades. The temperature built up in the valley during the daylight hours, and early evening was often the hottest time of the day. But the desert was deceptive, dangerously so sometimes. It could cool off very quickly after dark.

Removing his suit coat, Jack tossed it nonchalantly over his shoulder. With his free hand, he undid his tie and rolled up the sleeve of his dress shirt. Switching his coat to the other shoulder, he rolled up that sleeve, as well. He happened to glance down. His cordovan shoes were already covered with a layer of fine red dust.

He raised his head and took a moment to study the quaint house in front of him. Real adobe was too expensive and too susceptible to water damage to be used as routine building material. But in Diana's case, he had no doubts this was the genuine article. God knows, his ex-wife could afford adobe if she wanted it. She had inherited money from grandparents on both sides of the family, and, in addition, had come into a hefty trust fund at the age of twenty-five. During the time he'd known her, Diana had always had plenty of money. She'd insisted on shopping at the "right" stores and buying only the best designer labels.

Jack shook his head. He was still marveling at the fact that this was Diana's house. A one-word description for it was rustic. There was a latticework of weathered spruce enclosing the patio and a primitive stone fountain in the Spanish-style courtyard. A huge stone sculpture of an animal was tucked into one corner between several large, potted plants and a collection of waist-high earthen jars. A pigskin loveseat and an assortment of old wooden chairs were arranged around a massive antique table.

The rustic adobe house wasn't even remotely like the place Diana had owned when they were married. In those days, he had somehow been made to feel like a guest in his own home. Truth to tell, he'd hated the luxurious condo on sight. He'd just never told Diana how he felt.

But this house in the desert—a man could relax here and put his feet up. A man could live in a place like this and call it home....

Even with the dark glasses he was wearing, Jack was forced to shade his eyes with one hand as he stood there and gazed into the distance. The sun was setting. It was a large red ball in the sky. Soon the heat of the desert day would give way to the cooling breezes of the desert night.

Abruptly he turned and grabbed his briefcase from the back seat of the Mercedes. Leaving one window rolled down as a safety measure against the heat, he slammed the car door shut and walked toward the adobe house.

He pushed open a wrought-iron gate and entered the shaded courtyard. The front door was nearly hidden under a canopy of white roses that grew around and above and over a trellis alongside the house. He knocked. There was no sound from within. And no answer. He tried again, with the same lack of response.

Noticing the door was slightly ajar, Jack pushed it open another inch or two and poked his head around the corner. "Diana?"

After a moment he heard her voice coming from the opposite end of the house. "Jack, is that you?"

"Yes!" he called back.

"Please come in and make yourself at home. I'll be with you in a minute."

Jack stepped into the house and closed the door behind him. He found himself standing in an entryway, the living room to his right. It was filled with green plants, Western paintings and clean, comfortable furniture. The focal point of the room was an old Mexican carousel horse.

To his left was a book-lined room that seemed to be part library and part office. He sauntered into the latter and looked around, grateful for the cool air inside the house.

In addition to a thousand or two volumes, there was an oversize desk in the far corner covered with stacks of paper; a giveaway glass from McDonald's stuffed with an assortment of ballpoint pens and sharpened pencils; several dictionaries, one lying open to the *S*s; a well-thumbed copy of Roget's *Thesaurus*, a computer keyboard and monitor, the screen lit and covered with print. Diana must have been working when he'd driven up.

He strolled toward the bookcases and read a few of the authors' names aloud. "Robert Heinlein, Arthur C. Clarke, Isaac Asimov, Frank Herbert, Ann Maxwell, Joan D. Vinge, Jayne Ann Krentz, Philip Jose Farmer, Piers Anthony."

The shelves were overflowing with the type of science fiction and fantasy novels that had been Diana's favorites when they were married. Apparently she hadn't changed that much. He wondered if she still watched reruns of *Star Trek* and *Dr. Who* on television.

Next to the science fiction was a bookcase of travel guides. He scanned the first row of titles. *Who Goes Out in the Midday Sun?, The Sun Never Sets On the British Empire, The Cry of the Kalahari, Stonehenge, A Book of Travellers' Tales, Ancient Cities of the Southwest.*

Diana had always said she was an armchair traveler at best. Other than to visit the deluxe hotels of Europe or to take the occasional cruise on a luxury liner, she hadn't wanted to give up the conveniences of home to travel. She didn't care to rough it or worry about the water or the required shots or poisonous snakes or whatever went bump in the day *or* night. She'd claimed that her imagination and a good book could take her any place she wanted to go. So she'd stayed home and read about the Belly of Stones while he'd traveled halfway around the world to see the vast expanse of sun-petrified ground along the Nile.

It was a crying shame, in Jack's opinion. Maybe it was safer to stay home, but he couldn't help feeling that the only way to really see the world and experience all its wonders was to do it firsthand. He was afraid that his darling Diana had always been something of a coward when it came to life—and love.

Spotting an unusual piece of sculpture on a table by the front window, Jack walked across the room to take a closer look. It was a carved piece of stone that he knew instinctively was native American Indian. It was a mesmerizing interpretation of a Madonna with child, or perhaps it was a young Indian woman with her baby. Either way, the sculpture was stunning.

"I see you like Alvin Marshall's work."

Without turning, Jack said, "It's incredible."

Diana's voice came nearer. "Yes, it is. I'm very lucky to have that piece."

"Native American artist?"

"Navajo. He grew up on the reservation that borders Arizona and New Mexico. As a boy, Alvin Marshall was a shepherd. Whether it was all the time he spent alone while he herded his animals, or the hours he spent studying the forms of nature, his honesty and strength come through very clearly in his work."

"Has he had any formal training as an artist?"

"Essentially he's self-taught, although I understand he was able to travel to Italy recently, where he studied the great masters, in particular Michelangelo."

At last Jack straightened and turned. Diana was crossing the room toward him. Her face was scrubbed clean of makeup, and her hair was tied back into an unpretentious ponytail that swayed from side to side as she moved. She was wearing a light cotton shirt and pants, and her feet were bare. Her only ornamentation was a silver and turquoise bracelet pushed halfway up her right arm. Her usually long, elegant fingernails were cut short and devoid of polish.

"There's something different about you. . . ."

5

SHE SHRUGGED. "Maybe it's the fact that I'm not smoking."

"You mean you quit?"

She nodded. "Three years ago."

"Three years ago," he echoed.

That wasn't it, Jack decided. Maybe it was the way she was dressed. Or maybe it was the fact she wasn't wearing even a trace of makeup. Or maybe something less superficial, less obvious than mere appearances had changed.

"It could be the outfit," she was saying as she frowned and glanced down at the plain pants and shirt. "I was working at my desk and lost track of time. I'm afraid I didn't have a chance to change into anything more appropriate before you arrived," she added apologetically.

Jack found himself studying her. Then he declared in a slightly husky tone, "There's nothing wrong with your outfit. Nothing at all."

Diana decided it was time to change the subject. "What's in the briefcase?"

Judging by the puzzled expression on his face as he glanced down at the expensive case in his hand, Diana knew Jack had forgotten he was carrying it.

"Catalogs."

That wasn't what she'd expected him to say. "Catalogs?"

"Catalogs. Promotional brochures. A few samples. Some leasing agreements."

In two giant strides he was across the room. He set the briefcase on her desk, turned the tumbler lock to a preset combination, threw the bolt and flipped open the lid.

He took out a professionally printed booklet and gave it to her. "Hot off the press, our new fall catalog."

Diana glanced down at the publication he'd handed her. On the cover there was an artist's rendering of a fisherman standing in midstream—water-resistant hat, hip boots, red plaid shirt, fly rod and all. The background scene was an autumnal one. Across the top, in big bold letters, was printed *The Outdoorsman*. Underneath that, in slightly smaller letters, was the tag, Jack Royce's Wisconsin Wilderness Wear.

"You have a company?" Diana finally asked.

"The Outdoorsman." Jack pointed to the name printed across the front of the publication. "We design, manufacture and sell hunting and field gear, tropical and desert wear, some arctic wear, camping equipment and survival kits."

Diana's brows came together. "You don't just dress like a businessman, do you? You are a businessman."

"Yes, I am."

Bits and pieces started coming together for her. "You've started your own company."

"Actually, I bought my dad's old army-navy store and built from there."

She wanted to know more. She wanted to know everything, Diana realized. But all in due course. She was forgetting her manners. Her guest was still standing with his suit coat draped over his arm.

She reverted to the role of the perfect hostess. "Would you like something to drink?"

Jack looked inordinately pleased. "I would love something to drink. I'd forgotten how parched your throat can get when you're not used to the dry desert air."

"Have you had any dinner?" Diana asked, suddenly realizing that somehow she'd missed both lunch and dinner.

"I thought I'd grab a bite on my way back into town," said Jack.

There was really only one thing to do, Diana rationalized. Before she could consider the wisdom of her actions, she heard herself suggesting to Jack, "I have two steaks in the freezer I can defrost and cook. And I always keep the ingredients on hand for a salad. How does a grilled steak and a tossed salad sound for dinner?"

By the time she'd finished relating even that short menu to her ex-husband, he was grinning from ear to ear. She found his reaction charming and downright disarming.

"Like heaven."

As an afterthought, she suggested, "Why don't you give me your suit coat? I'll hang it up in the front closet for you."

He handed it over to her with polite thanks and turned to shut his briefcase.

"Bring that to the kitchen with you. I'd like to hear more about this company of yours," Diana added as she hung his suit jacket on a hanger, shut the closet door and indicated he should follow her toward the back room of the house.

The kitchen was Diana's favorite room. It was a unique combination of modern conveniences and Southwestern-style Spanish architecture. The floor and the countertops were done in an unglazed Mexican tile. The ceiling was raised and beamed with natural vigas—large, unfinished logs that served as supports for the roof. Against one wall was a rustic sideboard cluttered with woven baskets, Indian pottery and a collection of candlesticks, ranging from matched pairs in polished brass and silver to one-of-a-kind, more primitive renditions in ceramic and wood.

In front of a floor-to-ceiling window, there was an eating area furnished with a dining table and four chairs. The view from there was magnificent. The room overlooked the desert and the mountains beyond.

Diana stopped in the middle of the kitchen. "Please take a seat and make yourself comfortable."

"Mi casa, su casa," Jack suggested with an affable smile.

Her house was most certainly *not* his house. Not anymore. But instead of debating the issue with him, Diana chose to ask, "What would you like to drink?"

"Whatever's convenient," he answered as any congenial houseguest would.

Peering into the cupboard that served as her liquor cabinet, she said, "I have bourbon, Scotch, gin, vodka, tequila, brandy, Canadian Club, Kahlua—" she opened the door of the refrigerator and added "—and cold beer."

It came as no surprise when Jack responded, "A beer would sure hit the spot." Some things never changed, it seemed.

Jack reached up and loosened his tie a little more. The briefcase ended up on the floor near his feet as he accepted a can of cold beer from her. He was just settling himself into one of the chairs at the kitchen table when she thought to ask, "Would you like a glass for that?"

Shaking his head, Jack declined with a thoughtful, "No thanks." He was staring at the label on the front of the beer can. After a moment, he pulled the flip top and brought the can to his mouth. He took a healthy swallow and sighed contentedly. "I see you haven't forgotten the brand I prefer."

Diana deliberately played dumb. "Is that the kind of beer you used to drink?" she said in an expressionless voice. The question was a rhetorical one; they both knew that.

Taking two T-bone steaks from the freezer, she popped them into the microwave on the counter. She pressed the buttons for the defrost cycle and programmed in the amount of time required before helping herself to a glass of mineral water. Then, leaning nonchalantly against the refrigerator door, legs crossed at the ankles, she watched Jack as he drank his beer.

He looked tired. And hot. But not as tired or hot as he had a few minutes before. It must have been a rough day for him. From what he'd told her last night on the telephone, she surmised that he'd had one meeting after another scheduled, starting first thing that morning.

Diana glanced down at the catalog that she still had in her hand. She skimmed through a few pages, noting the quality and variety of the merchandise for sale and the prices. Apparently wilderness wear didn't come cheap.

This, she thought with growing amazement, was what Jack had been doing for the past three and a half years. He'd been building a small business empire. The idea was definitely going to take some getting used to! And now was as good a time as any to find out exactly how he'd done it.

"I'm very impressed by your catalog," she said, shaking her head in wonderment.

"It took us months to put it together," Jack confessed as he leaned back, balancing his weight and that of the chair on its two hind legs. "We worked our tails off, I'll tell you."

"Who's we?"

"Primarily the graphics-design firm I hired to help plan the layout of the catalog—and me. Although my two older brothers and my father had some input into the merchandise we're offering."

"Earlier you said you started out by buying your father's army-navy store."

"Yes, I did. When I moved back to Wisconsin a few years ago—" his eyes glazed over for a second or two "—I decided it was time to put my knowledge of the outdoors to work."

Jack had begun his story without once mentioning their divorce, Diana noticed. For that, she was grateful.

He went on. "I probably told you a long time ago that I got my first fly rod when I was only six years old."

"No. You never did." The oversight, however inconsequential, bothered Diana more than it should have.

Jack looked at her and said frankly, "I guess there were a lot of things we didn't tell each other."

"I guess there were," she said, stricken by the fact.

"Anyway, I suppose that's when my interest in the outdoors began, when I was just a kid. Hunting, fishing, camping, hiking, boating—our family did them all."

"Your mother was quite the outdoorswoman, too, wasn't she?"

He gave a playful snort. "Yes. She was the best fisherman of the five of us. And the best shot. Still is, for that matter."

"She must be an unusual woman," ventured Diana.

"That she is," agreed Jack wholeheartedly. "She's had to be to survive in a household of men like ours."

Almost wistfully, Diana added, "I would like to have met her."

He shook his head as if the idea was crazy. "Trust me. The two of you have nothing in common. You're as different as night and day."

She disagreed, and said so. "Maybe we aren't as different as you seem to think we are, your mother and I."

He studied her for a minute at his leisure, then conceded, "You may be right about that."

She urged him to continue his story. "So your interest in the outdoors began at an early age."

He nodded. "It started out as a pastime; once I was in high school it had become my passion. Like many a homegrown Wisconsin boy, I spent more hours tramping through the woods during deer season than I did in school." He rubbed the back of his neck and said self-critically, "When I look back now I realize it was a miracle I ever got my diploma. The week after high-school graduation, I hiked all the way to Washington State to climb a mountain." He shook his head and laughed reminiscently. "I sure had more brawn than brains in those days."

She liked this man, Diana realized. She genuinely liked him.

He sat forward in his chair now and leaned his elbows on the table. "I kicked around from one place to another along the West Coast. Saw most of Washington, Oregon, California, a little of western Canada. One thing led to another, and the next thing I knew I'd signed on to work a tramp steamer on her way to Singapore."

This part of the story she'd heard bits and pieces of before, but it was still fascinating. "You must have been how old at the time? Eighteen? Nineteen?"

"As a matter of fact, I turned nineteen somewhere out in the middle of the Pacific Ocean. From Singapore I went on to Kuala Lumpur and from there saw the rest of Malaysia, eventually ending up in Manila that trip." He took a drink of his beer. "The thing is, you see, that way of life becomes addictive after a while. The thrill of new places, new people and new experiences, the surge of adrenaline that shoots into your bloodstream like a potent drug when you know damn well you've pitted yourself against overwhelming odds and still come out on top."

"It sounds like a coming of age, a rite of passage, a test of manhood," Diana murmured perceptively.

"Sometimes it was a test of your survival skills. Winning simply meant staying alive. You know most of the story from there up until the past few years," he said, deliberately circumventing the subject of their marriage and subsequent divorce. "I started out my first year in the business by buying overstock, manufacturers' closeouts, whatever quality merchandise I could get my hands on. Then I started designing and manufacturing my own line of wilderness wear based on personal experience, like padded knees in a number of my pants. That came about as a result of a three-hundred-mile canoe trip I once took."

"Perhaps experience is really the mother of invention," Diana interjected.

"Function comes first for an outdoorsman, form second. Last on the list is fashion. But the darnedest thing has happened, Diana. The majority of men who are buying my clothes have never set foot in the wilderness." He rubbed his chin introspectively, as if that fact still had him confounded. "I'm even getting requests to do a line of women's clothing."

"Move over, Banana Republic," she warned.

At that Jack laughed good-naturedly. "We're hardly in their league."

"Yet."

He shrugged. "I suppose anything's possible. I know we can't keep up with the demand. I've got my whole family involved in the business and half the town of Walleye Lake,

Wisconsin, and I'm still working eighteen hours a day, seven days a week," he admitted wearily.

That worried her. "How long has it been since you've had a vacation?"

He snorted. "This is my vacation."

"Your trip to Phoenix?"

His forehead wrinkled. "I meant sitting here drinking this can of beer."

She wasn't his mother. She wasn't his wife. Not anymore. It wasn't her place to tell Jack Royce that he was working too hard, Diana reasoned. But she had to bite her tongue until the urge to lecture him had passed.

Then, as she took lettuce and tomatoes and cucumbers from the crisper drawer, she asked, "Would you like another beer while I make our salad?"

"I'll help myself," Jack volunteered, getting to his feet and rummaging around in her refrigerator while she washed the fresh vegetables in the kitchen sink.

He wasn't having any difficulty making himself right at home, Diana noticed. Not that she really minded. Never in a million years had she ever imagined she and Jack could be so comfortable together, so companionable. Maybe they'd both changed more than either of them realized.

"So why the trip to Phoenix, then?" she said, tearing the head of lettuce into bite-size pieces. "Besides the obvious reason, of course."

Jack closed the refrigerator door and stood there with a frown on his handsome face and a can of beer in his hand. "The obvious reason?"

She started in on the ripe, red tomatoes, cutting them into thick wedges. "Kit's wedding."

The frown disappeared. "Right."

What other reason could there be, Diana wondered before her attention reverted to the cucumber waiting to be sliced.

"I'm looking into the possibility of opening a West Coast operation," Jack finally elaborated as he sipped his drink. "We ship a lot of merchandise to this part of the country. As a matter of fact, half our customers live west of the Rocky Mountains. It makes a lot of business sense to be closer to where the action is."

"Why not California?"

He shook his head. "Too expensive. Besides, we feel the image of our company would be better suited to the up-and-coming, entrepreneurial spirit of the Phoenix area, rather than the laid-back California style, or high-tech Silicon Valley—or, God forbid, Hollywood." He shuddered.

Diana shuddered right along with him. She'd never known anyone who was more the antithesis of Tinsel Town, with its bright lights and tawdry glamour, than Jack Royce. He was a man without artifice, a man devoid of pretense. He was willing to put everything up front and expected the same of others. His handshake meant something; his words even more. In the truest sense, he was an honorable man.

"I suppose opening a West Coast division of The Outdoorsman would mean that you'd be dividing your time between Wisconsin and Phoenix for a while."

"I suppose it would."

"Will your . . . family mind?"

"Nah."

That certainly didn't answer her question. She'd have to try again. "Won't they miss you?"

"Actually, I think they like it when I'm gone. You see, I have a tendency to forget that there's more to life for them than the company," he admitted sheepishly.

"Doesn't your wife mind that you're away?" Diana blurted out.

"Nope."

"Why not?" When they were married, she'd hated every minute that they were apart.

Jack's eyes narrowed. "Because I don't have a wife." He expertly extracted the paring knife from her grasp and laid it on the countertop.

"But I'm all wet," she objected as he pulled her hands toward him.

Her protest was ignored. The water dripping onto the tile floor was equally ignored as Jack placed his left hand—palm down, fingers splayed—across both of hers. "See. No ring."

His touch sent a jolt through her. Diana wondered if he could tell she was trembling. He must be able to.

Her stomach lurched precariously, but somehow she got the nerve to point out to him, "The absence of a wedding ring doesn't necessarily mean a man isn't married."

"In my case, it does."

Diana believed him. She said so. Her voice was husky. She hadn't meant it to be.

She dropped his hand and returned to her task. "You've never remarried."

"No time. No inclination. No interest, I guess." Jack polished off the last of his beer and deposited the empty can in the trash. Then he simply stood there, watching her.

Diana wasn't used to having someone in her kitchen, observing her every move. It made her nervous.

"Do you know how to start a gas grill?"

"You dare to ask that of a man who once started a fire without even two sticks to rub together?" Jack teased.

As the tension between them eased, Diana countered, laughing, "Well, do you?"

He shrugged his broad shoulders. "What's there to know?"

She raised her eyebrows heavenward. "Men! They're as helpless as kittens!"

Jack spread his hands. "Hey, we try."

"Do you think you could manage to slice the rest of this cucumber for our salad?"

He took the paring knife from her and sniffed, "Of course I can. Anything else you want done, just let me know."

Diana's skepticism revealed itself. "First, we'll see how you do with the cucumber," she cautioned, opening the drawer beside the kitchen sink. She took out a long, rectangular dish towel and instructed him. "Raise your arms, please."

He looked at her askance. "What's that for?"

"To protect your clothes," she said, reaching around him from behind to tie the towel at his waist.

"It's a damned apron," Jack scoffed.

She tried to explain to him in the same way she would have to a small child, speaking slowly and using plain, simple vocabulary. "No, it isn't an apron. It's a dish towel. We wouldn't want to get anything on your lovely, expensive suit trousers, now would we?"

Jack was still mumbling under his breath as Diana took a box of matches from a kitchen drawer and headed out the back door in the direction of the gas grill.

"I think I did a pretty good job with the cucumber," he informed her when she returned from lighting the fire.

She peered into the large wooden salad bowl sitting on the counter. "You did a *very* good job with the cucumber," she said, patting his arm solicitously.

He beamed at her. "Anything else you want chopped, sliced or diced, ma'am, I'm your man."

She decided to take him up on the offer. "Perhaps we should throw in a couple of carrots, maybe a little celery, some green pepper, a few radishes . . ."

"Whoa! Whoa, there! I'll be chopping, slicing and dicing all night at that rate," protested Jack.

Diana looked thoughtful for a moment. "You're right. We'll leave out the radishes."

DIANA LOOKED UP from their dinner and complimented Jack. "Your salad is delicious, even without the radishes."

"I think the crowning touch is the dressing," Jack claimed with no small amount of personal pride.

She was puzzled. "Didn't you use the bottled salad dressing in the refrigerator?"

"Yes. But it's very important to know exactly how *much* dressing to use. Too little or too much can ruin an otherwise perfect salad."

Diana laughed. He was preposterous.

Jack put another bite of steak into his mouth and chewed for a minute, then exclaimed, "Great steak! It's cooked just the way I like it."

Diana glanced down at the half-eaten T-bone on her own plate. There was a large piece she hadn't even touched. "I can't finish mine. Would you like it?"

Jack didn't have to be asked twice. He reached across the cozy kitchen table and speared her meat with his fork, pausing only long enough to double check. "Are you sure you don't want it?"

"Positive," Diana assured him, sitting back a little in her chair.

She watched in amazement as Jack neatly consumed what was left of his dinner and hers. She'd almost forgotten what a healthy appetite a big man like her former husband could have for food, for life, for lovemaking. . . .

Sex. She'd discovered a thing or two about herself since the breakup of her marriage, Diana thought candidly as she sat across the table from Jack. She was fundamentally, it seemed, a one-man kind of woman. She was afraid she always would be.

It wasn't that she hadn't tried dating. She had. But on the few occasions when she'd agreed to go out to dinner, or a concert, or a movie with a man interested in her, she'd found herself *un*interested in him. Her dates had been unspectacular, if not actual failures.

Men had kissed her, of course, had tried to make love to her, but she'd always stopped them well short of the consummating act. It had never felt right to her. Always wrong. What it had felt like, Diana realized, was adultery.

"What are you thinking, Diana?"

She looked up, and there was Jack watching her intently. Her face went a flaming red. "Oh, nothing in particular," she fibbed.

He let it go at that. "Nice place you've got here," he said, looking around.

"Thank you. I like it," she replied mundanely.

"How long have you lived out here?" he asked as she poured each of them a cup of after-dinner coffee.

She shrugged, added a teaspoon of sugar to her coffee cup and stirred. "About two and a half years."

"Kind of far to commute to your downtown office, isn't it?"

"I don't work downtown anymore."

Jack was visibly confused. "Did your office move?"

Now he had her confused, too. Her forehead wrinkled in thought. "No."

"How are things at the magazine, then?"

"I'm no longer employed at the *Arizona Magazine*. I haven't been for almost three years."

It was obvious he still didn't understand. "Aren't you writing?"

Diana's hands flew to her mouth. "Oh, damn, I left my computer turned on." She jumped to her feet. "Excuse me, Jack. I'll be right back."

He probably thought she was rude, or just plain crazy, dashing off and leaving him alone like that at the table. But she had bigger things to worry about, Diana feared.

"I only hope I haven't lost any pages of my manuscript," she moaned as she made a beeline for her office.

6

FIVE MINUTES LATER Diana walked back into the kitchen with a gigantic and rather silly grin on her face. Let the man sitting there with a curious expression on *his* think she was crazy if he wanted to. At the moment she was too relieved to care what anyone thought.

"I'm sorry about running off like that, but I'd forgotten all about my computer."

"I noticed it was on when I first arrived. I meant to say something to you. It slipped my mind."

"At least there was no harm done." She refilled their coffee cups and sat down again at the kitchen table. "I was lucky this time."

"You were lucky this time?" he echoed.

"I didn't lose any of the writing on the screen."

"Computers can be fickle things, can't they?" he commiserated, without knowing the details. "In the mail-order business we have to deal with them all the time. Some days they're a mixed blessing at best."

Diana agreed wholeheartedly. "I was working one day last winter when there was a momentary brownout. The electrical power went off—" she snapped her fingers together to illustrate "—and then came back on in a flash."

"And you lost all the data on your computer screen."

"At least twenty pages, maybe even thirty were gone in an instant. Eventually I did try to reconstruct from memory the material I'd lost, but it proved impossible."

He was sympathetic. "Couldn't you use your notes to redo the article?"

"It wasn't that simple." Apparently there were a few things he didn't know about her. "It wasn't an article I was writing, Jack. I'm not a journalist anymore."

He raised an eyebrow. "What are you?"

"I'm a free-lance writer. I was writing a story."

"A story?"

She clarified that. "Well, a novel, actually."

"A novel! Exactly what is it that you do?"

There was no reason not to tell him. "I write sci-fi books."

A very small feather, Diana suspected, would have knocked her former husband over at that point. She could see he was dumbstruck by her announcement.

"You write science-fiction novels?" he repeated after some time.

"Write them, and even more important, sell them."

"And so you've been published, I assume."

It was the question most frequently asked of her as soon as someone found out she was a writer. "About a dozen short stories in various sci-fi magazines and periodicals, and two novels," she said proudly. "I'm working on a third book now."

Jack nearly fell over backward in his chair. "Well, I'll be a son of a—" He cleared his throat. "Congratulations, Diana."

She was pleased. "Thank you."

"I guess you were always destined for success."

"I don't know about destiny, but I have worked long, hard hours to get where I am." She paused for a second. "I don't need to tell you about what it takes to be successful." Not when the evidence of his success was right there on the table in the form of the Outdoorsman catalog.

Jack gave her a knowing glance. "I've discovered everything has a price tag attached to it, Diana, including success. The question is are we willing to pay the price, to do whatever it takes to get what we want."

"Sometimes the price we have to pay is high," she stated in a raspy voice she scarcely recognized as her own. "Too high."

Jack nodded and continued in the same vein. "I understand something about success that I didn't before. The real pressure comes not from what other people expect of us, but from what we expect of ourselves. It's tough being successful. As tough as trying but not succeeding, and a hell of a lot tougher than not trying at all."

So Jack did understand. She had wondered if he would. At one point in their lives he hadn't understood at all, of course.

Diana folded her hands in front of her on the table and studied her unadorned nails for a moment. "People assume that because I was born with the proverbial silver spoon in my mouth, I haven't had to work for my success. Nothing could be further from the truth. Sometimes writing really does take blood, sweat and tears. I often have to put in long hours at my computer when I'd much rather be doing something else like reading, or watching television or going out with my friends—"

"Or sleeping?" he interjected with mild humor.

She laughed lightly. "Or sleeping."

They both began to yawn, and ended up laughing together.

"There never seems to be enough *time* anymore," Jack observed with a shake of his head.

"You've noticed that, too, have you? It's not the hard work I mind so much as the lack of time to just do *nothing* once in a while." A funny smile formed on her mouth. "Maybe I'm getting lazy in my old age."

"I hardly think that's possible. First, you don't look any older than the day I met you. And, second, you always were a damn hard worker." The former was the nicest kind of compliment for a woman to hear. "But there are times when I ask myself if it's worth all the sacrifice, the hard work and effort. I believe we've both come up with the same answer: yes, it is."

He finished his coffee and stretched long legs out under the kitchen table. Diana could feel his trousers rub against her pant leg, and she had a momentary vision of those long, muscular limbs, bare, browned by the sun, as Jack strutted across their room toward the bed where she lay waiting for him.

She thought of the times when she'd awakened to find her legs entangled with his and the crumpled sheets wrapped around them, dampened by their lovemaking; his warm, naked body beside her.

She remembered what it had been like to run her hand up his leg: the smooth length of skin and bone; the soft, dark hair from ankle to crotch; the power implicit in the muscular thighs; her never-satisfied curiosity about what most made him a man, at least physically. His body could be hard and soft, demanding one moment, malleable the next. Endless fascination, that's what she'd felt for her lover, her husband.

"I'd like to read one of your books sometime, if you'd allow me to," Jack requested, breaking into her intimate daydream.

Diana's eyes blinked open. She hadn't realized they were closed.

"Read one of my books?" she repeated in a just-awakened monotone.

How could she possibly stop him? It was a free country. He didn't need her permission. At the same time, could she explain to him the grave reservations she had about letting him do just that?

Diana tried. "Having anyone read your writing is nerve-racking. Having someone you know read your writing is—excruciating. It's like trying to show off a new baby. You desperately want everyone to say yours is the most beautiful baby ever born, yet you're half afraid they'll tell you it's the ugliest."

"I promise I won't critique a single word of what you've written," Jack vowed. "I'm curious, that's all."

Still she hesitated. Like any good writer, she'd invested a great deal of herself in her stories and books: her thoughts, her feelings, her ideas. Did she want to give Jack that kind of intimate glimpse into the workings of her mind, into her very heart and soul? After all, this was the man who'd once broken her heart into a thousand tiny pieces.

Diana corrected herself. This was the man she'd *allowed* to break her heart.

Jack didn't seem to notice her hesitation. "I confess I know next to nothing about science fiction," he told her. "What kinds of things do you write about in your books?"

She'd keep it short, Diana decided. She'd tell him just enough to satisfy his curiosity.

"I don't try to do the futuristic Star Wars kind of science fiction, as much as I love it as a reader. I'm more interested in telling a story about the relationship between man and woman, between man and his world, between man and the unknown."

He cocked his head. "The alien unknown?"

"No. The unknown that's all around us and inside us. Why do we have problems communicating with each other? Why do we destroy the natural resources we need in order to survive? Why is it so difficult for us to love each other? To make a commitment to one another? Why must we always lose something before we can appreciate its real value?" She paused to take a deep breath.

Jack winced as if she'd hit on some truths painfully close to home. "It doesn't sound like fiction to me."

"Fiction based on fact, that's where I like to start a story. But I'm also interested in drawing from old legends, native American Indian and otherwise, prehistoric cultures and myths, the half-forgotten stories of ancient times when magic was as much a part of daily life as eating, or sleeping, or sheer survival. The elemental, eternal struggle between good and evil. The forces of wind and fire, water and stone, sea and sky."

Jack was enthralled by her words, mesmerized by the dulcet tone of her voice, the flush of excitement on her cheeks, the flash of blue fire in her eyes.

"Tell me about one of your books," he urged.

"My first full-length novel is about a woman who goes back in time. She wants desperately to relive part of her life, to do things differently the second time around."

Jack was hanging on her every word. "And?" he prodded.

Diana looked at him dumbly. "And?"

"And what happens?"

"In a nutshell, she discovers that the past isn't hers to change, only the future."

"She's right." His voice sounded strangely hoarse to her. "God knows there are plenty of us who'd give anything to be able to go back into our own pasts and correct the mistakes we've made." Jack sat up straight in his chair and reached across the kitchen table for her hand. All of a sudden Diana knew he wasn't talking about some fictional character in a book anymore; he was talking about him, about them. "I was crazy for you, Diana. You were crazy for me. I know you were. Damn it, how could something so right go so wrong?"

Hadn't she asked herself that same question a hundred times or more?

"I don't know what went wrong, Jack," she admitted, then immediately contradicted herself. "So many things, I guess."

"I want to know. I need to know," he said in a tone reinforced with steely resolve.

She looked up. He was watching her with an unwavering gaze. She had to look away. "Surely the post mortem can wait. Isn't it enough to know that both of us have changed? That we've grown up in the years since . . ." She swallowed hard.

His eyes never left her. "You can't say it, can you, Diana? The word you're afraid to use is divorce. It's not a pretty word, but then divorce isn't a particularly pretty thing, either."

Sudden tears pooled in her eyes. Were they tears of sadness? Tears of anger? Tears of frustration? In the end, Diana supposed it didn't make much difference. They were undoubtedly a little of each.

She bit her bottom lip, sinking the sharp edges of her teeth into the tender flesh until she was certain she had control of her emotions once again. She would not make a fool of herself in front of Jack.

When she finally looked up, her eyes were clear. "Divorce is an ugly word with ugly connotations. It's a word that means failure somehow. I've never cared for failure in any form."

"Especially when you're the first member of your family to fail at marriage, to go through a divorce." He cut through to the heart of the matter.

"Yes."

"I imagine your parents and your sisters were upset."

"To put it mildly."

"That still doesn't tell me where we went wrong," he pointed out.

Diana sighed. Surely this whole exercise was academic. What could Jack hope to gain by raking a long-dead relationship over the coals?

Reluctantly she ventured an opinion. "We were young and a little foolish, I think."

"I'd say more than a little. I'd say a lot."

"A lot, then."

He continued. "We were great together and we were awful."

She nodded and took it a step further. "We should never have got married." Jack's fingers closed around hers. That's when she realized he was still holding her hand. "We should have had a love affair and ended it at that," she concluded, prying her hand loose.

"But I wanted to marry you," he proclaimed.

"And *I* wanted to marry *you*."

"But . . ."

"We wanted to *get* married. I don't think either of us really wanted to *be* married." She threw up her hands. "Let's face it, Jack. We had vastly different expectations. I thought marriage was what my parents had: the husband worked hard and came home every night for dinner. The wife created a home, had a job perhaps, mothered her children and served as the guardian of the family's mental, physical and spiritual health. The man took his wife out to dinner on Friday evening and dancing on Saturday night. They attended church together on Sunday. They entertained their friends in their home. They supported their community through volunteer work and financial help. A husband and wife worked together. They played together. They stood by each other through thick and through thin."

"And since we weren't like that ideal of marriage, you felt we'd failed."

"Yes. I was caught up in my career at the magazine, and you kept taking off for parts unknown. We never gave ourselves the chance to create our own kind of marriage. We never did have a great deal in common, and we just kept drifting further and further apart, it seemed."

"You've obviously spent some time thinking about us, about where we went wrong," he observed.

"Any writer worth her salt is going to try to analyze, or at least try to understand, something about men and women, life and death, love, power, sex. Even divorce."

Jack was silent for a minute. Then he confessed to her, "For a while after the divorce, I tried to convince myself that I hated you."

As long as they were baring their souls . . . "I know how you felt. I hated you, too."

"Still mad about me, are you?" He tried to flash her one of his old smiles.

"Still mad *at* you is more like it," she replied dryly. "But not often. Not anymore. Anger is self-destructive. You taught me that."

"I did?"

She tempered that with, "Well, your leaving did, and our divorce."

His eyes narrowed. "Tell me now what you wouldn't the night of Kit's wedding. Why didn't you ever write to me?"

Diana winced. It was going to be a painful post mortem, after all. No stone would be left unturned. No raw nerve left unexposed. No illusions intact. There didn't seem to be any way to avoid answering.

"As far as I was concerned, when you left that last time, for the Amazon, it was a trial separation. When you didn't come back and I never heard from you, I was honestly at a loss to know what to believe. I didn't know where you were or what you were doing. I didn't even know if you were dead or alive. I used to have nightmares about it. They were always the same. Your body was somewhere on the bottom of a swampy river with an arrow through the heart." Diana's voice broke on the last word. She wasn't sure she could go on. Taking a deep, fortifying breath, she tried. "Then I got the note you sent me from Wisconsin. Naturally I was relieved you were alive, but I assumed you wanted me to read between the lines."

"I did," he said softly.

She was uncomfortable. "I waited several months and when I never heard from you again, I contacted a lawyer."

Jack shot back, "Why didn't you write back, for God's sake, before you had your lawyer contact me about a divorce?"

His anger was rubbing salt into an open wound. It was a minute or two before she said, "There didn't seem to be anything left to say at that point. You were home. But you hadn't come home to me."

Lord, don't let me break down now, Diana prayed. *Don't let me cry in front of this man.*

There was a stony silence between them.

How could she tell Jack that he'd hurt her too badly, that she'd had to gather her pride around her like a protective shield just in order to survive? How could she explain that she'd used her anger, her rage, her resentment as a daily reminder that she was still alive?

She'd been numb at first, dead inside, except for the awful, heavy weight that pressed down on the center of her chest. It had taken months for the physical discomfort to go away, even longer for the emotional pain. But in the end she'd learned that strength came from sorrow, determination from failure. She could survive anything now.

And she knew at last what loving Jack Royce had cost her. Gone forever were her girlhood dreams of love and romance. Shattered were any illusions she may have had about men and women, love and marriage, commitment and happiness. There was no such thing as happily ever after. At least not at the end of her story.

Suddenly Diana knew she couldn't sit there across from Jack for even one more second without bursting into tears, or venting her anger by shouting at him. She pushed her chair back and got to her feet. She wanted to run just as fast and as far as they would carry her. But she knew from experience that it was never fast enough and far enough to let her escape her own thoughts.

She walked to the large picture window and stood staring out at the night. There were a few lights twinkling in the distance and a thousand stars in the desert sky overhead. The shadowy shape of the mountains loomed on the horizon, and nearby, the outline of a solitary saguaro cactus, its arms raised toward heaven.

Diana shivered and wrapped her arms tightly around herself. For the first time since the day she'd moved in, the adobe house closed in on her. It seemed too small and cramped.

She heard a chair leg scraping along the tile floor and watched in the window as Jack walked up to stand behind her.

Any woman who stood five feet nine inches tall in her bare feet rarely had the opportunity to look up to a man, but Diana raised her eyes. Jack was nearly a head taller than she was. His silk tie was hanging loosely around his neck. The collar of his dress shirt and the first two buttons were undone. The sleeves were rolled up to just below the elbows. The material fitted snugly across his chest and shoulders and tapered at his waist, outlining his strong body. He thrust one hand into his thick, dark curls and the other into the pocket of his trousers. Jack's expression was grim, his eyes hooded.

Lifting his face, he spoke to her reflection. "I know the last time I went away I didn't come back, but so help me God I never meant to hurt you, Diana. I was like a wounded animal myself at the time."

"Why did you have to go away?" The words were torn from her. "Why couldn't you have stayed with me?"

He glanced down at his feet for a moment, shaking his head as if to say it was useless to try to explain. It always had been. "You never did understand." He sighed.

"I wanted to understand," Diana cried out softly. Then she pleaded, "Help me to understand."

She could feel the tension radiating from his body. "All right, I'll try. Again." He paused, searching for the right words, marshaling his defenses. "I guess I felt like a kept man, damn it. It was your house, your car, your money, your friends, even your town. It wasn't *our* life, Diana. It was *your* life. I was just passing through."

She stood there, trembling, her heart swelling painfully in her breast. Her intuition had been correct: Jack would never have survived her world for any length of time. In those days, he'd been like a caged animal—a leopard with its unchangeable spots—that should have been allowed to roam free.

He'd been reluctant to begin this conversation. Now Diana didn't think she could stop him, even if she'd wanted to.

"I went away all those times because I had to in order to survive. I didn't—I still don't—have your education. What was I supposed to do? Hang around Phoenix and hire myself out to do odd jobs? Or would you have preferred that I live off you like the gigolo, the opportunist that your parents assumed I was, anyway? It was my job to guide hunters in Alaska, fishermen in Colorado, anthropological students through the Central American jungle. That's what I did for a living. You knew that when you married me."

"Why do men always fall back on 'you knew what I was like when you married me' as an excuse for their shortcomings? The truth is men think of commitment only in terms of what *they* want—their dreams, their plans, their jobs. Not in terms of a woman or children."

"You think I was afraid of making a commitment to you?"

Diana didn't spare Jack's feelings. She told him the harsh truth, her version of it, anyway. "I think yours was a half-hearted commitment. I was someone to come home to *when* you felt like coming home to someone. A woman to call your own on those occasions when you wanted to be bothered with a woman. Usually you were off doing something important, something macho or life-threatening or adventurous, something that tested your strength and survival skills. You always were more a man's man than a ladies' man."

"Would you have wanted me any other way?" he challenged. "I've always known what the initial attraction was between us, Diana, even if you haven't. That old cliché about opposites gravitating to one another, like the magnetic pull of north and south on the needle of a compass, was true for us. I was the uncivilized and unshaven man fresh from the wilds of Africa, and you were the oh-so-rich and sophisticated—and undoubtedly bored-to-tears—debutante."

"I was never a debutante!"

"That is a matter of opinion. Face it, honey. You were drawn to me from the beginning because I wasn't one of your fresh-faced tennis boys in immaculate white shorts who drove around in a BMW or a Mercedes or a Corvette convertible."

"And what did you drive up in tonight?" Diana blurted out before she put her hands over her ears and squeezed her eyes tightly shut. "Oh, God, why do some people seem made for each other? Why can they love one another for their whole lives, and we can't even be civil to each other for one lousy evening?"

The room grew progressively quieter until the only sound was their breathing interspersed with the rhythmic tick of the clock on the kitchen wall.

"Only one thing mattered then, and matters now," Jack said in a low, husky baritone. "I did love you, Diana."

She felt as if she'd been cut with a knife. She even opened her eyes and glanced down at the tile floor, half-expecting to see it running bright red with her blood.

Wheeling, she accused him, "You don't fight fair, Jack Royce!"

"I was trying not to fight at all," he said reasonably, bringing his hands to her shoulders.

She pushed out with her arms, as if trying to struggle through an invisible barrier. "I, ah, I need some fresh air...."

Diana ran as fast as she could and as far as the back door. She pushed it open and escaped into the desert night, stopping only when she reached the adobe wall encircling the house and yard. She stood there with her body pressed to its cool earthen surface.

She could still feel the imprint of Jack's hands on her shoulders. The heat of his touch seemed to have burned right through the thin cotton shirt she was wearing to the bare skin underneath. The sensation of warmth lingered, even while a cooling breeze caressed her face. The wind tousled the loose hair that had escaped her ponytail; a few wisps strayed around her face and at her nape. She pulled a long strand away from her lips and watched as a firefly lighted its own way through the dark.

Jack followed her at a slower pace. He halted somewhere a foot or two from the adobe wall.

His tone bordered on the ironic. "We may be older, my dear Diana, but we're just as foolish as we always were." Then silence for a moment. "I apologize if I upset you or hurt your feelings. I didn't come here tonight with that intention."

Diana relented and offered her own apology, then asked, "What were your intentions in coming here?"

She heard him take a step toward her. "I wanted to see you again. I wanted to talk with you. Maybe I hoped to put a few ghosts to rest, as well."

She stayed where she was, her back to him. Her voice sounded calm and strangely disembodied. "Are you haunted by ghosts, Jack?"

"Memories. I'm haunted by memories," he admitted.

"Memories of what?" she dared to inquire, without turning around.

He hesitated, came to a decision, it seemed, and answered under duress, "Memories of a golden-haired beauty who could love a man to distraction, drive him to sell his soul for her, make him crawl to her on his hands and knees across the burning desert sands." This time it was Jack who mesmerized her with his words and the mellifluous tone of his voice. "'Sweat of the sun; tears of the moon,'" he murmured, touching first her golden hair and then the silver bracelet on her arm. "Do you remember what I told you that quotation meant?"

She nodded and answered as if from a long way off. "Yes, I remember. That's what the ancient Incas of Peru called gold and silver."

"You do remember." Jack sounded pleased. Almost as pleased as he was by the fact that she'd quit fighting him. "I've always loved the color of your hair, the feel of it...do you remember that, as well?" He reached up and untied the elastic band holding it in place.

Her hair flowed over his palm like spun gold, reaching to her shoulders and beyond. He buried his fingers in it, reveled in the silky texture, combed through the tangles until he had it soft and manageable.

Diana could feel her scalp begin to tingle. Her skin was aglow. She was sensitive to the slightest touch, the merest movement. Only one man had ever had that effect on her. That one man was Jack Royce.

He came up directly behind her, touched her shoulders briefly and then slowly wrapped his arms around her, saying, "I wanted to see you. I wanted to talk to you. But most of all I wanted to put my arms around you, Diana, and just hold you."

It had been so long since a man had held her, had made her feel . . . cherished. Diana rested her cheek on his forearm, not caring anymore if Jack could feel her tears as they dropped one by one onto his bare skin.

"We always seemed to communicate better when we didn't talk," Jack pointed out gently.

She didn't need to be reminded that all he'd had to do was kiss her, take her in his arms and make love to her and the world went away. Their differences disappeared, and their problems vanished. Nothing else existed during those moments but a man and a woman who shared an insatiable hunger, an unapologetic passion for each other.

Jack turned her to face him. "So many nights all I could do was dream about kissing you. I want to kiss you now," he murmured persuasively.

"No." She sniffed. "Not like this. Not crying." She wiped her eyes with the back of her hand.

And then Jack kissed her.

It was the blessing of rain after a long drought. It was the spring thaw on the heels of a cold, harsh winter. It was something Diana had convinced herself she'd have to live without for the rest of her days: Jack's arms around her, Jack's kiss on her lips.

It began simply enough, a man trying to comfort a crying woman. It deepened as he tried to apologize for making her cry. Then both tears and sympathy were forgotten. Suddenly it was like setting a match to dry kindling. He touched her, and she went up in flames. The match had been lit—the fire had been started. All they could do now was watch it burn.

Jack sighed into her mouth. "Oh, my lovely Diana."

Her arms went around his neck.

Diana inhaled deeply. He smelled faintly of coffee and after-shave and the dark summer night, Jack did, but mostly he smelled like a man, and that was far more intriguing than any artificially produced scent.

He trapped her face gently between his hands. The breath from his lips stirred the fine blond hair that fell in natural waves on either side of her face. He kissed her again and again. She kissed him back with equal fervor.

Then he parted her lips with a single thrust of his tongue, and she was lost.

Something in her heart had always hoped that this was the way it would be. Three and a half years ago, Jack had walked out, and there had gone a large part of her life. Now he was back—for whatever reason—and Diana rejoiced.

But her joy was mixed with fear. Surely they were playing with fire.

He set her blood on fire, she couldn't deny that. Diana groaned in silent frustration as Jack raised one hand to cover her breast. She could feel the peak tease his palm through the soft material of her shirt.

He trailed his lips along the sensitized skin of her face and neck with a concentration that nearly drove her mad. He knew exactly what pleased her, what excited and aroused her. His thumb found her nipple and flicked back and forth until it was hard and erect. A small moan of intense pleasure escaped Diana's lips, telling him she was nearing the point where pleasure became inexorably mixed with pain.

Part of her—the sensual woman who had dreamed of him night after night—would have liked nothing better than to be swept off her feet, taken to bed and made love to until the brilliant colors of tomorrow's dawn lighted the desert sky.

Part of her—the woman who had cried over him sleepless night after sleepless night—was tempted to tell him to take his kisses and his caresses back—she didn't want them.

But the more rational part of her—the woman who had grown out of those sleepless, dream-filled nights—that woman knew she had to be very careful if she wasn't to have her heart broken all over again.

She was an intelligent woman. Hadn't she learned anything from her mistakes? Physical passion had betrayed her the first time around. She and Jack had rushed into a love affair, followed by marriage, and she'd lived to regret it.

"Oh, God!" She tore her mouth away, then stood there gasping for air, her eyes filled with regret.

For a minute or two Jack simply stood there, too, staring at her. Diana knew that his heart was racing fast and furious in his chest, that his breathing was shallow and slightly labored, that his body stirred with arousal. She'd tasted the hunger in his kiss, sensed it in his touch.

"You must know that I want you," he said without apology.

"Yes." A tremulous hand pushed the hair away from her face.

"And I know that you want me," he said, insisting on the whole truth and nothing but the truth from her.

"Yes, I want you, too. But that isn't enough anymore."

His eyes were nearly black. "You've changed."

"I told you I had. I'm not the same woman you left behind, Jack, when you went off to the Amazon. I'm older and wiser now."

"And far more cautious."

"That, too."

He turned and looked toward the horizon. Diana watched him in profile. She wondered what he was thinking.

"Time. We'll have to give each other some time," Jack finally announced, as if she'd been privy to his thoughts. He faced her. "I'm going to be in Phoenix for the next few weeks. May I come see you again?"

She hesitated. "Yes."

They retraced their steps to the adobe house.

"Will you have dinner with me on Saturday night?" Jack asked as she was taking his suit coat from the front closet.

"I don't know what time I'll be back on Saturday."

"Where are you going?"

"I'm driving up to Flagstaff on Friday evening. First thing the next morning I have permission to go onto the Navajo Indian reservation. I'll be there all day researching some ancient ruins."

He opened the front door for her and then followed her out onto the rose-vined patio. They walked toward his car.

Jack opened the back door and tossed his jacket and briefcase onto the upholstered seat. "Would you mind having some company this weekend?"

"Company?"

"I'd like to come along with you to the ruins."

"Are you sure you wouldn't be bored? I mean, I may have to be there most of the day, and I wouldn't be much of a companion," Diana warned him.

"I won't be bored, and I don't expect to be entertained. I'd like to see the place, that's all."

She knew she was taking a chance, but she agreed. "Then you're welcome to come with me."

Jack opened the front door on the driver's side and got into the Mercedes. He turned the key in the ignition and pushed the button to lower the power window. "What time will we leave on Friday?"

Diana bent over and peered into the car. "I want to be on the road shortly after lunch. I have a room reserved for Friday night at a local motel. I'll call and get a second room for you."

She noticed Jack didn't blink an eye when she mentioned two separate rooms for the night.

"What time will we start out on Saturday morning?"

She thought for a moment. "Just before dawn. Say around four-thirty, five o'clock."

Jack groaned quietly. "Four-thirty?"

Diana smiled. "Don't tell me that's too early for an old, experienced outdoorsman like yourself?"

"Oh, no, that's not too early," Jack reassured her with a slightly stiff answering smile.

"I feel I should warn you, it's pretty rough terrain where I'm going. The trail is steep and rugged. It will take a good three hours round trip to hike in and out again."

He kept a smile plastered on his face. "I'm sure I can handle it."

"I'll see you on Friday afternoon, then." She stood to one side and waved as he turned the car and headed toward the main road.

He'd be up with the damned birds on Saturday morning, Jack thought with a grimace as he drove south along the highway in the direction of Phoenix.

Of course, he consoled himself, they said it was the early bird that got the worm. . . .

7

DIANA WAS CHECKING over the supplies in the back of her Jeep when she glanced up and saw Jack coming out of his motel room. It was still dark at ten minutes past four; they seemed to be the only two patrons at the Grand Teepee Motel who were up and about.

"How'd you sleep last night?" she called out quietly.

"Like a rock."

There was something in his tone that kept her from asking if he was talking about how well he'd slept, or if he was describing the mattress in his budget motel room.

"Anyplace a man can get a cup of coffee around here?" Jack muttered, stroking the stubble on his chin.

"There's a large thermos of black coffee on the passenger seat. Help yourself."

"You seem mighty wide awake considering the hour," Jack commented dryly as he filled a Styrofoam cup with steaming hot coffee. He strolled over to watch as she secured a five-gallon jug of fresh water to the other supplies already in the back of the Jeep.

"I'm used to getting up early," Diana remarked as she continued to work quickly and efficiently.

He eyed her with skepticism. "Get up at the crack of dawn often, do you?"

"I like to get a head start on the day. Most mornings I'm at my computer by daybreak."

"The next thing I know, you'll be telling me that you've already had your coffee and a hearty breakfast of steak and eggs."

Diana wrinkled her nose in distaste. "A banana and half of a high-energy all-natural granola bar." She reached into the front pocket of her cotton fatigues and came up with the other half. "Would you like to try it?"

Jack regarded the granola bar with suspicion. "What's in it?"

"Wheat germ, rolled oats, honey, almonds, unsweetened coconut, raisins, rolled whole wheat and kelp."

"Kelp? As in seaweed?"

She nodded. "It's very good for you."

"I'm sure it is, but I think I'll pass this time."

"There are two bananas left if you're hungry," she said, plopping her favorite hat on the top of her head.

It was a curious piece of headgear. Natural in color and constructed of lightweight straw, it was styled in the tradition of a Panama, with a hint of the Western Stetson thrown in. She'd bought it last year on a trip to the Yucatan Peninsula in southern Mexico.

Coffee cup in hand, Jack leaned against the frame of the Jeep and casually crossed one ankle over the other. "What happened to the Diana I knew who loved to sleep in until noon every chance she got?"

"I suppose she went the same way as the Diana who used to smoke."

"It still seems strange to see you without a cigarette in your hand," he confessed.

"That may be the least of the strange things you'll see today," Diana murmured a few minutes later as Jack went to fetch himself a refill on the coffee.

"You say this is going to be quite a walk this morning?" he verified when he returned.

"Yes. It isn't the place for a tourist out for a Sunday stroll. You have to be in top physical condition, carry your own water and supplies and be alert to any hazards—rockfalls, unexpected drop-offs, flash floods—that might crop up on the trail." She took a sheet of paper from the breast pocket of her shirt and said briskly, "Let's check our list one more time—hiking permit, map, water, rations, canteens, flashlight, poncho, sunscreen—"

"Sunscreen?" Jack repeated, interrupting her.

She looked up. "With an SPF of 15. We don't want to take any chances. Haven't you read the latest medical reports linking skin cancer and sunburn?"

"Can't say I have, but I'm aware of the connection."

"Here—" she handed him the plastic bottle "—rub some of this on. Don't forget your ears," she tacked on. "Let me see. Where was I?" she murmured, tapping a fingernail against her bottom lip.

"Your checklist."

"Right. Hiking permit—"

"You were down to sunscreen," Jack reminded her as he squeezed a small pool of cream onto his palm and began to apply it to his face and ears.

"So I was," she said, flashing him a smile. "Hiking shoes." She glanced from her own ankle-high walkers to the paramilitary boots Jack sported. "Long pants and long-sleeved shirt," she read next. "Sunglasses. Hat." She looked up at his bare head. "Where's your hat?"

"Right here, ma'am." Jack took a well-worn safari hat—à la Indiana Jones—from his back pocket and plunked it down on his head.

Continuing with the last few items on her checklist, Diana read: "Compass. Matches. First-aid kit." She refolded the piece of paper and returned it to her shirt pocket. "I think we have everything."

"Everything but the kitchen sink," Jack muttered under his breath.

Diana chose to ignore the remark. Instead she goaded him a little. "I hope you've kept in shape, Jack. Like I said earlier, this isn't going to be a casual Sunday stroll in the park."

He gave her a toothy grin. "I'll manage to keep up somehow." Then he paid her back in kind. "What about you, Ms Quick? I seem to remember you had a nice figure, but you were hardly what I would call the athletic type."

Diana leaped to her own defense. "I walk two miles every morning. I'm vice president of our local hiking club. I have a stationary bicycle in my bedroom and a ten-speed in the garage that I use on a regular basis. I've also been doing some weight lifting at the gym." She watched his eyebrows go higher and higher. "Any questions, mister?"

"No questions. No, sirree," Jack said with a straight face.

"Then let's get this show on the road," she said, climbing behind the wheel of the Jeep and securing her seat belt.

Jack settled himself on the passenger side. As they pulled out of the parking lot of the Grand Teepee Motel, he raised his arm and drawled in his best John Wayne imitation, "Wagons ho!"

The morning sun was climbing into an azure-blue Arizona sky before Jack said to her, "Tell me something about the ruins we're going to see."

Diana swept a strand of blond hair away from her face. "The Southwestern desert is home to a number of strange phenomena, not the least of which are hundreds of ancient cliff dwellings, all abandoned centuries ago."

"There's some mystery as to what happened to those early cliff dwellers, isn't there?" he said, taking a pair of dark glasses from his shirt pocket and slipping them on.

"Yes. The group I've been concentrating on are the Anasazi. Some time around 1300, they simply deserted their settlements. No one knows quite why even today."

"I seem to remember reading about the Anasazi," Jack murmured, rubbing his chin. "Aren't they the tribe the Navajos call the Ancient Ones?"

"Yes." The hair on the back of Diana's neck suddenly stood on end, and she shivered in spite of the desert heat. "I met an old Navajo once who claimed that he'd heard the voice of an Ancient One speaking to him. At the time, of course, I thought he was simply being fanciful. That was before I'd ever seen the silent cities of the Anasazi, before I'd stood in the vacant rooms of their cliff palaces and felt the dust of centuries beneath my feet." She shook her head and laughed self-consciously. "Now I'm the one who's being fanciful."

"Hey, a lively imagination must surely be a prerequisite for a writer."

But Diana became practical again. "There are a few things I should remind you of before we enter the Navajo reservation. We're here by permission only. If we meet any Navajos on the trail, we will courteously show them our permit and tell them where we're going. We have to be sure to stay clear of their hogans, and to close any gates we may open. I don't need to tell an outdoorsman like you that at all times we should move as quietly and unobtrusively as possible. We'll build no fires and carry out everything we take in. We should drink only the water we bring with us, and leave no sign that we've even been there. And watch out for poison ivy and biting red ants," she warned in conclusion.

"Got it," said Jack as they entered the Navajo National Monument.

Diana pulled up in front of the headquarters building. "We need to stop here first and check in with the park ranger, since this area is officially protected by the National Park Service. Then we'll drive on a few more miles to the reservation itself."

An hour later, they reached their initial destination within the Navajo reservation. Diana parked the Jeep, and they began to unload their backpacks and canteens.

"It's significantly cooler up here," Jack observed. "What's the elevation?"

"Over seven thousand feet." Diana adjusted the straps of her backpack. "Of course, at this time of year the temperature in northern Arizona can run a good thirty or forty degrees cooler than down in the valley."

Jack looked up for a moment at the innocent white clouds overhead and the endless expanse of blue sky. "It's going to be a perfect day for your hike."

"I certainly hope so," she replied as they double-checked their equipment. "Ready?"

Jack nodded wordlessly.

"We'll pick up the trail about two hundred yards north of where we're standing right now," she said.

Then they were on their way.

Diana could tell that Jack's instincts took over once he was in his natural element, the outdoors. He moved quietly, in long, easy strides, and spoke only when necessary. The sleek muscles of his back and shoulders were outlined in detail as the material of his cotton shirt grew damp with sweat and clung to his upper torso. The strength in his thighs and legs was evident as he tirelessly made his way along the trail in front of her.

Although it was a cool, clear morning, they hadn't gone far before the perspiration started to run down the middle of Diana's back, as well. Not that she minded. It felt good to walk, to use her arms and legs in demanding physical exertion.

She supposed she had Jack to thank indirectly for her current state of good health. Their separation and subsequent divorce had done a great deal to make her grow up and realize she was responsible for herself, mentally and physically—no one else.

That, and turning thirty the year before last, Diana recalled with a wry smile. There was nothing quite like a landmark birthday to make one sit up and take notice.

They were halfway up a steep, rocky incline when Diana paused and untied the kerchief from around her neck. She motioned to Jack to take the lead while she took half a minute to wipe the perspiration from her brow. She retied the cotton kerchief and followed him.

An hour later, as they were approaching a small, level clearing, Diana suggested, "Why don't we stop here for a few minutes? I'd like to check my map before we approach the next canyon, and I could use a drink of water and a short rest."

"So could I," Jack admitted.

Diana sank down on a nearby ledge and took a piece of folded notebook paper from her pocket. She sipped a little water from her canteen and nibbled on a strip of beef jerky while she studied the rough, hand-drawn map spread across her lap.

Jack stood a short distance away, gazing out over a red rock canyon. A hundred feet or more below them was a thick forest of trees. Above them and to one side was a boulder the size of a small mountain. There was a deep gash in the rock, worn smooth by wind and weather. Veins of subtle colors, like an artist's palette, ringed its surface.

After a few minutes, Jack turned and said, "I'm curious about something."

Diana looked up. "What?"

"You obviously know a lot about this country, particularly the cliff dwellings. Why are you doing more research?"

"Not far from here are two of the most spectacular cliff dwellings ever uncovered: the Betatakin Ruin and the Keet Seel Ruin. Both are completely excavated and open to the public. They were the inspiration for the book I'm writing. Now I find the main character in my story has stumbled upon an ancient city that has lain half-buried and in ruin for centuries."

"So for the proper inspiration, we're on our way to an *un*excavated cliff dwelling."

"Exactly. The trail we're following has been almost lost in time, forgotten even by the majority of Navajos. Official maps of this area don't exist."

Jack took off his sunglasses and looked down at her. "How did you get your hands on one, then?"

"A friend of mine in Phoenix has a grandfather who still lives on the reservation. He was willing to tell her the details so she could sketch a rough map for me. Then I was given special permission by the tribe to spend the day up here."

Shaking his head, Jack muttered, "You've turned out to be an amazing woman, Diana Quick."

She was flattered. "It's time we were on our way," she said, tucking the precious map into her pocket and getting to her feet.

They walked for some time before the trail narrowed; it cut a sinuous path through an even narrower canyon no more than twenty feet across. The canyon walls were thickly forested with pines.

Small animals scurried in the underbrush, and the harsh, raucous call of a crow or two echoed from the treetops. The scent of pine needles permeated the air, and the sound of rushing water could be heard ahead.

Diana's heart was pounding in her breast. Her pace became faster and faster, until she was nearly running by the time she reached the end of the canyon trail.

She stopped dead.

For a moment the only sound audible to her was her own labored breathing. Jack came up beside her, and she heard him gasp in astonishment.

They were looking out over a sandstone canyon of mammoth proportions. Below them, on the canyon floor, a bright blue ribbon of water wound its way through a forest of disheveled loveliness: half-toppled aspen and Douglas fir, oak and juniper.

On the far side of the canyon, rising three or four hundred feet or more above them, was a natural amphitheater, its sheer size dizzying.

And there, set against the amphitheater's back wall, bathed to the color of warm gold in morning light, seemingly carved from the very stone itself, was an ancient cliff palace!

Jack was the first to speak. "My God, Diana, did you know this was here?"

She nodded, then shook her head. "Not really. The old man thought he remembered hearing stories as a boy of abandoned ruins tucked into a remote canyon, but I never expected anything like this. It's . . ."

"It's magnificent."

"Yes, it's magnificent. I wish I had my camera," she said wistfully. "But no picture taking was part of my agreement with the Navajos."

"A photograph could never do it justice, anyway."

It was some time before Diana ventured, "How far would you estimate it is across the canyon floor?"

He removed his dark glasses, pushed his hat back off his face and squinted into the bright sunlight. "Maybe half a mile. No more."

"Let's move closer," she suggested.

It wasn't just that the great stone amphitheater and the long-abandoned Anasazi dwelling were larger than life, Diana discovered as she and Jack made their way toward the other side of the boxlike canyon. The ruins were somehow "other" than life. They were like something from an ancient dream reaching across the bridge of time.

Diana could almost picture an Indian woman, her hair fashioned into the elaborate coiffure preferred by the females of her clan, carrying a large woven basket on her hip as she returned home from visiting another nearby Anasazi settlement.

She could imagine the joy, the excitement, the sense of homecoming the woman would have felt as she entered through the narrow canyon and saw her people farming in the valley below, their homes high above in the community built into the stone overhang.

The Anasazi were intelligent and artistic, a peaceful society of farmers who also displayed an ingenious knack for building.

An unbelievable knack for building, Diana decided as she and Jack drew near the narrow steps leading to the ruins.

"You stay here," Jack insisted. "I'm going to scout ahead and test the footing."

"But—"

"No buts, Diana. I know what I'm doing. So let me do it."

She backed off. "All right, Jack. But be careful, please."

He nodded and began to climb the stone steps. Diana watched, her heart in her throat.

Within five minutes she'd developed a healthy respect for her former husband and for his skills as a mountain climber. He was as nimble as a mountain goat, as graceful as a dancer and every bit as light on his feet.

It dawned on Diana that for most of his adult life, this was the kind of work Jack had been paid to do. She hadn't appreciated the skill, the know-how, the expertise it took until now.

Something else occurred to her. She was loving every minute of this adventure. No wonder Jack had kept seeking new challenges, new experiences, new thrills. It was exciting. It was exhilarating. It could, indeed, become addictive.

Five more minutes passed, then ten. She was getting impatient. "What do you think?" she called up to Jack. "Are the steps strong enough to support our weight?"

"The steps seem sturdy enough. But before you come up I want to take a closer look at some of the buildings, or what's left of them. These rocks are the perfect hiding place for rattlers." With that, he disappeared behind a remnant of stone wall.

Diana shifted her weight from one foot to the other. She took a drink of water from her canteen. She retied the kerchief around her neck and began to pace.

Jack reappeared.

She stopped pacing. "Well?"

"The structures are surprisingly sound. Actually, it's amazing when you figure they're held together with mud that's hundreds of years old."

She grew more impatient. "What about rattlesnakes?"

"No sign of snake on this side," he said, pointing to his left. "A few sidewinder tracks about forty feet north of that embankment. They're a day or two old, but I'd stay clear of that area."

"Can I come up now?"

"Be my guest. But only as far as this level," he cautioned, holding out his hand to her. "The walls and partial structures seem stable enough, but don't take any unnecessary risks by leaning against them. Individual stones may still have worked their way loose over the years."

Diana scrambled up the steps. She slipped the backpack off her shoulders and took a pen and notebook from one of the large, outside canvas pockets. Closing her eyes, she inhaled deeply. "You can almost smell it, can't you?"

Jack looked at her. "Smell what?"

"Sagebrush. That's what the Anasazi would have burned." Her voice grew dreamy. "I can almost see a full moon on the rise and countless small campfires on the canyon floor below. I can hear the rhythmic beat of the ceremonial drums and the eerie sound of the tribal chants."

Jack stood perfectly still. "There is something kind of haunting about this place." He gave himself a shake. "Well, you've got ruins to explore and notes to take. We don't have all day, so you'd better get started."

Diana glanced down at her watch, then frowned. "It took us longer to reach our destination than I'd planned."

"Almost three hours one way. We have to assume the hike back will take even longer since we'll be tired, at least in comparison to what we were when we started out this morning. We have to allow plenty of time to get to civilization before dark."

She saw his point. "Then I'd better get a move on."

"I'll leave you to your research until it's almost time to go," Jack volunteered.

"What are you going to do?"

"Explore a little farther. If I find anything unusual I'll let you know."

"You can find me in this area. I'll either be poking my head around corners, or in doorways, or jotting down ideas as they come to me."

He nodded and moved away quietly, carefully, as skillfully as an Indian.

Diana explored the first level of the cliff palace for the next half hour. She discovered a house—it had no roof and only part of two walls remained—with a stone bench inside.

She sat down on the large, rectangular-shaped boulder. The warmth of the sun was on her face. The heat of the stone penetrated her cotton fatigues. A fine layer of dirt and sand dusted her hands and clothing where she touched the ancient chair. She put her head back and basked in the sunlight.

In ages long past, had some other woman sat in this very spot and looked out over the landscape? What had she been thinking? Feeling?

Surely in ages yet to be another woman would sit here and wonder who had come before her to this place. What would she be thinking and feeling?

Diana felt a strange chill course down her spine.

Perhaps this place of the Ancient Ones did bridge time. But they were long gone, the men and women who had built this city out of the earth's stone and mud. They were dust unto dust, leaving behind their buildings, a shard of pottery, an arrowhead, perhaps, needle-sharp and shaped like a leaf. That's all that remained.

Who remembered their pain, their joy, their sorrow, how they loved, *who* they loved? Who remembered if they were kind to their children? Who knew the secrets of their hearts? Had they loved wisely and well?

As Diana sat there in a meditative state, her eyes closed, she suddenly saw what the world would be like without Jack in it, without her in it. It was clear to her as never before: they were just one man and one woman. They were nothing, and yet they were everything.

Human life was painfully short. There was no time for pride or anger or the past to get in the way of living. The past was done. The future was yet to be. All she had was now. All anyone had was now.

JACK FACED THE ANCIENT RUINS and wondered—if not for the first time, then for one of the few times in his life—if he was a religious man.

He had to admit he'd only said a prayer once or twice in his thirty-five years. Maybe when he'd been in that tight spot in Bangkok and hadn't been able to see a way out. Or the night he'd lain in the grip of a deadly jungle fever and hadn't been sure he'd ever see home again, or even the light of another day. Maybe then he'd prayed.

Without putting it into words, Jack knew one thing: he was thankful, grateful, to someone, some thing beyond himself for allowing him to see this place.

He climbed higher and higher, picking his way, testing the stone stairs as he went, step by step, until he was standing on a rise overlooking the canyon below. From this vantage point the trees looked like matchsticks, the rushing stream a mere thread of blue.

This was big country. And big country could make a man feel small, insignificant in the grand scheme of things. It wasn't the first time Jack had been aware of that essential truth, but he'd forgotten it somewhere along the way.

The mountains, the stone canyons, the deserts beyond—stretching as far as the eye could see—they'd been here for millions, perhaps billions of years. Three score and ten. That was the span of a man's life on earth. It was no more than a split second in comparison to that of the life around him.

What was there for a man in those few brief moments of his life? Work that gave his years some purpose, some meaning. Dignity in the way he treated others and they treated him in return. Love. Love of family. Love of country. Love of God, whatever form he took. Love of a good woman.

Diana.

The thought of her filled his mind; the remembered scent of her, his nostrils; the feel of her, his hands; the love he had for her, his heart.

None of it mattered, Jack realized, not one damned bit, not even this magnificent place preserved by the dry desert air, if Diana wasn't there with him in life.

WHEN DIANA FOUND JACK he was standing on a rise looking out over the valley far below. There was a nobility about him that made her think of an ancient Anasazi who would have stood in that spot and watched his people working in the fields, carrying water from the stream to their village above.

She climbed higher.

Jack had removed his sunglasses and his hat. They were at his feet, along with his backpack. Now she could see the sweat running down his face.

She came closer.

She looked again and wondered if those could possibly be tears on his face.

She'd never seen her husband cry. Not before they were married, not in all the time they'd been together, not when they were happy or sad, making love or quarreling. Not once. But he was now, and she wanted to take him in her arms and hold him, hold him to her and never let him go. The urge, the need, to do so was almost overwhelming.

Instead she approached his side and said, touching his arm, "Jack, are you all right?"

He didn't answer right away. When he did, she knew by the fullness in his voice that at least some of the moisture on his face was, indeed, from tears.

"Yes. I'm all right. Better than I've been in a long, long time, I think."

She understood. Perhaps that was the true wonder of this ancient place, the effect it had on those who came here. The air seemed clearer, the sky bluer. The sun shone more brightly. The senses were alert to every sight and sound and smell.

And Diana knew somehow that she loved the man standing beside her. Loved him with all her heart. Perhaps she'd never stopped loving him. Perhaps she'd fallen in love with him all over again. Where and when wasn't important anymore, only the fact that it was.

"Jack, I think it's time for us to leave."

He looked down at his watch. "Yes, it is."

By the time he'd strapped his backpack on and retrieved his other belongings, he seemed to be in full control of himself once again.

Ten minutes later they were retracing their steps to the lower level of the ruins. They didn't stop again until they'd reached the narrow canyon passageway.

"It's like a fantasy, a dreamworld," Diana murmured as she gazed at the ancient cliff dwelling one last time. Then they turned and began the long hike back to civilization.

Diana was close to exhaustion when the welcome sight of her Jeep greeted them nearly four hours later. They quickly stowed their equipment in the rear and prepared to depart from the Navajo Indian reservation.

"All I want is to go home, take a hot shower and fall into bed," she groaned wearily.

"You do look dead on your feet," Jack commiserated. "Give me the keys to the Jeep. I'm driving."

Diana was too tired to argue with him. She crawled into the Jeep, snapped the seat belt around her waist, promptly yawned and murmured sleepily, "I want to go home, Jack. Will you take me home?"

He watched her for a moment and then said in a tenderhearted voice, "Yes, darling, I'll take you home."

8

HE WAS BEAT, Jack admitted to himself as he parked the Jeep in the garage behind Diana's house.

He flexed his shoulders. He was stiff and tired and a little sore all over.

He glanced down at his watch. It was too dark to see the face, but he knew it was late, middle-of-the-night kind of late.

He looked over at Diana. She was still sleeping. She'd awakened once or twice during the evening and had asked where they were, how he was feeling, had offered to drive when she couldn't even keep her eyes open. But he'd told her to go back to sleep; he didn't mind being behind the wheel.

The funny thing was, he really didn't mind driving. In fact, he'd enjoyed the trip south from Flagstaff. The quiet hours on the open road, no traffic to speak of, no appointments to keep, no need to talk, no one to talk to. Yet he'd still felt Diana's presence, and that had been companionship enough for him.

He'd stopped a couple of times, once for a cup of black coffee and a sandwich, ham and cheese on stale rye, and once for a break at a rest stop, where he'd stretched his legs and used the facilities. Otherwise they'd been in the four-wheel-drive vehicle since earlier that evening.

They'd left the Navajo Indian reservation just as the sun was setting, streaks of scarlet and crimson across a navy blue sky. It was the perfect ending to a perfect day.

Jack wondered why he and Diana hadn't spent more days together like this when they were married. Maybe if they had, they would have become good friends, the best of friends, and they would still be husband and wife today instead of another divorce statistic.

It had been one hell of a day, all right, thought Jack, shaking his head. He hadn't realized how much he'd missed getting away from civilization until they'd hiked into the backcountry that morning. It was clear to him now: in the past several years he'd spent too damned many hours stuck in an office behind a desk, or sitting around a conference table.

That was going to change.

The Outdoorsman was important to him, but not as important today as it had been yesterday. He'd been making a good living, but he'd been forgetting how to live. Hell, he couldn't even remember the last time he'd had a date, taken a woman out to dinner, gone to a movie, seen a parade. He was due to make some changes in his life again. Past due.

The woman beside him stirred.

He turned off the ignition and reached out to touch her arm. "Diana?"

"Hmm . . . where are we?" she mumbled, rousing.

"Home."

She sat up before she opened her eyes. "Home?" The word was repeated in the form of a question, as if she didn't quite comprehend its meaning.

"Yes. We're back at your house."

Slowly opening her eyes, she said, "You drove all the way."

"Yes."

"You must be exhausted."

"I'm a little tired."

"I should have stayed awake. I should have helped drive. I've got to unload my stuff," she announced in slightly staccato tones, opening the door on the passenger's side.

Jack got out of the Jeep and came around to where she was struggling with a rope that had been tied around the supplies in the back.

"Can't the unpacking wait until morning? There's nothing here that's going to run off or spoil or turn green."

She looked up at him with a blank expression on her face. "Turn green?"

He smiled wearily, affectionately. "Never mind, sleepyhead."

"I can't leave my research notes in the Jeep," she protested, rummaging through their gear.

Brushing her feeble efforts aside, Jack assured her, "I'll get your notes." He located her backpack and his, and swung both effortlessly over one shoulder. "Is there anything else that has to be unloaded tonight?"

Diana shook her head and allowed him to guide her toward the house. They made their way along the adobe wall and past the gas grill to the back door.

He stuck out his hand, palm up. "Key?"

She dug around in the pocket of her cotton fatigues, paused for thirty seconds or so, knitted her brows in a studious frown, seemed to remember something important and then reached above her head to feel along a small ledge that ran the width of the door frame.

Triumphantly she held up a brass key ring. "I almost forgot where I put it. I was afraid I'd lose my key if I carried it around in my pants pocket."

Jack took the house key from her, unlocked the door and escorted her inside before he turned and secured the lock behind them. "I'll go out the front door when I leave," he offered by way of explanation.

Diana flipped on the light switch, stopped in the middle of the kitchen and blinked at him. "Are you planning to drive into Phoenix tonight?"

He glanced down at his watch. "Technically it's not night anymore. It's morning."

She stared at him, swaying on her feet, her eyes glazed over with fatigue. "I'm exhausted. You must be, too. You're welcome to stay in the guest room." She gestured toward the bedroom wing of the adobe house. "It's the least I can offer when you were kind enough to do all the driving."

Jack felt a yawn coming on and couldn't stop it in time. "If you're sure you don't mind."

Diana yawned, too. "I don't mind. The bed's already made up, and there are clean towels in the adjoining bath. If you need anything else, please ask me."

"Don't worry about playing the perfect hostess with me, honey," he said, taking her by the elbow. "I'll manage. Why don't you get undressed and crawl into bed?"

"I want to take a shower first," she muttered.

They reached the hallway that led to the bedrooms. Diana's was off to the right; the guest quarters were on the left.

Jack dropped the canvas backpack with her precious notes inside on top of the cedar chest at the foot of her bed. "Can you manage on your own?"

She nodded and began to fumble with the buttons of her long-sleeved shirt, first those at the cuff, then the row down the front. The edge of her bra and the rounded curve of her breasts were showing when she finally realized he was still in the room. Her hand froze.

Tired as he was, Jack became aware of desire, lazy and long-forgotten, uncurling in the pit of his stomach. There was a corresponding tightening in his groin. He would have liked to have adjusted his pants; they suddenly seemed too small. There was both pain and pleasure in the sensation. He groaned and wondered if Diana heard him.

"I can manage on my own," she said at last, her fingers playing with the remaining few buttons.

There wasn't anything left for him to say but goodnight. So he did, adding, "I'll see you in the morning."

"Later this morning," he heard Diana correct him as he closed the bedroom door.

Morning or night, it made no difference to him. But they'd both be better off with locked doors between them, the way he was feeling. Five days ago he had told Diana that what they needed was time. He knew damn well she didn't want to rush into anything, especially with an ex-husband. He was pretty sure five days wasn't long enough. She would suspect he was trying to hustle her into a love affair if he made his move now.

Was he?

Jack ran his hand back and forth along his jawline as he sauntered across the hallway to the guest room. He needed a shave and a shower.

Hell, what he needed was his wife. No matter how he sliced it, he wanted her so badly he could feel it in his gut like a red-hot poker. But he wasn't going to get her. Not tonight. Not tomorrow night. Maybe never. That's what happened when a man burned his bridges behind him.

Jack dropped the backpack on the floor beside the bed. He sank down on the edge, his weight making a sizable impression in the mattress.

The truth was he wanted to see that special look again in Diana's eyes when he made love to her. The one that said her world began and ended with him, the one that said all she'd ever need was air to breathe and him beside her. Was that asking so much?

It was asking too much. And he knew it.

Jack stood up and started to undress. It was time to stop thinking, to stop torturing himself. What he needed was a shower. An ice-cold shower.

DIANA WATCHED as Jack walked out of her bedroom, closing the door firmly behind him. For a minute he hadn't wanted to go. She'd seen it in his eyes. It was a look she'd seen before; a look, God knows, she'd never forget. It said he wanted her, needed her, desired her on some elemental, primitive level. And no other woman on earth would do. Only her.

There had been times during their marriage when Jack had been away for weeks on end, when she had wondered if he'd reached out to find momentary satisfaction in the arms of another woman. She'd had her share of doubts about his fidelity. What wife didn't wonder about her husband from time to time?

Jack was one hell of a good-looking man, after all. Not to mention the fact that he possessed an indefinable charisma. She wasn't blind. She'd seen the way others of her sex looked at him, flirted with him, tried to come on to him. Jack had always reassured her—not in so many words, but in his hunger for her, his need for her—that there was no one else, could never be anyone else for him.

Diana thought about that as she finished undressing and took a hot shower. At thirty-one, she was older and wiser. She could step back and reflect on the past with a certain amount of objectivity. Jack had always been, and still was, too fundamentally honest to cheat at anything, and that included his marriage vows.

"I do promise before God and these witnesses to be thy loving and faithful husband as long as we both shall live... with this ring I thee wed, with my body I thee worship..."

She repeated aloud the words he'd said to her that day in the wedding chapel in Las Vegas. Some might call her foolish, some merely naive, but she believed Jack had been faithful to her while they were married. Since then . . .

Since then was none of her business.

She threw her hair back over one shoulder and let the hot water run down her body. Taking a bar of soap in her hands, she rubbed them together until they were covered with the fragrant lather. She used the lather to wash her face, her arms, her breasts.

It reminded her of the times when she'd showered with Jack. He'd loved to wash her from head to toe with his bare hands. She could remember the feel of his callused, slightly roughened palms on her wet breasts, how they'd grown and swelled under his tutelage, how her nipples had hardened into two erect nubs, how she'd thrilled to his ministrations as one soapy hand glided over her abdomen, down to her pelvis and into the triangle of darker blond hair between her thighs.

How could she ever forget the erotic sensation of his fingers entwined in her wet curls, his thumb finding that most sensitive spot as he stroked and caressed her, his mouth seeking her breast, his tongue licking the droplets of water from her nipples even as he spread her legs and entered her first with one fingertip and then another until she was whimpering with need, pleading for satisfaction?

Diana lifted her face to the warm spray and let her groan of dismay drown beneath the sound of rushing water. She was being seduced by her former husband, and he wasn't even in the room with her! Jack was obviously not the only one who was haunted by memories. She was thoroughly and completely aroused by the memory of his lovemaking.

She had to face a few truths about herself. She was in love with Jack. Still. Again. Once more. And she wanted him in every way a woman could possibly want a man. What was she going to do about it?

There was no quick or easy answer to that question.

Drying off, Diana slipped into the cotton underwear she'd got into the habit of wearing to bed at night: a pair of bikini briefs and a matching tank top.

She was tired but not sleepy. Not anymore.

She was restless, aroused, hungry. At least she could do something about the hunger.

Grabbing a summer robe from the hook on the back of the bathroom door and her notes from the backpack on the cedar chest, Diana padded barefoot down the hallway to the kitchen. As she passed the guest bath, she could hear water running. Apparently she wasn't the only one who'd decided to take a shower before going to bed.

Opening the refrigerator, she studied its somewhat meager contents. On the first shelf there was a baked chicken breast and a small container of green beans left over from Thursday night's dinner. Half a cantaloupe, two slices of watermelon and a few strawberries were on the second shelf. The third was bare. She reached for the fruit.

Diana ate her impromptu supper as she stood at the counter, glancing through her notes. She'd been inspired to write several paragraphs on her latest book while they were at the ancient cliff dwelling. She read through those, as well.

At least she wasn't hungry anymore, Diana consoled herself some ten minutes later as she rinsed her plate in the kitchen sink. She was still wide awake, however. And restless. And aroused. She poured herself a glass of white wine and decided to take it with her to bed. On the way to her room, she took a brief detour, stopping in her study long enough to pick up a manila envelope that had arrived the day before yesterday from her publisher.

As she walked by the guest room, balancing the glass of wine in one hand and the envelope in the other, she could hear the shower still going.

She removed her robe and tossed it over the back of a chair, then settled down for the night. Sprawled across her bed, a pillow tucked under her for support, she read through her notes for a second time, occasionally reaching for the wineglass she'd set on a nearby table.

Something made her glance up a few minutes later... and there was Jack standing in the doorway. He was leaning against the jamb, arms crossed, chest bare, wearing a pair of faded Levis and nothing else. He was watching her.

"Working at this hour?"

"Looking over some notes."

His eyes never left her. "I thought all you wanted to do was take a hot shower and crawl into bed."

"The shower woke me up. I got hungry and went to the kitchen for something to eat." It was her turn to interrogate him. "I thought we were both exhausted. What are you doing up?"

"I'm thirsty. Thought I'd mosey along to the kitchen and get myself a drink."

The words hung in the air between them, stretched along a line of tension that reached from one to the other like the taut wire of a tightrope walker.

It was a moment Diana knew she would be able to recall in every detail even years later: the tired lines around Jack's eyes, eyes that were intense and on fire with desire; the way he unconsciously splayed his hand across his abdomen, an abdomen that was taut and muscular and without a bit of spare flesh on it; the tanned arms and chest, the strength inherent in them, the whiter skin of his bare feet; the clean-shaven face, the neatly trimmed mustache, the drops of water on his dark hair, the mouth with its fuller bottom lip and the haunting memories of what he could do to her with that mouth, those teeth, that tongue.

"Thirsty?" Diana heard a low, sultry voice repeat the word and scarcely recognized it as her own.

But she knew exactly what she was going to do.

Almost in slow motion she rose from her bed, notes in hand, and walked toward him, the wineglass extended slightly in front of her.

"Would you like some wine?"

Jack accepted the fluted glass and raised it to his mouth. He drank.

"What are you reading?" he asked as he took the papers from her other hand.

"My notes from yesterday."

Diana thought of the words that had flowed from her pen to fill the page. Let him read them. Maybe they would tell him what she couldn't.

Jack scanned the first sheet of paper. Then she watched as he began to read aloud:

> The frontier of her homeland was a foreboding, jagged, natural stone fortress that rose up out of a bittersweet blue sea. The only way on and off the rock island was on the back of the giant elos, the large half-bird, half-reptile creature, gargoylelike in appearance, that had served her clan for generations.
>
> She had traveled the great deserts, the tallest mountains, the rain forests of her world. She had seen them, taken them in, made them a part of herself until they had changed somehow and become the land-

scape of her imagination, the unique expression of her heart and soul and mind. She would remember them, recall them in every detail as she sang her songs and told her stories to the People.

That was why she had been sent away. It was the way of all Tellers of Tales.

But she had been gone so long. Longer than anyone had planned, and she had traveled farther than anyone else of the Clan. Would she remember the ancient song that called the giant elos from its slumber?

She brought her hands to her mouth and formed a cup. Taking a deep breath, she emitted the first, tentative note of the Calling Song. She took another breath and began again. This time her voice was sweet and clear and echoed from stone wall to stone wall.

She waited. She heard the flap of giant wings. The elos was, indeed, coming for her.

The journey across the Void left her safely on the other side.

Then Jana Clearmountain stood tall on the mesa top and gazed out over the desert canyon below. This was her land and her people, she thought proudly. This was her place. There was no more she could wish for than to be here.

But in her heart Jana knew she wished for more. She remembered, and she wished for the love of Keet Longstrider and the children she would never bear.

She remembered well, and she wept....

Jack took another drink of wine and looked into her eyes. His were clouded with pain.

"Is that how you feel?" he said hoarsely.

After a long moment . . . "Yes."

"Do you weep for me, Diana, and the children we never had?"

Her hands were shaking as she took the sheets of paper from his grasp. "Sometimes."

She stood beside him, could feel the heat emanating from his body. Of its own volition one hand reached out and touched his arm. His skin was feverish.

Her blue eyes darkened to midnight. "Are you all right?" He didn't answer, and she tried to cover her confusion, going on in a faltering voice, "You . . . you feel so hot, like you're burning up."

He finished off the wine and set the glass down on a small table just inside the bedroom door. He moved toward her, his intent clear. "I am burning up, inside and out, for you, Diana. For you."

She momentarily lost her nerve and fell back a step or two, exclaiming with alarm in her voice, "Jack!"

That stopped him cold.

He raked his fingers through his dark and unruly and still slightly damp hair. "Damn it, I know you're exhausted. You said so yourself, honey. Part of me knows I shouldn't take advantage of that, but so help me God, Diana, I want you so badly it hurts."

"You want me that much?"

He swore under his breath, then reluctantly admitted, "Yes. I want you that much."

Bravely she closed the distance between them. The papers in her hand fluttered to the floor. "Life is short, too short, and we've wasted more than enough time already, haven't we, Jack?"

He nodded. "Yes. As I was standing on top of that mountain of stone, looking down into a red rock canyon centuries old, I saw how much precious time I've wasted on things that didn't matter. For us, every day—and every night—counts." He took a deep breath. "I want you, Diana. I need you. Now. Tonight."

"Tuesday night we agreed to give ourselves some time and not rush things."

"Is that what you want?" Jack demanded to know.

"I thought I did, then."

"And now?"

"Now I know that time is an illusion, an invention, a man-made device used to give some structure, some semblance of order to our lives. But all we mortals ever truly have is this moment, this one moment we call the present. Nothing is promised us beyond that. We can't change the past. We can only hope that we have a future. What we do have is *now*."

His shoulders relaxed. "I want to go to bed with you, Diana. I want to kiss you, touch you, make love to you. There is no yesterday for us. No tomorrow. There is only this night."

Jack came toward her until they were standing no more than an inch apart. In anticipation, the tips of her breasts puckered beneath the thin cotton tank top she was wearing. They poked him in the chest. He reached out and cradled her hips in his hands. He began to move in a languorous and suggestive gyration.

There was something she wanted him to know. Diana tried to keep a clear head long enough to tell him. It was important to her.

"There has never been anyone for me but you, Jack. Not in all the days and months since we were last together."

One callused hand reached up to cup her face as he gazed down into her eyes. "All the time we were married, you were the only woman for me. Hard as I've tried, that's still true. Some species in the wild mate for life. Some men and women are the same way. I'm that kind of man, Diana."

"And I'm that kind of woman."

His mouth was so close to hers that she could savor the sweet wine on his lips. She used the tip of her tongue to explore the tantalizing taste and texture of him. His hands tightened their hold, one at her chin, the other at her hip.

With an intimacy that literally stole her breath away, his tongue found her lips and surged beyond them into the warm, welcoming recesses of her honeyed mouth. Her heart was pounding madly. Her breasts were flattened against the hard wall of skin and bone and muscle that was his bare chest.

Diana wanted to wrap herself around Jack and hold on for dear life. She wanted to become so much a part of him that whether they were together making love or far apart—even halfway around the world from each other—he could still smell her on his skin, feel her inside his head and heart, know that she was with him always.

He was devouring her. His lips and teeth and tongue were on her mouth, her ears, her partially bare shoulder, the sensitive pulse point at the base of her throat. His passion overwhelmed her. She was suffocating, and didn't care. She was content to die right there in his arms.

His hands were nearly bruising her hipbone. His fingers sank into the soft curve of her buttocks and urged her closer to him, letting her know how aroused he was, allowing her to feel the strength in his body, the hard flesh that rose between them as if with a will of its own.

Diana's fingers snaked between their bodies. She tried to undo the snap at the waist of his Levis. Jack stopped her. Covering her hands with his own, he pushed them lower. She could feel the hard, throbbing outline of his erection. She caressed him through the denim material, caught him in her grasp, ran her nails along the length of his manhood. He moaned. She moaned, as well, remembering, always remembering.

Carefully she undid the zipper down the front of his jeans and released his swollen shaft into her waiting hands. This was the glorious paradox that had always fascinated her: he could be so soft and vulnerable one minute, so very hard and powerful the next. Life stirred in him. The beats of his heart could be counted as blood pulsed through the tiny veins covering his feverishly hot skin.

"Diana." Her name was scarcely audible, although his mouth was only inches from hers. She touched him again. An expression of pain mixed with pleasure flickered across his face. He fairly shouted her name. "Diana!"

Had she inadvertently hurt him? "Are you all right?"

"No."

"Are you in pain?"

"Yes. Terrible, glorious pain. Help me, darling. Only you can help me."

She understood.

The words shot from his lips as he went on, "It's been so long since you've touched me, sweetheart. If you keep this up, I'm not going to last worth a damn when we make love. I won't be able to help myself. I want you to stop. I want you to go on touching me. I shouldn't be a selfish bastard about it, but I am. I am."

"Don't you know that it doesn't matter? I want to touch you. I want to give you pleasure. Just having you in my arms again, feeling your body against mine, is enough for me."

"It's not enough," Jack growled as he picked her up and, in three easy strides, carried her to the bed.

He laid her down on the sheets and kicked off his jeans; his manhood sprang forth with vibrant life. He eased the tank top over her head and dispensed with her cotton panties. Testing her readiness, he touched her between her thighs. His fingers came away hot and sticky with the melting response of her body.

"Love me, darling," she urged, opening her arms.

"I am. I swear I'll try. But I'm afraid I won't last very long the first time," he warned.

In one beautiful, fluid movement, Jack surged into her, striking deeper and deeper, until every inch of her seemed to be filled with him. There was not a word left on her lips, not a thought remaining in her brain beyond the realization that Jack had truly come home to her in every sense of the word, in the most intimate sense of the word.

They lay there, their bodies joined, not speaking, not moving, the only sound their harsh breathing. Diana opened her eyes and looked up at her husband. His slowly opened, and he gazed down at her.

"God, how I've missed you!"

"And I've missed you!" she cried out softly.

Their eyes closed again, and they were both lost to the world of physical sensation. He kissed her eyelids, the delicate shell of her ears, the hollow of her throat. His tongue teased and tantalized her skin. His teeth sought the rigid tip of her breast: he nibbled gently, then almost painfully. She couldn't take any more and arched her back, driving her nipple into his mouth. He sucked on one breast and then the other. Her head went back, her mouth opened slightly, and an aroused moan escaped her lips.

All the while they were intimately joined, her body stretched to accommodate his. She wanted what he had to give, joyfully took every inch of him into her.

Then Jack poised his body above hers and began to move, slowly at first and in long, languid strokes that drew the last breath from her body. The blood vessels on his arms stood out from the exertion; there was a light film on his face; his body was hot and damp. Almost as hot and as damp as her own.

Diana's hands went to his chest. His skin was silky, his hair sleek and smooth like the pelt of a leopard. With her tongue she found one small, pebbly male nipple and encircled it, exciting it. She opened her eyes and watched as he made love to her. He was, indeed, like a magnificent animal in action, with his head thrown back, his eyes closed, body flexed, muscles straining with a very real power.

His thrusts became faster and faster. He drove into her, ever harder and deeper. As the world around her began to spin out of orbit, she held on to him tightly. Then she was swallowed up by a pleasure so pure, a sexual climax so intense that she could only cry out his name again and again.

Hers became a trumpet call, a triumphant crescendo of sound on his lips. "Diana. Diana. Diana!"

With one final thrust of his hips, he shouted and emptied himself into her, then collapsed onto her prone figure.

Diana wrapped her arms around him and held him close. A sense of peace and utter contentment crept over her. She dozed, unaware that Jack rolled off her inert form, gently touched her cheek and promptly fell into an exhausted sleep beside her.

They awoke at dawn and made love again, slowly at first, certainly thoroughly, a little wildly in the end. They rediscovered all the pleasures and special joys they knew how to give each other.

THE NEXT TIME DIANA ROUSED, it was midday and the sun was already a bright yellow ball in the Arizona sky.

She could smell the rich, inviting aroma of freshly brewed coffee. She pried open her eyes. Jack was propped up in bed beside her, drinking a mug of coffee.

The manila envelope from her publisher was torn open and tossed onto the cedar chest, just as she'd left it last night. Cover drawings for a two-book series she was writing lay across Jack's lap.

He looked down at her and smiled. "Good morning, sleepyhead."

"What time is it?" she asked, taking the coffee mug from his hand.

"Almost noon."

Diana groaned. "Noon?"

"We had a late night," he reminded her unnecessarily.

She stretched like a cat and inquired, sipping his coffee, "What are you doing?"

"I found these on the floor this morning." Jack held up the book covers. The artwork on the first was a strange, primitive rendering of a tribal mask stamped in gold leaf. He read the title aloud, "*Gold: Sweat of the Sun.*" Then he examined the second cover. The illustration showed an exotic woman with long, flowing, white-blond hair. There was a large silvery teardrop on her cheek. "*Silver: Tears of the Moon.* You really didn't forget, did you?" he murmured with bemusement in his voice.

"I told you I remembered." She knew the titles would have a special meaning for him.

He read the print across the front of the art. "'Book one in a new series by best-selling science-fiction author, D. K. Quick.'"

"Diana Kingston Quick."

"I know. I know," he said softly. "You should be very proud of what you've accomplished. I may not be much of a critic, but I am a reader. Your stuff's good, Diana, damn good."

"My writing has kept me sane. I can do it anyplace, anytime, anywhere I want to. How many professions offer that kind of freedom?"

"Not many," he agreed.

Jack was silent for a minute or two. He put the drawings down, took the nearly empty coffee mug from her grasp, finished off the last drop in the bottom and set it on the bedside table. Then he gathered her in his arms.

Diana snuggled beside him, fitting her body to his.

"Content?"

"More content than I ever remember feeling." She pressed her lips to his chest, kissing him above the spot where his heart was. "We were good together last night."

"We were *very* good together this morning." He corrected her, then added after a moment, "I've been thinking."

She knew it. She still recognized the signs: the utter stillness of his body and the way his eyes went dreamy and seemed to focus on the horizon. In fact, what surprised her most was how much she remembered about Jack, about herself, about the two of them together.

"Don't wrinkle your eyebrows like that," she scolded affectionately, reaching up to smooth his forehead with her fingertips. "You're getting a permanent groove between your eyes."

Jack tried to relax his facial muscles. The frown came right back. "I've been thinking," he began again. "I have to return to Wisconsin in a couple of weeks . . ."

Diana could feel his heart pounding in his chest.

"Yes?" she prodded when he failed to go on.

Turning her in the circle of his arms, Jack looked long into her eyes. "I'm not going to be afraid to say it. I'm in love with you, Diana. I think I've been in love with you since the first night we met." He held up his hand. "And that's God's truth. I know we've had our problems. But I've changed. You've changed. Maybe this time we could make it. I want to give us the chance to find out. I want you to come back to Wisconsin with me."

How many times during the four years of their marriage had she hoped and prayed to hear those words from this man? But he'd never said them to her, never asked her to go with him. So she'd stayed behind, alone. Now he was finally asking. What would her answer be?

Jack didn't wait for a response. He went on, quietly, eloquently, "I learned something on my last trip to the Amazon."

A sharp pain coursed through her. "The Amazon." She repeated the word as if it were a dark curse.

He continued. "I found out that I wasn't invincible, that I could die and nobody would give a damn; no one would know what had happened to me. There wouldn't be anyone to bury my body and mourn my passing."

Perhaps at last she would understand. "What did happen?"

A cold sweat broke out on Jack's brow and ran down into his eyes. He wiped it away with the back of his hand. "I was all alone in a remote region of the jungle. I caught some kind of tropical fever. I still don't have any idea how many days I walked before I finally collapsed. A tribe of friendly natives found me. I was damned lucky they did. They usually hunted closer to home, but game was scarce that season. Anyway, they found me, took me back to their village and cared for me. They said later I called out your name a hundred times or more that night." He laughed, and it was a terrible sound. "They thought I was praying to my god, or cursing the god's name. I was delirious, you see. Out of my head. They didn't know if I was going to live or die."

Diana felt as though her worst nightmare had become a waking dream. "I—I had no idea you'd been sick."

Jack's eyes narrowed. He didn't say anything for a minute. "Once I was able to stand on my own two feet again, I headed back to civilization and hopped a plane for the States. I swore once I got out alive, I'd never go back. And I haven't. I want you to know that. If you come with me, I won't leave you. I don't go running off to the far reaches of the globe anymore. I do a small amount of business traveling, and that's all."

She didn't know what to say. "But my house, my writing, my life is here."

"I'm not asking for a long-term commitment, just this: come to Wisconsin, spend some time with me, write in the privacy and seclusion of my cabin by the lake and see what happens from there. I promise we'll take it one step at a time, one day at a time."

"One day at a time. . . ."

"You don't have to decide right now. Think about it for a few days." He threw one last factor into the equation. "You should have been introduced to my family years ago. You're right about that. Maybe it's better late than never. They'll be gathered together for our annual Fourth of July celebration. The timing's perfect."

Diana knew some of the reasons she'd never met Jack's family, but she was pretty sure she didn't know all of them. "After we eloped you didn't tell your parents about us right away, did you?"

"No. I thought it might be best to wait for a while."

Curiosity got the better of her. "Why?"

He tried to explain. "Not everyone can jump on an airplane whenever they feel like it. The Royces were plain, simple folk, honey. Still are, for that matter."

"There's nothing wrong with being plain, simple folk."

"I know. There was more to it than that."

"What was it, then?"

He rubbed the back of his neck. "Well, when we were first married you were pretty busy with your career."

"And you were always off to Alaska or Central America or some jungle," she shot back.

Jack frowned, then admitted, "I guess that's true."

He was holding something back. Diana knew it. "What else?"

"I suppose I didn't want to upset my folks." He obviously hated digging up old dirt. "About the time we got married, my oldest brother was going through a real ugly divorce. His wife—his ex-wife—was a lot like you. In appearance, anyway. She was tall, blond, beautiful, came from a well-to-do family. A hothouse flower with no staying power, that was Deidre. She made my brother's life a living hell for five years, then just up and walked out one day, leaving him with two small children. A few months before we eloped to Las Vegas, Deidre reappeared and decided she wanted the kids, after all. There was a nasty court battle."

"And?"

"And my brother lost custody of his children."

"Oh, no." Diana groaned.

"Oh, yes."

"And you figured your family would take one look at me and see another Deidre."

"Something like that."

Diana felt an odd tightening in her chest. "I wish you'd told me at the time."

"I can look back now and realize how stupid I was about the whole thing. You weren't, you aren't, anything like my former sister-in-law. My family would have been smart enough to see that." He paused. His voice changed. "Tell me, Diana, how does a man apologize for failing to live up to his promises? How does he correct the mistakes he's made with a woman?"

"It's never a one-way street. We both made mistakes."

His eyes darkened. "I underestimated you, Diana Quick."

"And I underestimated you, Jack Royce. If only I'd known then what I know now."

"Regrets?"

She sighed. "Plenty of them."

"Me, too."

"We should have known that any two people, especially a man and a woman, think differently, express themselves differently. We didn't talk to each other, Jack. We never learned how to communicate." He raised a dark eyebrow. "Yes," she acknowledged with a light laugh, "we communicated on a physical level. But why didn't we tell each other what we wanted and needed and expected from our marriage? We weren't mind readers, after all."

"We weren't even friends, were we, Diana?"

That flash of insight on his part surprised her.

"No. I don't think we were."

"Friends or lovers, you ruined me for any other woman," he admitted, dropping a kiss on her bare shoulder.

"And you ruined me for any other man."

He smiled. It seemed he couldn't help it. "I'm glad."

"So am I."

"Will you at least consider coming to Wisconsin with me for a few weeks?"

"I'll think about it." Then she remembered. "I should tell you, though, I'm going to England for the month of September."

Jack was surprised. "Why?"

"My publisher is sending me on an eight-city tour to promote my latest book. While I'm there special arrangements have been made for me to study at Stonehenge."

"Stonehenge? You mean the megaliths, the druids and all of that mumbo-jumbo?"

She nodded. "Whoever the architects of ancient Stonehenge were, they must have been a tribe, a clan, of sorts. Think of what their religious beliefs must have been in order for them to build such an amazing structure." Diana knew her enthusiasm for the subject was showing. "I confess I'm fascinated by the inexplicable, by the mystical aspects of clans, whether they be ancient Native American or ancient Celt. I've been wanting to do a new interpretation of the Arthurian legend, of Merlin and the knights of the round table, perhaps set in a far distant past, or in a far distant future."

"I understand. I understand." Jack quickly dismissed the conversation as he started to fondle her breasts. "You have to go to England in September."

But September was months away, he rationalized to himself. What mattered was the fact that they were together now. Diana had said it best. Today was all they had, all they were sure of having. Not tomorrow. Not the day after. Only today.

He began to make love to her. She made love to him in return. And time stood still as it did for special lovers.

9

"NERVOUS?" INQUIRED JACK as he pulled out of the long-term parking lot at Milwaukee's General Mitchell International Airport and pointed the four-wheel-drive Bronco south.

Diana glanced down at the shredded tissue on her lap. "A little, I guess. How many people did you say will be at this family get-together tomorrow?"

"Let me see. There are my parents. My oldest brother, Judd, his two kids, visiting for the summer, and his fiancée. That's six. Then there's my other brother, Bret, and his family. He and his wife, Julie, have three children. Plus the two of us—" Jack scratched his chin "—makes thirteen."

A baker's dozen. That wasn't much of a crowd.

Diana relaxed and even managed to joke, "I hope thirteen isn't an unlucky number in our case."

Apparently she spoke too soon. Jack wasn't finished.

"That's only my immediate family, of course. Then there are all the aunts and uncles and cousins on both sides, and any other relatives that happen to be visiting in the area for the annual Salmon-A-Rama."

"Salmon-A-Rama?"

"It's the big fishing tournament held every July along the shores of Lake Michigan. Brings in quite a crowd of sportsmen, too. The winners take home some impressive prizes—pickup trucks, campers, the like."

Diana dismissed Salmon-A-Rama and tried to pin him down on numbers. That's what she was interested in, numbers.

"So how many Royces and assorted relatives do you estimate will be at this Fourth of July picnic?"

Jack shrugged and turned onto the main highway going east in the direction of Racine. "Last year's turnout was kind of puny. There weren't any more than seventy-five or eighty in attendance."

"That's puny?"

"The year before last we must have had close to a hundred. Mom and Dad think we could set a new record this year."

"I'm going to meet one hundred of your relatives all at once?" Diana swallowed hard. "You didn't tell me it was going to be baptism by fire."

He grinned at her. It was almost infectious. "Don't think of it as baptism by fire; think of it as safety in numbers." He reached for her hand and tried to reassure her, saying, "There's no need to be nervous, honey. My family doesn't bite, you know."

Easy for Jack to say.

She wadded the shredded tissue into a small ball and stuffed it into her handbag. "Weren't you just a tad apprehensive at the prospect of having dinner with my parents this past week?"

"Yeah, I'll admit I was." Jack's eyes were fixed straight ahead on the road; every now and then he glanced in the rearview mirror. "But after the first few awkward moments, I think the evening went well. It helped that I was dressed appropriately for a change. At least in your mother and father's opinion."

Diana didn't quibble with his logic. Clothes didn't make the man, especially in Jack's case, but they did endow him with a certain air of prosperity and respectability.

"My father gave you a hard time, didn't he?"

"Only in the beginning." Then he added, "Harry's not so bad."

She stared at him in amazement. "I'm surprised to hear that coming from you. After all, it was my father who was so dead set against it when we wanted to get married."

"Looking back, I can't say I blame Harry. I was pretty lousy husband material for you seven years ago. You said yourself I was irresponsible and afraid to make a commitment. And I showed no signs of trying to support you in the style you were accustomed to. I spent most of my time wandering around the world like I was still nineteen years old, footloose and fancy free." Slowly he shook his head. "Hell, if you'd been my daughter, I wouldn't have approved of me, either. I was always off doing one foolhardy thing after another, instead of settling down with my wife and starting a family like any sane man would have."

Their conversation was turning out to be far more revealing than Diana had dreamed it would be. There was one point she took exception to, however.

"I never expected to be kept in *any* style by my husband. I have always been perfectly capable of taking care of myself."

"Maybe so, sweetheart. But a man has his pride. I can tell you one thing: I wouldn't be with you right now if I weren't a hell of a successful businessman."

She was temporarily speechless. "Why not?"

Jack didn't mince words. "I wouldn't have tried to see you again, that's why not."

"Ever?"

"Not until I had something more to offer than I did the first time around," he said, deadly serious.

She nearly flinched as she said, "What if I'd remarried by the time you'd decided you were successful enough to approach me?"

"Then I would have had to learn to live with the fact, even if it killed me. Either I came back to you on my own terms, Diana, or not at all."

She was stunned. "It sounds like your terms included being my lord and master."

His eyes narrowed. "Not your lord and master—" a faintly amused smirk formed on his mouth "—however tempting the prospect may be at times, but at least your equal."

"You were always my equal," she argued.

He wouldn't budge. "Only in some things, and only in some ways."

Diana was suddenly irritated with him. How dare he allow their entire future together to hinge on money, or the lack of it? Who cared where the darned stuff came from, or how much they had?

Another thought occurred to her. What if it were less a matter of dollars and cents and more an issue of misplaced masculine pride? Well, as far as she was concerned, to hell with pride, whether it be Jack's or hers.

Then her anger began to dissolve, and she realized she was proud of her former husband and his accomplishments. He'd worked his tail off, as he put it, and some of the blame and credit was indirectly hers.

She was touched by what he'd just confessed to her. Whether Jack fully understood the implications of that confession was another matter. This man had spent three and a half years salvaging his pride and marshaling his resources so that he would, however subconsciously at the time, be considered worthy of her. No man had ever don as much to gain her favor. He'd worked damn hard, fro what he'd told her. She wasn't about to throw it back i his face.

There was a conciliatory tone to Diana's voice when sh said, "I'm sure that my parents' opinion of your ambitio has improved drastically since they've seen how we you've done with The Outdoorsman."

"They seemed pretty impressed." He gave her a quic sideways glance. "But the only person's opinion that matters to me—that has ever mattered to me—is yours."

"Don't you try to sweet-talk me, Jack Royce," sh teased.

He smiled at her. "Who? Me?"

"Yes. You. That's how I got into this predicament in th first place."

He was innocence itself. "Predicament?"

"Yes. Predicament. You and your sweet-talking ways ar the reason I'm on my way to your house in Wisconsin about to meet one hundred or more of your relatives tomorrow, instead of being back home in Scottsdale doin what I do best."

"I think we both know what you do best," he murmured in a suggestive tone.

Diana felt her face turn red. "I'm glad we got to see Ki and Eric at least once before we left Arizona."

"Not that they really noticed anybody but each other, Jack said meaningfully. "At the rate they're going, Eric wi be an old man before his time."

"Old before his time?"

His voice was laced with sexual innuendo. "Your siste is wearing the guy out. Believe me, I know from persona experience how he feels." He frowned, adding, "It mus run in your family."

Diana nearly choked. No one needed to inform her that ıe had a healthy sexual appetite. She was well aware that ıe did. At least when it came to this particular man.

"I'm amazed by how lush and green everything is in 'isconsin," she commented, deliberately changing the ıbject.

"It's beautiful country. That's why I wanted you to come ıck with me, to see my home state, to get to know my lks, to show you what living here is like."

As he turned onto what appeared to be a main thor- ıghfare, Diana caught a glimpse of a winding river and ɔzens of sailboats and yachts anchored in berths along ıe crowded banks. The city of Racine had the appear- ıce of being old, but it was quite picturesque.

"That's the Root River," said Jack. "It winds back and ırth throughout the entire county. A lot of boating en- ıusiasts from southeastern Wisconsin, as well as Illinois ıd even Chicago, rent slips along these piers."

He headed north, out of the city limits, cutting down arrow roads that skirted vast fields of corn and cab- ages and the occasional farm with its herd of Guernseys.

Diana recalled her high-school geography. "Wisconsin the dairy state, isn't it?"

Jack nodded and gave her a few facts. "We produce the est cheese in the entire country. Racine is also famous for unique Danish pastry made here, called Kringle. Frank loyd Wright designed several building complexes in this ɔrner of the state, and it has a real future as a recreation rea. You'll see what I mean when we get over by Lake lichigan."

They turned down a tree-lined street. On either side 'ere neatly kept homes, white picket fences and stretches f manicured green lawns, with an abundance of blue

spruce and clumps of white birch, pots of colorful flowe
and an array of blooming bushes.

A plainly printed sign warned of the dead end straig
ahead. Then there it was, directly in front of them, a pa
oramic view of a vast and seemingly endless stretch of a
ure-blue water.

The breath caught for a moment in Diana's throa
"It's—it's beautiful!"

"Yes, it is."

She leaned forward in her seat. "Is that really Lake M
chigan?"

"None other than."

She sat there and stared out at the horizon. There wa
nothing but blue as far as the eye could see. "Why, it ha
waves just like an ocean."

"And whitecaps and sea gulls," Jack added as he pulle
into a parking area that overlooked the lake.

They sat there for a few minutes without speaking.

Diana was mesmerized. "It really is like the ocean."

"I've been coming here since I was a boy, and I've nev
grown tired of looking at Lake Michigan, not in all the
years. It's never the same twice."

Spotting a point of land that jutted out into the lake, sh
asked, "What's that white tower?"

"The Wind Point Lighthouse, built in 1880. It's the ol
est and tallest lighthouse still standing on the Great Lake
The tower was sealed in 1964, but there's a public go
course and a number of piers where the public is allowe
to fish. We'll walk along the beach below my house onc
we're settled in."

"Beach?"

He laughed. "Yes. Beach. You know, as in sand."

"Your cabin must be right on Lake Michigan."

"Prime lakefront property, complete with house, large ooded lot, sandy beach and its own pier. That's how the al-estate agent described it when she first told me the operty was for sale." Jack pulled out of the parking area d headed along a winding two-lane road.

Diana divided her attention between the front window the Bronco and the side window. "I had no idea that utheastern Wisconsin was so scenic."

"See, you didn't even know what you were missing."

"It's so different from the mountains and the Arizona sert. All that gorgeous blue water," Diana murmured, ill entranced by the sight of the lake. She looked at Jack. ou love this place very much, don't you?"

"Yes, I guess I do. But I didn't really learn to appreciate until I went away and then came home again."

Jack took the next right-hand turn and maneuvered the onco along a narrow driveway. It was partially conaled by a canopy of weeping willows, overgrown honsuckle and towering pine trees. Underbrush covered the ound in a profusion of blue chicory and white and yelw wildflowers.

Through the open window, Diana felt the coolness of e shade and the forest. She wondered just how far back the woods this cabin of Jack's was.

They reached the end of the drive, and the house sudenly appeared in front of them.

It was an intriguing combination of naturally treated ood and quarried stone that soared two stories and more to the air. The architecture was modern and elegant and pen. The blue of Lake Michigan and the late afternoon y could be seen behind it, as well as through its numerus walls of glass.

Diana turned to him and exclaimed, "You call *that* a bin?"

Jack pulled up in front of the three-car garage. "I gue I picked up the habit from the original owners. They a ways called it 'the cabin'."

"How long have you owned the house?"

"It'll be a year in October." He got out of the Bronco ar came around to open the door for her.

"It's so private, and there are so many trees." She wa looking around at the forested lot.

"You should see it around here in the fall. It's magnif cent when the leaves start to change color."

"It must be breathtaking," Diana agreed as they en tered the ultramodern structure.

From the entranceway, she could see directly into th living room. The far wall was two stories of glass pane overlooking a stretch of green lawn and the blue on bl of the July sky and Lake Michigan. The floor was po ished hardwood, the decor plain and sparse, the furnitu masculine. At one end of the room was a large stone fir place. There were several pieces of African art on th walls.

Jack gave her the nickel-and-dime tour of the first floo Besides the living room, a sparsely furnished formal di ing room and a kitchen, there was a laundry area, sever bathrooms and a storage space.

An elegant spiral staircase led to the second floor. Th master bedroom had a vaulted ceiling with a Casablan fan at its peak. The floor was hardwood partially cover by an area rug. The room was furnished with a king-si bed, an armoire and an overstuffed chair. There were thr other bedrooms, all standing empty. Jack muttered som thing about the house needing a woman's touch. Dian was inclined to agree.

"My home office," he pointed out as they entered a win built over the garage.

Diana peered around the corner into the room. It looked ke a busy executive's office.

There was one more room on the tour. Jack opened the oor and stood back, letting Diana enter first. It was an-ther office, but this one appeared to have been recently emodeled. The walls were painted pale blue. The iden-cal color was picked up in the Oriental carpet on the oor. The furniture—an elegant desk and chair, two ookcases, several ceramic pots containing silk cactus and ne mini-blinds on the window—were all decidedly fem-ine.

On the wall opposite the bookcases was the latest in omputer equipment. There was an assortment of office upplies in a French-style cabinet that matched the desk nd chair. Through an open doorway Diana could see an djoining powder room and kitchenette.

"It's lovely!"

Jack seemed pleased. "I'm glad you like it."

"That shade of blue is my favorite color..." It sud-enly occurred to Diana what he'd done. "Jack?" She urned and looked up at him.

"What?"

"You had this office done especially for me, didn't you?" omehow she knew it was true.

"I figured you'd need a place to write while you're here."

"But how did you manage all this?"

"Through the miracle of modern communications. I elephoned a few people."

"A few people! It must have taken an army."

He cracked a smile. "Only a small army."

She was momentarily at a loss for words. "It was a very houghtful gesture, but—it looks so permanent. You did ay we'd take this one day at a time."

"We will. We'll take it one day at a time, one step at a time just like I promised," Jack said in a mollifying tone, looping an arm around her shoulders. "Now, let's go unpack the Bronco and get settled in. Then I'll take you down and show you my beach before we get some dinner."

Despite his reassurances, Diana was apprehensive. She'd agreed to spend a few days, perhaps a few weeks, here in Wisconsin, but that was all. She wasn't about to be rushed, or pressured, into doing something she'd regret later. Her heart had once been broken by this man and the promises he hadn't kept. She'd decided to give him—them—a second chance, but she was still skittish, still skeptical.

Damn it, she had a right to be, Diana told herself.

Good intentions weren't enough anymore. Sex was never enough, no matter how great it was. Even love wasn't enough this time around. She needed understanding and commitment and maturity from a man. She wanted children and a home and a marriage to last a lifetime.

Yet they were two different people from the Diana Quick and the Jack Royce who'd met and eloped more than seven years ago. They'd been so young and foolish then, rushing into a marriage neither was ready for. Perhaps they'd changed. Perhaps they could make it work this time. But she had to be very certain.

First, Diana reminded herself with no small amount of trepidation, she had to make it through the celebration tomorrow and meeting one hundred of Jack Royce's nearest and dearest.

"EXACTLY WHAT DO YOU DO at these family gatherings?" Diana was asking late the next morning as they made their way from the Fourth of July parade to the picnic grounds.

"Eat, drink and be merry."

"That I could have surmised on my own. What else?"

"Gossip, although we prefer to think of it as catching up on each other's news. Look at photograph albums. Play softball and volleyball. A few of the older men usually bring out a game of horseshoes before the afternoon's over. Some play cards, pinochle mostly. There are sack races and balloon races and the like, with prizes for the kids. It may sound corny, but at the end of the day we form a circle, link arms and sing, 'Now the Day is Over.' It's become something of a tradition over the years."

"I don't think it sounds corny." As she smoothed the skirt of her plain cotton dress, Diana noticed her hands were shaking. "Any last-minute advice?"

"Don't worry about offending anyone. It's impossible not to when this many people get together."

"That's a big help."

He tried again. "Just be yourself and have a good time. Oh, and watch out for Cousin Bernie. He likes the ladies."

"Likes the ladies?"

"Actually, he pinches them."

"Cousin Bernie pinches the ladies?"

He nodded. "I think the poor old geezer is senile."

"How old is this Cousin Bernie of yours?"

"Eighty-nine, and he's hard of hearing."

Trying not to laugh, she went on, "Do you have any other eccentric relatives I should know about?"

"Nope. I guess Cousin Bernie pretty well does it." Jack hesitated, scratched his head and said, "Except for Great-Aunt Addy, of course."

"Great-Aunt Addy?"

"Actually she's my great-great-aunt."

"What about her?"

"She's a mite outspoken. Thinks it's her God-given right for having survived so long."

Diana sighed. "Just how long has Great-Aunt Addy survived?"

"Ninety-one years, she claims. But we all know she's knocked a few years off for good behavior. I suspect she's closer to ninety-four, maybe even ninety-five." Jack stroked his chin. "Anyway, for some reason I've always been Addy's favorite. And ever since she found out I was married she's been pestering me to bring my bride to the family's Fourth of July celebration. She couldn't figure out why I never did. Then we got divorced, of course."

In a flash of insight, Diana ventured, "Great-Aunt Addy blames me for the divorce, doesn't she?"

"Like I said, I've always been her favorite."

"I suspect she's not the only one who thinks it's my fault."

They exchanged glances.

"I didn't tell you any of this to frighten you off," Jack said.

"I'm not going to be frightened off," Diana assured him. "But if it gets too rough I can't promise I won't try to get lost in the crowd."

He tried to console her. "My parents don't blame you. They know I was as much at fault as you were, if not more."

Diana willed her shoulders to relax. "When are we supposed to meet your parents?"

Jack checked the clock on the dashboard of the Bronco. "I told them we'd be at the picnic grounds shortly before noon. Dad said they'd have a couple of tables staked out and saved for the immediate family."

"I'm a little nervous about meeting your parents," she confessed as they pulled into the parking lot. "What should I call them? Mr. and Mrs. Royce sounds so formal, but Mom and Dad is too familiar, considering we've never even met."

"Why not simply stick to Mary and John?" Jack suggested.

"Mary and John," Diana murmured, satisfied with the compromise.

They got out of the Bronco and gathered up the wicker hamper Jack had packed earlier that morning. It was filled with his contribution to the picnic: hamburg and hot-dog buns, potato chips and popcorn.

"We'll drop the food off at the shelter house before we go looking for Mom and Dad," he informed her as they cut across a wide expanse of grassy lawn.

"I don't think we're going to have to look far. There's someone waving to us, and I'll bet it's your father."

10

THE FAMILY RESEMBLANCE was uncanny, Diana decided as she and Jack walked toward the middle-aged gentleman standing by the picnic tables.

It was easy to see where her former husband got his tall, dark good looks. John Royce was at least six feet two inches, broad of shoulder and narrow of waist. He was graying at the temples, but the rest of his thick head of hair was as black as coal. Diana knew from Jack that his father was sixty years old, but the man certainly didn't look his age. There was a strength and vitality to Jack's father that were sure to carry him into his later years with grace.

"I see you picked a nice shady spot, Dad," Jack called out while they were still fifteen or twenty feet away.

"Just following your mother's orders," the man answered with a broad smile. He came toward them, his hand outstretched. "You must be Diana. You're just as pretty as Jack said you were."

She felt her face flush. "Thank you."

He seemed bound and determined to make her feel at home. Pumping her hand enthusiastically, he declared, "I'm John Royce. You can call me whatever you like, but John's okay with me."

Diana's mouth turned up at the corners. "All right, John."

"Where is everybody?" inquired Jack, looking around at the picnic baskets and the empty lawn chairs.

"Judd's making sure the cans of soda and beer get unloaded and packed in coolers. His boys are helping Susan in the shelter house. I think they're sorting plastic silverware and paper napkins." John turned to include Diana as if she were part of the family. "I don't know if Jack has told you, but Susan is Judd's fiancée. She's a nice young woman. A schoolteacher. I think you'll like her." He went on. "Bret and Julie called the house just as we were leaving to say they were going to be a few minutes late. On their way home from the parade, one of the boys took a tumble and scraped his knee." John looked over at his son and shook his head. "I remember when your mother and I went through the scraped-knee and banged-up-elbow stage with the three of you. It seemed like a daily occurrence, but it was sure a lot easier to handle when I was younger." He politely motioned Diana to one of several lawn chairs. "I'll tell you what this family needs," he confided as he sat down beside her.

She laughed. "What?"

"Girls."

"Girls?"

"Mary and I have five grandsons." The man held up the fingers and thumb of his right hand. "The good Lord knows I got nothing against boys. We had three of our own. But this family could sure use a couple of cute little girls in blond pigtails for a change. Every one of those grandsons of mine is a hellion, I'll tell you. I don't envy their parents."

Clearing his throat, Jack interrupted without ceremony, "By the way, where's Mom?"

"Your mother went to find a pay telephone. She's arranged a surprise for the younger children, some kind of clown who does magic tricks, pulling rabbits out of hats or something. Anyway, she wants to make sure the guy is here at two-thirty on the dot." John turned back to Diana. "Mary will be upset that she wasn't here to greet you the minute you arrived. She's been looking forward to meeting you for a long, long time."

There was a special emphasis placed on the last three words. John Royce stared at his son meaningfully. Jack leaned against a tree trunk and pretended not to understand.

Diana was simply relieved. At least her former father-in-law didn't think it was her fault that it had taken seven years for them to meet. Not that he seemed to actually be angry with Jack, either. John was a teddy bear, a great, big, smiling, friendly teddy bear.

"Here's Mom now," Jack announced as a woman came hurrying in their direction.

Diana didn't know which surprised her most, the fact that Mary Royce appeared even younger than she'd expected, or the fact that she couldn't be any more than five feet two inches tall. She was a midget in a family of giants.

Slim and smiling, she was wearing a plain cotton dress very similar to the one Diana had on. Her hair was light brown and curled softly around her face. Her features were small and delicate; her eyes were a deep blue-green in color.

Mary Royce was a lovely, youthful-appearing sixty, Diana discovered as she came closer. She seemed to be without pretense. The only makeup she wore was a trace of lipstick. Her complexion was lightly tanned and flawless, with laugh wrinkles around the eyes.

"Hello," she called out as she waved to them. She went up on her tiptoes and gave her husband a peck on the cheek, then turned to Diana. The handshake she had prepared became a warm hug. "So you're Diana." The voman stood back and sized her up. "You're everything ›ur son said you were and more. Welcome to Wisconsin, ny dear, and to our family picnic."

"Thank you. I'm happy to be here."

"We want you to relax and have a good time today," her ormer mother-in-law went on. "It might seem a bit over-vhelming at first with all these Royces around, but you'll ;et used to us. And I'd like you to call me Mary. That way ve'll both feel comfortable."

"I will, Mary."

"And you." She finally approached her youngest son. 'Come here and give your mother a hug, you big lug."

Jack had to practically bend over at the waist to do as iis mother requested.

"How'd it go with the clown?" John wanted to know.

"Not a clown, dear, a magician. He promised me he'd ›e here on time. I only hope he means it."

Diana spoke up. "Is there anything I can do to help?"

"Not at the moment, but I'll take you up on that offer ater. We'll all have to pitch in once Judd and Bret and their amilies join us. It can get a bit hectic with five boys in the amily, when the oldest is nine and the youngest is still in liapers."

"I know what you mean," Diana murmured with feel-ng.

"I understand you're one of five sisters," Mary ven-ured as her husband stood and offered his wife the chair ›eside Diana.

"Yes, I am."

"Jack said your youngest sister was recently married."

Diana nodded. "Kit and her husband just returned from heir honeymoon, as a matter of fact."

"At least you're used to big families, although boys are 'ery different from girls, believe me."

"I think I'd like little boys," Diana speculated.

"We'll see if you feel the same way by the end of the day." And Mary laughed as the picnic area began to fill up.

Several other men who bore a striking resemblance to Jack were soon headed in their direction, with wife and fiancée and offspring in tow. One of the young women had a diaper bag over her arm and a small boy on her hip while the man beside her was carrying a portable playpen. Several of the other boys were giggling and teasing each other like half-grown puppies. They were all talking and laughing as they joined the adults waiting in the shade of the trees.

Diana found herself laughing and talking right along with them, grateful to be so readily accepted into the intimacy of the Royce family, content in the knowledge that she liked these people and they liked her.

"You go right ahead and play volleyball with your brothers," Diana was urging Jack several hours later. "I'm too full to move. I intend to sit right here in this lounge chair beside your mother and enjoy the view."

"Don't worry," Mary Royce piped up, "I'll protect Diana while you're gone. I won't let Cousin Bernie get within ten feet of her."

The idea of a woman who was a good seven inches shorter than she was, and no doubt twenty pounds lighter protecting her brought an amused smile to Diana's face.

"Wish me luck," Jack said as he bent over and kissed her.

She was pink in the face and out of breath by the time he lifted his head and took off after his father and older brothers.

"I'm very proud of my sons," Mary observed as they watched the men walk away.

"They certainly take after their father, don't they?" Diana said.

"Yup. Not a blond in the bunch. Except for us, of ourse," Mary said as if her own light brown hair and Diana's golden blond hair somehow made them comades-in-arms.

Diana leaned her head back and put her feet up. She ighed contentedly.

Mary was watching her. "Tired?"

"A little. We left Phoenix rather early yesterday morng."

"Plus you're in a new place, meeting new people, seeing new faces, learning new names. It can be wearing on the nerves."

"It helps that you've made me feel so welcome, such a part of your family."

"You are part of our family. To John and me, you always have been."

Diana tried to swallow the lump in her throat. "I wish Jack and I had visited you after we were married."

"I suppose you both had your reasons. Now that I see you I suspect Jack's were somehow involved with the awful trauma we were going through at the time with Judd and his first wife. You bear a striking resemblance to Deidre, but I'm sure that's where the resemblance ends."

"Jack told me a little about her."

"My former daughter-in-law has caused us a great deal of pain and heartache. Not that Deidre can be blamed for all of the problems between her and Judd. Marriage—and divorce—are never a one-way street. Either way it takes two, both the man and the woman."

"Jack and I both made our share of mistakes. Looking back, I realize we weren't prepared to make the kind of wholehearted commitment it takes to make a marriage work."

"It may be romantic for a young couple to think thei marriage is made in heaven," Mary responded though fully, sharing some of the wisdom of sixty years of living "But the truth is a good marriage is made right here o earth. It simply takes time and attention and a great dea of love."

"Often love isn't enough on its own," Diana mur mured.

Mary nodded. "John and I were madly in love when w were married. I remember we went through a real roug spell about four years after the wedding. We had Judd an Bret by then, of course, and Jack was on the way. Eve pregnant, with two babies, I was thinking about divorc ing John."

Diana was shocked. "You seem so devoted to eac other."

"We are. We'll celebrate our forty-first anniversary thi October. But anyone who's been married very long know that there are always ups and downs, peaks and valleys i a relationship. I don't know any happily wed couple wh haven't considered divorce at one time or another during their marriage."

"Jack and I should have tried harder. Maybe we wouldn't have had to go through a divorce."

It wasn't meant unkindly, but Mary informed her, "It nearly killed Jack, you know."

Diana was taken aback. "You mean the fever he contracted while he was in the Amazon?"

"I meant your divorcing him."

She stared down at her hands. "It was the hardest thing I've ever had to do."

Her former mother-in-law reached out and patted her arm. "Nobody blames you, Diana."

She tried to make light of it. "Not even Great-Aunt ddy?"

"Great-Aunt Addy is always the exception to every rule. ut the immediate family—Jack's father and I, and his others—we certainly never blamed you. We knew our ungest son was a roamer. Never could get that boy to ay in one place long. When he called to tell us he'd got- n married, we hoped that might change things. When ck didn't settle down then, we were worried it wouldn't st."

"And it didn't."

"Sometimes *believing* a marriage will work is all a man d a woman have to cling to."

"Maybe Jack and I didn't believe hard enough."

"You've got to stick with it through thick and through in, that's for sure. I think marriage and divorce finally rced Jack to grow up. It was going to do that, or kill m." Mary hesitated, then added, "If history were to re- at itself, it would be the end of him."

Diana didn't say anything for a moment. "I know," she ally whispered.

They watched the rest of the volleyball game, cheering udly when the occasion called for encouragement from e sidelines.

As the afternoon warmed up, several of the men, in- uding Jack, slipped their shirts off and played bare- ested. Even from her vantage point, Diana could make ut the crisp, dark curls on his upper body and the corded uscles of his arms as he struck the ball. It was a joy to atch him move.

"Do you love him very much?"

The question caught her off-guard. She turned to Mary d saw only warmth and affection and concern in the oman's eyes. "Yes. I do. Jack is the only man I've ever loved. That isn't the problem. I just don't know if we ca survive living together."

"Men—that old saying about not being able to live wi them or without them still applies." The older woma sighed.

"That's for sure."

"Does Jack know you're still in love with him?"

"I haven't told him in so many words. I want to be ve sure this time before I commit myself."

Apparently his mother thought that was enough pr ing for one day. She changed the subject. "What do y like to do for fun?"

Diana welcomed the diversion. "Back home I belong a hiking club. I walk every morning and work out at gym. And I bicycle."

The other woman wrinkled her small nose. "Soun more like exercise to me than fun. I know you're not he for a vacation. Jack has told us you have a book due your publisher before the end of the year, and you have be left alone to write. But I'd like to take you fishing f salmon on Lake Michigan, if you think you'd enjoy it."

"I'd love to go fishing with you."

There was a twinkle in Mary's green eyes as she sai "You might be interested to learn that fishing for chinoo salmon is very similar to handling a man."

Diana laughed. "All right, I'll take the bait. How a they similar?"

"You have to get a salmon—or a man—on your lin show him who's boss and then land him," Mary claime tongue-in-cheek.

They could see the men coming toward them, jostli and gesturing animatedly, a cold beer in each of the hands.

"What have you two been up to?" Jack wanted to know

Diana shielded her eyes with her hand and looked up at m. "Talking."

"Girl talk," his mother expanded.

John Royce nudged him playfully in the side with his elbw. "That means mind your own business, son, in case u didn't get the message."

Jack was suspicious. "You were talking about us, weren't u?"

Mary lifted her chin. "Actually, Diana and I were talkg about salmon fishing."

"Salmon fishing?" Jack hooted.

"When are we going?" John spoke up.

"Yes, when are we going?" Jack joined in, a smile hoving at the edges of his mouth.

Mary glanced up at the two handsome males towering er her. "Diana and I are going whenever she feels she can ke a break from her writing. I don't remember inviting ther of you to come along, however." She turned her ad and said to Diana, "Sometimes the Royce men think ey can lord it over a woman because they're so big. Don't u pay them any mind. If you have any problems with y son, just call me."

"I'll do that," Diana said, smiling conspiratorially.

"That's what happens when you leave women to their wn devices too long," his father warned Jack, raising his rk eyebrows in an exaggerated arch.

The younger man ran the cold beer can over his chest. ell me something I don't know."

"Isn't it about time for that clown to do his show?" John ondered aloud.

"Magician, dear," Mary corrected her husband again she rose from the lawn chair and looked across to where group of children were gathering. "The man is a magian."

"What man doesn't have to be a magician if he ev hopes to understand women," Jack muttered as the headed for the shelter house....

"I LIKE YOUR FAMILY," Diana was telling him later that da

"They like you, too."

"You're so much like your dad. Not only in appea ance, but your mannerisms, too. And your mother is . .

"Outspoken."

"Yes, but she's far more than that. Mary is straightfo ward and doesn't mince words. I like that. She's strong an independent. I like that, too. She's lived in a mal dominated household for years and yet she manages hold her own. I have nothing but admiration for yo mother."

"How'd you hit it off with Great-Aunt Addy?"

"She started by informing me that at least I showed th good sense not to shout in her ear like some of the young generation were doing. It annoyed her that she was bein treated like an old lady who'd lost her hearing along wit her eyesight."

Jack sympathized. "It's Addy's pet peeve."

"She was as proud as a peacock when she informed m she still had all of her own teeth. I commented that I onl hoped I could say the same when I was ninety-one. That when she lowered her voice to a rather theatrical stag whisper and confided she wasn't ninety-one like everyor thought, but ninety-five."

"I told you so," he said, slightly smug about it.

"She asked me if I wanted to know the secret of ho she'd lived to such a ripe old age. I said, of course I did Diana ticked the points off on her fingers. "She nev smoked, never touched alcohol and never worried abo things she couldn't change."

"Sounds just like Addy."

"She also informed me you were quite a man."

"What did you say to that?"

"I agreed."

"I'm flattered."

"She pointed out that you hadn't looked at all well about three years ago. She figured it was my fault."

He hesitated. "What did you say?"

Diana looked at him with clear blue eyes. "I told her that it was partly my fault and partly your own."

"True enough," Jack said as he guided her toward the pier on the lakefront of his property.

A pale moon was on the rise over Lake Michigan. They were going to watch the annual fireworks display as soon as it was dark.

"Your great-aunt had more to say," Diana said as Jack's arms went around her waist.

"Sounds like you had quite a chat with Addy."

"I did. She wanted to know if I was staying here in Wisconsin. I told her I was for a while, anyway. That's when she asked me to promise her something."

"Promise her something?"

Diana took a deep breath. "She asked me not to break your heart again."

There was dead silence. She could feel Jack's breath on her cheek and along the side of her neck. She could sense the tension in his arms as they tightened around her.

"Did you promise?"

"I said I'd try, but it wasn't only your heart that had been broken. Mine was, too. That's when she gave me the key to a long and healthy life. She said that she'd loved only one man during all of her years. Sometimes he was good and sometimes he was bad, but she always loved him."

For a long time they didn't say anything. The waves lapped at the shoreline, and the wind gently rustled the pines. Then there was an explosion of color and light in the sky above their heads, a great fountain of green and red and blue sparkles.

"It's beautiful." Diana found she could scarcely breathe. "It's so beautiful, it's frightening."

"Yes, it is," Jack murmured.

His arms tightened around her as if he never intended to let her go, ever again.

THINKING BACK to that Fourth of July, Diana wondered if her comment about the fireworks had meant something more to Jack. Sometimes being in love was beautiful and frightening, she knew. Dear God, how well she knew.

But commitments were commitments, and promises were promises, Diana reminded herself as she curled up on the living-room sofa with her book. She'd promised her publisher she would go on a two-week promotional tour of England, and that's just what she was going to do. She was also committed to two weeks of study at Stonehenge. A lot of people had gone to a lot of trouble arranging it for her. She couldn't back out now. Of all people who should understand, it was Jack.

But he didn't.

If only he'd try to understand. She didn't want to leave for an entire month and have their parting be one of bitterness. If Jack was angry with her for going, how could she possibly return once her trip was over?

And what about her home in Arizona? And her family? She had a life beyond this house in the woods, much as she'd grown to love it. She had a life outside Wisconsin and Jack's family, as fond of both as she'd become.

The problem was, Diana realized as she gazed out the window at Lake Michigan, the shoe was on the other foot now, and Jack didn't like it. Not one bit.

"What are you doing, honey?" The sound of his voice startled her. She hadn't heard him enter the room.

"Reading a book."

"What's it about?" He sat down beside her on the leather sofa.

"*Celtic Myth and Legend, Poetry and Romance.*" She read the title off the cover.

"Sounds utterly fascinating," he said with a mild attempt at humor.

"Actually, it is fascinating."

He moved closer and slipped an arm along the back of the sofa. "Not as fascinating as a certain lovely lady I'd like to take to the movies this evening."

"I wish I could go...."

He frowned. "I think I hear a but coming."

"But there's so much background reading I need to do before I leave on my trip. I don't think I'll have enough time as it is."

His frown turned to displeasure. "Seems like a damn waste of time to me."

"It's not a waste of time," she countered gently but firmly.

Jack drew a breath and tried a different tack with her. "You never used to be interested in trotting off to the far reaches of the earth."

Diana turned sad, understanding eyes on him. "And you never used to be interested in settling down and staying home. You said it yourself, Jack. Times change. Circumstances change. People have to change along with them."

His gaze darkened. "I don't want you to change."

"You can't stop it. I already have. I've been trying to tell you I'm not the same woman you married seven years ago, and I'm certainly not the same woman you left behind when you took off for the Amazon."

His tone became dry and slightly brusque. "What happened to the Diana who was content to be an armchair traveler?"

She was more than willing to tell him. "That Diana finally learned not to be a coward about life and all it has to offer."

Jack winced, no doubt recognizing his own words on the subject. "You used to claim that all you needed was your imagination and a good book. You said they took you any place you wanted to go."

"And you used to tell me how much I was missing out on," she shot back. "You said the only way to really see the world and experience its wonders was to do it firsthand. Well, I finally decided to try it your way, Jack. And it seems you were right all along."

He realized she'd turned the tables on him. It was difficult, if not impossible, to argue with his own logic. "You're really going, then."

She sighed wearily. "We've been over this again and again in the past few weeks. I told you long before I agreed to come to Wisconsin that I had this trip in September. I thought you of all people would understand. You know what it is to have commitments that mean you have to go away. You used to do it all the time when we were married."

That wasn't what Jack wanted to hear. "Yes, I had commitments that took me away from home. But that was different."

"Yes, it was different." Diana's voice vibrated with long-buried emotions. "You were the one leaving, and I was the one staying behind."

His eyes took on a hard sheen. "Are you doing this to give me a taste of my own medicine?"

Her words were scarcely uttered above a whisper, but they were weighted with determination. "No, I'm not. It doesn't have anything to do with you. I've tried to make you understand and you simply don't want to. This is strictly business. And part of my business is to cooperate with my publisher when it comes to promoting my books. The reservations were made months ago. People are counting on me, and I'm not going to let them down."

"You'd rather let me down instead."

"That was a rotten thing to say," she said, the quaver in her voice matching the tremor that ran the length of her body.

Jack relented. "I'm sorry, honey." His face was gray with strain as he admitted, "It's just that I'm afraid."

Diana turned to him. "I know you are."

He tried to smile and failed. "Is this the way you felt the times I went off to some godforsaken place?"

She couldn't make it easy for him. "Yes."

"How did you stand it?" His whole body was taut with tension.

She wouldn't lie to him. "I cried a lot. Didn't sleep well. Worried about you. Fretted and fussed and sometimes fumed. And in the end, I simply stood it because I had to. You will, too."

"I will, too," Jack echoed. He finally seemed resigned. "When do you have to start packing?"

"Not for days and days," Diana said as she put her book down and moved into the circle of his arms.

"ARE YOU almost finished packing?"

Diana looked up and saw Jack standing in the doorway of the bedroom they'd shared for the past two months.

"I just need to put in these two pairs of shoes and that handbag."

He came up beside her, bent over and kissed the sensitive spot behind her ear. "What do you say we forget about all of this for a while and go to bed?"

She knew Jack wasn't angry with her anymore, that he accepted the fact she was leaving, but perhaps he simply needed to reassure himself that in some ways she was always his, would always be his.

Diana turned in his arms and twined her hands around his neck. "Go to bed?" she repeated in a husky voice.

"Yes," he said, kissing her again and again, sliding his tongue into her mouth until she felt branded by him. His hands were on her breasts and hips. She began to move against him, rubbing her body along his.

Jack slowly and deliberately removed her clothing and his own, then pulled her down on the bed beside him. He covered every inch of her flesh with his kisses. His teeth nipped her bottom lip; his tongue flicked back and forth across her breasts, and that most sensitive part of her exploded into a shower of fireworks as he gave her the most intimate of kisses, of caresses.

Then he propped himself up on his elbows and gazed down into her eyes, apparently satisfied with what he saw there, knowing that she wanted him as much as he wanted her, that their desire, their passion, their need for each other was mutual.

Jack eased his weight from her and rolled over, taking her with him until she sat astride his body. He ran his hands over her silky smooth skin, looking up into her passion-glazed eyes.

Diana watched as her body was stretched above Jack's in offering. He reached up to caress the tip of her breast, then urged her toward him until the hardening nipple was pressed to his lips. He kissed it tenderly, worshipfully. He groaned and took it into his mouth, his tongue wrapping around the taut bud. Then he drew her closer, enfolding her in his arms as he found her mouth in a kiss that seemed to go on forever.

Diana clung to him, digging her nails into his shoulders as his hands trailed a fiery path from her neck to the rounded curves of her hips. His touch became more insistent, more demanding, perhaps even a little desperate; it carried her to a level of excitement she had never known before.

Then he shifted his body under her and drew her down onto his waiting manhood. A wave of pleasure coursed through them both.

Jack raised his hips and surged even farther into her body, exclaiming, "You're so tight, so sweet, so hot...."

Her muscles contracted around him as he began to move beneath her, movements that quickly caught them up in the natural rhythm of lovemaking. He thrust deeper and deeper as they reached for the moment of shattering oblivion together. They cried out in unison as they climaxed as one.

Later, as they lay with their arms wrapped around each other, Jack gazed into her eyes. "I love you, Diana. I want you to marry me. I want you to be the mother of our children."

Diana's heart was pounding in her breast. Was Jack willing to accept the fact that she'd changed? Could he make a lifelong commitment this time? Could she trust him to keep his promises?

She knew Jack believed what he was saying, but would he feel the same way in one month? Two? Perhaps a little time away from each other was what they needed right now.

Looking him straight in the eye, she said, "You've been the only man in my life since the night we met. We've made our share of mistakes with each other. We need to be sure we don't make any more. Marriage is such a serious step. We both know from experience that it takes more than love or good sex to make a marriage work. Think about it while I'm gone. I'll promise to do the same. When I get back at the end of the month, we'll see how we feel."

"God, it's going to be so lonely without you," he muttered harshly as he buried his mouth in her hair.

"I know, darling," she murmured. "I know."

She did. She remembered the loneliness. She would never forget how empty their apartment had seemed when he was gone. All the nights she'd called out his name and he hadn't been there. Now the shoe was going to be on the other foot. Now Jack would know the awful emptiness.

"I'm going to miss you more than you know," he confessed as they fell asleep later that night.

"I'M GOING TO MISS YOU," Diana told him the next morning as they stood at the gate waiting for her flight to be announced. "I'll call if I can. Do you have the emergency numbers I gave you?"

"Yes."

"Take care of yourself," she whispered as she brushed her lips across his. Then she turned and ran down the ramp toward her plane.

"Vaya con Dios, my love," Jack murmured as he watched her disappear from sight.

He knew Diana was coming back to him. She'd promised. But all the same some part of him died as she walked away from him. Some irrational part of him was afraid he would never see her again.

JACK SHOT UP IN BED.

He was covered with sweat. The sheets were soaked through. His heart was pounding in his chest, and he was breathing heavily.

He'd had the dream again. Nightmare, really.

It wasn't the first time. It had been occurring more and more frequently since Diana had gone away.

He struggled to his feet and made it to the bathroom. He turned on the faucet and filled a glass with cold water. He drank it down in one gulp. Then he bent over and stuck his head under the faucet.

He returned to the bedroom and walked out onto the second-story deck. The evening was surprisingly cool. There was the smell of autumn in the air. He stood there and looked out at the lake, watching one wave after another wash into shore.

His dream was always the same. He was back in that hellhole of a jungle. The sun was white and burning; his mouth was dry and swollen. The mosquitoes were chewing on his sunburned flesh as he lay in his hammock. He remembered the mangrove trees, the mango and the acacia.

There were necklace-length centipedes crawling across his body, and ants as long as a man's thumb and black scorpions to sting a man's vulnerable flesh. Sloths hung in the trees above. Crocodiles sprawled in the sun, some with their mouths agape, and small birds hopped in and out picking food from their teeth.

He finally managed to climb out of his hammock and start through the jungle, using his machete to cut away the thicket in front of him. That was always part of the dream.

He was in agony. His body was on fire. He'd known pain but never a pain like this. It consumed a man and threatened to drive him out of his mind. He kept going somehow, though his clothes were torn from his body. It rained, and he could find no shelter. The humid air dripped with sultry heat, and he could find no relief.

He was delirious and he knew it—sometimes. He had to go on and couldn't remember why. He asked himself what was the use, and there was no answer. But he kept moving all the same. There was a vision of a blond-haired, blue-eyed angel before him. She seemed to be saying he must follow her; he must not give up or he would die and then the angel would cry.

He tripped over a root, fell flat on his face and couldn't get up again. He wanted to cry and didn't have the energy. He put his head down in the soft, odoriferous humus on the jungle floor and waited for death, wished for death, prayed for death to come and make quick work of his misery.

He recalled opening his eyes for a moment when the Indians found him, but it meant nothing to him.

He opened them again later, waking from a raging fever, and found an old, weather-beaten man leaning over him. The old man smiled, and Jack saw that he had no teeth.

Days later—in the dream he now recognized as the living and waking nightmare of those last few weeks in South America—Jack would awaken and see the local padre bending over him. The man smelled of onions and was wearing the distinctive heavy brown cassock of his order. No doubt he'd saved Jack's life, this man of God who was e one the Indians had called when they'd found the ringo in their midst.

He remembered the priest asking him, "Are you Catholic?"

"No, padre."

"I will pray for your soul all the same, my son."

He clutched the sleeve of the man's worn robe and demanded to know, "Diana. Where is Diana?"

That was the question he asked again and again.

The dream always ended the same way, Jack realized as e gazed out over the dark lake in front of him.

He would awaken—as he had tonight—and Diana wouldn't be there. He would find himself all alone.

He wasn't sure which vision was the real nightmare: the one he had while he was sleeping, or the one he found once he awakened.

11

SHE'D FLOWN OUT OF HEATHROW that evening at eig o'clock. It was nearly nine hours later before she ma aged to get a seat on a connecting flight leaving New York La Guardia Airport for Milwaukee, with intermedia stops in Pittsburgh and Cincinnati.

The flight arrived at its final destination shortly aft midnight. By the time a rental car had been signed for ar charged to her American Express card and directions s cured to Highway 94 and points south, Diana had bee traveling for almost twenty-four continuous hours.

She was exhausted.

But she wasn't about to stop now. Something drove h on, some sense of urgency, of foreboding, perhaps. Som ill-defined feeling that she must get home and see Jack.

She couldn't explain it without sounding as if she taken leave of her senses. So she hadn't tried to explai She had simply apologized to her hosts, saying there ha been a change in her plans and she must return immed ately to the States.

In a matter of an hour or less, she'd gathered up her r search material and her notes, her camera and her lu gage and had caught the next train for London.

She was dead tired by the time she pulled up in front Jack's house. She got out of the rental car, taking time on to grab her handbag and lock the doors. The rest of h things could wait until morning.

The solitary light shining in the black of night spot-hted the far end of the garage and part of the forested vn. The house itself was dark.

Diana took out the latchkey that Jack had insisted she ep with her and unlocked the front door. She stepped o the entranceway, closing the door behind her. There sn't a sound to be heard. The silence was eerie.

The soles of her walking shoes made a strange, squishy ise as she crossed the slate floor toward the staircase. e paused at the bottom of the steps and listened. There s only the wind in the trees outside the window and the unding of Lake Michigan as tons upon tons of icy cold ter were thrown against the giant boulders close to ore.

She started up the stairs.

Diana was halfway to the top when she heard some-ng. She stopped dead in her tracks and cocked her head one side. The sound came again. It sent strange chills her spine. It sounded . . . inhuman, like an animal in in, or some nameless creature of the night that moved rough the darkness like one of the creations in her book, pecter, a wraith, a shade.

All was silence again.

Diana continued up the steps until she reached the nding above.

She suddenly felt very foolish. What in the world was e doing sneaking around Jack's house in the middle of e night? And in the dark, no less. She should at least turn ight on so she could see where she was going.

What were her intentions? To undress and crawl into d with Jack and shout "surprise" in the morning when awoke to find he wasn't alone? How could she explain at she'd flown back a week early because she'd had a ange sense of foreboding?

She stood in the hallway outside his bedroom and d
bated with herself as to the wisdom of her actions. Not th
she was thinking very clearly. She was so tired that s
leaned forward and rested her head against the doorjam
for a moment.

That's when she heard it again, a strange, frightenin
wordless cry. It came from Jack's bedroom.

Her head shot up. She was wide awake now. Every sen
was alert: sight, smell, touch, taste and hearing. S
opened the bedroom door and peered into the darknes

For a moment she couldn't see anything. Then she ma
out Jack's form on the bed. He was thrashing from side
side, his arms flailing the air as if to ward off some my
terious and invisible attacker.

She moved closer. The sheets were tangled at the bo
tom of the king-size bed, imprisoning his ankles. The p
lows were tossed helter-skelter. The spread and lightweig
blanket left over from summer were strewn across t
floor. She tentatively reached out and touched the shee
It was damp. Outside, it was a cool night in late Septe
ber.

Diana tried her voice. It came out as a whisper. She tri
again a little more loudly. "Jack."

There was no response.

There was only one thing to do, Diana decided. S
turned on a small lamp in the corner. It sent a soft glo
into the room. She walked toward the bed. There w
something wrong.

The sweat was like rain on Jack's naked body. It gli
tened in the lamplight and was beaded on his forehead a
his upper lip. It ran between the crisp, dark curls on h
chest and down into the indentation of his abdomen.

He grew quiet for a moment, and she reached out and uched the skin of one thigh. His flesh was on fire; he was urning up.

"Oh, my God!" Diana whispered to herself.

It must be the strange jungle fever Jack had contracted the Amazon. She'd read somewhere that once a human eing caught a disease like that, it could recur without arning.

She remembered something else. The last time, he'd early died from it.

What if she'd waited too long to return to him? What if e died before she had a chance to tell him that she loved im and wanted nothing more than to be his wife, the other of his children?

She tried to place her hand on his forehead. Jack twisted round, and his mouth began to move. He seemed to be ying to say something. Diana bent over to catch the hispered word.

"Diana."

It was her name. She nearly cried out with joy.

"Diana. Diana. Diana."

She remembered what her husband had told her about he night he'd almost died. How he had called her name ver and over. The Indians had thought he was praying o his god, or cursing the god's name.

"I'm here, Jack. I'm here," she repeated.

With a jolt and a strangled cry, Jack tore himself from er embrace and sat straight up in bed. She sat back and vatched as he buried his face in his hands for a moment. Then he slid off the bed and staggered toward the bath-oom, cursing under his breath words she couldn't quite nake out.

Diana heard water running. Jack had turned on the aucet in the basin.

She stood up and waited. She was certain now that wasn't in the throes of jungle fever, but a very bad drea And she was equally certain that he hadn't realized she w in the room, the house or even the same country as he wa

Jack appeared in the doorway between the bathroo and the bedroom. Diana could only stare at him. In h nudity, he was everything a man was meant to be—stron muscular, powerful, beautifully formed from the shape his head to the lean lines of his torso to the distinctive o line of his manhood. He was partially aroused.

He stared at her as if she were an apparition conjur up out of the night and his dreams. She knew he didn't b lieve his eyes. She could see he was afraid that his nigh mare had taken him over the edge, that he was mad, qui mad.

"Diana?"

"Yes, Jack. I'm here."

"Are you a figment of my imagination, or are you real

Slowly she moved around the bed toward him. "I' real, darling, very real." She stopped a foot from hi "Reach out and touch me. You'll discover just how rea am."

For a split second he did nothing. Then one arm ca up, and a hand was extended toward her. He touched h breast, and she felt her nipples tingle and grow taut b neath her blouse. Jack felt it, as well. He brought his oth hand up and covered both breasts. Her pulse becan wildly erratic.

"You are real," he murmured as he drew her to him. H was fully aroused now.

"Yes, I'm real."

"You're home."

"Yes, I'm home."

That seemed to be enough talk for Jack. He took her in s arms and kissed her as if he'd dreamed of nothing else ery minute of every day and every night since she'd gone vay three weeks ago.

Diana went to him willingly. She had missed his kiss, s touch, more than she could ever have imagined. There as plenty of time later to talk, to explain. Right now all e wanted was the man holding her, making love to her.

In the dim glow of the lamplight, Jack unhooked the row buttons down the front of her blouse and reached be- nd her to undo the clasp of her bra. He nudged the othes aside and bent his head to trace the outline of first ne breast and then the other with his tongue. Her nip- es tightened until they were two hard nubs and she was egging him for release.

"Please, Jack."

"Please what?" he drawled.

"Please take me into your mouth."

"Like this?" he asked, grasping one taut peak between s teeth and biting down gently.

"More. Please more," she pleaded, her head thrown ack.

"More like this?" he went on, flicking his tongue back nd forth across her sensitized flesh.

"Yes. No. More. Please."

He finally took pity on her and drew her breast into his outh and sucked long and hard like a starving man. Di- na opened her mouth, releasing a groan of arousal mixed ith pleasure.

When it became apparent that she could barely stand n her feet, he slipped the blouse and bra from her shoul- ers and placed her in the center of the big bed. His hand ent to the waist of her slacks. He didn't immediately ndo the button or the zipper, but ran his hands over her abdomen and down to her pelvis and the juncture of he thighs. He gently massaged the bone there, and she felt he body instinctively arch against his hand.

Her skin was on fire, her eyes feverish as she gazed u into his. "Undress me, Jack."

Slowly he loosened the waist and eased her slacks dow and off her legs, taking her shoes and socks with them. Sh was left wearing only a pair of bikini panties.

His eyes grew darker as he looked down at the woma stretched beneath him.

He reached out with one hand and tugged at her panties until they, too, joined the rest of her clothes in a forgotten heap on the floor.

Kneeling above her, he straddled her body. He wa hard. More aroused than Diana could ever remember i all the times she'd seen him in a state of sexual excitement She took him in her hands, holding him between he palms.

He gasped. "If this is a dream, I hope I never wake up.

"This is no dream," she told him, and she bent an kissed his tender flesh.

He slid between her legs and nudged at the feminin opening. She was ready for him; he slipped into the velvet softness of her body. Her muscles contracted aroun him and drew him deeper, ever deeper.

"This is real. You are real," Jack said, as if he were jus beginning to believe it.

"Yes, darling. We're real," Diana reassured him as sh moved her hips beneath his.

Then the rhythm picked up as their bodies began th primal male-female dance. Every thrust, every parry every caress brought one or the other or both even greate pleasure.

Then Jack began thrusting into her faster and faster, and her mind was gone. Her body seemed to follow him to some exquisite place she'd only dreamed of before.

Jack shouted her name. "Diana. Diana, my love!" With that, he thrust one last time.

Almost immediately afterward they fell asleep, their bodies damp and exhausted, in the soft glow of the lamp left burning in the corner. The wind whistled through the treetops, and the dark lake below flowed into shore...but the sounds were only soothing now. They lulled the lovers to sleep.

"I THOUGHT IT MIGHT BE A DREAM, after all," Jack confessed after he'd opened his eyes the next morning and found Diana beside him, watching him quietly, contentedly.

"It was no dream."

His eyes went dark and thoughtful for a moment. "For a while last night it was a nightmare," he admitted.

She turned over onto her stomach and rested her chin in her hands. "Was your nightmare about the jungle?"

He looked vaguely out the window to the clear blue of the sky. The sun was already high over the lake. "Yes, it was about the jungle."

She was concerned. "Sometimes it helps if we talk about our dreams. Do you want to tell me about it?"

Jack seemed to consider her offer. "I think I would like to, actually," he said, stuffing a pillow behind his head and half sitting up in bed. "I won't start at the very beginning. I was in the Guiana Highlands by that time, heading toward the mouth of the Amazon. I needed a guide to take me the rest of the way through the jungle. A man named Sadio volunteered in exchange for a small bag of gold dust. That's gold-mining country," he explained.

"The legends of El Dorado."

"Exactly. Anyway, we'd been out about three days when Sadio started acting a little nervous. He wouldn't tell me why, but I should have suspected something was wrong. I awoke the next morning and found that he'd taken most of our supplies and vanished."

Diana jerked her eyes up to Jack's face. "You mean he ran off and left you?"

Jack shrugged as if to say it was a reasonable guess. "Maybe he got scared. There are those who believe evil spirits live in the jungle. Or maybe he was simply a thief who hoped to sell the stuff he stole from me. In the end, it was all the same: I was deep in the jungle with only the food and supplies I was carrying on me."

"What did you do then?"

"I struck out on my own. It's all in bits and pieces after that. I was coming down with fever, you see."

"Malaria?"

Again Jack shrugged. He rubbed one hand back and forth across his bare abdomen in an absentminded gesture. "They say that no one escapes without a taste of malaria. The damned thing comes and goes as it pleases, too." He shook his head. "I knew whatever else was true, my will to survive was the key to getting out of the jungle alive."

Diana inhaled a slow, trembling breath and listened.

"I was feverish by that time. I'd lost count of the days since Sadio had run off. I saw your face before me. You talked to me, told me I had to keep moving or I'd die. You said if I died, you would weep for me."

"Jack." Two large tears welled from her eyes and ran down her cheeks.

Jack wiped them away with the tip of his finger. "I slept on the jungle floor. It was cold and damp."

Diana's eyes were growing larger and rounder with horror. Without being told, she knew somehow that a lesser man than Jack wouldn't have survived. "What did you eat?"

"I picked berries—juicy, purple berries—and ate my fill. I got awful stomach pains, though, and became light-headed. I collected nuts and ate them. I tried to make tea from *quina-quina* bark. At one point, I sensed an animal was tracking me. I never saw it and never knew why it didn't take me, when I was so weak by then. It finally rained, and I opened my mouth and drank."

Diana thought of last night, of how Jack had awakened and raced to the bathroom sink to gulp down a glass of cold water.

"Later, after the Indians found me, I seem to remember there was a bony mongrel sniffing around my hammock. I tried to make a fist and strike out at him. I was too weak to even defend myself against a skinny, starving dog. A small boy assigned to watch over me finally chased him away with a stick. There were flies everywhere. And mosquitoes." He scratched his arm as if merely talking about mosquitoes made his skin itch. "I don't want to go into every gory detail."

Diana said to him as calmly as she could, "I don't mind if you talk about it. I want to share everything with you. Friends share the good times and the bad."

Jack rubbed his jaw and frowned in thought. "I thought I was over it, that the dream was part of the past I could put behind me."

"You can now," she said soothingly.

"I believe I can, although I've had that same dream so many nights I've lost count. Each time I wake up calling your name, and you aren't there. Last night I woke up, and you were there. I've finally come full circle, honey. Something tells me I may never have the nightmare again."

She was a little shaken. "If you do, I'll be there, Jack. I promise."

He finally seemed ready to put the dream behind him. He sat up straighter in bed and gazed down at her, his eyes clear. "You aren't due back from England yet. What are you doing here, anyway?" He quickly amended that. "Not that I'm complaining, mind you."

"I didn't think for a minute that you were," she said saucily. "Actually I decided to catch an earlier flight."

He laughed. "I'll say. About a week early."

Diana rested her chin on his bare chest and twirled a soft strand of hair around her fingertip. "I got lonesome. I missed you. So I decided to come home."

His eyebrows rose fractionally. "How did the book tour go?"

"Fine. Tiring." She looked up at him. "The food was heavy, all meat and potatoes and gravies. I've been dreaming about a fresh salad made with crisp lettuce, luscious red tomatoes and cucumbers for the past three weeks."

Jack put a hand to his stomach and claimed, "Stop! You're making me hungry."

"I've got coffee brewing downstairs," she said enticingly.

"In a minute. In a minute," he admonished. "Tell me first. Did you finish your research?"

"Nope."

He was obviously surprised. "No?"

"I decided it could wait until another time." She combed through his chest hair with her fingertips. "Maybe we can go to England together sometime."

Jack smoothed the hair back from her face. "Did you really miss me that much?"

She let it show in her eyes and in the way she stroked his chest with a gentle, caressing touch. "I missed you more than you'll ever know."

"And I missed you," he said in a husky voice.

Wrapping part of the sheet around her, Diana sat up in bed beside him. "It's just no good, Jack. Nothing is any good if you aren't with me. For three weeks—it seemed like months—I dragged myself from luncheons to book signings to teas. I sleepwalked through the daylight hours and lay awake half the night. It was awful. It was worse than awful. I've been miserable and grouchy and out-of-sorts with everyone. The longer I was away from you, the worse I was getting."

He smiled at her sympathetically. "I know. I haven't been worth a damn to anyone, including myself, since you left."

She knew her true feelings and she wasn't going to hesitate to tell him, now that she had the chance. "I discovered something while I was away from you." She looked him straight in the eye. "You are the most important thing in my life, Jack. You're more important than my career. You're more important than wealth or fame or power. You're more important to me than all the other people I love put together." Her voice cracked for a moment. "I don't want to live without you. And I can't imagine how I've survived without you for the past three years."

He was very quiet. When he caught his breath, it sounded like a groan. "God, how I wish we could go back and live the past seven years all over again. I would do things so differently the second time around," he declared with great feeling.

She sighed. "We can't change the past."

"I know. Like you said about the character in your first book: she found out that the past wasn't hers to change, only the future." Jack looked at her with an intensity she'd never witnessed before. His voice was strangely hoarse. "I'm still crazy about you."

The breath shuddered in her lungs. "And I'm still crazy about you."

"Maybe something so right won't go wrong a second time."

She moistened her bottom lip. "Maybe it won't if we invest the same time and energy in our relationship that we give to our careers, if we work at it with the same dedication and single-minded determination that we've both brought to success."

Jack reached out for her hand. He held it in his. "This time I solemnly promise that I will be there in the good times and the bad, for as long as we both live. So help me, God."

Her voice caught a little as she declared, "And I promise that you will always be first in my heart and in my soul and in my mind."

He gave her a penetrating look. "I want to try again."

"So do I."

He took a deep breath. "Will you marry me, Diana Quick?"

"Yes. Will you marry me, Jack Royce? Will you be my husband, my lover and my best friend for the rest of our lives?"

He nearly lost his composure then. "I will. I've changed. You've changed. I guess people can change more than we realize. Yet one thing has never changed. We love each other. We were meant for each other. You are my destiny, Diana."

"And you are mine, Jack. I believe our love was a true love, after all."

"And they said it wouldn't last." He laughed lightheartedly.

The tension eased from Diana's body. All of a sudden, she was feeling downright cheerful. "I think our families will be happy for us."

"Are you kidding? They'll be thrilled. At least mine will be. My father is counting on us giving him several granddaughters."

"With blond pigtails." Her brows arched. "We should have at least one boy for my father's sake. After all, he's put up with a household of women all these years."

"A girl for Grandpa Royce and a boy for Grandpa Quick." Then his expression grew serious for a minute. "Do you want to have children? We never talked about it when we were married before."

"Yes. I want children, if they're yours."

Her words acted like a trigger release. "I want us to do all kinds of things with our kids," Jack envisioned.

"We'll take them hiking and camping and boating and fishing," she said.

"We'll visit the Wisconsin Dells and take them to Disney World and Six Flags America and the state fair," he enthused. "We have so much to talk about, Diana."

"And all the time in the world, darling," she murmured as she ran her hand down the sheet covering his leg. "Later."

That didn't stop Jack. "I think we should have a church wedding this time, with our families and closest friends in attendance. Maybe we could hold the ceremony in that smaller chapel at your church."

"You want to get married in Arizona?"

"Of course. Arizona will be one of our two homes. You place in the desert and my place by Lake Michigan. They'l be both of our homes now."

"Talk about opposites."

"Talk about opposites attracting," he corrected.

Together they looked from her female body to his mal body. Hers was soft and yielding. His was hard and de manding. Her skin and hair were as fair as the golde sunlight. He was as dark as midnight.

Day and night.

Champagne and beer.

Yin and yang.

Man and woman.

"There is definitely something to this idea of opposite attracting," Jack murmured, nuzzling her neck and the sof flesh of her bare shoulder.

"And I intend to enjoy the differences between us to th fullest," Diana declared as she snuggled down beside him urging his body toward hers.

Jack threw out a sexy laugh, his hands covering he body. "Maybe ours is a match made in heaven, after all.'

"I only know that I'm in heaven when I'm in your arms,' Diana murmured, intending to keep his arms around he forever. . . .

New York Times Bestselling Author

HEATHER GRAHAM POZZESSERE

Heat up your night reading this October with

SLOW BURN

The Players: *Spencer Huntington*: Rich, recently widowed, longtime friend—and onetime lover of David Delgado.
David Delgado: Born on the wrong side of the tracks, ex-Miami cop, now a P.I., still carries a torch for Spencer.

The Plot: A year after his death, Spencer's husband's murder remains unsolved. And now *her* life is in danger. Enter David and a passion that cannot be denied.

The Result: Miami—just got hotter.

Reach for the brightest star in women's fiction with

MHGPSB